CW01651317

BONDS OF BLISS

Allie concentrated on calming herself. She had been unprepared for the harsh realities of her action, and for the fear that had charged through her as Rat had woken, furious in his bonds. Now, however, she felt powerful. Rat outweighed her by at least four stone and had twice her strength, yet lay helpless, spread for her enjoyment. She had wanted to show him how it felt to be blindfolded and defenceless, hoping that he would recognize the humiliation and be kinder to Hope if he tried it again.

'What are you going to do?' Rat sounded nervous.

Allie drew her palm over his chest and stomach, then cupped and squeezed his most intimate part through the cloth of his shorts. She stroked gently until she felt him respond. When he was aroused she let go, pleased at his small whimper of disappointment. She tucked her fingers under his waistband and tugged, until he raised his hips and let her slide his shorts to mid-thigh . . .

Also in New English Library paperback

Rock Hard
Midnight Blue
Interlover
Satisfaction Guaranteed
Dangerous Passions

Passion Quest

Virginie LaRue

NEW ENGLISH LIBRARY
Hodder and Stoughton

Copyright © 1997 by Virginie LaRue

First published in 1997 by Hodder and Stoughton
A division of Hodder Headline PLC

A New English Library paperback

The right of Virginie LaRue to be identified as the Author
of the Work has been asserted by her in accordance with
the Copyright, Designs and Patents Act 1988.

10 9 8 7 6 5 4 3 2 1

All rights reserved. No part of this publication may
be reproduced, stored in a retrieval system, or transmitted,
in any form or by any means without the prior written
permission of the publisher, nor be otherwise circulated
in any form of binding or cover other than that in which
it is published and without a similar condition being
imposed on the subsequent purchaser.

All characters in this publication are fictitious
and any resemblance to real persons, living or dead,
is purely coincidental.

ISBN 0 340 68483 6

A CIP catalogue record for this title
is available from the British Library.

Typeset by Hewer Text Composition Service, Edinburgh
Printed and bound in Great Britain by Clays Ltd, St Ives PLC

Hodder and Stoughton
A Division of Hodder Headline PLC
338 Euston Road
London NW1 3BH

Chapter One

The article was three pages long; commanding in magazine terms. It meant the publisher felt the subject newsworthy. Plus there were two pictures. A large one depicted a woman caught in frozen stride in a city street. She looked belligerent, her chin thrust forward aggressively, her briefcase on the upswing and her forward foot lifted in a parody of a high-kicking step. The tailored Chanel suit clung perfectly to her curved contours and the silk blouse cleaved just enough to show the reader she had soft, generous breasts. She looked feminine in spite of the grim determination in the set of her mouth and the narrowed intensity of her hazel eyes. Her long hair was loose, dark blonde and swept back by the momentum of her onward march. The caption underneath the photograph questioned, 'And who is The Cannibal setting out to devour today?' The article was headed *Hope Springs Eternal*.

'Not any more,' she muttered, before reading on.

> If you get a call in the night from Hope Andrews you either hand in your resignation or leave town. No self-respecting company turning over more than one billion pounds should hesitate to check their assets the next day: it is certain that the boardroom will lack a powerful resource by noon.

The article listed her successes. Names in the City whom she had hunted and persuaded into alternative boardrooms, dangling before them extra incentives, added status and greater power and wealth. None of her 'victims' were unhappy and most of the companies she deprived were also her clients. Shifting people at the top was an age-old tradition in London which often demanded the interpolation of a headhunter. One of the most successful now sat slumped in her chair, wondering if her career was at an end. Publicity negates the ability to act covertly and Hope's successes were based on relative secrecy.

'Such is life.' She sighed irritably and pushed the magazine aside.

It had always been a risk. She dealt in giddy circles, high society, and mingled with the jet set. That she had escaped serious attention from the gossipmongers for her ten years with Pursuit was a miracle and she had had a good run. The thing which most angered her about the article was the second picture. Salvatore, the flamboyant pornography baron whom she had tracked and netted in Buenos Aires. Richards had wanted him on the board prior to the launch of his new magazine and, having been himself hunted by Hope, elected that she should capture Salvatore. She succeeded, in a round of glittering parties, offshore lunches and shameless compliments. What really burned her was that she had had a good time, the first in years, but she had not succumbed to the rampant wiles and passionate, dark attempts at seduction by her quarry. Night after night she had retired breathless with frustration, the need for Salvatore boiling in her blood. With the image of his dark, brooding eyes before her, she would thrust her fingers rudely between her thighs until orgasm. She never felt wholly satisfied and always dreaded the next day when she would have to face him again and refuse him again. It was because he could not have her, although he was totally aware that Hope was smitten with lust, that Salvatore took the position she promoted.

'If your work means that much to you that you deny your most dire needs, then I think I should take it seriously.' Salvatore had whispered these words while running a soft finger over Hope's cheek.

It was their only physical contact, but the caress was caught by the photographer. There was no caption, nor a need for one. The naked lust betrayed in Hope's glistening eyes and parted, swollen lips provided all the statement needed. Gazing at the picture she relived that moment. She could feel the velvet graze across her cheek, smell the rich, sweet odour of the bougainvillea on the terrace mingle with Salvatore's earth scents. His body had been close, his lips almost upon hers. That was all that happened. He had then stepped back and Hope, trembling and faint, had slumped against the rail of the balcony. Had the moment lasted, she felt sure she would have thrust herself shamelessly upon him, her discipline shattered. Looking back she knew that he was aware of her rampant need for him and had, in spite of his reputation, let her go. She did not know that Salvatore's want had been as great as hers. Afterwards he had vented his frustrations on a famous Latin singer, whom he had wrested from the stage and dragged, unprotesting and delighted, to ravish in her dressing room. It was as close as Salvatore had ever come to a proposal of marriage. Now, however, Hope felt bitter. The picture was merely three months old, barely long enough for her body to lose its yearning. She could have had him, shed five years of celibacy in the olive embrace of the lover most hot-blooded women would die for. The desperate irony was that the article was printed in the magazine for which she had hunted Salvatore and it was his perfect white smile and burning eyes which graced the front cover. Despite her feelings of betrayal, Hope's treacherous body responded to the sight of his photograph. She had no doubt her career was ruined by exposure but it left her free. Perhaps, she reasoned, she should cast herself before him and demand the succour she had previously refused. It was a wild thought which she dismissed before it blossomed. She threw the magazine across the room. When the telephone buzzed she had reduced her anger to cold calm. An old trick she had learned in her psychology training. Once you know the facts do not fool yourself with the fancies, she admonished herself as she lifted the receiver.

'He wants you up top,' the elegant voice of the chairman's assistant enunciated before the line went dead.

Hope took her time. Her secretary had disappeared for lunch and left Hope logged onto her terminal. Normally Hope would chastise an assistant for this transgression but this time she was thankful. It took her three minutes to type and print her resignation, then she took the elevator to the penthouse to face her employer. Reggie conducted interviews in his lounge. He would ease his corpulent frame into a large leather chair, behind a massive mahogany desk, and wave his guest to the padded, sleek sofa. The trapped air of the cushion always escaped in embarrassment: an effect seemingly lost on the flatulent chairman. Hope wondered if it was intentional. He put himself at a disadvantage, being clearly uncomfortable, but imposed the greater mischief on his hapless victims. Hope knew this, so she perched gingerly on the edge of the seat, then slid back softly. It deprived Reggie of the noisy expulsion of air and gave her a sense of evil satisfaction. There was little in her life of which Reggie was not aware and they had long ago stopped pretending she was a nice little girl.

'Did you fuck him?' He gestured to the magazine, a copy of which lay open on the mahogany surface of the coffee table between them.

'No.' Hope placed her unfolded letter of resignation to cover the article.

Reggie grunted and leaned forward to pick it up. He studied it for a moment then crumpled it into a ball and tossed it on the floor.

'Pity.' He was referring to Hope's abstinence and she suspected he was a dirty old man who wanted to conjure the images of the two in sexual congress, had she confirmed his fears.

'Doesn't matter, I have a job for you.'

'I thought the publicity would negate that.'

'Got to send you undercover, old girl. Sorry.'

Hope sighed. She should have expected it. It was not that Pursuit kept their operatives secret, just that untoward exposure ruined their prospects. Clients felt that their discretion was compromised. If the person was valued the company simply found them less public tasks. In this case it turned out to be to seek a special placement for a company called Blain, LeChange and Partners. Reggie explained they were a new client, netted two billion per annum turnover and made their money dealing.

'They want a hacker.'

'As in computer hacker?' Hope did not keep the surprise from her voice. 'Are they nuts?'

'Give a damn, they're rich. Some bright young fellow thinks that a hacker is the best chappy to install the securities on their system. They want their network hacked and then the perpetrator to come fix it.'

'People have tried that logic before and got burned. Why don't we just get Rat to bodge it and run consultant on this one?'

'Suggested that. No, they want their own pet hacker. They think that they need to keep the securities constantly changing. Let slip that their dealing is sensitive.'

'This is not really my style, Reggie. I know my businessmen, but these underground types are aliens as far as I am concerned. I don't think they fall for Chanel suits and champagne.'

'I know, my dear. You must realize that we don't want to lose you and this rag . . .' he waved at the magazine, 'must be sorted. Until then this is important. I am not just handing you a dog. Blain, LeChange need this character. All I ask is that you stay to do it.'

Hope studied her employer earnestly. In a way he was confirming his faith in her. The type of prospect sought was clearly out of her range but he felt she could swing it and, if not, he would understand. She had done some swift calculations in her mind as the elevator carried her to the penthouse. With the earnings she had accrued over the last ten years, little of which had been spent, due to her generous expense account, she could live comfortably off the interest for the rest of her life. It had been a relief to proffer her resignation, it offered the freedom to do exactly as she pleased. Even get laid. However, apart from that titillating thought she had absolutely no idea what she would do. Her work had claimed her life, allowing her to form no lasting relationships with men or even girlfriends. Nor had she an interest in sports or hobbies. The most Hope did before she fell asleep was to read a book or masturbate gently to ease her stress. As Reggie and she gazed at one another they both knew this would be her last project for Pursuit. It was a respectable and lucrative task which would not sully her professional reputation, even should she fail. She could not help but rise to the challenge.

'I shall go and see Rat.' She rose as she spoke and Reggie grimaced a smile before reclaiming the magazine.

As the elevator doors closed she heard him chuckle. Yes, she thought, he would be impressed. What was bad for Hope might just be good for Pursuit. Strangely, she felt no anger, just a sad sense of letting go.

Rat operated from the cellar. It seemed apt, given his nickname, but in fact Hope knew that was a diminutive of 'Raith'. She had visited his nest once before and found it a confusion of strewn cables, dim lighting and the odour of stewed coffee. The only decent glow was from the computer screens and an expensive, adjustable desk lamp, which now cast a pool of light over cascading computer printouts. Rat was not expecting a visitor, much less Hope, and was in his typical pose. He slouched back in a swivel chair, feet propped on his desk, with a cold, half-full mug of coffee clutched to his chest. He stared at a terminal screen with an intensity which should have scared information from the databanks. For all intents and purposes he was lost in some nerdy world. Coincidentally, he was daydreaming about Hope. He had seen the magazine article. The offending publication was resting in a corner where he had tossed it in anger after dwelling on the caress of Salvatore.

Rat was heavily in lust with Hope. He had resigned himself to an unrequited passion but his daydreams were rampant with sweaty success and impossible penetrations. At this moment he was thrusting between her glowing bumcheeks as she arched and gasped broken demands. He could clearly envisage the slim line of her spine and the blossoming pinkness of her jostling globes as his penis rode, glistening with her generous, slick pouring. It was Rat's favourite dream. Hope, leaning on straight arms over his desk, the mute glow from the screen casting a pale halo over her naked shoulders. There were variations, some of which woke him in shamed and sweaty ejaculation in the night; some were more romantic.

Rat rued the day he had cast eyes on Hope. He felt obsessive and worried about his dark lusts. All he longed for was to muss her perfect hair, force up her skirt and rip her pants before plundering her ice-maiden calm with the sheer power of his hard, pleasure-giving rod. Right now, he was uncomfortably aware of the hardness trapped in his jeans and had laid one hand on the denim bulge comfortingly. He resolved to complete his fantasy and stroke to the final crescendo of her cries of release. It was when he sneaked a shifty look sideways to ensure his privacy and became aware of a silent presence that Rat erupted from his chair in shock, swearing. He stared in slack-mouthed surprise at Hope who stood, wide-eyed in the deluge of his curses. Her stare, drawn to the course of spilled coffee seeping down his tee-shirt, could not fail to take in the bulge of his flies; his clearly-stated arousal. She blushed, cursing herself for a schoolgirl reaction, but noted, once she dragged her eyes back to his dismayed expression, the echo of colour staining Rat's cheeks.

'Sorry, I didn't mean to startle you.' It was inadequate. She shuffled and stared at the floor. 'I mean, I should have warned you.' She gave up.

Rat stared at her. Hope had always projected an air of collected, cold confidence. Not unfriendly, just businesslike. Now she was wriggling in his cellar like a miscreant child. Before he had thought her merely icily beautiful. Now, with the pink glow of embarrassment, she was ravishing. A wild thought crossed his mind that perhaps she could be within his reach, now that she appeared human.

'I need your help.' Hope was appealing to him.

'You got it.' *Go on*, he willed, *tell me to kill someone, leap off a cliff, chop off my own dick*. He swiftly censored the last instruction and placed himself as her willing, but still able, slave. 'Anything,' he muttered, as she strained forward to hear.

Rat dropped swiftly into his chair and winced as his now half-erect penis caught viciously in the clench of his denim crotch. He wriggled until it seemed easier and looked expectantly at Hope. Before, when requesting his help, it had been for information and he, fingers poised over the keyboard, would trace the password of the Governor of the Bank of England, should she so wish.

'No, not data. A hacker. I need a hacker. The best hacker there is.'

Hope gazed at Rat. She guessed him to be in his mid-twenties. He was attractive in the way that men who devote themselves to something other than their appearance can sometimes be. His hair strayed around his shoulders in unruly curls, black and swept untidily from his forehead by irritated fingers. He tended to stoop and she wondered if it was his height or constant, bent attention to the computer screen that caused his shoulders their imagined burden. Long legs. They seemed impossibly so, as if it was only the weight of the soiled tennis shoes that disciplined their gangly progress. Now he had tucked them under the table she presumed their restraint allowed the gesturing of his hands.

There was a nervous energy in Rat that seemed to contradict the still hours in front of a screen. To Hope, he kept moving. If his hands weren't flying with his words, or constrained on the keyboard, his face was mobile. It was his eyes that were startling. The palest blue, almost lost in their white surround. Curious, searching and intelligent eyes that settled in earnest inquiry, then rode the waves of thought once the information was gleaned. Were he not a computer nerd, she reasoned, he would make a great inquisitor in the fine Spanish tradition.

In response to Hope's request Rat had stared into her eyes as if seeking more depth of information. His mouth, in repose, was wide, with a generous lower lip that he now tucked between his teeth as if the imprisonment would aid his thought process. For a moment he seemed very still, then he was all small movements. He shifted abruptly in his chair, swept his hair from his forehead and glanced at the screen before peering up at her.

'Hackers do not want to be found.'

She shrugged, 'I guessed that much. Do they want to be rich, though?'

Hope perched against his desk for two reasons. One, she found Rat's upward gaze disconcerting, so she wanted to lower herself to the level of his eyeline, and, two, her feet hurt. To further assist, she kicked off her shoes. They made small clicks as the steel-tipped heels struck the floor, drawing Rat's attention. He immediately wanted to suck her toes through the sheer denier of her stockings. While Hope had almost succeeded in reaching his eye-level it was, unfortunately, her breasts that settled at that height, as he found when he glanced up. His yen for Hope's toes was swiftly replaced by a greater hunger for her nipples, which accused him in the cool air of the cellar. He swallowed back the saliva that had suddenly flooded his mouth.

'No . . . sometimes.' He was losing her, she would go away if he could not help, so he added, 'But the best hacker is Willincough. I have to tell you, though, that if you are head-hunting him, Willincough's not moving'.

Any final reserves were shattered when Hope placed her hand on his naked forearm. He stared, his gaze riveted as she murmured.

'Please, Rat, will you try to get hold of him? At least get him to talk. It would really get me off the hook even if he says "No"'. She squeezed, her manicured nails curving along his flesh.

Nails he wanted raking along his back as her legs clung to his waist, her hips bucking in frenzy.

'Yes. You can't watch though. Sit somewhere.' Even as the words emerged he realized their stupidity. The cellar was devoid of chairs apart from the one he occupied. He pulled a crumpled sleeping bag from beneath his desk and thrust it at her.

'You use this?' Hope queried as she spread the bag on the floor and settled on it, after stripping off her suit jacket. She stretched her legs and leaned back on her elbows. Her breasts protested at the tightened silk of her blouse. She seemed not to realize that a button had popped open under the stress and Rat could view the lace-encased mounds, the valley tempting between. 'Yes.' His mind conjured an image of his penis, erect and purple with angry demand, sliding between the pale cushions, his hands pressing the giving orbs together.

'When I work late I sometimes sleep under the desk.' When he came, he decided, his white glue would arc over her face. He imagined rubbing his waning prick softly over her cheeks, smearing his liquid gift, as her tongue chased it to capture a taste. She could lick him clean, as if she were savouring a lollipop. Rat shook his head to clear the scene and swiftly dialled numbers into a mobile phone, listened a moment and muttered, 'Rat needs Willi on boobers, try 880011.' He disconnected and swung to a terminal, typed swiftly and then cocked his head to listen as a modem chirruped and trilled.

'You know him?' Hope began to feel impressed.

She knew that hackers were moles, cybertunnellers who journeyed through virtual mazes that were almost impossible to follow. If Rat could merely make a telephone call to contact one then it was more than likely he was a fellow hacker.

'Yes, I know him.' Rat watched the screen, then his fingers raced over the keys. He paused, then swung to face Hope. 'I am trying to get him to join a chat forum. That was a password.'

'I am impressed.' Hope's eyes were alive with curiosity.

She knew better than to ask questions but her estimate of Rat's abilities rose. When he remained silent, his face serious, she began to realize that he was taking her into his confidence. She nodded, as much to herself as to reassure him, and lay back on the spongy fabric. She felt strangely tired.

'I handed in my resignation.' Hope could not see Rat's expression, she spoke to the ceiling. 'Reggie would not accept it. We both know that this is my last project with Pursuit.'

She wondered why she was telling Rat. More than that, she found it difficult to trace how she had ended up lying on the cellar floor, barefoot and jacketless, on a sleeping bag impregnated with the odours of a colleague she barely knew. It was strangely peaceful in the dim glow of the computer light, the electronic hum louder at floor level. Without conscious thought she curled on her side and closed her eyes. Rat watched her for a while. He supposed Hope had gone to sleep. Her breathing had deepened and her eyelids fluttered then stilled. Her skirt had ridden up as she curled foetal-like and he could see the clips of her suspenders lying high on the backs of her thighs. As if in answer to his dreams she shifted, drawing her knees higher, and offered him the cup of sheer, white panties. He could just make out the darker shadow of the cleft between her bumcheeks. He slumped in his chair, his long legs stretched towards Hope and rested his chin on the steeple of his fingers, studying her minutely. She seemed so vulnerable. Her blouse had rucked and now the neckline was open, revealing a translucent lace-edged bra. The dark stain of her areola held his gaze.

'Uh oh,' he whispered.

An idea was taking shape. Rat longed to cross the space, kneel beside the sleeping woman of his dreams and slide his hand between her naked thighs, in that space where the stocking tops ended. He did not feel gentle. He wanted to cup her corolla hard and feel her juices soak through the white crotch and stain his palm, just before he twisted the thin fabric and forced his fingers past its barrier and straight into her wet cave. She would sigh, shift in her sleep to lie on her stomach, and part her legs for him. There was a small vent in the back of her skirt. The tantalizing vee that designers left to allow easy movement. It would be easy to rip the seam from there. The image of Hope, her skirt torn open and peeled back to expose her pristine white panties and lacy suspenders, rose in his mind. He would push the crotch of her panties to one side, cover her from behind and plunge in without preamble.

That was when she would wake, panicked at his invasion, and he would pin her arms, his weight pressing her down, and keep thrusting. Soon she would whimper and rise to him, slippery and swollen around his bursting cock. Hope, lost in rapture, her hands scrabbling to free her breasts so she could pinch at her swollen nipples, knead her bulging orbs harshly and delight in the pain. He would have a hard time staying mounted, so hard that he would slide from her and her demand would then be loud for a different plunging. Her bottom would weave before him and he would strip her sodden panties to her thighs, part her bumcheeks and force firmly past the star-pucker to invade her more secret canyon. Oh yes, his head rang with her moans and rampant, wild demands as he tupped forcefully.

'Harder, harder!' It was Rat's own voice that whispered harshly.

His hand was tight and working furiously around his shaft, the foreskin rumpling and stretching under his ministration. He spurted with a groan and kept stroking until the last quivers stilled. He felt shocked, his blood rang in his ears and his breath was harsh and uneven. At some stage his fantasy had overtaken him and he had released himself and wanked, wide to Hope's view. He blinked and swiftly stuffed his waning member back into its denim prison. Afraid, he stared at Hope. She had not moved, her breath still flowed evenly although she seemed unnaturally still.

'Oh, Jesus,' he whispered softly and ran his hand over his face. 'I must be going crazy.'

He knew, however, that he would stop at nothing to seduce the woman on the floor. Now he had the means available. 'Willi,' he muttered, 'you are damned well going to move for me.'

The computer beeped and he swung to face it. Concentrating on the scroll. With his hands still trembling he started typing. He heard the shift of fabric as Hope woke but did not turn around. He was afraid of what would show in his face. Hope had not been asleep. She drifted but became aware of Rat's scrutiny and, beneath lowered lashes, had watched his progress. When he ripped at the buttons of his jeans and freed his hard rod she had barely restrained her gasp. He had worked at himself like a starving man, pounding his flesh mercilessly until she almost cried out her concern. She longed for him to cross the space and sate his hunger at her fleshy altar. She could feel her need flush through her and seep between her thighs and she clenched rhythmically to try to press herself to release as his groans presaged his coming.

Hope was not successful and a sick disappointment washed through her. At one point she almost rose to join him, her mouth wide and hungry for the occupation of his rosy bulb, her tongue swollen and tender and her saliva as copious as the pale custard slicking her thighs. The event seemed like a dream and she was painfully aware that her provocation was not without design. The whole day had been bizarre. It felt as if she was shedding skins and leaving her sophisticated shell behind. At some time, perhaps when Rat had feasted his eyes on her breasts, she had started to want him, recognizing his ill-concealed lust for her. She knew when her buttons had opened and when her skirt had risen, yet she had not wanted to make more direct moves. It seemed inevitable to her that they would mate. Some part of her thrilled to the game: she would hunt him and, like the businessmen she pursued, he would be a willing victim. She adjusted her clothing and rose as Rat stopped typing. He switched off the terminal and swung to face her, now composed.

'Willi wants to talk. He is in Eire and you have to go there but in secret.'

'*We* have to go there,' Hope placed deliberate emphasis on the plural, then stooped to pick up that magazine, 'and I have the perfect place to meet.'

Chapter Two

'. . . far from the crowds you can find a tranquillity and beauty that allows you to face your sea-change, gather strength to continue in your life without the stresses and pressures that have so far bested you.

In a small group of peers, guided by hosts Karen and Brandon Ormandy, we promise healing and personal growth. Perhaps you merely need to retrace your steps, return to your centre – or maybe you just need a pause from the rat race . . .'

'It is a retreat,' Hope observed, and continued reading. 'Look – in a stone house on an island in Loch Derg in Ireland.' Her finger traced the lines, as she bent to share the magazine with Rat.

Rat half-listened, far too absorbed with the facing page that carried the 'kiss of Salvatore' and the elegant passage of Hope's manicured fingernail along the text. Far from taking a lesson from his recent exposure, he found himself obsessing anew, imagining that finger tracing a pathway down his chest, over his stomach, and . . .

He curtailed his thoughts irritably, shifting in his seat as if a sudden physical change would reintroduce reality. The ploy failed when his shoulder bumped sharply against

Hope's breast. She straightened swiftly, a small crease of pain flitting across her face, and her hand rose instinctively to cup her injury. Both blushed and, to cover his confusion, Rat fixed his attention on the advertisement.

'It sounds naff,' he muttered gruffly, aggressively embarrassed, with an after-image of Hope, her hand massaging her soft breast. His treacherous imagination raced forward to savour a picture, stripped of clothing, in which a lusciously – endowed Hope masturbated passionately for his voyeuristic pleasure. He groaned.

'It's not that bad!' Hope stared at him, her breast smarting but now unattended. She chose to ignore the inadvertent transgression but was unsure whether his moan was related to his embarrassment or to the idea of the retreat. 'It's secluded and, by its nature, supposedly secret – so it is perfect for Willincough. Anyway, I like the idea of a pause from the rat-race.' She smiled encouragement at Rat.

Accepting her cue, he returned a grimace. 'I'll speak to Willi.'

'Great.' This time her smile was genuine. 'I'll telephone for details.'

Hope tore the page from the magazine, slipped on her shoes and jacket and left Rat staring at her photographed lust, regretting that he had not watched the passage of her bottom as she had exited the cellar.

'Okay,' he muttered, 'you get a pause but "rat race" is what you will have to do to get away from me on this miserable island!' His lame bravado did little to lift his despondency. For all his determination he feared that his obsession would make a fool of him whenever Hope was around. He twisted his head and sniffed, hoping for a whiff of perfume, a tangible reminder to accompany the imagined, soft warmth imprinting his shoulder. He leaned forward and began to tap impatiently on the keyboard.

Hope noted her e-mail icon flashing while she struggled to understand the information being given by a strong Irish accent over the telephone line. She read the mail as she listened and jotted notes on her desk blotter.

> 'Willi's in. Send me the details by return and I'll pass them on . . . Rat'

Hope leaned back in her chair and kicked off her shoes, recalling Rat slaving over his hard rod. Removed from the moment, she was amazed at her clear recollection of the length and angry purple demand of his penis; even more amazed when her thighs tightened in empathy. She slipped her hand beneath her skirt, confirming the dampness of her crotch. She had originally intended merely to satisfy her curiosity, but she found herself tucking her fingers absently under the white barrier. She let her mind wander back to the cellar, Rat's whispered desperation as he gushed and the sharp, hard connection of his shoulder on her breast.

Her fingers danced, forcing the material barrier aside and slipping back the tiny hood of her clitoris to press with an almost metallic intensity on her exposed nub. With her head back and eyes closed she recognized, before losing herself in the moment, that if Rat were to enter her office she would not hesitate to take him between her thighs, wrestle his shaft free and force him forward until he slid inside her. His own eager thrusting would then allow her to slouch back and concentrate on release.

Frustrated with the impediment of her clothing, Hope wriggled until her skirt rucked up over her hips, slid forward until her bottom was precariously perched and planted one heel on her chair so she could open her thighs more widely. Her pose left her wide open to observation, a fact Reggie enjoyed when he arrived moments later. He watched with pleasure the slow caress of her fingers, decided that Hope was lost in sensations, and then approached. When his fingers gently pressured hers aside, Hope started violently, shocked back into reality.

She looked with ghastly alarm at Reggie, who lumbered to his knees between her thighs, preventing the closure of her legs. He clamped a firm hand on her raised foot to thwart her attempt to dislodge it from the chair. With no purchase she was helpless to crawl from his approach.

'Shhhh,' he whispered, 'it's okay.' He stroked her inner thigh as if calming a frisky mare. 'Close your eyes.'

His voice, low with consolation, repulsed Hope, as did his florid face, his intense scrutiny of her quim, and his wet tongue darting along his red, fleshy lips. Shuddering, she closed her eyes to block the awful picture, and slumped into submission. She had withdrawn her hand, pressing it hard against her midriff as if to block the scene below, its reassuring press a retention of her integrity. Recognizing that the situation was beyond her physical control, Hope attempted mental control, forcing a picture of Rat into her mind. All she could conjure was the image of him standing, appalled, in her doorway, while he watched Reggie drench in her juices. She found this image inescapably arousing and her horror of her ageing, gouty employer seemed to contribute. A sick passion doused the last of her reserves.

Reggie, sensing the change, slid his hand to cup Hope's

fleshy nether lips. He pressed into the moist parting, then massaged, rhythmically and patiently. The sensation drew Hope to participate and her hips edged forward. Her hand fell from her stomach and lay loosely at her side and she offered no resistance when Reggie manipulated the buttons of her blouse with his free hand, merely moaned when the fingering faltered.

Reggie forced the lacy cup of Hope's bra from her right breast. It bulged from the cloth platform, uncomfortable and trapped. He sucked her nipple into his mouth, and worked it harshly, hungry as a baby, his breath escaping in wet slurps. He gripped and pinched Hope's other nipple harshly. Her small cries were pained and encouraging. When he suddenly thrust two fingers into her vagina, he bit on her nipple and she jolted towards him with a loud groan, her hand swiftly rising to clamp his head hard into her breast.

Reggie pulled away and watched his fingers work her cave, fascinated by the increasing flow and grabbing demand. This was Hope, his little blonde employee, and he felt the conflict rise and titillate. With her severe grey suit awry, a breast poking lewd and blushing and her thighs parted, she was whorish and exposed. As he thrust experimentally, she mewled, her lips slack and mouth open, tongue working. Her pudendum was swollen, lubricated and lush, wisps of pale hair curling wetly. His fingers, square and slightly gnarled, buried in her soft tissues, then stilled, and Reggie bent to taste.

He lapped at her, sweeping her musky juice into his mouth and delighting in the push of her against his lips and her increased, now strident call for release. Her vaginal walls had opened widely and were smooth and hungry. He rued the flaccidity of his age even as his surrogate rods consumed her space but, with the inventiveness of experience, bent his thumb to push at her anal pucker as his lips trapped her swollen clitoris. She rose slightly, with a gasp, as he entered her rear. Then she stilled, her breath caught, and he could feel the tremble and gulp inside her forcing along his fingers as she came. Hot fluid spurted around his fingers and into his mouth, giving proof of her woman's ejaculate. Her moans faded and she slumped, breathing heavily.

Reggie licked her softly, eased from her and quickly left the room. He understood that her libidinous transformation might lead to remorse and disgust, a matter she would wish to resolve without his presence. He paused outside the door and said kindly, his words loud enough to penetrate into her office, 'Pretend it never happened, my dear. Pretend it was just a fantasy.'

But, she reasoned as she tugged her clothes straight, it was not a fantasy. She removed her panties, screwing them into a sodden ball that she threw into the wastebasket, and patted herself dry with tissues before tugging her skirt down. She considered her aversion to Reggie, whom she had regarded as a sly and disgusting old man. He had tendered to her needs, whatever thrill he had enjoyed in so doing. Her orgasm had been a satisfying release, although her body still hungered for a larger penetration. He had instructed her to pretend. Hope recognized that his words were well-intentioned, but her newly-emergent needs were pressing. She could think of no reason why their intimacy could not recur. Each had enjoyed the event, and the illicit relationship between colleagues seemed a minor barrier to overcome by consent. It did not escape her attention that she simply liked the idea of being pampered and submissive.

Submission did not mean, she reasoned, that she had to lie back and think patriotic thoughts while a man plundered her body, and it had not been like that with Reggie. It was her power, her womanhood and her wet, swollen readiness that had summoned him to her need. If anything, it was his ministry that had been submissive. Had he stayed, perhaps the roles would have reversed and it would have been she who bowed to his control. Dark desires swept over her.

Her years with Reggie had revealed him as astute, a powerful man who was, at times, unscrupulous and manipulative. He had peddled Hope's successful combination of beauty and predation but she knew that he had employed women of a more sensual persuasion on some projects. Perhaps, had she been more sexual in her approach, her services could have been earthier and exposure by the magazine avoided simply because to reveal her would indict all those involved. It was a form of protection that it was not too late to introduce. This was her time of change.

A vague memory rose and she leaned forward, frowning with concentration. She had visited a gypsy three years earlier and had her Tarot read. One card stuck in her mind, the last laid on the table. It depicted a young woman, bound and blindfolded, surrounded by swords that lodged points downward in the wet soil around the woman's naked feet. She learned that the card was not as negative as it appeared, but heralded a sea-change for Hope, a time when she would escape a difficult situation by cutting her bonds. Three years would pass before she had to face this event.

Hope, sure in her career, had dismissed the prediction,

preferring to deal with her demanding present. Now, however, facing the demise of her career with Pursuit three years later, she felt chilled at the recollection, although it was the symbolism of the bonds and blindfold that held her mind in thrall.

It seemed that her search for Willincough barely camouflaged her growing enthusiasm for the Retreat in Ireland. Booked in for a fortnight, she had a mere two days to prepare for travelling. Part of that process involved the cutting of ties and the development of different goals for her future. Reggie was somehow associated with her liberation; he had controlled her life for the last ten years.

The card had depicted submission but the portent was one of liberation through escape and the confrontation of choices. It was Reggie who would have to release her bonds and, she thought excitedly, with her passive participation he could endorse her emergence and set her free.

She e-mailed Rat with information concerning the Retreat, advising him that he and Willi should book independently to retain anonymity but that she would reimburse them from her expenses, then she slipped a cheque into an envelope with a handwritten registration. As she bent forward to place the letter in the out-tray for her secretary, she glimpsed the ball of her panties in her wastebasket.

She thought for a moment, then plucked the garment from the bin and pushed it into a padded, internal communications envelope and addressed it to Reggie. He would receive it that afternoon: a blatant, sexual invitation. Caught up with symbolism, Hope fancied that the message was more profound. She was offering her intimate self, supplicating Reggie and thanking him. She was risking herself in the form of a symbolic surrogate which presaged her own surrender to his power.

She was deep in thought when her secretary slipped into her office and lifted the envelopes from the tray. She cast a quizzical look at Hope and offered her coffee, then stood embarrassed under the continuing scrutiny.

Hope wondered that she had never actually noticed the girl before. Granted Amy had only worked for her for two months, but she had never really looked at her properly. She was startled to note that the girl was slim and attractive, shy and eager to please. Hope had been too engrossed in her work, or too often absent from her office, to form a relationship but that did not seem to her to excuse her sheer bad manners. She felt guilty, especially when she found herself gazing at the small slope of breast and tight waist of the girl hovering before her. She smiled, disliking herself, but unable to avoid her new predatory bent.

'Yes, Amy, thank you – coffee would be nice.' She paused, raising a delaying palm as the girl turned to leave. 'By the way, I have a special project to do, if you want some overtime?'

Amy nodded eagerly. She learned it would entail night work, at Hope's flat – after a day of shopping. When she left the office, carrying the package for Reggie, she had little doubt of Hope's intention; women had looked at her that way before. She smiled to herself as the lift rose to the penthouse. While she had been scrutinized before, she had never responded, but with Hope, whom she admired, she had every intention of throwing herself fully into her work. She prodded the small bag addressed to Reggie, then noticed it was not sealed: only a butterfly grip held the edges together. Curious, she straightened the wings and eased the padded lips of the envelope apart, reached in and drew out the panties. She stared for a moment as the wet garment slid over her fingers, then she lifted it to her face to bury her nose in the white folds, took the crotch into her mouth and sucked. Sex traces mingled with her saliva, earthy and foreign. *There*, she thought as she tucked the panties back into the envelope, *you get two for the price of one, my dear Chairman*. She sauntered into Reggie's office, grinning, and tossed the package onto his desk.

'Looks like you have an admirer, dad.' She left before he could retort.

Reggie pulled the damp fabric from the envelope and sighed. He recognized the gesture and the farewell it indicated. He had savoured the flavour that remained in his mouth after he left Hope and there was still an aftertaste, which he renewed by pressing his tongue into the moist fabric. He felt slightly uncomfortable with the knowledge that his daughter was aware of his liaison with Hope, but not sufficiently so to avoid dwelling on their next encounter. He had already been advised, by his assistant, that Hope had scheduled an appointment for four o'clock. Obviously she had expected her panties to be firmly plastered against his face prior to her visit, so whatever he might do would come as no surprise. He at least knew that she would be naked under her skirt. He decided to presume Hope's supplication. With her departure from Pursuit he had little to lose in so doing, therefore he would concentrate on imposing his preferences.

Reggie flicked the intercom.

'Connect me to that shop in Soho.' He waited, sensing the disapproval of his assistant, until the burr of an outside call interrupted, followed by the sound of the receiver lifting. 'I need some stuff,' he said, 'but only if you can get it to me within the next two hours.' It was unnecessary for Reggie to identify himself: he purchased a lot of interesting products from Kinks of Soho. After he replaced the receiver, he viewed the room critically, rose and then pulled the large leather chair from behind his desk to position it carefully in front of the large windows.

There was a man gazing through the windows of a high-rise building opposite. He watched Reggie with interest, waving when the older man turned to face him. The stranger smiled with anticipation when offered a thumbs-up response. He had witnessed this scene before. He gestured to his wristwatch and signalled an acknowledgement when Reggie held up four fingers. The man then walked over to his liquor cabinet, checked the contents and sauntered to his desk, where he began making telephone calls.

Hope viewed herself critically in the mirror of the *en suite* powder room attached to her office. She barely recognized herself. Her basic features remained unchanged, the slant of her cheek and soft wave of her blonde hair, but her eyes sparkled and the contours of her face seemed softer. She felt different.

After Amy had left her office to deliver Reggie's envelope to him, Hope had experienced severe misgivings. Her hand had strayed towards the telephone several times, her intention to cancel the afternoon appointment almost successful. Each time, she had balked. She felt confused. A barrier between work and play had been breached and her resolution to keep the two distinct created a conflict. Her imagery, the symbolic cutting of bonds, now compounded her confusion.

Peering at her reflection she saw an expression mirrored, one she recognized when facing a head-hunt quarry. She recalled her observation at these times – will he jump, or won't he? There was a magical moment when she knew she had successfully landed her quarry – when the target blinked, took a deep breath and acceptance dawned. She watched herself progress to this point, took a deep breath and offered her reflection a rueful smile.

Hope stripped until she was naked, wadded some paper hand-towels and held them under the warm flow of the basin faucet. She cleaned herself, drawing the damp pad over and around her breasts, beneath her arms and along her taut stomach. She placed one foot on the edge of the basin, feeling the tight stretch of her inner thigh muscles, which protested at her exaggerated stance. She re-wet the paper wad and watched herself dab and stroke over her open and exposed quim, marvelling that she was ministering to the place at which Reggie had supped; a place which seemed strangely remote from her, although the frisson of pleasure as she washed lent it reality.

Rat was not far from her thoughts. He seemed a later treat, reserved for Ireland. A fanciful image arose, involving a parade of men bent between her thighs, their mouths eager – Rat's long hair flowing; Reggie's sparse dome, an imagined Willincough. Merely the backs of heads; parading future patrons. As her thoughts wandered, she stared at her quim, parted the lobes with her finger and dipped into herself, wondering at her new lusts and the strange power she now felt she possessed. A power, she allowed, that would enable her to seduce

Amy and lend her the determination to feast at the young woman's altar.

She slipped her moistened finger into her mouth, curious to taste the dew that men desired. It was strange and pleasant, fresh, rich with musk, like a foreign sweetmeat. As she drew her leg from its raised position, Hope determined that she would test the flavour of Amy, ascertain if she differed. Her own sap left a cream in her throat, and a longing to garner a more generous helping from her secretary the next evening.

Hope also felt nervous, a slightly bewildered excitement, as she redressed. She stood in her white bra, suspenders and stockings, peering down at the freshly puffed hair of her mound as if seeing her body for the first time. When she exited the office, her pudendum naked under the straight, strict line of her grey suit, she did so with the knowledge that the next eyes to peer at her private places would be those of the Chairman of Pursuit, her employer and sudden lover.

She felt dream-like as the elevator rose, opened and allowed her into the penthouse. Reggie's assistant was absent, which was a relief, and to knock on the door to his office seemed absurd, so Hope opened it softly and stood quietly inside the threshold, waiting to be noticed. She kept her head lowered and her hands clasped loosely in front of her.

Reggie studied Hope, unable to avoid a comparison with her earlier visit to his office. She had strode in, her chin high, exhibiting a belligerence which he recognized as her strength and had grown to admire. She had been businesslike and had dealt with him as an equal. She had not demurred, philosophical about any damage wrought through her exposure by the magazine article.

He needed Willincough, and her fall from grace enabled him to send her underground. He felt no guilt and had merely taken advantage of an opportunity, as he had when he chanced on her masturbating in her office. Now he would also take advantage of her sexual emergence and her supplication to him. It was how Reggie operated, how he had built the wealth and strength of Pursuit, and how he intended to continue a proven formula.

He observed the lowered slope of Hope's shoulders, her glance roving the weft of his carpet and her hands, clasped softly at her mound. It confirmed her attitude and endorsed his reading of the situation. While he was not given to introspection, Reggie did wonder what had transpired to produce the startling changes in Hope. He dismissed Rat as a catalyst, but accorded him a measure of provocation, on the basis that she had been pleasuring herself subsequent to her visit to the cellar.

No, he reasoned, it was Hope herself who had rung in the changes. He admired her all the more for her ability to adapt and shed her cloak of celibacy to bask in a sexual spotlight. Were he a humble man, he would savour the privilege of the invitation she offered him, to play his part in her emergence. However, he shrugged dismissively, he was not that humble and was simply content to take advantage of yet another surprising opportunity.

'Please take off your clothes, my dear. That's right, just leave the bra and stockings.' Reggie leaned against his desk, fully clothed, and watched Hope slowly unbutton her blouse. Although she could not see through the large picture window, he noted that a small group had assembled;

men of power, voyeurs who understood Reggie's little treats to be 'sweeteners' that required a return. They milled idly, as if at a cocktail party, drinks in hand, awaiting his signal. He could see the good-natured smiles and laughter.

Hope remained by the door, her blouse and skirt puddling around her feet. Reggie appreciated her beauty, the swell of her firm breasts above the rim of the bra and the puff of hair gracing her pubic mound.

'Come to me'. He drew a large square of black silk from his pocket, the signal which encouraged the watchers to take their seats. 'At any time, should you wish me to stop, you merely have to say the word "cave".' He ensured eye contact, 'Say it please, now – so I can remember how it sounds when you pronounce it.'

'Cave.'

'And again, please.'

'Cave.'

'Okay, that is your safe word, my dear. It is very, very important to remember it. You see, to say "no" is part of the fantasies and games we can play.' He tied the band around Hope's eyes, turned her from him and propelled her towards the window, stationed her in front of the chair he had positioned earlier and then left her.

'Take off your brassiere, please. I would like very much for you to fondle your nipples to peaks'.

Hope unclipped and slid the scanty garment from her breasts. Unfettered, they jounced, firm and rounded, until she caught them and hefted them in her palms as if showing prize melons to a competition judge. She captured her nipples and rotated them in her fingers, found it awkward, then slipped her fingers into her mouth to wet them and resumed the ministry. Her areolae bloomed, the sharp exclamation of her nipples a confession of her growing arousal. Her hands wandered, sliding over the globes, kneading and stroking. Her lips parted and her breath quickened.

Reggie approached. 'Enough,' he whispered, 'now part your legs for me. That's good; wider, please.' He kneeled and clasped a leather band around each of Hope's ankles, then attached a bar between the bands, which prevented her from drawing her feet together. Her balance was compromised and she swayed and uttered a small cry of fear.

'Shhhh, it's okay.' He grasped her waist from the rear, and slid his hands to cover her breasts, to enjoy the pucker of nipples on his palms. Thrust tight against Hope's back, he licked her shoulder, savouring the light salty flavour of her skin, pleased that she had avoided perfume. She leaned into him, thrusting her breasts into his palms and he quickly pinched hard on her nipples, delighting in her swift moan.

'I am going to let you go now, and I want you to stretch your hands forward. That is good, lean now and you will feel the window. Okay, bring your hands together.'

Hope felt cold metal surround her wrists and heard the unmistakable click as handcuffs tightened. She felt afraid and uttered a cry of protest.

'Trust me,' he commanded. 'You will be safe, but if you attempt to move your hands you will fall because your feet are manacled.' His voice was stern and he gave her a sharp smack on her bottom which caused her to jolt with surprise, but she held her stance. He did not inform her that, were she to fall back, she would be saved by the sturdy chair.

'Good,' he praised. 'Now keep very still.'

Reggie licked the nipple clamps before clipping them to Hope's breasts. He tightened the small, winged screws and tugged gently to ensure their attachment, then ran the light chains to the bridge of the handcuffs, securing the end with a clasp.

'If you move a lot, my dear, you will start to enjoy the pull on your breasts but, for now, keep still.'

Hope experimented. She leaned her bottom backwards and felt her breasts tug, pulled forward by the chain; the clamps hurt her nipples but felt good. The sharp sting of Reggie's hand on her bumcheek reminded her of his instruction to remain still. She felt the imprint burn and then the caress of his tongue on the heat.

'More!' she demanded. The sensation was wonderfully intense.

'This once I will indulge you. After that you behave.' Reggie laughed.

She was prepared and, as he swung his hand, she jutted her rear. As his palm met her cheek, her breasts were pulled, nipples sharply snagged. Her cry was pitiful but her deep moan which followed, as pleasure rode the waves of pain, was heartfelt.

Reggie felt absurdly proud when he observed the handclapping of the watchers. He smiled at the assembly and executed a small bow, as if he had choreographed the event. Hope exceeded his expectation. He suspected that she had not experienced bondage before and her immediate, pleasured response was rewarding. He tapped the microphone attached to his lapel, peering at the man, and received a nod which confirmed that the audio was working. They would have appreciated her vocal response. He needed them to know that this show was not rehearsed.

'Hope,' he murmured, his breath softly brushing her ear, 'have you ever done anything like this before?' Reggie ran a finger along her spine, cupped a bumcheek and squeezed.

She shook her head.

'You enjoy it, don't you? You trust me?'

'Yes.' Hope's voice was low.

'You know that, if you are good, I will reward you by showing you new pleasures?'

'Yes.'

'Good. So far you have been very, very good. So I am going to do something nice for you.' Reggie withdrew and there was a silent pause during which Hope strained to hear, her head turning, blindly seeking clues to prepare her for her next experience.

She had relaxed, no longer fighting the darkness or the restriction of her movement. The clips holding her nipples felt comfortable and now that the muscles of her arms had eased, she felt poised. Her rampant arousal had lessened to pleased anticipation. She realized that she was enjoying her submission. She had been forceful in her career, independent and manipulative, with a cultivated charm that allowed her to control her quarries. Now she was stripped and free, feeling the emergence of a glorious womanhood and a pride that her firm body and moist willingness was all the reward that her dominator required of her. 'Being good' was natural to her, all that had passed before was a game that she had played well. She knew that, in time, she would learn to be naughty – provocative, so that the reward would be the freedom to punish her. She shivered, her mind racing with possibilities, already recognizing that Reggie's expertise was a wonderful introduction to a new beginning, one that felt so natural that she wondered that she had not known of it before. But it was only one half of an equation: the other was to be found in Ireland when she had distanced herself from the past. For now it was sufficient to experience this new adventure. She smiled.

'Why are you smiling?'

'Because I want to please you.' The conviction in Hope's statement surprised Reggie. Perversely, he cursed the magazine and Salvatore, recognizing that the short time he had to enjoy Hope would create no lasting bond. He was to be master for a session, but to discover the natural slave in Hope was a precious coincidence. He could prepare her, however, and ensure that her next experience would add value. He paused, staring at the audience. All sophisticated in the art of domination, there was one man seated slightly apart from the rest, his legs stretched casually forward, an arm draped over the back of his chair. A man completely at ease, yet alert and judging.

That man would recognise the potential of the lovely woman, bared to him across the small expanse between the buildings. If Reggie could manipulate the situation then he was sure he could surrender Hope into the care of this stranger and, in return, he would gain a powerful ally in the business arena.

'How do you think you can please me, Hope?' Reggie stood back to admire her. He glanced at the stranger. The man had leaned forward, his elbows resting on now bent knees. Hope's answer was critical.

She was glorious. Instinctively her head was bent, her body open to his ministry, whatever act he might choose to inflict. Her response had been full of quiet passion, a confession that her submission was true to her, not merely a contrived attempt to parody the art. He was sure that her sexual emergence would continue to be full of wonder, that she would experiment; perhaps she would also discover an ability to dominate that would exceed the expectations of her supplicants. Hope, poised on the edge of discovery, was stunning.

She was humble in her awareness of her own beauty. It was for his enjoyment. Her sexual passion, the wet response between her thighs, was an instant endorsement of her giving of pleasure. She stilled in thought and, when she responded, Reggie knew that her words reflected her deep self-search.

'I can please you by being proud of who I am – a woman who will be at your bidding.'

'Do you know my bidding?'

'No, it is your pleasure to know your bidding, mine to accept and learn it – not to presume.'

'Take your hands from the window.' Reggie commanded.

Hope shivered, paused for a brief moment, bent her elbows and pushed, hoping the backwards momentum would carry her weight until she could stand straight. For a moment it seemed that she would succeed. Her thigh and stomach muscles knotted with effort and she bent her knees slightly, but her blindness was disorienting and, with no visible reference, she began to topple forwards. She raised her imprisoned hands to cover her face; with her feet barred she was vulnerable. She gasped as her breasts swung free, the clamps biting anew.

Her trust in Reggie was absolute and her faith rewarded when his body broke her fall. He staggered slightly as she landed against him and she cried out when her nipples pressed into his chest but her main feeling was one of gratitude accompanied by the concern that she was inconveniencing him with her weight. Although she anticipated more pain, she slid along him until she crouched, her face hard in his groin when she dropped her hands between her knees.

He allowed her a moment, knowing that her harsh breathing was a result of her effort to accept the torment of the clamps. When she seemed to ease, he stroked her head, his fingers lacing through the blonde waves. The heat of her gasping felt pleasant, penetrating the fabric which covered his groin. He was surprised that he hardened but dismissed his response: it had little to do with his plans and he had no intention of employing his penis for her pleasure. He bent to slip his hands under her armpits and urged her to rise.

'Okay, lean against the window again.' His voice was soft and caring, betraying his pleasure.

Hope was flushed with pride as she complied. She felt his tongue circle the clamps and then the soft gust of his breath. The pain eased to a pleasant ache and the cool dampness he invoked was a kindly-meant gift.

'Thank you,' she offered.

'I told you that if you were good, I would reward you.' He glanced through the window and was satisfied to note that the stranger had resumed his casual pose but was now smiling his approval.

'Hope,' Reggie's tone was now conversational, 'there were many things I planned to do to please you but I think we both know that anticipation is often more exciting than the fact, so our time is nearly up.'

Hope moaned her disappointment. Her loins had woken and were aching for attention. He smacked her breast sharply, hard enough to leave a pale pink imprint of his fingers. He moved to her side, faced her and studied her reaction. As the pain receded, Hope felt a delicious warmth which spread through her swollen nether lips. She longed to be able to shut her legs, to tense her muscles and squeeze to ease her throbbing need. She felt her wetness build and a sexual ache start to torment her. When he next spoke, Reggie's words thrilled her.

'You have been so good that I am going to do something very nice for you, my dear.' His words presaged the warmth of his hand as it travelled softly over her waist. It felt as if he was rolling soft balls along her and she delighted when he traversed her mound, then tucked his fingers into her crease, manipulating the squashy spheres until they slipped inside her. She mewled with pleasure, then disappointment when his hand left her. She felt a presence but it was inadequate to her needs. Moments later, however, she trembled when a small vibration started, increasing in strength until she could hear a muted hum and feel a jostling inside herself.

'These are sponge duos,' Reggie explained, 'the wetter you are, the more they will swell. I hold a remote control that will start and control their vibration.' He turned the balls off and Hope concentrated, her breath quickened, and noted that she felt fuller. 'I am going to give the control to a special man and you will have to seek him in order to obtain pleasure. Nor am I prepared to allow you to remove the balls.'

Hope felt Reggie pass something between her thighs, then draw flaps up to her waist. She heard sharp clicks and tried to imagine what encased her. It felt uncomfortable and unyielding, heavy and constricting. Not tight, but with little space between the swell of her pudenda and the harsh gusset.

'You are going to want to pee. You therefore have a choice. Either you can wet this garment or you can seek the gentleman and hope he feels kindly enough to free you, perhaps even use the remote to please you. I would suggest that you seek him fast – it would be unseemly to wet your panties, unless that is his preference.'

Reggie crossed to his desk and pushed a button, causing heavy drapes to draw over the window and dim the room. He returned to Hope and propelled her gently across the room, allowing for the awkward stagger caused by the ankle bar. He drew her to a halt before a full-length, gilt-framed mirror and took off her blindfold.

Hope's first act was to peer down to identify her encasement. She stared at the heavy black leather chastity belt with wonder. It seemed ugly and bulky on her pale body, the silver padlock mocking. When she raised her eyes, she met her reflection. Her arms hung down, wrists cuffed, and her hands were gracefully clasped, resting in front of the leather belt. Her breasts, pushed together slightly by the hang of her arms, bulged. The clamps glinted dully, the silver chain snaking loosely.

Hope felt distanced from the woman she viewed. She found the image bizarre but appealing, aesthetic in the dim, silvery light. Reggie stood beside her, holding her arm to help her to balance. Of all the paraphernalia, she found the ankle bar most distracting. The picture presented seemed skewed by the unnatural parting of her thighs. But it was a good way to expose her secret places, notwithstanding her inclination to hide shyly. It was this that made her finally aware that submission was not the surrendering of her power, but the means to enforce it. The statement embodied in her stance was celebratory, an assertion of her womanly parts and her glistening beauty. It invited control yet rendered the controller helpless.

'Disarming,' she at last commented.

'Yes.' Reggie knelt at her feet and unclasped the ankle bands, rose and unlocked the handcuffs, and partially unscrewed the clamps. He gently cupped Hope's nipples, keeping the clamps in place. 'Wait a moment, let the blood flow, and then remove them.' He let go, ensured the clamps would not immediately fall, then lifted her hands in place.

The handcuffs were loose but remained around her wrists, so the chain would not drag the clips from her. She paused, shuffled her feet together and sensed the balls inside her as her thighs met, slightly impeded by the leather gusset. She was reluctant to shed her bonds, aware that to so do would render her more naked than were she simply without clothes. Without her fetters, she felt she would be more exposed – they were symbols that lent her an identity but, like the woman portrayed on the Tarot card, she needed to be set free. There was fear of the unknown. However, the promise implicit in the chastity belt was reassuring, she knew it would allow her to exit Reggie's office with a sense of freedom yet allow her to seek new goals. It helped that there was a stranger whom she could approach to gain a clearer definition of those goals. She dropped her hands and the clamps fell away. Her nipples were red and angry and she wet a finger and gently patted them, enjoying the residual pain. The handcuffs slipped from her wrists and fell to the floor to join the ankle bar, the silver chain coiling and clinking sharply as it met its metal companion.

'Remember this number.' Reggie quoted a portable telephone number and made her repeat it back to him.

'When you want to complete your liberation, seek release from the belt and shred any remaining reserve, use that number.' He helped Hope to dress, easing her skirt over the chastity belt and leaving her silk blouse loose, to cover the betraying outline. 'I will keep your stockings. I want you to imagine the next woman I tie up; her hands will be bound by them.' He lifted the fine wisps to his nose and sniffed appreciatively, 'I will, perhaps, tell her about you.' He paused, cupped her chin and peered deeply into her eyes, his expression serious. 'I want you to remember what I first told you. The safe word is "cave" and the man you seek will know that.'

'Thank you.' Hope knew that her experience with Reggie was over and, more intuitively, she realised that it was unlikely they would ever meet again. Gratitude warred with sadness as she left the penthouse and returned to her office. Without hesitation, she immediately lifted the telephone receiver and dialled the number she had been given.

Chapter Three

Hope left the offices of Pursuit immediately after replacing the receiver. She flagged a cab and, while the driver negotiated the evening traffic jams, considered the man to whom she had spoken. His voice had sounded strange, as if disguised, and his instructions had been terse. It was obvious to her that, in the short time between leaving Reggie's penthouse and her conversation on the telephone, he had been appraised of the situation. Or perhaps, she mused, staring blankly through the cab window, it had all been pre-arranged.

The chastity belt felt uncomfortable, the wide gusset chaffing, so she sat with her legs parted and her skirt pulled up to mid-thigh. She did not care if the driver could see her unladylike pose, nor the belt. In a way she welcomed his stare. Her exhibition marked her 'coming out' and established her sexuality.

As the cab rolled around corners, she leaned with the motion against the curve, her pelvic muscles tensing, and she felt the spongy balls shift inside her and swell as her pleasure increased. By the time the driver drew the vehicle to a stop in front of a discreet Victorian townhouse, she was roused and eager to meet the stranger. She paid the cabby and mounted the wide steps to an imposing oak door, lifted the grinning brass gargoyle knocker and rapped twice.

The door was opened by a young woman. She was dressed in maid's attire, a black, high-necked dress with white lace collar, the dress material caught into a tiny waist then flaring into a generous skirt which fell below the knee. A white lace-edged apron was tied at the waist. While it was not uncommon for the London gentry to perpetuate the dress code for domestic workers, it *was* unusual that the girl was barefoot, and that a delicate gold slave-chain glinted at her ankle. She beckoned Hope through the foyer and ushered her into a room, then drew the heavy doors closed.

The drapes were drawn. A single spotlight cast a shaft over a maroon velvet covered stool that was stationed in the centre of the room. Anticipating her role, Hope crossed the polished wooden floor and stood in the light. She thought she was alone until a voice instructed her to sit on the stool. When she had obeyed, perching gingerly on the edge, she strained to make out the features of the man who addressed her. He was sunk in shadow, an impression of disembodied legs that stretched from the darkness of a corner. While the light was not harsh, it was sufficient to cloak him in secrecy. His voice still seemed disguised, slightly mechanical.

'You do not stare at a man,' he instructed, 'unless invited so to do.'

Hope blushed and averted her head so her gaze settled on her feet. She had automatically crossed her ankles and loosely clasped her hands in her lap. Her back was straight, her breasts proudly thrust forward.

'Reggie is right, you are very beautiful – perhaps a little superficially proud, but that is to be expected.'

Hope remained silent and the minutes passed. She hardly dared breathe as the suspense built. Then she heard the man rise and tread softly towards her. He stood before her, two paces between them.

'You may look at me.'

She peered up and gasped when she saw he was wearing a shiny black balaclava. The leather shaped his head perfectly, a silver zip tracking beneath his chin. There was a hard, round plug fixed into the throat – the device that changed his voice. His eyes glinted through holes, his nose was covered and his mouth exposed, his lips thin and slightly smiling at her discomfort. He wore tight black leather leggings, his genitalia clearly exaggerated by a moulded cup. His chest was bare, smooth and planed to a muscled stomach. He held a remote control.

He flicked the switch and a mild thrum started inside Hope's vagina. The sensation increased when he slid the bar upwards and then varied the intensity as he watched Hope respond, his eyes critical.

She held his gaze, her eyes widening as the balls expanded to absorb flow. Her lips swelled, parted and her tongue crept out to wet them and then she sighed, lowered her lids and surrendered to the pleasure building inside her. The vibrations ceased. With a moan of disappointment she opened her eyes to stare beseechingly at her tormentor.

'Stand up.'

Hope rose.

'What is your safe word?' He stared into her eyes.

'Cave.' Her voice was husky.

He nodded. 'Good, now don't look at me any more.'

She lowered her gaze.

He instructed her to remove all her clothing and soon she stood with merely the belt gracing her hips. He reached out and caressed her breasts and her nipples puckered with delight. He caught one between two fingers and gave it a hard pinch, starting the vibrating balls as the pain echoed through Hope. She cried out in delight.

'If you please me I will allow you to be serviced.' He came closer and pressed her shoulder so she sank onto the stool, her face now level with his groin. Without preamble, he cast aside the remote control, after ensuring the setting was at its maximum, hooked his thumbs into the waistband of his tight trousers and forced the fine leather over his hips.

'You may remove my trousers, then you may touch me.' Despite the disguise of the mechanical aid, Hope could hear the lust in his voice.

He assisted her very little as she urged his trousers down, her lips grazing along his thighs as she leaned closely into him, rolling the leather trouser legs over his feet, one by one. The belt impeded her movement so she slipped from the stool and kneeled, then lowered her head to dip her tongue between his toes. She slowly swirled it, sinking into the pleasure of washing him, stretching the service until she felt sated.

He parted his legs as she rose, his breath catching as her nose sunk into his groin. She cupped his testicles, hefting them slightly and massaging gently, and then drew her tongue around the base of his penis, slipped it along his smooth shaft and tucked its tip into his flange. To her immense gratification, he wore a Prince Albert. It was large and dully silver, a small drop of precum lubricating the thick metal. The ring disappeared into his penile eye, and emerged a little below his flange. She gazed hungrily at its possession of him, overcome with the desire to penetrate. She rubbed her cheek along his shaft, tapped lightly with her fingers around the base of his cockhead and then half-rose and quickly scuttled around him.

He remained still, his breath quickening and his midriff clenching, as Hope prised apart his bumcheeks and swept wetly down his crease, her tongue muscling at his anal pucker. Then he leaned forward and placed his hands on the stool, so his bum jutted obligingly for her repast. She jabbed her tongue quickly at the hole and rode his rear cavern hungrily, the strong need to possess him driving her wild, her hot breath and messy manner dragging an exulted, involuntary cry from him.

When her hand crept between his thighs, surrounded his cock and pumped harshly, he surrendered, moving with her until his ejaculate traced through the air and laced over the stool, leaving a milky, meandering trail over the deep maroon pile. He breathed roughly, appreciative of her now more gentle tonguing as his pulse slowed. Sensing he was replete, Hope drew back, once more aware of the throbbing balls which consumed her and her rampant demand for her own release.

The man straightened, turned and looked down at her. He laid his hand on her blonde, bowed head, caressing and kind. 'You are pleasing,' he said shortly, 'and I promised you service – so it shall be.'

She whimpered as he slipped past her to return to his shadowy corner. He pulled on a tasselled chord and, moments later, Hope heard the door open, a whispered command and a soft approach of footsteps. The mechanical voice instructed her to kneel.

A young man crouched in front of her. Their eyes met and she guessed him to be a mere eighteen years old, fresh-faced and gentle-eyed. He wore leather briefs and his penis, which rose as she stared, protruded from a strategically cut hole. He also sported a Prince Albert ring, impossibly large and weighting his erection to force it low. A bar pierced his nipple and studs his tongue and nose. He held a key between his fingers, with which he opened the padlock, eased it from its housing, then peeled the chastity belt from her waist. He helped her to her feet, then pressed her forwards until the stool met her knees. She lowered herself across it until her stomach bridged the velvet, the milky residue slippery against her skin, and she hung her head and let her arms fall loosely. Her bottom was exposed and her knees did not touch the ground so her legs could easily be parted, her feet placed to ensure she was openly displayed.

When the switch landed, she yelled with surprise. It was not painful, merely unexpected, and the ensuing pause was disturbing. The tension was oppressive, then her young tormentor relented and grazed the slim birch branch across her buttocks, drew it up her cleft, within which the balls still thrummed, and idly traced her bumcheek only to deliver a small, sharp tap. He repeated the process several times, his breath growing harsh with desire as he watched the thin red welts start to lattice Hope's pale rear.

Her bottom stung but Hope cried for more. The pleasure from the vibration inside her heightened as the short sharp bursts of the birch criss-crossed her bottom. When the striping ceased, she groaned, then purred when she felt a cool tongue trace along the burning trellis on her sensitive flesh. His moist breath helped cool the pathways and she could sense the sharp pattern of welts.

Fingers penetrated her, seeking, then tugging so the spongy spheres shifted and were drawn from her. She suddenly felt empty, the demand of her channel still there.

She wriggled her invitation, gratitude sweeping through her as she felt the tip of a metal-ringed clasp tap at her opening, then slide swiftly in nestle deeply. The groan reassured hear that the young man's want was as urgent as her own.

They paused. Apart from the hum of the discarded balls, vibrating wastefully on the wooden floor, their breaths and the sudden awareness of a loudly ticking clock, the room seemed still and isolated. Then they began a synchrony of movement, Hope flexing her cheeks to grasp at the thrust of his rod and easing with his withdrawal, tensing to take him in, then again surrendering to his exit.

Soon Hope lost all sense of the passage of time, the rhythm of movement a steady coursing. She learned to welcome his penetration, thrilling as his bulb pressed at the neck of her womb, drew deeply along her and then plunged to excite her swollen and weeping inner tissue. The heavy metal Prince Albert ring dragged and ploughed a furrow along her vaginal walls, creating an intense inner hunger for continuing cultivation. When her orgasm started it was a languid tide, a dull rolling which seemed to wrench at her solar plexus. Then a frisson began at her toes and her clitoris added its own sharp demand. She mewled, alerting her lover to her readiness.

He increased the force of his thrust, pummelling as she went limp in submission. He placed his palms on her bumcheeks, then delivered stinging, alternate smacks on her jouncing bottom, and her orgasm burst around his cock, gulping and sucking him, until he shuddered and spilt his cream to mix with Hope's copious fluids. He bowed over her, the heat of his flesh awakening her welts, until his trembling ceased. When he was done and her whimpers had died away, he slipped from her, eased back on his heels, then rose and quietly left the room.

Hope lay still, savouring the last tiny pulses of her coming, then the warm glow and mute awareness of her hot, latticed buttocks. She did not move when she heard footsteps, but listened dreamily when addressed.

'Those welts are light, but they will sting and chaff when you put your clothes back on. You must go straight home and soak on your tummy in a warm bath.'

She felt a hand caress her bottom, fingers slipping inside her to roam, and then an invasion. His penis was larger, the ring a more massive pressure. At first she felt little; a reluctance to accommodate at war with her desire to please. Time seemed to stop as his thrusting continued, the friction painful as her juices dried. Her cries of protest were futile as his tupping continued relentlessly. Then her fluids began to seep, her body responding even while she thought of the safe word, and her moans changed from despair to delight.

He grasped her hips, his fingers digging sharply into her tender flesh. His rod strove for depth, his bulb a ringed fist kneading deeply. A different, more fearsome hunger surged through her – a greed to consume him, swallow his largeness and remove his cream. To leave him drained and senseless; wring from him his life force, the fluid of his loins. She arched, her head flung up, her hands grabbing at the stool as she jerked back at him, met the power of his thrust and held him until, were he tempted to withdraw, he would fall back.

His fingers were a vice, the only means he had to hold himself in balance. He was forced to freeze. Then Hope squeezed, her pelvic muscles biting into the base of his shaft, her vaginal muscles rippling and sucking him in. His cries were almost pained, her nether throating dragging along his rod until it felt raw and trapped, but he thrilled as her womanhood hunted his sap. He swelled, paused and then spouted, his hoarse cry exultantly filling the room as her muscles continued to tear at him until Hope gloried in her own shuddering release.

He waned inside her, marvelling. When his penis was limp, it bundled and slid from Hope, sulking and heavy. He pressed against her, letting her last warm trembling shiver on his tender bulb.

'You are a natural,' he whispered at last, allowing a minute gap between their glistening genitals. He gently slid his fingers along their union, soaking in its spend, then he leaned over her, cupped her chin and trailed his gift over her lips. She slipped her tongue around his fingertips, tasting and savouring. He touched her tender corolla once more, this time for his own consumption, and she heard his eager suck and sigh of approval. He moved away from her with reluctance.

'I have another appointment. Next time you shall remain, but now you must dress and leave. I understand you will be absent for a fortnight. After that, you will wait until my call and then you will come swiftly.'

It was only much later that Hope realized his voice was no longer mechanical and there had been no distortion when he had approached her, after her young lover had serviced her. It had not occurred to her to look at him. Had she so done she might, later, have saved herself a considerable amount of disquiet and much that transpired would have made sense.

* * *

When Hope let herself into her apartment an hour later, she felt weary. The material of her skirt rubbed uncomfortably against the welts criss-crossing her bottom and she felt sticky and sex-stained. Dressing, entering the taxi summoned by the maid, travelling to her home, had all taken on a dreamy perspective. She dropped her keys to the carpet of her lounge and stood, gazing around as if the place were an alien planet. The minimalist furnishing, calm grey walls, shutters and absence of bric-a-brac made its own statement. To her, it seemed that her life had been devoid of colour, devoted to endeavour that held little real meaning. She felt a strong need to assert herself, inject personality – take a risk in exposing herself and those things that had value. First she had to establish her real identity, and her foray to Ireland seemed an ideal time in which to seek herself. The island retreat was becoming an overwhelming pull, whatever might happen about Willincough.

The light of the answerphone blinked furiously, drawing her to its side. She kicked off her shoes as she listened, loosened and allowed her skirt to fall, and unbuttoned her blouse. Her waist was chafed, a slight pinkness betraying the earlier presence of the chastity belt. She slipped a palm over her mound and felt a treacherous throb, a renewed demand for attention. Rat's distracted voice claimed her.

'Willi and I have arranged our travel. See you at the Piper's Inn in Killalloe on Friday evening.'

She imagined him, curled in his chair in the cellar, the telephone receiver balanced between ear and shoulder as he maintained a rhythm on the keyboard. Or, she smiled, perhaps her voice, her recorded message, had urged his hand to his crotch, where it palmed and squeezed – as did hers as the trace of him faded and the tape ceased. She played the message again, seeking his tone, and imagined that he had been concentrating his fantasizing attention exclusively on her, rather than dividing it between her and his computer.

She tested her still-sensitive nipples with gentle fingers and slipped her hand beneath her bosom to lift so that she could suckle at her own breast gently. The result was painfully sweet, a sharp reminder of the clamps. She imagined teaching Rat how to nip at her in a way that would please her, experimenting with small, sharp bites until she felt her nether lips swell, aching for an application of teeth.

True to the command of her recent mentor she ran a warm bath, adding mineral salts. As she slipped into the water, she gasped. The welts stung brutally for a few moments, bringing tears to her eyes, then the pain dulled. She forced herself to sink into the heat and peace, steam rising and cloaking her in perfumed sweat. She lay on her stomach, riding her bottom up and down so it cleared the water then submerged, each new dip painful, then healing. In the morning she knew she would sport pink lines but they would fade fast. She longed for a new birching, worried that her lust for marking would drive her frantic during her two weeks' absence from the stranger. She wondered what she could learn, of herself and her sexuality, to bring back as a gift to lay at his feet.

She pulled the plug and felt the water drain around her, leaving her shivering in the cold porcelain tub. She imagined that the fluid, swirling and disappearing, was her old life. The next day would again be a lesson, one to share with Amy, and following would be Rat and then others now faceless who would be unaware of their part in the forming of her new self, droplets in which she could immerse and eventually float.

Hope was not hungry for food and went straight to bed. She lay naked and damp as her mind reviewed her day with wonder, then drifted into sleep, her hand cupped reassuringly over her mound.

The ring of the telephone at her bedside woke her, dragging her from dream-strewn depths as she fumbled groggily for the receiver. A glance at the bedside clock assured her that she had slept soundly for twelve hours and was now late for work. A first. Amy's soft voice brought her awake.

'Hope, hello. I think I woke you and I am so sorry!'

'I slept in.' Hope shook her head in disbelief.

'So, where do you want me?' Amy reminded Hope of her plan for the day.

'Can you come here? We can decide as I breakfast. Quite honestly, Amy, I need your help.'

'Tell me about it when I get there. I cleared today with Reggie anyway, so I am all yours. I look forward to it.'

'So do I. Give me a moment to shower and dress and I'll be ready.'

'No way . . . I am outta here right now. Besides, I want to see you before you start the working day!' Amy flirted, her words teasing over the telephone.

'Right, then. I shall have some coffee and wait for you.'

As she replaced the receiver Hope felt amazed. Her interaction with Amy had taken on undertones, messages that could not be revoked. Inexperienced with women, in every sense, Hope could not identify the moment at which tacit agreement had been reached. It seemed that, from the dawning of her awareness of Amy the previous day, there had been no preliminary ground, merely a switch to intimacy. She hoped that she had not mistaken the invitation and reviewed the conversation to seek alternative meaning. As she pondered, allowing anticipation to build, she padded into the kichenette, set the percolator bubbling and leaned against the refrigerator while the aroma of fresh, wet coffee grounds swirled around her.

It suddenly dawned on her that she had intended, unwittingly, to open the door to Amy naked. A picture of her, turning to lead the girl into her bedroom, her pale, marked buttocks holding Amy's gaze, was tempting but inappropriate. To compromise but provoke, Hope selected a short black silk kimono from her bedroom. She relaxed on the sofa in her lounge until she heard the chimes of the doorbell and, pressing an intercom, Amy's confirmation that she stood at the front door to the apartment block. She buzzed her in, released her flat door from the latch and left it slightly ajar. She had time reoccupy the couch, curl her legs under her and lift her coffee cup before Amy tapped at the door.

Finding it open, her slight knock forcing it wider, Amy pushed the apartment door. It opened to reveal a small, bland lounge. The anonymity of the room served to highlight Hope's presence. She looked comfortable and sophisticated, draped on a small sofa, and Amy felt a twinge of anxiety. Her head had been full of titillating fancies that had given birth to a confidence that diminished now she was confronted by the reality of the woman with whom she had flirted on the telephone. She felt shy, especially when Hope rose and gestured at her coffee cup. The short robe fell open under its loosely belted waist to reveal a length of pale thigh and, Amy was almost sure, a glimpse of Hope's public vee. The blonde's breasts thrust at the material, her nipples sharply outlined and the valley exposed, the creamy swells revealed.

Amy caught her breath, unable to speak. She managed a slight nod and weak smile, accepting the offer of coffee, and watched Hope's swaying hips as she wandered into the kitchenette.

'The hell with it,' Amy whispered, and followed.

The room was small and the women were forced closely together. Amy, a head shorter than Hope, was painfully aware that her gaze rested level with the soft black clad-breasts. She licked her lips, a gesture not lost on Hope, who decided to hook and reel the girl in over the course of the day. If she was successful, she would not only prepare for her trip to Ireland on time, but also ensure she looked forward to an adventure that night.

'You needed my help?' Amy muttered in a low voice, her words addressing Hope's nipples while she fought to avert her gaze.

'Yes.' Hope shifted, tightened the belt at her waist and succeeded in drawing closer to Amy and ensuring the neckline opened further, the cloth now barely covering her areolae. 'It is going to sound stupid, I think, but . . . She stared as the girl swayed towards her, hoping that the red lips would seek her now rigid nipples, but Amy grabbed her coffee mug and swiftly returned to the lounge, blushing. Hope followed, continuing her sentence as if there had been no interruption, '. . . this new project is outside of what I know. I need clothes; an idea of how to dress!'

That much was true. Hope's wardrobe was devoid of

casual wear, her agenda usually demanding elegant suits or cocktail gowns. Invariably, she would strip off the finery and relax naked. Her intention to shop for sweaters and jeans was always thwarted by pressure of work. She hoped that she and Amy would spend the day in the city, secure appropriate clothes for Ireland, have lunch and share an afternoon bonding. She intended to treat her secretary to supper at a small, intimate restaurant, then serve her coffee and liqueurs at the flat. She had not formulated a plan after that because she had no real idea of how to proceed, merely an intention.

Amy's response was positive. She grinned widely, apparently on home ground around clothes shops. She seemed to come alive, no longer shy, and chattered about various stores, happy to assume that Hope had an unlimited budget, and made plans for their itinerary.

'Okay, if you are going to an island in the middle of nowhere to escape the crowds and have private space, you can lose the make-up you usually wear.' She cocked her head and stared at Hope. 'Anyway, you are more beautiful without it.' This time she did not blush, her compliment real, not flirtatious. Her natural sense of organization took over. 'So let's go, time's a-wasting!'

She followed Hope into the bedroom and curled on her bed while Hope showered. When she returned, damp and naked, Amy at first averted her eyes but, lulled by the businesslike actions of Hope who set about choosing day clothes purposefully, she allowed herself to stare openly. Hope pretended not to notice, simply moving to permit maximum scrutiny. She had checked in the bathroom mirror so knew that her welts were still visible but they excited no comment. Rather they imposed a silence.

She could not avoid formal clothes, the whole reason for this shopping trip was to procure more comfort, so she slipped on suspenders and stockings and donned a skirt and blouse. As Amy watched, she selected court shoes from the rack.

'You are going to die in those, walking around all day,' Amy observed dryly. 'What say we think about buying some jeans and loafers first and you change into them in the shop?'

Hope smiled her approval and quickly applied light make-up, brushed her hair until it shone and held out her hand to help Amy from the bed. She had begun to look forward to her shopping trip and was enjoying the company of the young woman, who seemed to feel no compunction in taking charge. Amy grasped that hand as freely as it was offered and they left the flat laughing and full of excitement.

The London streets sweltered in the summer heat, their surfaces bright and hurtful to the eye. Traffic droned around the pair as they strolled around the centre, after being released, already sweating, from the rear of the black cab. During the ride Hope had elicited the promise that Amy would regard this shopping trip as mutual: she would match Hope, purchase for purchase, at Hope's expense. Hope had expected an argument and was pleasantly disarmed when Amy cheerfully agreed, as if the practice was normal and comfortable. It was the first indication that the girl was accustomed to treats and not heedful of money.

Their first real contact occurred in the dressing room of the jeans shop.

'I cannot wear these!' Hope protested. She stood in her

lacy bra and panties as Amy held a pair of black stretch jeans to her waist. They looked absurdly small.

'Why not?' returned Amy coolly. 'You have the figure and I promise you will find them comfortable. Go on, live dangerously.'

Hope shrugged comically and tugged a leg of the jeans over one foot, grabbed Amy's shoulder for balance and struggled into the other. Sure footed, with the material binding her ankles, she leaned over and wriggled until the stretch denim covered her bottom. The flies gaped in a wide vee and Hope breathed in deeply and tugged the sides together.

'Go for the zipper,' she gasped, and Amy, who had idly watched Hope's reflected bottom wriggle as she pulled on the jeans, dipped her fingers to grab the zipper tab and pulled. She had to slide her hand under the fabric to avoid catching the fine hairs and pinched skin in the tracks of the zip as she pulled the tab up. Hope was straining to hold her breath, clasping the edges of the waistband together. Both caught their breath when their hands touched, Amy suddenly aware of the trembling, warm flesh beneath her caught fingers. She paused to savour the sensation, then slowly completed the task, her fingers stroking Hope's as she withdrew. They stared at one another.

'There,' Amy said, pointing to the mirror, 'see, they are perfect on you.'

Hope turned and viewed herself. The jeans hugged her tightly and comfortably. The seam of the crotch bit into her crease, exaggerating the lobes of her labia and causing a pleasant pressure. It was blatant and sexual, and delighted her.

'I look like a vamp,' she grinned and wriggled her hips suggestively at Amy, who stood behind her.

'Uh huh, so try this top.' Amy held out a small scrap, which turned out to be a halterneck bodice, secured with laces at the neck and back. It left the midriff bare. 'Lose the bra.' She did not wait but slid her fingers under the clasp and released the edges, which fell away to allow Hope's full breasts to bounce free. A puckered line remained as a legacy, surrounding Hope's torso. Amy rubbed it gently. 'Not good,' she commented, raising her eyes to meet Hope's. She slipped the top over Hope's head, and tightened the neck lace while Hope held her hair from her neck. With her arms raised, the bib of the garment falling free, her breasts were raised, jouncing while Amy worked. Hope could feel the tremble of fingers and turned, mischievously, so the material slid and Amy's hand brushed over the smooth mound. She drew her hand away as if socked, blushed and recovered, then slid her hands around Hope to capture the laces to tie around her back.

Amy had to work in reverse, operating by reflection in the mirror, and she was disadvantaged as she pressed lightly into Hope, her arms embracing her and her face a fraction from the valley between Hope's breasts. She fumbled but succeeded in securing the tie, and then withdrew slowly, her palms sliding from Hope's back and drawing around to cover her midriff. She slipped a finger under the edge of the top and wriggled it.

'There, not too tight.' She waited while Hope turned and examined herself, her skin alive to the touch and a pale bloom of arousal adding luminescence to her breasts. She liked what she saw, not merely the image of herself, but the reflection of Amy, close behind her, her lips swollen and her expression vulnerable.

'We've done well,' she praised, deliberately injecting ambiguity.

They left the dressing cubicle and earned the stare of two men, who were obviously waiting for their partners to try on garments. Hope immediately dropped her gaze and paused, to allow them the pleasure of looking. The action surprised Amy but she approved: she felt proud to be partnering this gorgeous, sexy woman and happy that she should be appreciated. She asserted her ownership by placing a proprietorial hand on Hope's bottom, propelling her towards the shoe racks. She selected colourful deck shoes and kneeled to slip them over Hope's toes, easing them over her heels with her thumbs. As Hope paraded, trying the shoes for comfort, Amy sat back on her haunches, eyeing the men surreptitiously. They stared with open admiration but were also guarded, noting Amy's physical involvement. There was envy in their eyes. Which, Amy chuckled inwardly, was daft. Even were she intimate with Hope, she would not object to sharing. Proprietorial she might be, but possessive she was not.

The touching increased as the day continued, until the contact became natural and was missed by both girls if the dressing cubicles were public and shared with other women. They lunched at a coffee bar, laughing and people-watching, and purchased glossy adult magazines in a shop in Soho, which they slipped into carrier bags containing baggy chinos, loose cotton tops, Levi jeans, voile blouses and billowing skirts, and T-shirts. Amy insisted on the purchase of two colourful leisure suits and aerobic slippers.

'If I am right, then you will be doing a lot of lounging about in company,' she stated.

At each shop she selected an item or garment she fancied,

and these were added to the carriers. They stopped at four o'clock for a coffee in Harrod's Circle Restaurant, then wandered around the elegant shop for an hour, managing to spend ten times the sum they had already frittered away during the preceding seven hours. It was Hope's second indication of Amy's disregard for money. She never looked at prices, merely tugged a couple of swimsuits from the stands and insisted they be checked out. They tried them on together.

Hope and Amy stripped, stood naked face to face, and drew the shiny scraps over hip and breasts, watching each other.

'You look gorgeous,' Amy breathed as her gaze drifted over Hope's body.

The thong bottom barely covered Hope's mound. A shining white triangle, it hugged the dome with small, dark blonde wisps escaping the edges. Amy leaned forward and tucked the wayward curls under the fabric. She tugged at the triangular patches covering Hope's nipples, brushing her hand over the peaks and drawing a finger down the valley. Seemingly lost, she then stood back, her hands hanging helplessly at her sides, unable to continue.

Amy was slim, her breasts small and pert. She had chosen for herself a one-piece suit, cut high in the legs, with a plunging neckline. It was a vibrant green, complementing her olive skin and black, shining curls. She was aroused. The day had been foreplay and flirtation and now she was unsure how to proceed. She surrendered control to Hope.

Hope stepped towards Amy and cupped her face in her palms. She stared, her expression serious and searching, then drew her hands down, caressing the slim neck and glancing over Amy's sharp collar bones. Her palms drew to a rest, cupping the young woman's breasts. Hope squeezed gently and rhythmically until the girl moaned and shifted into her and they kissed, their lips grazing softly. Then hunger forced their mouths wide and open, tongues writhing and wrestling. They clung together, their thighs pressed against each other and their eager breaths puffing and mingling. It was Hope who broke the impassioned embrace, shivering, her eyes fixed on Amy's until she calmed. She grasped Amy's upper arms, her fingers digging into the taut flesh.

'Later!' she gulped, barely able to resist the beseeching look on the young woman's face. 'We go home, change into something casual and new and then we go out and eat.' She lowered her voice to plead, 'This has to be done right, okay?'

Amy smiled weakly and nodded. She felt compelled to confess, 'I have not done this before, Hope. Not with a woman.'

Hope stroked Amy's cheek, 'Me neither, and I think we need to go back to Soho.'

'Why?' Amy was tired, she longed for a bath, a relaxing hour in which to cuddle with Hope, and she felt hungry, suddenly eager to share a supper table with her new partner.

Hope studied Amy's face, then said with deliberate inflection, 'Because I want to fuck you and I want something special for that.'

They returned to Soho in silence, touching and stroking openly in the rear of the cab, oblivious to the occasional interested glance of the cabby.

Chapter Four

They dined in a small Italian restaurant just off Piccadilly Circus. Candles burned low in wax-encrusted wine bottles, on tables covered with red-and-white checkerboard cloth that matched the waiters' aprons. Loud, friendly banter ricocheted around a room pervaded with delicious aromas, rising from steaming platters of sauce-doused pasta. Outside it was still light, the English mid-summer evening refusing to pale much before ten o'clock. Inside it simulated deep dusk, intimate with candle flicker and classical guitar music.

Hope and Amy shared a bottle of Chablis. They were seated at a table in an alcove and were able to view the bustle of the restaurant and still enjoy privacy. Their chairs were pulled close together and their knees touched. Amy leaned forward to rest her elbows on the table and stared into Hope's eyes. 'What did you buy?' She referred to their return to Soho. Hope had made her wait in a coffee shop while she made her purchases.

'Later.' She studied Amy's face with pleasure. Their physical contact was now easy, butterfly touches of promise, but they had not repeated their kiss.

They had returned to Hope's apartment and gloated over their purchases, choosing outfits for each other to wear that evening. Hope was wearing a soft burnt orange voile skirt and matching blouse that tied at her waist. Her face was devoid of make-up and her hair had been brushed until it gleamed. Her feet felt slightly cold in delicate sandals. As Amy had followed her from the cab to cross the street to the restaurant, she had noted how the material hugged Hope's curves, which were visible when backlit by the street light. The fabric was thin, almost transparent, as Hope's areolae testified. She looked soft and very feminine.

Hope had chosen a strapless stretch minidress for Amy, a mere tube of black that the girl had tugged over her torso and that remained in place with luck rather than any real securement. She was lithe and curving, her collarbones sharp and her neck long and slim: swanlike. Amy never wore make-up and the thin contours of her face were softened by a mass of tumbling, short curls and thick lashes that framed her sultry dark eyes. She wore no underclothes, fearful of spoiling the sleek hug of her dress. Now, she was careful to cross her legs at the knee in case she offered an inadvertent display to other diners, notwithstanding the generous hang of the tablecloth.

'A hint,' Amy prompted.

Hope laughed and leaned forward, her forearm resting along Amy's. The girl's olive hue heightened the effect of her own pale skin. 'Only that you will like it.' She drew back as their dinner arrived. Both had chosen carbonara and salads, and they relaxed to enjoy the simple repast. Neither wanted to gorge and both were already slightly tipsy. They ate in companionable silence for a while, allowing the sexual tension to build.

'Hope,' Amy said softly, at last, 'I want to leave.'

'No, not yet,' Hope had watched Amy's thoughts build.

The girl now played with her food, restless. Her head was swirling with images as she thought ahead to the time they would leave the restaurant and return to the flat. The wine had dissolved any remaining reservations and she had spoken when she noted the rise of Hope's nipples. She longed to unbutton the blouse, free Hope's breasts and bury her cheeks in the valley. She trembled, her lower lip pouting and red.

'Why don't you go on eating?' suggested Hope, seemingly brutal advice under the circumstances until she slipped her hand beneath the tablecloth and placed it high on Amy's thigh. 'That's right, one forkful.' There was laughter in her voice as her fingers slid upwards and under the hem of the short dress, to press lightly on the young woman's mound.

Amy unclasped her legs. Already roused and warmed by the alcohol, she felt impatient. The clamour of the restaurant was dulled by the pounding of her own blood in her ears and her world reduced to one of pure sensation when Hope, leaning further forward, slipped two fingers between her legs and stroked between her lobes.

'You're very wet,' Hope muttered, her own excitement mounting as she began to explore this new territory. Her mouth filled with saliva, her lips in empathy with her seeking fingers. Amy was right, they should have left, but she could not now withdraw, her curiosity and their mutual needs were too strong. She wriggled her fingers experimentally and was delighted to induce a small moan. Amy's fork clattered to her plate, drawing the waiter's attention, but neither woman noticed his approach, quick glance and dawning understanding.

The restaurant had quietened, the theatregoers having eaten and dashed away. A couple, four tables away, concentrated on each other and a small group chattered softly in the centre of the room. Elsewhere, waiters bustled to clear the tables and prepare for the next wave of diners. The pulse had slowed, which allowed the observant attendant to stand discreetly, obscuring the activity behind him.

Hope thrust her fingers into Amy, and the girl slid lower in her chair, her thighs parting and the dress slipping up, until she was exposed to Hope's view. She had tight lobes that pulled back to expose her swollen clitoris and delicate, moist inner folds. Thick, dark curls covered her slight mound, rising in a rampant pathway up her taut stomach. Hope stroked the mat, leaving a glistening trail, and wove her fingers among the curls, enjoying the silky tug of the soft hair. Amy pushed her hips up at Hope's hand.

Hope risked a quick glance at the room, thankful to note the broad, stoical back of the waiter. She gently shouldered the table aside and slithered to kneel between the girl's slim thighs, her blood pounding and senses lost. She eased Amy's labia further apart and stared. In the pale gold light of the candle glow, her corolla looked exotic, a shiny, delectable repast. Hope bowed into her and breathed deeply, inhaling her sweet, fresh aroma, before she brushed her lips lightly over the swollen, blushing marble. She tapped it gently with her tongue, pursed her lips to surround it and sucked softly. Amy pressed lower, her hips now edging over the rim of the chair, her waist curving and her dress riding high to settle at her midriff. Hope heard her small whimpers and realized that she would have to bring her to orgasm swiftly, or their performance would attract further, perhaps unwanted, attention. She slipped her fingers into Amy, attempting to create girth, and pressed into her, working at the girl's nub with grazing teeth and whipping tongue. The sweet sap leaked over her hands and drenched her chin and then she felt hands clasp her head to force her harder into the folds, until she was barely able to breathe.

Amy's passion was fierce. She was aware of her surroundings, thrilling to the public risk. She longed to kick the table, overturn it so that the wonderful woman at work between her thighs was exposed to view, the attention of other diners drawn by the crash of crockery. Her head rang with the newness of female feasting, the softness of the lips that had surrounded her bud and the slim, exploring fingers that she wanted to penetrate her more deeply. She lost herself in a frenzy of judders along Hope's face, now uncaring that the gasping below was for breath, as her blood quickened. She groaned, stalling, as she recognized the deep beat of her orgasm beginning, then gripped hard on Hope's head, clamping her thighs to increase the pressure.

Hope was helpless, caught in the vice of Amy's legs and unable to move. The young woman was stronger than she appeared and had trapped her. She recognized that Amy was close to coming and empathized with the new, languid movement of her hips and the increased pressure. A thrill shot through her, a powerful, jubilant realization that she had brought her quarry to completion, and she savoured the increased honeyed torrent and ringtug that trembled rhythmically along her buried fingers.

After a minute Amy's inner shuddering slowed, her thighs parted and only a mute throbbing remained; her blood drummed and her breathing evened. She peered down and watched Hope lap her juices tenderly. She felt splayed, warm and decadent, loose and grateful. She licked her dry lips, reached for her glass and sipped the last of her wine.

Alert to the clink of the glass, the waiter turned, assuming that the pair were finished. He stared with surprise at the blonde head, still bowed between the olive thighs: a shameless erotic image that caused his loins to stir pleasurably. When Hope edged back he could see Amy's blushing open pudendum. His eyes, reflecting admiration and approval, sought hers and met her sweet, smug stare of triumph. As he watched, Hope wriggled back into her seat, her expression bemused. She ran her hand over her face, slipping her fingers over Amy's wet benediction. The waiter offered Hope a serviette, which she accepted with a blush, and he then replenished their glasses.

Amy wriggled, easing her dress back over her hips. Her inner thighs were slippery with her juices, which cooled pleasantly in the aftermath. She felt sated and exhilarated, more at ease but still eager to return to Hope's apartment and claim her turn to feast. She kissed Hope's cheek softly, then settled back to savour her wine. Now that her initial furious demand had been satisfied, she felt relaxedly sensual, both anxious to continue the intimacy and aware that there was no need to advance at a such a furious pace. Her mind filled with delicious possibilities, treats she could bestow on Hope and an eager anticipation to share the sex-toys her lover had purchased.

The waiter, satisfied that he had no further reason to shield the pair, calmly accepted their order for coffee. He smiled as he walked away, resolving to take five minutes to ease his stiff member while the image of Amy's quim and Hope's slicked cheeks remained fresh in his mind. As he pushed his way through the swing doors into the kitchen a girl peered at him, unable to avoid noticing the thrust of his erection against the flies of his tight black trousers.

She stopped washing up and dried her hands carefully with a towel.

'The alcove table?' she queried with a smile. At his nod she took his hand and led him into the dry larder. Among the bulging sacks of flour and drums of sugar, she quickly lifted her skirt to offer him her plump, ready rear.

'I am sorry.' Amy faced Hope, 'I know you did not want to do that so fast but I couldn't wait any longer!'

Hope peered in surprise. 'As it happened, nor could I. God, you taste so wonderful! Sweeter than me, and so wet. I just want to get you into bed and lick you, stick my tongue into you and feel you come again and again.'

'And I want to suck your nipples so badly.' Amy moaned at the thought of Hope's breasts, her fingers barely in check. She cast a swift glance at the other tables and, satisfied that no one was looking, brushed her fingers over Hope's nipples, delighting in the sudden, hard response.

They had turned their chairs to face one another, their knees touching. Hope had shed her sandals and tucked her feet around Amy's ankle, wriggling her toes. Amy kicked off one small shoe and raised her foot, eased it under Hope's loose skirt and edged it up until it rested against her mound. Hope sighed and leaned back to enjoy the sensation as Amy pressed into her. She pointed her toes and eased the gusset of Hope's panties aside, then flicked her big toe along Hope's moist crease, pleased when her lover's eyes closed in bliss.

'Just keep that up like that,' Hope murmured, 'and you'll have me at you in the taxi!' She did not, however, pull away, merely parted her thighs to accommodate Amy's toes, amazed at their prehensile ability working along her. She felt a small, insistent penetration and sighed with pleasure. There was no urgency and she did not feel the need to assert her demand, merely to enjoy the foreplay. Amy could continue playing without Hope losing her senses, at least until they were safely in her bed. She sipped her coffee and watched her companion affectionately, while she continued to tease.

After leaving the restaurant, the women walked around Piccadilly Circus. They were eager to get back to the flat but more delighted to show themselves and their intimacy in public. They kissed at the foot of the statue of Eros, eliciting a round of applause and some catcalls from the motley assembly strewn on the steps.

'Yer want a real man!' a hoarse shout rose from the gathering.

'Shut yer gob, yer savage,' came a coarse response.

'Right on, sister!' A female voice.

'Get 'em orf, ladies!'

They left before the banter became harsh, dashed across Shaftesbury Avenue and managed to flag a cab, laughing and flopping back comfortably once directions had been given. Amy sighed and peered blindly through the window, then turned to face Hope with a quizzical expression.

'What?' Hope waited.

'It is just that I need to know something.' Amy faltered, uncertain about continuing.

'What?' Hope repeated.

'It is about my father; I just wanted to know what is happening.'

'Your father?' Hope looked nonplussed.

'Reggie. I know you are involved with him, I just feel odd about it.'

Hope stared at Amy. 'You don't have his surname.'

'I changed it because of business. You did not know he is my father?'

'No!'

'Does it change things?'

'Not for me – does it for you?'

'No.' Amy still seemed curious and Hope tried to sort her own feelings.

'Tell me,' Hope said cautiously, 'how did you know?'

'I only knew yesterday,' Amy confessed, 'I saw your panties in the envelope when I took them to him.'

'Does he know you know?'

'Yes, I think so. But he does not know about you and me. Still, I know my father is into some funny stuff . . .'

'You want to know what we did?' Hope looked at Amy, aghast.

Amy eased over to the cab window and stared out. She regretted starting the conversation. It seemed that all the intimacy that had built over the day had been jeopardized and, with her thighs still sticky, she felt remorseful. She dared not look at Hope, cursing herself for a fool and wondering what had induced her to stick her nose into an affair that was clearly not her business. The rest of the cab ride passed in silence and when they drew up outside Hope's building Hope stepped out and offered the fare through the front window. Amy remained in the rear seat.

'Amy?'

'I thought you might prefer that I went home now.'

'No, I prefer that you come with me.'

The cabby stared straight ahead, pretending not to hear, as he had done during their earlier conversation. He had heard it all before and only felt a mild curiosity about how it would turn out. He would wait a few seconds but would then have to reactivate the meter.

Hope got back in, grabbed some notes from her bag and pushed them through the sliding window. 'Please would you just drive around until that has gone?'

He looked at the bundle. 'I stop work in two hours.'

'Okay, until then, please?'

He peeled off some notes and tried to return them.

'No, keep them, this is important.'

He nodded, closed the partition, and pulled into the traffic.

Hope and Amy sat in silence for some minutes. Hope was unsure why it seemed important to calm the younger woman but she still remembered the sweet taste of her loins and suspected that it was lust, rather than emotion, that was driving her.

'I cannot tell you about your father, that is between him and me. I can tell you that I enjoyed it and would do it all again.'

'I am sorry. God! I seem to be apologizing all evening!' Amy groaned, suddenly turned to Hope and cried out, 'What can I do? I feel like such an idiot!'

She seemed so vulnerable, appealing to Hope with her dark eyes huge and contrite.

'You can take off your dress.'

Amy looked bewildered at this unexpected turn. Hope was leaning back comfortably, with an expression that was unsettling. Amy had seen it on her father's face when he watched women, part predatory and part calculating. She did not like it but something inside her stirred. She turned towards Hope, crossed her arms and hooked her thumbs under the top edge of the black tube of her dress under her armpits, and tugged it down. Her small breasts popped free. She knelt on the seat, swaying as the cab took a corner, recovered and pushed the dress from her hips and over her thighs, fell back and lifted her legs into the air, placing her feet on the ceiling of the vehicle to ease the stretchy material over her calves and feet. She lay like that for a moment, displayed for Hope, then brought her legs down and sat cross-legged, sideways on the seat so she faced her.

Hope unbuttoned her blouse slowly and slipped it from her arms. She unclipped the waistband of her skirt, eased down the zipper and rose slightly to ease it from her hips. The soft cloth slid from her and crumpled to the floor. She wore only a pair of white lace panties, beneath which Amy could see a mat of blonde pubic curls. She slid the panties off and they joined the discarded skirt. Hope placed one foot on the seat, leaned back and placed the other on the glass partition that separated them from the driver. She glanced at the rear-view mirror and caught the cabby's eye. He simply lifted his eyebrows and kept driving. She gazed at Amy, then reached down and began to play with herself one-handed, her fingers circling lightly over her labia. She grasped her breast with her free hand and lifted her nipple to her lips, tonguing around it until the areola puckered.

Amy uncrossed her legs and crept towards Hope, her bottom weaving, until she covered her, then she began to nurse at the free nipple, her little slurps eager. She sucked until the nipple hurt, her slim form swaying over her blonde companion. She buried her face between Hope's breasts, grabbing at them with her hands until they cushioned her, then kneaded until she heard a satisfying moan.

'Let me shift down,' Hope instructed softly. 'Then turn around and sit on my face.' She wriggled until she lay with her back flat, her legs still splayed, waited until she felt the tickle of Amy's muff and then began to lap with long, sweeping strokes at the pink tissues hovering over her.

Amy probed among Hope's folds, concentrating hard, but keenly aware of the street life passing outside, the traffic and pedestrians. Her prayers were answered when the cab was forced to stop at a red traffic light, drawing alongside a bus. A bored-looking young man peered into the taxi, and his eyes widened. Amy parted Hope's labia and slipped her finger inside, running it swiftly up and down the crease, then dipping into the deeper opening. When satisfied that her finger was fully coated she put it in her mouth, exaggerating the action, and sucked it with a rapturous expression. The young man mouthed at her, his lips twisted and leering, and she smiled and repeated the process. The lights changed and the vehicles remained together for a while, then the cab peeled off. Her last glimpse was of the voyeur struggling to the rear of the bus to catch a last look at her display.

Amy bent forward and stuck her tongue into Hope, burying it deeply and scooping the musky dew into her mouth. She feasted, nipping and sucking, her tongue whipping at Hope's clitoris until she felt her own excitement rising as the pale hips bucked for more. She rose and pushed her thumbs into Hope, her fingers tucking into the crease of her bottom and let the bucking find its own rhythm, until she felt the creamy increase and the expulsions of breath between her own legs that indicated Hope's muffled cries of lust. Unable to prevent herself, she ground into the heat of Hope's mouth, and then thrilled to the pulse of her coming at the same moment as she felt the clutch of vaginal muscles around her thumbs. She lifted her hips quickly, scuttled round to face the other way and lay on top of Hope, feeling the pillowing of breasts and the hard meeting of their mounds. Hope's legs curled around her and they lay joined until their cries softened. As the pounding of their blood eased they kissed each other's faces, small quick pressings against brow and cheek and a long, tender caress of tongues.

Some time later the cabby drew his vehicle to a halt and slid open the partition. 'Back home,' he announced cheerfully, staring forward. They tugged on their clothes roughly and spilled through the door. As he drove off, he peered in his wing mirror. The blonde woman was trying to open the door while the small dark one had stuck her head under her skirt and was tonguing her bottom.

'I'm surprised we made it up the stairwell,' Amy exclaimed.

They lay on Hope's bed, Amy naked and shameless, splayed, her curls clinging damply to her forehead and a sheen of perspiration glistening on her skin. Hope lay on her side, her leg thrown over the young woman's stomach, her hand gently stroking the small breasts. Strewn around them were the sex toys. An oyster-coloured vibrator lay between them, bent at an improbable angle at a pearl-filled joint at the base of the eight-inch-long penile surrogate. Earlier the phallus had throbbed and twirled inside Hope, a small vibrating protuberance thrumming at her clitoris. Amy had watched her face intently, memorizing her features when they contorted with passion as she came.

A glittering, colourful butterfly clung to Amy's mound, held in place by thin elastic strands that circled her hips. After Hope had attached the sequinned toy, Amy had danced for her, weaving and bobbing gracefully, delighted when the wings seemed to flutter and vibrations tingled through her sensitive flesh. She had pressed against Hope, sharing the tremors, clinging while their mouths met.

A dildo for two lay in the curve of Hope's back. They had faced each other, Hope's longer legs curving under Amy's, nipples brushing together, the slender rubber rod penetrating both of them. Amy had slid her hips, straddled Hope's thighs and choreographed the ride to a shared orgasm. A tube of KY jelly leaked its contents over the once-crisp sheets, the reasons for its purchase, two soft buttplugs, discarded on the floor by the bed.

They were exhausted and content, pleased with the sweat and sex smells that impregnated the sheets and the cream still coating their tongues. Amy lay back and sighed.

'You're leaving tomorrow.'

'Yes, catching the afternoon flight to Shannon. I have to meet the group in Killalloe.'

'Where's that?'

'I think, looking at the map, it is about fifteen miles from Limerick – a large town somewhere in the west of Eire. I don't know really, I have only ever been to Dublin.'

'Wish I was coming with you!' Amy sounded like a child, her voice full of hope in case her wish could be granted.

'It's work, Amy.' Hope rolled over to face her new lover.

'Can't you tell me about it?'

'I can afterwards but right now the fewer people who know the better. The guy I am going after wants secrecy.'

'Does Dad know?'

'Of course.'

There was a silence, a mute reproach.

'How long are you going to be away?' Amy attempted to break the freeze.

'Two weeks. But I will not be returning to Pursuit after that, whether my project is successful or not.'

Amy shot to a sitting position, horrified. 'Why?' she wailed.

Hope sat to face her, 'Because of Salvatore and the magazine,' she said gently. 'Surely you can see that my discretion is compromised?'

'I won't see you again? What are you going to do?'

Hope paused. She realized that she had no idea what would follow her return from Ireland. During her career, she had travelled widely and visited wonderful cities all over the world. The only reason she clung to London was Pursuit. With her job finished, she could choose anywhere to live, perhaps move around and enjoy herself.

She felt guilty as she gazed at Amy. She had not thought further than that night, while it seemed obvious the girl felt their relationship would continue. They barely knew one another and, for her, the intimacy they had shared was simply another adventure, sandwiched between Reggie and Rat. She believed it would aggravate the situation later were she not honest now.

'I don't know. I had not thought about what would happen afterwards.' She took Amy's hand in hers and looked into her eyes. 'I had not thought about *us*. I am sorry.'

The young woman before her suddenly seemed a total stranger. In fact, Hope realized, Amy *was* a stranger. For all they had shared, they were no closer in knowledge of one another than the day before when Amy had been her secretary. She was horrified to note that she was already thinking in the past tense, especially when she realized that they would not be likely to meet again to rekindle their lust. The only thing of which she felt sure was that the dominant stranger, who had mastered her the previous evening, would summon her on her return and that she was to await his call.

She was surprised at her union with Amy. They had loved as equals and Hope had not chosen a submissive or dominant role. Though they had taken turns to please one another, it was a sharing of power. It was only now, when Amy stared at her, eyes wide and hurt, that she understood the partnership was unequal, and that the balance of power lay in her hands. It was emotional, not free like the sheer physical conjunction between her and the stranger. She did not want any emotional commitment, especially with Reggie's daughter.

'No, I am sorry,' Amy once more apologized, 'I was racing ahead without thought.' She stared unhappily at the sheet. 'It is just that I never realized how good it could be with someone . . .' She faltered. 'Another woman.'

'Nor did I!' Hope smiled, hoping to ease the situation. But she was unsuccessful.

'Look, you have to pack in the morning and I'll just be in the way.' Amy imbued her words with cheerful bravado. 'I shall grab a taxi and go home.' Yet she dallied.

'You could stay, I would like you to. It won't take me long to pack and it would be nice to wake with you.' Even as she spoke, Hope realized she was lying. She wanted Amy to leave and preferred to wake alone. The thought of sharing her first moment of the day with someone was a romantic notion. She needed the space to prepare for her trip, arrange her thoughts and hug the memories of the past two days, before letting them go. To her regret, she understood that Amy would be an encumbrance and her preparations to leave would seem cold hearted to the girl. A part of her was horrified at the practicality of her thinking. Not least, though, she had not woken with someone in a very long time and it seemed too vulnerable a thing to do. One for which she was uncertain she was ready.

'No.' This time Amy smiled. 'I think it would be better if I did leave. I want to slip away now rather than say a proper goodbye when you have to dash for the airport.'

Hope cursed herself when a feeling of relief spread through her. 'Let's shower, then have coffee and talk.'

'Go on,' Amy suddenly grinned. 'Start without me.'

Hope kissed the tip of Amy's nose softly, feeling treacherous, slipped from the bed and within moments delighted as the soft warm downpour of the shower sluiced the stickiness from her skin. Amy took her time joining her and, when she had not appeared for ten minutes, Hope stepped from the spray, wrapped herself in a towel and peered into the bedroom. Amy had left. The bed was still in disarray, sheets twisted as evidence of their hours of pleasure. Only the butterfly was gone.

Hope leaned against the doorpost, feeling sad. The steam from the still cascading shower seeped into the bedroom, the drumming of the water not loud enough to drown the sound of the front door to the building slamming shut. She raced to the window in time to see Amy cross the road to a waiting taxi. The girl did not look back. Hope returned to the shower, turned the force to full and leaned her forehead against the tiled wall, allowing the needles to massage the sudden stiffness from her neck.

She changed the sheets on the bed, gathered the toys,

slipped them into her bedside drawer and set the alarm clock to allow her five hours of rest. She lay quietly, her mind coasting, and, before sleep claimed her, she forgave herself.

Hope was tired when she arrived at Shannon Airport. She had woken with the alarm and accustomed to travelling, had undertaken her packing, the trip to Heathrow and the flight itself with remote efficiency. Unlike on previous trips, for which she had dressed in couture suits, she had donned a pair of jeans and a loose sweater and had slipped into an economy, rather than first class, seat on the aeroplane. She did not carry a briefcase, had no papers to spread and work on and found herself distracted and restless during the short flight. Her head was filled with memories, replays of the previous two days.

As she collected her baggage from the carousel she finally allowed herself to sink into the warm, lilting Irish tones around her and let the bustle of London fall away. She found the conversations around her difficult to follow, the colloquialisms, the accents and the speed with which the sentences flowed. There seemed to be laughter everywhere and the pace was relaxed, forcing Hope to slow down and look around her. For the first time she started to feel as if she was really escaping.

She took a taxi from the airport, having realized that the cost of hiring a car for two weeks just to leave it parked on the banks of a lake was foolish and expensive. The driver was delighted with an easy fare and kept her entertained, pointing out Bunratty Castle, Durty Nellie's and regaling her with stories of the medieval dinners held there. They drove slowly through Limerick town and headed onto a peaceful country road to travel the fourteen miles to Killalloe.

The driver seemed unsurprised at her journey. He claimed to know Loch Derg well and had heard of the retreats. 'Secretive they are,' he claimed, 'but sure, you can do no better than spend time fasting and finding your spiritual self.'

'Fasting?' Hope had not anticipated that.

'Well, it's a retreat, you say. So I expect you'll be staying awake and walking around all night and not eating. It is to make you see clearer, you know.'

'I thought we would be just relaxing, taking time out!'

'Ah, well now, it may be different altogether.' He embarked on a tale of an acquaintance who had been on a retreat and Hope let his words wash over her. He seemed happy to keep up a one-sided conversation while she admired the scenery.

It was late afternoon by the time they drew through the town of Killalloe and took a road that hugged the shores of the lake. Hope caught a glimpse of a canal, bridged by disused iron walkways and lined with colourful barges. She learned that people lived on them. The lake was huge, in comparison with those she had visited in the Lake District in England, a wide channel opening into a large expanse in which wind surfers coasted, dipping and swirling their sails, like colourful butterflies dancing in the light wind.

They passed a small sports centre. A sturdy wooden jetty thrust into the lake, providing mooring for four launches. People heaved canoes, small sailboats and windsurf boards into the water and the shrieks of beginner sailors filled the air. Hope experienced a pang of regret, wishing that she were among them, losing her balance on the small boards and toppling into the clear, cool lake. She suddenly realized how sticky she felt in spite of the brisk flow of air rushing into the taxi through her open window. She longed to swim in the lake and share the innocent camaraderie of the novice sportsmen.

Shortly after the centre, the taxi driver turned off onto a dusty road that wound up the slopes of the low hills whose foothills curved to the lake edge, broken only by the ribbon of road tracing the shoreline. They pulled up in front of an unspoiled country pub, a plain rectangular brick building set in a scrubby space, seemingly in the middle of nowhere. It seemed deserted, the parking lot at the side empty except for a golden retriever who declined to look at them, as if the effort were simply too much of a bother. This was The Piper's Inn where the group was to meet and stay overnight before being transported to the island retreat the following morning.

Chapter Five

Hope entered the dim, cool interior of The Piper's Inn through a low-beamed door. She stood blinking on the threshold until her eyes adjusted to the gloom. Pleasant, silvery light flowed through leaded windows, mottling the rough white plastered walls and grey flagstone floor. Small round tables, surrounded by woven stools, took up the space between the door and the thrust of a solid bar that divided the room. Through the stalactites of bourbon and rye bottles, Hope could see benched alcoves. The wide passage at the end of the bar was occupied by dinner tables, set with place mats and solid cutlery.

The atmosphere was rustic and welcoming and, although she was alone, Hope felt comfortable. A clanging of pots and pans drew her across the room to seek the kitchen and she approached a door next to the far side of the bar. As she drew nearer she began to feel shy and, rather than intrude, she called out a greeting, hoping she would be heard above the clatter.

'Hi there!' The voice came from behind her.

Hope jumped, her blood pounding, and swung to face her assailant, who held up his palms innocently. 'Sorry!'

'You scared me!' she accused him, then became flustered. 'Where is everyone?'

'Do I count? I'm someone?' he grinned. 'Name's Rusty.'

He offered a hand that Hope took and was surprised by the limp, cool handshake. He was English, his accent North Country, Teesside, Hope guessed – he was also very beautiful. It was the only word that popped into her head as she studied him. He was tall, broad-shouldered and muscled under his tight cropped vest and cut-off jeans. His hair, a burnished red-gold, hung to his shoulders in a thick tangle of curls that Hope ached to tame with her fingers. His soft blue eyes were almost turquoise and edged with thick, coppery lashes. He had a wide, smiling mouth, set in a square jaw. He was barefoot and dusty, tanned, and smelled of coconut oil. She caught a glimpse of a knapsack, sandals tucked untidily under the flap, resting on one of the bench seats in an alcove.

Hope deposited her tote bag, thankful to be relieved of the weight, next to the knapsack. She was aware that he had been scrutinizing her with the same frank openness as she had scanned him. As if the mutual assessment was satisfactorily concluded, they both then peered at the kitchen door. He seemed ill at ease, so Hope pushed her way into the room and discovered a large bearded man wearing a frilly washed-out apron.

'Oh hi!', he said, beaming, 'you must be with the retreat group. I bet you're thirsty.' He ushered her back into the bar and then slipped through a flap in the counter. 'What's it to be?' He peered with mild curiosity at Rusty and settled his hands on the counter. He did not seem ludicrous in his apron, merely like a large, benign cartoon bear, and Hope warmed to his open, cheerful face.

'I would like a beer,' she chanced and, at his look of enquiry, sifted through the beer-pulls along the bar. 'The green one.'

'Good choice,' the barman teased. 'A pint of lager, then?'

'Why not?' she grinned at him.

'Come a long way?' he asked while he grabbed a pint glass from the draining board and poured the golden flow to the rim, leaving thin white froth on top.

'Just from London. My name is Hope and I am starving, by the way!' She cast a longing, theatrical glare at the kitchen door.

'Well, pretty lassie, you have an hour to go, but I can help you out.' He placed the glass to drip on a table mat and disappeared, returning shortly with a plate containing a cold chicken leg and slices of quiche. The informality of his offering pleased Hope.

'Hey, this is just like home!'

'We try,' he smiled. 'It is the way it should be. Now settle yourself in for a moment and I shall serve this young man and then show you your rooms in a while.'

Rusty, seemingly at a loss, rode on his heels and then settled for the same brew that Hope now sipped. She slid into an alcove and sighed, kicked off her shoes and drank deeply. She shared her platter with Rusty and both chewed silently. He was a delicate eater, tugging morsels of chicken from the leg with neat, tiny bites while she tore and gobbled. It dawned on her that, for all his beauty, he was nervous. She attempted to ease the situation with conversation and learned that he was from Teesside as she had suspected, but was living in London where he modelled for a men's fashion house, occasionally doing photoshoots for European publications. He was hoping the retreat would help him to improve his self-image. All the time he spoke, he gazed sincerely at Hope, as if seeking approval. He seemed uninterested in her details, but became increasingly confiding of his own problems, which had more to do with keeping in trim and his complexion clear than any apparent emotional distress.

Hope ceased listening. She was impressed with his good looks and happy to imagine the firm, warm flesh beneath his scanty top but loath to grant him more than half her attention. She wondered what he would be like in bed, suspecting that mirrors would have to be installed, not for their erotic ambience but for him to ensure that he disported himself with elegance. She could not believe he would easily abandon himself to passion, it would be far too mucky and ungainly. She was relieved, as she stifled a yawn, when she heard footsteps on the stone floor and a figure rounded the bar.

'Well,' she said, half alert, 'perhaps we shall get a chance to fuck again.' Even in her ears it sounded wrong but it took a glance at Rusty's shocked expression and the frozen figure now standing by their table to discover her mistake. She closed her eyes and leaned back, slapping her hand to her forehead. 'I mean *talk*. We shall get a chance to *talk* again!'

When she opened her eyes, it was to watch Rusty sliding from the alcove. He looked serious when he turned and said, 'Why do women always say that to me?' but the unfortunate response to his injured question was a gale of laughter from the newcomer.

'Go look in a mirror, silly, and think about it!' The rich Scottish accent sang with mirth and Rusty retreated.

Allie flopped into the seat vacated by Rusty and peered at Hope with owlish good humour. 'Reckon you soured your pitch there!' She kicked soiled tennis shoes from her feet and planted her soles on the cool floor, groaning with pleasure. A cap of short red curls plastered her forehead and sweat trickled from her chin to soak into a strappy stretch top. Her clothes were soaked. 'Hitched from Limerick,' she informed Hope, 'but had to walk from Killalloe. When I saw the sports place, I just ran and dived off the jetty!' A trail of freckles splashed her nose and cheeks, highlighting her pale but sun-flushed alabaster skin. She rooted in her knapsack and grinned while she applied a cream she had found. 'I burn easily,' she explained.

'I guessed,' Hope smiled.

'Oh no, don't tell me! It is the ghostly white skin?' Allie cawed with laughter and introduced herself. 'You are going on this retreat, aren't you? Just my luck to choose a genuine tourist and make a fool of myself.'

Hope nodded, 'I am going.' She took an instant liking to Allie, who seemed uncomplicated and friendly. She had tucked her slim legs on the seat and perched on her ankles, wiry and comfortable. 'Is he-man going?' she nodded in the direction in which Rusty had escaped.

'Yes, he is.' Hope grimaced. 'I upset him, I guess. Perhaps that is something we can work through on the retreat.'

'Oh, right!' Allie assumed a hurt expression and mimicked his accent, 'I just want to tell you all that Hope hurt my feelings by wanting to ravish my pecs!' She grinned as Hope laughed. 'It *was* his pecs you were after, was it not?'

'Absolutely,' Hope managed a serious expression. 'What else?'

'Ah, now, we shall have to investigate that further, to be sure.'

The bearded barman pushed his way through the swing

doors, introducing an aroma of delicious cooking smells. 'Right! This way to your sumptuous accommodation, Mademoiselle.' He acknowledged Allie with a grin, 'You, too.'

'I will not budge,' Allie stuck a small, determined chin towards the bar, 'until you hand me a pint of Guinness, my good man!'

'Ah, and I need to pay for the drink I had. What about registering?' Hope asked.

'Oh no, I will charge the drinks when you leave tomorrow. You've a slate. If it gets busy, just mark them off yourself.' He pointed at a book on the bar. One column headed 'Hope' showed her indebtedness. She was impressed with his trust. The next column showed 'Rusty'. 'I caught the model fellow taking the evening sun outside and learned his name,' he said.

Hope knew then that he had overheard some of their conversation. To know that Rusty was a male model, he would have had to be listening in. 'Just how much could you hear?' she demanded.

'Oh, enough.' He beamed at her. 'As Freud would say, "an eloquent sufficiency",' he misquoted, smiling as Hope blushed. 'It will make for a good evening,' he murmured reassuringly, 'and bring things down to earth.'

He chattered as he drew a Guinness and nodded his approval when Allie started her own column in the book. He also drew a pint for Hope. 'Try it,' he said simply. Armed with brimming pint pots and their baggage, the women followed him into a corridor and up a stairwell.

'It's pot luck,' he explained as he led them to rooms at the end of a landing. 'You want these, right by the bathrooms?' The doors had no numbers. 'That way,' he reasoned, 'if you get blasted, you know to hit the far wall and turn into the door beside you.'

'Yeah, but what about the rest of them? They'll miss their doors and we'll end up with strangers in our beds,' Allie muttered, while the barman remained silent and grinning. 'Oh, okay,' she conceded, 'just keep Mr Model on orange juice, will you?'

The rooms were basic: small single beds with hard mattresses, foam pillows, white cotton sheets and grey blankets. Small dressing tables with spotted mirrors and creaking drawers rested drunkenly beside lime-green stuffed chairs. Thin, leaning cupboards offered wire hangers and shelves covered with floral waxed paper. Two bathroom doors stood opposite, labelled with scrawling amateur paintwork.

'Grab a shower,' their host advised. 'The water runs cold if others get in first. I heard more arrivals, so by the time you get down again, we'll be thinking of supper.' He sped off to attend to his duties and Allie and Hope dashed to comply. The walls of the bedrooms were thin, and they discovered they could hold a reasonable conversation simply by directing slightly raised voices at the partition. The lack of secrecy was even more apparent in the bathrooms, giving rise to hilarity until each stood thankfully in the showers.

Hope was delighted. Despite the ramshackle appearance of the facilities, the cascade from the showerhead was impressive, massaging over her shoulders harshly and easing the grime and sweat from her hair in a torrent. She felt selfish, but stood to enjoy the flow as the water began to run cool. *Well*, she persuaded herself as she dried herself with a tiny, scratchy towel, *it will soon heat up again*.

Hope was accustomed to five-star hotels, with champagne

service, yet she felt she had never enjoyed a shower more. It was a relief to enter her small room and pull on jeans and a light sweater, without doing much more than running a comb through her damp hair. She felt free and natural, going to dinner without an idea of the menu and not dressing for the occasion. It seemed, as she joined Allie on the landing, that the Scottish woman never had reservations of this kind. She looked impish, lithe and tomboyish in faded chinos and T-shirt.

When they entered the bar, they found that seats were being taken at the dinner tables under the guidance of Bear as they had decided to name him and who responded to the nickname with smiling grace. He showed them to seats at the furthest head of one table, tucked into a corner. 'You get served here first, do you see? We work outwards.'

Rusty, apparently having forgiven Hope, appeared and took the seat to her right. Each table seated six and Allie was quick to ensure that introductions were made. Quinn sat opposite Hope, a stocky, soft-spoken American some years her senior. He seemed charming and had a habit of stroking his pale blond hair from his forehead. It would be a nervous gesture in someone less confident, but it lent import to Quinn's words.

Hope was relieved at the arrival of Rat, who smoothly usurped a seat next to Allie and offered a shy smile to the table. He introduced himself as 'Raith, from London – a geek,' and lapsed into silence after casting a warm look at Hope. Allie, not missing the glance, raised her eyebrows at Hope, leaned over and whispered loudly. 'What, another one you get to *talk* to?' The innuendo was lost on Rat but caused Rusty to giggle, which surprised the women into joining in with chuckles. It seemed that Allie had lost her earlier contempt for him and embarked on a lengthy conversation about his modelling, not sparing her compliments. 'Here,' she said to Hope, after talking across her for a while, 'swap seats, will you?'

Hope was happy to oblige and sit next to Rat. He remained silent but she knew he was pleased and she felt more at ease with him beside her, as if he was someone comfortable and familiar from back home. She spoke across him to Quinn, and then with a new arrival, the last to take a seat, who lumbered into the vacant chair with an awkward jutting of elbows and knees. Ruari, as he introduced himself, looked painfully embarrassed at being the centre of attention. He had a rich accent, initially hard to follow, and claimed to be from the City of Cork, and a craftsman bookbinder. He seemed to Hope to be more suited to labouring, his hands rough and fingernails broken though clean. He was large. 'Built like a brick outhouse' as Allie commented later. His dark hair escaped loosely to almost obscure heavy eyebrows and flashing, dark brown eyes. 'He's what they call a "black Irishman", I think,' Allie added. 'Not the skin tone but a general swarthiness. Lord knows where they get it, something historical, I imagine.'

His choice of seat was fortunate as it emerged that Quinn, while American, resided in Dublin and they shared a knowledge of the nightclubs along Leeson Street. With Allie seducing Rusty, it allowed Hope space to murmur a conversation with Rat. She learned he had driven over, taking the ferry from Liverpool to Dun Laoghaire and driving across to Limerick. He was late because he had stopped in Killalloe seeking directions and got caught up in sightseeing.

'It is a great place,' he enthused softly. 'They serve cream teas at the hotel.' He fell silent, suddenly aware of Hope's thigh pressed along his, although it was simply the crush of the small table that caused her nearness. Rusty and Ruari, both large men, had a more significant problem with lack of space and seemed to be a perpetual juggle of elbows, until Allie sensibly swapped seats with Rusty. She sat opposite Hope and offered her an exaggerated wink, then cast sly looks to her left and right, glorying in her male phalanx. Rusty blushed and Ruari sniggered with pleasure, responding with good-humoured Irish banter to Allie's increasingly outrageous patter.

They worked their way through well prepared standard fare, offered without a menu but with easy, laughing service and quick attention to their needs. Melon preceded roast chicken and vegetables, followed by apple pie with cream. Each course was served with glasses of chilled white table wine and by the time dessert was placed before her, Hope was feeling tipsy. The volume of conversation around her had grown, her fellow diners growing similarly inebriated.

She leaned back in her chair, edging around so she could examine the people at a neighbouring table, and was surprised to find there were only three. A girl with long, curling black hair and wide, shy eyes, a petite woman with long, straight ash-blonde hair and ice-blue eyes who laughed a lot, a tinkling, flirtatious chuckling; and a man. As a third table held six people, obviously windsurfers if the logos on their T-shirts were to be believed, Hope assumed that the three were part of the group intended for the retreat. She returned her attention to the trio.

The man was mature, immaculately dressed in a polo shirt and dark trousers. A heavy gold Rolex watch gleamed at his tanned wrist. He was slightly built, wiry. His hair was slicked back from a broad forehead and trimmed straight at his collar. His eyes seemed black in the dim light. He leaned politely towards the blonde woman, listening intently and laughing while her giggles punctuated each of her sentences. The young, gypsy-looking girl seemed unhappy, more so when the man deliberately included her in the conversation, an act equally distasteful to the blonde, who frowned. He mollified her with a light touch on her shoulder and glanced at Hope, then settled back in his chair and cocked his head to one side, as if to study her better.

Hope felt chilled. There was something unsettling and predatory in his eyes. He suddenly smiled softly and tilted his glass in salute, then murmured to his companions and came to crouch beside Hope's chair, his breath brushing her cheek as she turned.

'I think we know each other. My name is Mallot and I believe yours is Hope Andrews?'

'Yes, I am Hope, but I do not think I know you.' Her eyes met his and she felt repulsion war with a strange longing. He had an hypnotic, reptilian gaze, and eyes so black she could not make out his pupils. She blinked and turned away.

'That's okay.' He rose. 'We met only briefly.' He asked if they could extend the circle, so that all those gathering for the retreat could sit together. Once chairs had been shuffled, the dark girl found herself wedged between Ruari and Allie. She introduced herself as, 'Elsa, from County Cork,' then fell into happy chatter with Ruari when they discovered mutual acquaintances. Allie seemed content to flirt with Rusty, who took this as his due and appeared unaware that her comments were growing increasingly outrageous.

The ash-blonde ice-maiden was Angela. From closer, Hope could see the fine lines etching her eyes, the careful outline of her lips and clever application of make-up. She was older than she at first appeared. Her mannerisms were charming and, Hope believed, cultivated. Angela had succeeded in staying next to Mallot, her seat set hard against his, and their thighs locked. She looked subtly triumphant, especially when Mallot, forced to create space to enable her to reach forward for her glass, placed his arm over the back of her chair. He looked amused when she took the opportunity to press closer against him.

Rat contributed little to the general conversation. He was uneasy in crowds and was overcome with the closeness of Hope. His main concern centred on her thigh, which pressed warmly against his. Each time she moved the denim of her jeans rode slightly along his bare flesh, clad as he was in worn denim shorts. It took little for him to imagine her naked heat sliding along him. He ate little, finding it hard to swallow, and shuffled as much as he could, without raising suspicion, to enjoy an occasional increased pressure. He drank more than he was accustomed to and welcomed the large mugs of coffee that rounded off the meal.

When the music started, he jumped, startled from his daydreams. A fast fiddle, accompanied by an expertly wielded piano accordion and flute, played a lively jig. The volume was sufficient to drown the possibility of further conversation and the diners were encouraged to find seats further from the musicians, who normally utilized the space occupied by the dinner tables.

The pub had filled with people. A throng hugged the bar and all the stools were full. People leaned against the walls and the benches in the alcoves were overfilled. Left with their chairs, the group slid them in a large semicircle around the players, then sat and clapped, tapping their feet in time to the music. The tables were stacked against the wall and, when the jig drew to a halt, the musicians moved into the space created, smiling at the applause and bantering with the crowd.

Hope chose that moment to lean across and whisper in Rat's ear, thrilling him after the disappointment he had experienced with the move which had taken her thigh away from his.

'Let's go outside and talk for a moment.' She turned to Allie and made an exaggerated gesture, drawing the back of her hand across her forehead as if suffering from the heat, then rose and pushed through the crowd to the front door.

Hope found it surprisingly chilly after the heat of the pub and was glad that she had chosen to wear a sweater. She felt a pang of sympathy for Rat, who followed shortly, bearing two pints of Guinness. He was wearing a baggy T-shirt, shorts and scuffed sneakers. Her concern seemed unwarranted when he muttered, 'Thank the gods!' and settled onto the step, as if unaware of the cold. He carefully placed the pint pots on the ground and lifted the hem of his shirt to wipe his brow, then gave Hope a sudden, brilliant grin.

'Made it!'

She joined him on the cold step and they sipped at their brew. Accustomed to the brightness of city nights, the blackness of the sky over County Clare seemed impenetrable and alien. Hope suddenly realized she was far from home with a near-stranger who lusted for her, in a location known only to Reggie and possibly to Amy. Light spilled from the leaded windows of the pub, shedding golden puddles over the small pebbled front path and tipping into the road.

The music throbbed, not clear and barely covering the clapping and stomping of the patrons.

'There's a bench just under there.' She pointed at a window near the end of the building. 'Shall we?'

Once settled on the wooden slats, Hope felt warmer. She leaned back to admire the stars and allowed the peace to overtake her. She still felt slightly tipsy and a little reckless, aware that Rat was staring at her, trying to make out her features in the glow from the window. She held his gaze until he was forced to turn away and pretend an interest in his glass.

'I think this is all of us,' Hope said. 'Any ideas on which is Willincough?'

'Huh?' Rat was surprised back to reality.

'Well, I suspect Quinn. He is a bit older than I would have thought for a hacker but he has soft hands and he lives in Ireland, whereas Ruari really does have the hands of a labourer, not like a keyboard jockey.'

'There's nothing to indicate that Willincough is a male,' Rat pointed out reasonably.

'Of course! Sorry.' Hope apologized to all her sisters in strife. 'Not Elsa, though, I think.' She picked the only other Irish resident.

'There's also no reason to suppose Willincough is Irish, or even operates from Ireland!'

'You said he lived in Ireland. Anyway, it was you who used the male gender.'

Rat sighed. 'Well, it is easier than constantly saying "he or she"! And, while he may live here, it is most likely you would find no trace of his operation through Irish communications channels. Hackers route deviously . . .' He stopped when Hope giggled.

'What?' He demanded crossly.

'Sorry, just sounded like a logo on a T-shirt. "Hackers root deviously"!'

'Nah,' he said, 'you're thinking of "Hackers do it through a dongle".' He sniggered.

Hope chuckled, relaxing. 'I expect Willincough will make himself known when he wants, or she wants. I must confess I just feel like unwinding for a while. Pursuit can wait a day or two.'

'Speaking of work, I saw Amy before I left this morning. She brought me a cheque to cover the expenses and seemed pissed off that I was coming here.' Rat neglected to tell Hope that he had crowed about the trip, showing off and insinuating that he proposed to enjoy a closer relationship with Hope by the end of the fortnight.

'Oh? What did she say?' Hope studied her glass.

'Something to the effect that I was a sad, geeky bastard and should have my balls removed.' He sounded mournful and Hope could not avoid laughing.

'Which no doubt you did not provoke?' she guessed.

'I think she is odd. Anyway, you were with her yesterday, what did you say to make her angry?'

Ah, thought Hope, *I simply said I like the taste of her juices as they stream from her cunt, the give of her tissue under my tongue and the feel of her soft lips suckling at my nipples*. To Rat, she said 'Nothing at all. Anyway, forget Pursuit. Let's pretend we're on holiday, except for seeking Willincough. London seems very far away, and tomorrow it will seem even further.'

Rat fell silent at the reference to the retreat. He could

think of nothing better than to be stranded on an island with Hope.

'You look great without make-up and clothes, by the way.' He suffered in the pause before Hope laughed and thanked him. His gaff reminded her of her earlier slip and she told Rat about it to amuse him.

'You said "fuck"?'

'Is that not permissible?'

'Say it again!'

Hope tucked her legs under her and leaned towards Rat until her lips were close to his, her expression sultry. She mouthed softly, 'Fuck,' then whispered again, her breath a caress on his mouth, 'Fuck'. She drew back slightly, her lips parted, and studied the effect on her colleague.

He seemed frozen, then groaned and leapt to his feet. 'I have to go back inside!' he growled, and sped from her.

'Now, there's a turn up for the books,' Hope muttered to herself, grinning. She sat to enjoy the rest of her Guinness before rising to rejoin the group.

The music had quietened and she entered to a sweet sound. A clear, high voice accompanied by a guitar. When she sought the singer, her blood aglow with sudden yearnings and her heart mourning, she was amazed to see that Elsa had taken a position amongst the musicians, and that it was she who thrilled the silent watchers. Her voice rose, loud with an historical Irish pain and lowered, whispering the grief of an enslaved people. Hope was shocked, her eyes filling with tears as she froze in the doorway. She barely listened to the tormented words, her heart laden and the tones filling her with remorse. When she risked a glance around the assembly, she noticed that her fellow listeners seemed as affected as she. When the last plaintive notes died away and Elsa fell silent, a hush descended, held for a moment, then exploded in violent applause and cheers.

Hope felt confused and emotional as she watched. Elsa smiled sweetly and surrendered the guitar to its owner, who forced it back on her. The musicians held a hurried, whispered conversation and then readied their instruments and suddenly broke into a cheerful, popular Irish folksong that encouraged the audience to sing along. The contrast was startling and left Hope feeling even more confused, her heart now buoyant. She felt vibrantly alive, the flagstones beneath her feet throbbing to the beat of the music.

If this was the heart of the Irish, she thought as she crossed to her group, Lord help us on the island. Mallot and Angela had disappeared, Rat was leaning against a far wall and Allie and Rusty had crammed into an alcove with the windsurfers and were engaged in serious drinking. Quinn and Ruari seemed to have their full attention riveted on Elsa, hypnotized by her skill and the beauty of her voice. Gone was the shy country girl they had first encountered. She sat among the musicians, her head thrown back, hair tousled and gleaming under the light and her eyes flashing. Over the din of the massed singers, Hope could hear her strong, vibrant tone, confident and alive, and she felt humble with admiration.

She also felt exhausted. With the thin walls of her bedroom, she had little hope of sleep while the revelry continued, but she ached to lie down. According to the instructions, the group would breakfast at eight o'clock and had to be prepared to transfer to the launches an hour later. She was shocked when the lights blinked to denote closing time, and glanced at her watch to confirm, surprised that many drinkers made no move to finish up and merely settled in more solidly while Bear slammed the bolts shut on the exterior doors after those departing had waved a farewell. The musicians disbanded, gravitating to the bar with Elsa in their midst. They were joined by Ruari and Quinn, who bought them a round of drinks.

Hope smiled at Bear and joined Rat. He seemed distracted and Hope supposed he had been as moved by the music as she had. She had noted how uneasy he was in company and how a space seemed to exist around him, even when he was jostled by passers-by. Wherever he was, his gaze had sought and found her, and now he peered at her with strange, bright eyes in which she noticed a feverish passion. Tired as she felt, her pulse responded and they stood staring at one another as if isolated, while the conversation poured over them.

Hope broke the contact. She blinked and ran her tonguetip over her lips, which seemed tender and dry. She eased past Rat and walked slowly along the corridor and up the stairs, aware that he trod softly behind her.

Rat felt strange. He believed that they had made a pact with their shared look, but it seemed too soon to consummate. He longed to push Hope to the thin carpet of the corridor, rip her jeans from her as she lay, face down and helpless, and bare her derriere. With her legs trapped he would sink into her flesh and ride hard until he spurted while she mewled and came. Yet she seemed vulnerable, pale and disarming as she walked trustingly before him, and his dangerous passion was made helpless. He would kiss her, he decided. At least he would place his mouth on hers and cement his claim, test if her lips were as soft as he had fantasized and her breasts as cushioning against his chest as he had dreamed. However, he was afraid that were he to lay hands on her he would surrender to his primitive drive. He was debating the wisdom of even thinking of a goodnight kiss when he walked into her, staggered and then clutched at her to prevent them both from falling.

Hope suddenly stopped when she passed the bathroom door. It was ajar, and Mallot was sitting on the edge of the bath, nonchalantly smoking a cheroot, his trousers puddling around his ankles – while Angela sucked hungrily on his large, swollen cock. The picture was so unexpected that Hope stood and gaped until the image resolved in her mind. Then she was fascinated, watching the silky ash-blonde sway of Angela's hair as her head bobbed.

Hope hardly noticed that Rat had not released his grasp of her waist after preventing their fall. She felt connected to the scene being played out before her, reluctant to withdraw her attention, and she felt an empathy with Angela's ministering mouth, now playing and sucking along the erect smooth shaft of the seemingly unaffected Mallot. Hope licked her lips, her mouth filling with saliva. She trembled. It was only Rat's restraining hands that prevented her from surging forward to claim her place between Mallot's thighs to worship with her tongue and fingers.

Rat felt her shiver. He was impressed with Angela whose consummate skill had at last provoked a sigh from Mallot, a sigh which was echoed by Hope. He was swift to take advantage of Hope's distraction and slide his hands beneath her sweater, groping for her breasts which he kneaded passionately, unable to temper his touch, having at last achieved first station. In his sudden quest he had forced the hem of the garment up and his furiously working hands could be clearly viewed by Mallot. It was this sight which brought him to the brink, caused him to lay his hand on Angela's head and tangle his fingers in her silken hair to force her to swallow his length. He half-rose from the rim of the bath and pumped his hips harshly, his eyes fixed on Hope's breasts. He withdrew from Angela's mouth as he came and his spinning cream arced and traced over her delicate cheeks while she wriggled to capture it. He at last looked at her with an expression of mild interest, then grasped his waning erection and rubbed his tip over her face, smearing his come.

Hope had been tense, straining under Rat's hands before Mallot came, then she slumped, as if it were she who was drained of precious fluids. She turned to face Rat, her eyes unfocused, and leaned against the wall, limply submissive as he continued, more gently, to massage her breasts. She felt aroused but distant and had Rat been as selfish and assertive as his fantasy self he could simply have taken her for his own pleasure. Her lack of involvement unnerved him, although he could see the desire in her eyes. He let go and gently, with reluctance, tugged the sweater back down to cover her breasts. She seemed to emerge from a trance, offered him a small, puzzled smile and eased away to enter her room.

As Rat watched her door shut softly he realized that he had, after all, not managed to kiss her. He heard a rustle of cloth and the sound of a zipper being drawn closed and resolutely kept his back turned on the scene in the bathroom. He wondered at Hope's fascination and dreaded the idea that it had something to do with Mallot, preferring to believe that it was the transfixion of voying.

'You can play with her, but she is mine.' The voice insinuated through Rat's denial.

'I think it may just be the other way around,' he muttered, but realized he was too late: the footsteps were receding and, when he turned, the corridor was empty.

Chapter Six

Hope missed breakfast. She woke, feeling hungover and drained, to a banging on her door that turned out to be Allie, bearing a mug of coffee and a plate of dry toast. She seemed unconcerned by Hope's nudity.

'Thought you might need this,' she said. 'Not really a drinker, are you?'

Hope grunted her thanks, pulled on a pair of panties and slouched on the bed while Allie regaled her with stories of the night's revelries. It emerged that she had stayed up all night, won a 'yard of ale' contest and earned Rusty as a prize. He obliged by stripping to the buff, accompanied by a mournful dirge played by an inebriated fiddler. She was lyrical in describing Rusty's attributes.

'He is very, very pretty. Had there not been a crowd, I would have jumped his bones. Mind you, there was a lot of encouragement.' She frowned, 'I do not know if it was the drink, but he was limp.' She crooked a finger downwards in parody. 'Anyway,' she concluded, 'what did you and the slab of nerd get up to?'

'Not a lot,' Hope told her. 'First stations.'

'Now that brings me back to schooldays. He grabbed your tits?' Allie peered at Hope's breasts, grinning.

'More like he prepared them for baking in a bread tin!' Hope protested.

'Kiss better?' Allie bounced onto the bed and planted small kisses on the mound of each breast.

Taken by surprise, Hope laughed, then settled to enjoy the sensation, especially when she felt her nipples surrounded and gently sucked. She murmured her pleasure.

'Trouble is,' Allie pulled away, 'you have two minutes to get up if you want to catch the transport to the launch.' She laughed at Hope's rueful expression. 'We have two weeks, during which time I shall hang off your nipples any chance I get.'

'Tease!' Hope cupped Allie's chin and kissed her hard, until the young woman opened her mouth. While they kissed passionately, Hope rolled over to straddle the lithe body. When they broke free, they were breathless, staring at each other with lust-filled eyes. Neither had noticed the small knock on the door, nor when it opened, but both suddenly registered the frozen presence of Rat in the doorway.

He stared in incomprehension for a moment, then muttered, 'Sorry,' but failed to leave. Hope slid from Allie, sat on the edge of the bed and contemplated Rat. Allie, unconcerned and unrepentant, rose and started tucking Hope's clothes into the tote bag.

'You now have no time at all.' Her words were emphasized by the blare of a horn. 'That must be the bus!'

'You're a lesbian?' Rat's voice was very soft as he addressed Hope. 'Is that what it was about last night – not Mallot, but Angela?' His expression was difficult to read.

Hope needed to reassure him. He seemed very vulnerable, his tone angry and frustrated. She rose, lifted his hand and placed it on her breast, then pulled him towards her and very gently slipped her lips over his, a feather-light promise. He trembled and groaned softly, and slid back to rest against the doorpost, his hand falling from her.

'I am only learning what I am,' Hope murmured. 'But I start off with being free. Now let's get that bus.' She quickly pulled on the clothes she had worn the previous night and they dashed down the stairs, Rat carrying her tote bag.

A minibus waited in front of the inn. The seats were already filled by the rest of the group, who shuffled to make space for the newcomers. The driver, a young man wearing skimpy shorts, checked they were all present, then announced, 'We're going to the sports centre, where we'll board a launch. The trip to the island takes two hours normally, but we will be stopping off for a picnic lunch. Also, we cannot dock at the island because of rocks, so you'll be ferried by a motorboat in relays from a dropping-off point. I will be with you all the way, so if you have any questions just ask.' He slid behind the wheel, then twisted in the seat and added, 'Oh, it is going to be damned hot today, with only a force two breeze, so I would advise you to change on the boat into swimming costumes. I will stop at a little bay so you can take a dip.'

Allie and Rat squeezed into a space at the rear of the bus. He remained silent, savouring the image of Hope bent over the redhead, her breasts naked and her lips swollen. The trip to the centre took a couple of minutes, during which time he daydreamed about sliding onto the bed behind Hope, then lifting her bottom to slide her panties from her so he could enter her while she licked Allie's breasts. He had just reached the stage where Hope thrust back, moaning with pleasure while he pummelled and prepared to feast on the damp offering between Allie's slim thighs, when the bus drew to a halt. He felt rampant, frustrated and irrationally angry and pushed his way through the bus to stalk to the end of the jetty.

Hope watched him race away. She sympathized, wondering how many of her fellow travellers had noticed the sharp exclamation mark of his erection pushing against the fabric of his thin Bermuda shorts. She sought Allie, who grinned at her, eyebrows raised, then fell into step as they crunched over the gravel, trailing behind the rest of the group.

'You are going to have to do something about that young man,' Allie said, 'and soon. The way he is carrying on, he will damage himself.'

Hope nodded. She recalled the strength of Rat's hands, kneading her breasts while she watched Mallot and Angela. There was pent-up passion in his roughness, a frustration that excited her. The contrast between Mallot's almost bored acceptance of Angela's ministrations and Rat's furious grabbing caused a conflict in her. She longed for both the older man's studied domination and the eager, spontaneous eruption of Rat. She also longed for the butterfly kisses that Allie had bestowed, and the sweet nectar promised between the slim woman's thighs. Like Rat, her imagination had been caught up with images, not much different from his and, like him, she felt roused and impatient.

It seemed this condition pervaded the group. Angela succeeded in staying next to Mallot, who seemed unaffected although he grabbed her breast when they were boarding the launch. She managed a look of mock-concern before laughing happily and disappearing through the cabin door. Elsa, flanked by Quinn and Ruari, looked flushed and happy but kept her gaze fixed on the boards of the jetty rather than brazenly facing her companions. Rusty seemed alone. He had taken station at the prow and tugged off his vest, baring his muscled torso to the early morning sun. He stood, an Adonis clad in running shorts, to be admired.

'I think I shall just go get a bit of that,' Allie observed, and leapt nimbly aboard to join him.

The driver had introduced himself as Sean as they were leaving the bus and had been joined on the jetty by a twin. 'Call us both Sean,' he had called out diplomatically. They were identical, bronzed and lithe, with copper-coloured hair and piercing blue eyes. They ferried provisions in polystyrene cool-boxes from the centre to the launch.

'Lunch,' Sean One informed Hope, as he strode past her to pass the boxes to Sean Two.

She took advantage of the time allowed by their industry to join Rat at the end of the dock. They stood together and gazed over the lake. A low mist shifted over the surface of the water, creating a wonderworld of swirling white patterns. The far shore was softened with an artist's light, appearing like a canvas backdrop rather than reality. Hope could see the slope of a slip and, surprisingly, the blurred shape of a large deer.

'The lake is over a quarter of a mile wide at this point,' Rat advised, 'according to the guidebook I bought in Killalloe yesterday. A private deer park has been created on that side and the owner refuses sightseers.'

'What about the people who surf and boat, they must be able to get over there?'

'Well, the main channel for the large, motorized boats and barges runs near that shore so I think it is kept reasonably clear of sportsmen.'

They stood companionably to enjoy the calm, comfortably aware of each other but with an unbridged gap which Hope chose to cross.

'Rat,' she turned and looked into his eyes, 'we are going to make love sometime. I just thought you should know that I am aware of that.'

His mouth tightened and he ground out, 'I don't want to make love.'

Hope was so amazed, that she felt no pain of rejection, 'Why not?'

'I don't think I can make love to you.' Rat's body was taut, betraying tension, then he exhaled sharply and grabbed Hope's shoulders, glaring at her as his words whipped. 'You see, I want to fuck you, not make love. I have spent hours, days, weeks thinking about how to dunk you. Christ! I want to rip off your clothes and suck your cunt, ram into you and ride you until you beg for more.' He let go of her shoulders and rubbed his temples, 'I am obsessed with you and have been for a very long time. And what happens? I find you sucking flesh with some woman!' He turned to leave her.

Hope grabbed his arm roughly and pulled him to face her again. 'Oh no, you don't. It seems too damned easy for you to run away, mister! First of all Allie is not "some woman"! Secondly, I am free to suck whatever I want with whomever I want. Third, fine, we fuck!'

They glared at each other until the absurdity of her words struck Hope and her lips quivered, then bowed into a wide smile. She sniggered, unable to stop herself, then burst into laughter, gasping an apology. It was a while before she realized the shaking of Rat's shoulders was not from anger but mirth. She reached blindly, as the tears began to stream, and clutched at Rat, who drew her to his heaving chest. When the gale died, she pressed into him, enjoying his strong embrace and hot, musky aroma. Rat sighed deeply, his hand sliding under the curtain of Hope's hair to rub the back of her neck. He planted a soft kiss on her bent blonde head. 'Yeah,' he mused, 'we fuck.' He rubbed her back briskly, pushed her away and studied her face, smiling softly, 'Now?' Despite the humour, Hope saw that he was serious.

'I want it now, too,' she confessed, 'but there's a boatload of people watching us.'

Rat reddened and turned to face slow applause. The group were lined up on the deck, striking exaggerated poses of patience. Sean One leaned against the bridge, arms crossed, and Sean Two held a mooring rope loosely, whistling at the sky. The rear of the launch, already untethered, started to swing away from the jetty, causing Sean Two to pull hard on the rope.

'Get on board, you two,' he called cheerfully, 'or hold these damn ropes for me!'

Rat blushed furiously. 'How much did they hear?' he hissed at Hope.

'Nothing,' she grinned, 'They just watched.' She grabbed Rat's hand and tugged him along the jetty.

He bounded over the rail and onto the deck, then lifted her on board, laughing when she tripped and stumbled against him. Allie clapped him on the shoulder.

'Way to go, Tarzan!'

Rat shrugged nonchalantly and wandered off, then turned to execute a small bow, earning further applause. His steps had brought him abreast of Mallot.

'Play away,' the man whispered meaningfully, then turned away with cool indifference.

Rat shrugged. He needed to be alone and savour the promise of fulfilling his lust. His quest took him into the cabin and through a door marked 'Head'. In the tiny cubicle, he leaned with one hand on the wall, slipped his shorts down and stroked his hard rod until he burst, with the image of Hope, supine and splayed beneath him while he geysered and shot his thick, white come over her trembling stomach. Afterwards he sat, breathing harshly, on the tiny toilet and surprised himself with the image of Allie, bent over his softening prick, licking hungrily at his bulb. He sat, waning, listening to the bustle in the cabin as people took turns to change into cooler clothing.

Hope and Allie stood aft, a cool breeze playing around them. As Sean had promised, the day was growing hot, the sun burning in a clear sky. Both women had taken the opportunity to change, Hope slipping on the white bikini that Karen had chosen for her and tugging a pair of denim shorts over the thong bottom. Allie wore a tight vest that hugged to her waist and the bottom of a bikini. They leaned against the safety rail and gazed over the boat.

'I cannot stay out here long,' Allie said, 'or I'll burn to a crisp.'

Hope studied the flat plane of her new friend's pale stomach, her eyes narrowed, then swivelled to watch the wake. 'Turn around,' she instructed softly, 'and come closer.'

Allie obeyed, puzzled until she felt Hope's palm smooth over her stomach. Hope tucked her hand under the rim of the bikini bottom and pushed, until her index finger rested in the moist crease below. She kept her gaze on the wake, semi-hypnotized by the small, curling waves that peeled at the edges of the trough. She enjoyed the symbolism when her finger grew wet with Allie's response.

They stood on a narrow plinth at the rear of the launch, between the rail of the deck and low roof of the cabin. There was a window behind them but, as they were sailing westwards, Sean had drawn the thin curtains so the direct morning sun would not stream in and overheat the cabin. Allie sighed, leaned back against the cabin and eased her head back eyes closed.

'Part your legs for me,' Hope said and slid to face Allie. She drew the straps of the vest from Allie's shoulders and tugged until the top nestled around the redhead's waist, gently binding her arms at her sides. Anyone looking aft would see a naked back and assume Allie was tanning her breasts. If anyone came closer, Hope would be revealed, kneeling between Allie's thighs, her mouth working at the sheer cloth of the bikini bottom.

Hope traced her tongue over the slick material, pushing until it tucked into Allie's cleft. She felt the seep of the young woman through the fabric, then tasted musk and pushed her nose into the cloth to inhale deeply. She sucked until traces of Allie's dew mingled with her saliva, and she savoured the aroused tang. She grasped the bikini bottom with her teeth and drew it down slowly, unveiling Allie's mound, to stare at the innocence of the bald pubis and the clam of swollen lobes. She drew her finger softly over the join, pressing until the edges took her in, then rubbed along the wet crevasse, fascinated as the thick lips hugged damply then swelled, opening to reveal Allie's pearl. Hope took it between her lips, pursed to surround it tightly and suckled, like a child at a teat. She had not realized how much a clitoris could swell. It felt like a small erect penis in her mouth.

Allie had curved her hips forward, to allow Hope easy access, and further parted her legs. Hope placed her palms together and steepled her two forefingers, easing the spire into Allie's wet cave. She kept her fingers still while she mouthed Allie's clitoris rhythmically, soon feeling the suck of vaginal muscles on her fingertips. Hope leaned back to watch, tamped her thumbs into the crease below the nub and seesawed into Allie, setting a beat as the girl's hips rode.

Hope looked up to watch Allie's flushed face and wide eyes. Her pupils had widened until they almost blotted the clear blue with black, and her mouth was stretched in a grimace of pleasure. They held the stare until Hope felt a soft explosion tug along her fingers and Allie shut her eyes tightly and moaned. As she subsided she watched Hope, who slowly withdrew her fingers then licked the thick dew from her fingertips with an expression of bliss. She parted Allie's lobes and swept her tongue along her with long laps, ensuring that she scooped up all the thick, creamy residue.

When Hope withdrew she noticed, through the vee of Allie's legs, that the curtains had been opened and Rusty's handsome face was outlined in the window. She placed her sticky palm flat on the glass and smiled when his tongue swept over the pane in an attempt to share the liquor. She rose and tugged Allie's top up while the young woman yanked her bikini bottoms back into place.

'Rusty was watching,' Hope whispered.

'Did he have a hard-on?'

'Couldn't see.'

'Pity. Next time, perhaps.' Allie caressed Hope's breast, 'I want him to watch, where I can see him.'

'Likewise Rat.'

'Do you care who fucks who?'

'Not as long as I can watch.' Hope smiled, complicity achieved.

Rusty appeared, swaying to the smooth dip and rise of the launch, making his way over the roof of the cabin. He sat on the edge, his legs dangling, and studied them.

'How much did you watch?' Allie asked at last.

'All of it, I think.'

'Who else?'

'No one. Rat was in the head and the others are driving Sean crazy on the bridge.'

Allie turned and wriggled between Rusty's knees, placing her palms high on his thighs so her thumbs edged beneath his shorts. 'Did you like what you saw then?'

He nodded matter-of-factly, 'Sure, you've a pretty cunt.'

Hope watched, amazed, as the conversation continued. She compared this Rusty with the blushing, injured man who had swivelled to face her after her gaff the previous day, and could not reconcile the two.

'So, you would like a bit of that, would you?' Allie circled her finger softly over the crotch of Rusty's shorts.

'Sure,' Rusty responded calmly. 'You want a bit of what you saw last night?'

Hope guessed he was referring to his striptease and realized that their interplay had started hours before.

'I do indeed, but I think we have to add a little starch.' Allie smiled away any insult.

'Takes something special to do that.' Rusty grew serious, his expression calculating.

'Nasty special or nice special?'

'Nasty.' Rusty, feeling he had said too much, scrambled to his feet to bring the conversation to a close.

Allie shrugged as she watched him walk away. 'Pity,' she muttered, 'I don't do "nasty".'

'Surely it depends on what it means?'

'I think I know what it means. Still, I won't give up just yet.' She kissed Hope abruptly. 'Let's see if there is anything to drink.'

'Anything more, you mean!' Hope grinned and licked her lips.

They linked arms and staggered as the launch changed course, heading into a small bay. A small sandy beach with a tiny mooring slid into view and they coasted towards it. Hope had an opportunity to admire one of the Seans as he leapt to secure the ropes. When the engine cut out, the silence was broken by the soft chatter of birds and lap of water on the hull.

'You guys swim or tan. Whatever you want,' Sean One shouted. 'We'll call you for lunch.' He helped the group to disembark, then disappeared into the cabin. Sean Two made sure the aft mooring was secure and clambered back on board. One of them emerged shortly afterwards with a coolbox that he suspended over the railing until Mallot took it.

'Drinks,' advised Sean.

Mallot opened the box and revealed a layer of bottles of white wine, a corkscrew and plastic tumblers. 'Rumour has it,' he said, as he opened two bottles and passed them to Angela who doled out glasses and filled them, 'that there will be no liquor on the island. So enjoy, this is our last opportunity to get blotto for a couple of weeks.'

Hope shook her head when offered wine. She was thirsty, and preferred a cool drink. She peered into the box and was delighted to find cans of sparkling water, took one and sat on the hot sand, slaking her thirst. It was only ten o'clock and the sun was merciless. She resigned herself to a wait for lunch, deciding to explore and swim.

Allie and Rusty curled up in a patch of shade and appeared to drift straight off to sleep. Not surprising, Hope figured, if they had been awake all night. She thought they created a vibrant picture, Allie's wild red curls and ghost-white skin resting alongside Rusty's coppery-gold locks and tanned flesh. Mallot and Angela had stripped to their swimming costumes. He wore a brief spandex scrap and she a one-piece swimsuit that seemed to comprise less fabric than Hope's daring bikini. Again, the contrast was startling: Mallot's onyx against Angela's ice. Quinn, Ruari and Elsa disappeared along a trail, melting into the conifers that tracked almost to the water's edge. Rat slumped down beside Hope.

She wondered what picture they projected, his litheness against her rounded femininity, his tousled brunette to her golden blonde. He was loose-limbed, and she tucked in and controlled. Hope envied him his boneless ease, resolving to move less purposefully and not commandeer and manipulate the space around her. She leaned back to rest on her elbows and lifted her face to the sun, enjoying the spread of heat on her exposed neck. The sand was sharp, gritty and hot, and dug into the sensitive flesh of her under-thigh.

'You should put on suntan lotion,' Rat remarked, producing a bottle. 'Neither of us are used to this.'

Hope was reminded of Rat's lair, deep in the offices of Pursuit. She glanced at him, trying to reconcile his sprawl of limbs with his sharply focused concentration over a keyboard.

'Do you miss your computer?' She knew that this was his life, hours and hours spent in front of a screen.

'Brought a laptop with me. It doesn't seem so bad, though. This is the first holiday I have had since I was twelve and went to Spain with my parents.'

'Me, too, I mean the holiday. Although I have travelled a lot I never got to relax. It feels odd to lie here in the sun, as if I should be working.'

'Well,' he rolled over and grinned at her, 'we *are* working!'

'Any more thoughts on Willincough?'

He shrugged. 'No, but as I said, I believe he will make his presence felt when the time is right.'

'Well, he knows who we are, presumably. I think he is Quinn, although I feel appalled at the idea that the next likely candidate is Mallot.'

'Why Mallot?' Rat sounded surprised.

'Oh, I don't know. He just seems so sinister and mysterious. I guess I think a hacker would match that description.'

Rat burst out laughing. 'Actually, the hackers I know are all thoroughly charming. You would not be able to pick them out at a dinner party.'

'If you have a computer with you because you are a nerd, then I think it is likely Willincough will have one too. I just need to look through the luggage.'

'Hope, why don't you stop? Let it rest. Besides, it would be a violation to go through people's private stuff!' Rat protested.

'Okay, okay. You're right.' Hope felt restless. Work had been her life for the past decade and setting it aside was difficult. Although she wanted Rat, it was also a problem to see him other than as a colleague. 'I am going to swim,' she announced, deciding to follow Rat's advice and let it go.

Hope shed her shorts and dashed into the water, leaving Rat with a tantalizing glimpse of her bouncing bottom. She struck out for the lip of the bay, moving effortlessly through the water, and emerged, dripping and refreshed, to throw herself down, spread-eagled, on a patch of grass. She felt slightly disappointed that Rat had not followed her but noticed him edging his way through the scrub that marked the border of the sandy beach and making his way towards her. His progress was slow, hindered with natural traps such as fallen trees and swampy shoreline. By the time he arrived, his legs were badly scratched and his feet and ankles muddy.

'I cannot swim,' he informed her.

'The water is quite shallow just here, so you could just dip to cool down and wash off.'

'The last time someone said that to me I believed them so I went in, to disappear in a bottomless well!' Rat was reassured by the stones he could see below the surface but, two feet further, the water became murky and the bottom invisible.

Hope laughed and paddled into the shallows, held out her hand and said, 'Trust me.'

With my life, Rat thought, staring at Hope. She stood with the water lapping around her calves, her hair slicked in a golden cascade over her shoulders and her breasts glistening. The bikini was wet, almost transparent, and her areolae were revealed, her nipples jutting sharply at the sheer white lycro. Dark blonde curls escaped around the small triangle of the thong bottom. The vee had tucked between her labia, exaggerating the soft, nether lips. Her legs were slightly parted for balance, and with her arm stretched towards him, she appeared like a siren, urging him to his watery demise.

This is it! he exulted, *this is when I take her. If I drown in the process, I will never die happier*. He stepped into the water and, ignoring her hand, waded until he stood close enough to feel her breath on his face as she peered up at him. They stood silent, the breeze chasing around them and the lap of the water on the shore a backdrop, as they read each other's expressions.

Hope saw in his the resolution to satisfy his lust for her. Although he seemed young, his expression was serious and composed, with a mature determination. Were she to demur, she felt sure he would not resist the surge of his blood. Her gaze roved over his torso, noting the sleeping strength in the etch of his muscles. Despite his sedentary lifestyle, he seemed fit, possessing a wiry strength that she knew would easily overcome any resistance. A tremor of fear shot through her, thrilling her, and suddenly Rat was no longer her colleague but a stranger in a lonely place. One who would brook no refusal. She clasped her hands loosely behind her back, baring herself in submission, and looked into Rat's face with full acceptance.

When he began to speak, she let his words caress her and her own desire rose until she lusted for possession. His voice was soft but tight, betraying tension, and he seemed unable to hold back the flow. She did not move or interrupt, even when his breath grew harsh and his last words panted from him, nor did she drop her gaze from his. She felt hypnotized and enthralled as she learned of his lust for her.

'I've dreamed about you for so long, the heat of your cunt around my prick, fucking you while you begged for more, then sucked me until I creamed in your mouth.' His eyes narrowed. 'I've buggered you in alleyways, shot my wad over your tits in bus stops. I've woken to your mouth on my cock and your tongue in my arse. I've whispered to you while you flashed your fanny in the office, lain awake at nights feeling so bad with lust I wanted to die.' He faltered, shutting his eyes and ground out his words. 'I've screwed other women and seen only you. Jesus,' his voice broke, 'I've even knelt by your chair and buried my face in the seat to sniff your muff-scent.' Rat clenched his fists, breathed deeply and threw his head back, eyes screwed shut.

Seconds passed while Hope studied him, feeling strangely remote. Her anticipation dissolved into acceptance. Whatever Rat chose to do, she would submit and act only to ensure that his fantasies proved themselves in reality. All he had described was lust, in which her part was token. Rat's obsession with her was entirely in his head and she was merely the vehicle through which he imagined his release. Her head spun with the images: Rat pushing into her in the dimness and stench of a dustbin-strewn alleyway, her skirt yanked to her waist and a cacophony of voices reaching through the open rear doorway of a pub; Rat with his face pushed into the seat of her office chair, his chest heaving with deep breaths in an attempt to garner her scents. She recognized his need: it was the same she had felt for Salvatore.

When Rat dropped his head to look at her once more, his expression was vulnerable. He unclenched his hands and flexed his fingers. He seemed at a loss now he was confronted with the object of his desire, his harsh daydreams at odds with the water lapping gently around their calves. The setting was romantic and disarming, not full of harsh, crazed brickwork and stench. It seemed insufficient for the raging lust that rode in him. Hope, devoid of make-up, a pink flush on her cheeks, was too girlish and not the dismissive, suited ball-breaker about whom he had fantasized. His intense drive wilted and his frustration warred with remorse, but he could not touch her, not while she was submissive – it would disappoint.

'Not like this.' He took the risk and, with it, made his final confession. 'Do you have any work clothes?' He watched understanding dawn in Hope's eyes and held his breath while her gaze flickered in thought.

The realization that it was Rat who wished to be controlled astonished her. With the hard drive of passion, she had assumed it would be *she* who succumbed to *his* will and his question at first bewildered her. She quickly reviewed their interaction at Pursuit, finally piecing the whole. All Rat had ever done was cater to her bidding, her sometimes terse commands for information and assistance. The beast had raged within him, but under her control. Now, while she was attempting to breach the work barrier, he was enforcing it. It was she who held all the power, and he who wanted it that way. Her working clothes were a uniform, one that she had not brought with her. She sorted through the options and eventually realized that the only person who could possibly provide her with the outfit she needed was Angela. It did not take long for her to recognize how she could arrange to borrow an outfit from the woman. It would be a deal, like any other she had manipulated throughout her years at Pursuit.

'Yes,' she said at last, glancing dismissively at Rat, as she would have done were they at the office. She turned and dived into the deeper water, surfaced and floated on her back. 'I think you ought to be getting back to the launch, lunch must be almost ready.' Without waiting for his response, she rolled over and struck out towards the beach in a slow crawl. *Soon*, she thought, *I had better be prepared for his beast to emerge*. She could play this game but her dominance was by permission, and fragile. The thought of a power-game was intensely pleasing, even though she knew its conclusion.

Rat watched her swim away and felt that he had aged suddenly. He had lusted after Hope with a boyish innocence, no matter how deviant he felt his imaginings to be. His communication with her had shattered his illusions, invoked a role-play in which he had to play his part. He wished he could swim, then he could reach her in the deep water, drag her down and rip her bikini from her, plunging heedlessly while she struggled to rise. At some point she would thrill to his manhood, her legs would clasp his waist and she would expel her breath and float in fluid sensations until he was sated. Rat felt slightly sick with excitement at the idea of her struggle for breath and release, and his benevolence when he freed her. He would be magnanimous, a life-giver, and the one who emerged victorious even while her reciprocating greed drained his cock-fluids. This is a war, he resolved, and victory would be Pyhrric. He smiled without humour as he thought of the adage 'It is not about winning or losing, it is how you play the game'. While he mused, his hand crept beneath his shorts, grabbing harshly until the pain of his forced coming offered an apt conclusion.

Hope reached the beach and flopped down to dry and watch Rat make his way back. Mindful of her observation, he paddled through the shallows and made easier progress than he had on the outward trip. He paused, once he set foot on the shallow strand, to stare at her, then made his way down the small jetty to the launch. Sean appeared as Rat boarded and shouted that lunch was ready.

Allie and Rusty woke with the summons, and Elsa, Quinn and Ruari suddenly scurried from the trees and leapt into the lake, hot after their intrepid voyage into the interior. There was no sign of Mallot and Angela, a puzzle that resolved itself when Hope clambered to the deck and found them looking smug, splayed naked on the cabin roof. She was not alone when she gawped at Mallot's generously displayed manhood. His groin was clean shaven, his large rod peacefully curled on its smooth bed. Angela, catching Hope's expression, smiled smugly and ensured that her tight pink pudendum was clearly seen. As intended, Hope wondered how the pale, slim woman could accommodate the large intrusion. Also, she presumed, it was intended that her own response should be one of urgent desire. When she raised her eyes, it was to find Mallot smiling at her with arrogant awareness.

Rat noticed the exchange of glances and the widening of Hope's eyes as she stared at Mallot's genitals. He felt a sudden flush of rage, resolving that, whatever the resolution of his lust for Hope, he would compete and win against Mallot. Any last vestiges of innocent youth dropped from him. He had succeeded, with his dedication to computing, in avoiding the exigencies of the real world throughout his twenty-five years, and now the politics and muck of human stuff drenched his senses. Naïvely, he had supposed his intellect would carry him through conflict, but now a tiny gut-warning bade him to watch and wait. One thing he could not alter was his isolationist temperament and therefore it never occurred to him to seek allies to further his quest. He would tackle Mallot alone. The spoils, he thought, looking at Hope, far outweighed any risk.

Lunch was simple and satisfying, comprising freshly poached salmon sandwiches, fruit, and thermos flasks containing strong coffee laced with thick, creamy milk. Sean took the opportunity, while people finished the meal, to address the group.

'We'll leave here after eating and reach the dropping-off point in one hour.' He consulted a clipboard. 'I was told to let you know that you will arrive at the island mid-afternoon and should assemble in the lounge of the house, where the housekeeper will meet you to discuss accommodation arrangements. After that you will be told by her what to do.' He glanced around the group with a smile, 'I will collect you in two week's time.' He dropped the clipboard to the deck and leapt onto the jetty, calling for Sean Two to prepare to sail and when the engines turned, caught and hummed, he cast off the moorings and nimbly reboarded. The only ones not to watch the receding shoreline were Mallot and Angela.

Hope curled up on a seat in the cabin and snoozed, lulled to sleep by the slow roll of the launch as it carved a path to their destination. She was woken when Sean shook her shoulder gently.

'We're here,' he said softly. 'Most of the others have already been relayed to the island. So if you don't want to be left behind, let's go.'

'All of a sudden,' muttered Hope, 'I like the idea of being left behind!' She was amazed that the original idea of the retreat had become so clouded. It seemed to be turning into a quest and the need to work her way through a series of complicated games and human puzzles. She followed Sean onto the deck.

The launch bobbed at its anchor line, lakeward of a large bay. They were surrounded by rocks, some of which pierced the water-line, others visible beneath the surface. When she looked aft, Hope wondered that they had managed to sail as close as they had. A rope ladder eased over the edge of the deck, dropping to a motorboat, manned by Sean Two, that bobbed companionably alongside and held Rat, Rusty and Allie. Hope descended the ladder gingerly and was helped on board by Sean, who grasped her waist and swung her easily to sit next to Allie.

The island became clearer on approach. It was larger than Hope had expected and consumed a large part of the bay, whose shoreline seemed hostile and uninhabited, thronged with trees and wild, tangled scrub. The island was embraced by the arms of the bay, the entrance guarded by an army of rocks. It lay low in the water, bare except for stunted trees, rocks and an imposing stone house that grew from its centre. They rounded the island to gain access to a weathered stone quay, the steps covered with algae but firm underfoot.

There was nothing tangible to support the negative feelings that rose in Hope, so she brushed them aside as fancy after she had mounted the quay to join the assembled group. She watched the motorboat make its way to the launch and the now small figure of Sean climb aboard and secure the boat aft. The transport then left, the mute hum of engines dying away, to be replaced by liquid slapping on the sides of the stone pier and the monotonous sound of dripping from the steps. She turned with her peers to study the house. Closer, it did not seem as forbidding. The grey stone was splashed with the muted greens and browns of lichen and a large oak door was open in welcome.

Mallot had already hefted his bag and was trudging up a cobbled pathway to the entrance, followed by Angela who was bowed with the weight of two large suitcases. They had donned shorts to eat lunch but Hope envisaged them naked, buttocks swaying, like Hansel and Gretel, vulnerable and about to enter the witch's house. She hung back with Allie and Rat to watch the others merge with the interior gloom.

An attempt had been made to landscape the garden to one side of the pathway but all it supported was wiry lawn and a weathered wooden bench. The other side was strewn with rocks and dotted with patches of hard earth that gave way to a wedge of sand at the water's edge. Half the island was in shadow, courtesy of the rearing hills which climbed westwards from the bay. The south-facing front aspect of the house peered moodily over a short expanse of rock-infested water at the tangled bay shore, which was mirrored to the north.

Hope judged the island to be a quarter of a mile in length, but was unable to gauge the width. She resolved to commandeer an east-facing room, determined that she should at least wake to the cheer of sunlight and a view of the lake. She was last to enter the hallway and pleased to find the sombre promise dispelled. The bare board floors gleamed with polish and an oriental carpet runner traversed the hallway, then travelled up a stairwell directly opposite the front door, held in check with gleaming brass rods at the base of the risers. An old-fashioned mahogany tallboy and choir bench flanked the open door of a lounge, through which Hope could see the group, reclining on comfortable armchairs. The room was fully carpeted in dark green deep-pile fleck and furnished sparsely with armchairs and sofas. The windows framed views of the bay that, seen from the cheer of the room, now seemed peaceful rather than bleak.

A hatchway slid open to reveal the interior of a modernized kitchen, allowing Hope a glimpse of a range and coppered extractor, before a head appeared. The woman stared at the company in the lounge.

'I won't be a minute,' she said and, true to her word, appeared at the lounge door moments after shutting the hatch.

She was a small woman, middle-aged and spry, wearing a pair of denim jeans and a T-shirt covered with a large apron. 'I am Mairead, and I am the housekeeper. You won't see much of me and I just have to tell you the set-up so you can make yourselves at home.' She bustled into the room and perched on the edge of a windowsill. 'Okay. I know there are no married couples, and if you are paired up then I must tell you that the Ormandies want you apart for the fortnight. So each of you is alone in the bedrooms, which are all upstairs. You can choose which you want.' She paused and checked they were listening.

'The door opposite is the dining room where I will serve all your meals, and you must eat together. There is a list in the bedrooms to show the times. If there is to be any deviation it will be decided by the Ormandies and, if you miss a meal, you may go hungry.

'I will make up your beds and clean your rooms and the bathrooms each day while you are in session, but would ask that you keep your clothes and personal possessions tidy, and use the liners for the bins.'

'We have electricity but there is no television or radio, and the only telephone will be in the Ormandies' room, which is not on your floor.

'You are welcome to help yourselves to drinks from the kitchen during the night but there is no liquor and during the day you must ring for me if you want anything. Please feel welcome to do that: I will be happy to serve you,' she flashed a sincere smile. 'I will be serving dinner at seven o'clock.' She wandered to the door, turning back, 'Welcome to Retreat House. I hope you will enjoy your stay. The Ormandies will be joining you for supper and tonight is your first meet,' she added formally, then disappeared.

Hope shrugged her shoulders, lifted her tote bag and exited, intent on securing her east-facing bedroom. She was closely followed by Rusty, Allie and Rat who, she assumed, shared her quest. The wide stairwell curved at a large mullioned window and rose gently to a wide landing. To Hope's delight a curved dome, set in the roof, rained prisms of coloured light onto the bare floor. Doorways stood open, revealing the comfortable interiors of elegant bedrooms, and she chose one next to a bathroom and crossed to look through the window at the lake. The island sloped steeply away beneath her, stones and earth giving way to the water. Beyond, the mouth of the bay framed the wide expanse of the lake. With the sun lowering behind her, a glittering ribbon of light played over the ripples creating a silvery pathway to her window.

An interconnecting door revealed access to the bathroom and, as she examined the claw-footed white porcelain tub and bronzed, sunflower-shaped shower head, Allie joined her.

'My room is on this side, so we get to share this bathroom.

As far as I can make out, we also share it with Rat and Rusty, who've taken bedrooms either side of us. The others have the same set-up, except that Mallot and Angela have disappeared up some attic steps. This place could take double the numbers.' She perched on the edge of the bath, swinging her heels happily.

'You know,' Hope said, 'this place is very elegant, and I only brought casual clothes.'

'Well, the way things are going, I don't think we'll be wearing much anyway.'

They grinned at each other, Allie sobering to gaze at Hope intently.

'I owe you a thorough cleaning,' she said mischievously, 'and I would suggest you drop your knickers and get under this shower!'

At which point Rat entered the bathroom, closed the door behind him and leaned, his arms crossed over his chest, against the wall.

Chapter Seven

'On the other hand, maybe not,' Allie stated, arching her eyebrows. She slunk dramatically to the door, tossed her head and slid through to her bedroom, turning to blow a kiss as she shut the door softly behind her.

'Didn't interrupt anything, did I?' Rat inquired sarcastically.

'Yes, actually you did.' Hope stared at him until his glance fell.

'Sorry,' he said, 'I was just checking the place out.'

Hope forgave him. She was more intrigued with the prospect of meeting the Ormandies, and learning what the next fortnight would entail, than concerned about Rat. She felt nervous at the prospect of interacting closely within a confined group, but reasoned that it had to be far worse for Rat who was more of an isolationist. They still wore their swimsuits and, however casual the retreat promised to be, she felt certain it would not extend to beachwear at the dinner table.

'We'd best change for dinner,' she said. 'Why don't you check back when we need to go down? It will be less daunting if we are together.' Hope smiled at Rat's expression of relief, then entered her bedroom and closed the door softly. She dug a small, battery-operated alarm clock from her bag and allowed herself two hours sleep, dropping off immediately.

When she woke, the house seemed silent around her, the thick walls shrouding the noises generated by her peers.

She showered, then unpacked, smoothing and hanging her clothes on wooden hangers in a deep wardrobe. After staring for some minutes at the meagre offering, she eventually settled on a pair of black leggings and a cerise voile overblouse, eschewing a bra. Her reflection in a full-length mirror attached to the rear of the wardrobe door revealed that her areolae were mistily visible, but the soft fabric felt so good against her nipples that she decided to ignore the blatant display. She twisted her hair into a topknot and stood back, pleased with the effect. Whether the group was casual or formal, her attire would be appropriate and her skin, graced by the sun, was already lightly tanned. She looked healthy and vibrantly sexy, without appearing vampish. As she slipped delicate sandals on her feet, a bell resounded through the house. The summons, she presumed, to dinner. Moments later she opened her door and found Rat standing moodily on the landing. His eyes widened with pleasure, an innocent, spontaneous compliment.

'Ready?' she inquired, stood back to admire him and then slipped her hand through the crook of his arm.

He had donned a pair of black denim jeans and a black silk shirt. With his hair hanging in loose, glowing waves around his shoulders, he looked handsome. The slip of silk under her hand emphasized the nearness of his warm flesh and, as they descended the stairwell, Hope rubbed his sensitive inner arm sensually. While he glanced sharply at her, Rat assumed her action not to be deliberate. He did notice that her voile blouse floated softly over her nipples, causing them to button slightly, and he nearly missed a step.

Angela and Allie stood at the bottom of the stairwell, watching their descent.

'I hate to say it,' stated Allie, as they joined her, 'but you two look gorgeous together.' She nudged Rat. 'And you sure tidy up well!' She had slipped on a pair of colourful Indian pants and a black tank top and looked intriguing.

Angela snorted; a small, disapproving expulsion of breath to signify her disdain of Allie's cheerful compliments. She turned and stalked off, her trim figure displayed in a pale blue sheath, her hair an ice-blonde shimmer. Hope had noticed the hard calculation in Angela's expression as she had swept Rat with her gaze. He, however, seemed oblivious and Hope decided that she had to mate with him before he lost all innocence to the ice-maiden. She had the horrible premonition that, while Angela would add significantly to his experience, she would destroy something valuable in the process. Hope did not want to compete with another woman but snuggled into Rat to endorse her prior claim, an action that surprised and thrilled him. Allie hooked her fingers around Rat's free arm as Rusty joined them.'

'I see, what am I, chopped liver?' He nodded at Rat and peered with mock sharpness at Allie's hold. He looked stunning, like a centrefold from a woman's new-wave magazine. A sheer white net T-shirt hugged his muscular chest and tight black trousers his thighs. His burnished copper hair was pulled back into a low ponytail and he had not shaved so his cheeks and chin were covered with fine gold stubble.

'Rat, you're gorgeous,' Allie rose to her toes and dropped an apologetic kiss on his cheek, 'but this here is my nasty pin-up boy!' She relinquished her hold on Rat and transferred it to Rusty, who pretended to flex with pride, serving only to make himself look more desirable.

They entered the dining room laughing, to find the rest of the group seated and Mairead hovering. The large square mahogany table comprised two leaves that would accommodate an extension for larger parties. A large window framed a view of the bay, now golden in the rays of the late evening sun. The room seemed huge, the walls decked with oil paintings and the ceiling sculpted with plaster cornucopias. On the far side of the table, seated beneath an imposing reproduction of Edouard Manet's *Déjeuner sur l'herbe*, were the hosts. Hope slipped into a seat directly opposite Karen Ormandy and gazed into the serene dark face. Even seated, the American woman's height was apparent and Hope guessed her to be over six foot.

'Hi, you must be Hope,' she said. 'I was just explaining to everyone that I am of Mexican descent.' She smiled warmly and Hope was reminded of a toothpaste advertisement, responding herself with a more mute version.

Karen looked impressive. Her skin was a gleaming coffee colour, her cheekbones pronounced and eyes soft and almost black. She spoke with a smooth, low drawl, as languid as her movements when she nodded thanks to Mairead, who set a plate before her. Her hair was swept back from a high brow and fell in a sheer onyx river past her shoulders.

Next to her, Brandon Ormandy looked slightly drab. A sprawl of loose limbs, gangling joints and sparse salt and pepper hair. His beard was overwhelming, a multithreaded, well-tended bib. He smiled a welcome to the newcomers and tucked into his first course with intense concentration. It was his eyes that compelled, warm brown and sincere:

eyes to trust. It seemed obvious that Karen would lead the team; she was charming and voluble and set the diners at ease with practised skill. Mallot, seated on her left, kept her entertained with a low conversation involving his travels in South America, to the chagrin of Angela, who flirted with a tongue-tied Ruari in an abortive effort to rouse jealousy.

Rat ate with the same silent remoteness he had exhibited the night before in The Piper's Inn. Hope, not inclined to conversation, was happy to watch the group. Brandon and Karen had eased in comfortably, not seeking to control. They were merely another couple at the dinner table. Hope brought herself up short with that observation. It seemed that they had all already accepted the union of Angela and Mallot, Rusty and Allie, and herself and Rat. Elsa was pocketed with Ruari and Quinn, the older man like a benign uncle, the younger like a shy suitor. She studied the Ormandies, wondering why they had organized the unchaparoned overnight stay in Killalloe and what they had hoped to achieve by it.

They worked their way through cool cucumber soup, grilled salmon and lemon mousse, drinking spring water in lieu of wine. After the meal they were directed into the lounge where they drank coffee and relaxed. The furniture had been rearranged to form a rough circle and Karen and Brandon Ormandy sat in two straight-backed chairs which flanked an Inglenook fireplace. Mallot and Angela sat to Karen's right on a small two-seat settee, and Quinn, Elsa and Ruari on a larger neighbouring sofa. Allie dropped into an armchair and Rusty nestled at her feet, leaning against an armrest. This left Hope and Rat to complete the circle by taking the last settee, the twin of that occupied by Angela and Mallot. While they sipped their coffee and basked in the aftermath of a friendly dinner, the atmosphere was relaxed but once the cups were removed by Mairead the group became self-conscious, casting glances at the Ormandies.

'Let's get formalities over with,' Karen said, smiling gently. 'There has to be a focus for the fortnight but it is the group that must discover it. Brandon and I are merely here to facilitate, by which I mean that we will make sure that whatever you choose for examination and growth we shall be here to assist you. Brandon's particular skill is dream therapy and this includes daydreams as well as nightmares or those confusing jumbles from which you wake and wonder if you are truly going bananas.

'We work within this group, never on a one-to-one basis. The idea is that you learn to trust your peers and they learn to be supportive. If we see things going terribly wrong then we will guide, otherwise this is *your* voyage of self-discovery.'

Karen gazed around the group, her expression serene, and Hope realized that she instinctively trusted the American woman. It was not the impressive list of qualifications that followed her name but the easy manner in which she addressed the group. Hope had feared a coldly analytical approach and now Karen seemed more like an older, wiser sister.

Brandon took over. 'We have plenty of time and we don't want anyone to feel under pressure. In these early hours it is a good idea to learn a little more about one another and to get used to operating in a group. There is no reason to decide a theme to this retreat this evening – unless something clicks.

'We will meet each morning at ten o'clock and work together until lunch, at one o'clock. It is very, very important that we are all here, and on time. That must be considered an inviolate rule. If there is unfinished business then we will regroup after lunch to resolve it, but will always close the sessions by three o'clock. Unless this happens, your afternoons are free and we shall meet again after supper.' He looked enquiringly at the group, seeking questions, but none arose.

Karen said, 'This island is remote. Exploring the interior is fine but the vegetation is inhospitable and once you are among the trees it may be disorientating. Please, therefore, pledge that you will not stray, because we do not wish you to place yourselves at risk.' She leaned forward with an expression of sincere concern and was rewarded with murmurs of consent. 'Good! I'm afraid there are no televisions or radios but there is a wonderful library. There are no watersports facilities but there is a cleared area near the quay where you can swim.

'Okay,' Karen paused and leaned back, 'Those are the formalities over and done with! What if we start by going around the circle, with each person introducing themselves and saying why they are here and perhaps what they hope to achieve before they leave?' She looked expectantly at Mallot, on her left.

He paused as if thinking hard and Hope decided that he was allowing himself time to prepare lies. It was an ungenerous thought, but she felt sure that he wanted to generate an air of mystery. She was pleased that she was on the far side of the circle, and thought that the members of the group would not listen to Mallot anyway. They would be concentrating on their turn and they would not listen afterwards because they would be too relieved that the spotlight had passed. Mallot, however, would set the initial level of confidences and Hope was certain that, whatever he said, it would be designed to gain the maximum advantage over the rest of the group. It was, for him, a game. On the other hand she was pleased that it was he who had been put on the spot. Were it the shy Elsa or reticent Rat, the process would be far more painful. While she herself was comfortable with speaking in groups, this forum was much more open and personal, thus nerve-racking, even though she had nothing to hide. The matter of Willincough was the only secret, and that had nothing to do with the group.

'My name is Mallot,' he began, 'and I am a businessman. I needed a break but I also wanted to get away from the public eye because, wherever I go, people in the same trade know me. When I saw this advertisement in the magazine . . .' he suddenly looked straight at Hope, who dropped her gaze in embarrassment, 'I thought it would be a good idea to purge my system of the crap that accompanies high-pressure business, get back to grass-roots and meet real people.

'Of course,' he added, 'it does not hurt to be among beautiful women!' He nudged Angela suggestively and gestured at Hope, smiling when Allie snorted her disapproval. He had clearly finished his introduction and ended on a note that was intended, as Hope saw it, to distract attention from himself and cause the group to focus on the female flesh present. Now all the men were studying Angela whose tight dress had ridden up sufficiently to allow a peek at the darkness of her vee, a tantalizing, shadowy place that left them wondering if she was wearing panties or not. Then their gaze swivelled to Hope, their eyes resting on her breasts beneath the sheer voile of her blouse. While Angela revelled in this lascivious attention, Hope felt like curling up and covering her breasts. In other circumstances she might feel proud to bare all, but with Mallot's manipulations she felt vulnerable. She glanced at Rat to find him staring intently at her breasts and she felt herself respond, her nipples hardening as he licked his lips. When she looked at Mallot, angry that he had engineered the spectacle, he was staring at her and she again received the impression that she seen his disconcerting dark gaze before. His reference to the magazine had unnerved her, marking his awareness of the article concerning her and Salvatore. She filtered through those who had been present at the time she had recruited the porn baron, and still failed to connect Mallot with the entourage. Fortunately, Karen diverted attention to Angela by thanking Mallot and looking expectantly at the slim blonde.

Angela acted flustered and wriggled in her seat, tugging the hem of her dress down and sitting straighter. 'I am Angela and I was divorced two years ago. I needed to get out in the world, make new friends and start a social life.' She paused to peer at Mallot, as if seeking approval. 'I lack confidence, so I thought that if I started with this retreat I could learn to be in company again.' She blushed prettily, glanced around the group from underneath lowered lashes and pouted becomingly.

Hope suspected that there was not a man there who had not been taken in by her atrociously feminine ploy, nor one who did not wish to take her into his arms and reassure her. Not one except for Mallot, who looked amused, more so when Angela gazed up at him to indicate that, while she wanted to circulate, her attentions were focused on him.

'But,' Angela continued, 'I don't want anyone to think that I am a wimp! I have worked my way into a good position in the last two years and I have my own little business. It is just that I have not been in male company for such a long time that I feel quite at sea.' She sighed. 'It is so good to have such nice men in this group. I hope you will all help me.'

Hope risked a look at Allie, who was staring at Angela with an expression of total amazement. Then, meeting Hope's eyes, she squinted comically. The redhead stifled her laughter but Hope had to cover hers with a coughing fit. She felt sure that their hosts saw through Angela's shallow act, but both were smiling encouragement. In the meantime, the ice maiden's teasing invitation hung in the air and, from the looks of speculation and male musing, Hope felt certain Angela's expectations for the fortnight would not be disappointed. Even Rat seemed riveted, his eyes drawn between Angela's thighs as her dress rode higher to reveal her crotch. This time Hope swore that she caught a glimpse of Angela's pink clam.

Quinn was next. He cleared his throat to speak. 'My name is Quinn. I am married but my wife and I have irreconcilable differences and I needed space to deal with them.' His admission was risky and genuine, earning him Hope's sympathy, and successfully reduced the effect of Angela's insincerity. 'I am not sure how much of the problem is my fault, so I hoped to find points of reference in a group, get feedback from other folk that would perhaps give me a new perspective.'

Karen said, 'Thank you, Quinn: in the next few days I feel sure that you will get really good feedback from all the group and we look forward to sharing your story so we can help.' She looked at Elsa, who blushed a deep red.

'I am Elsa.' She stopped and clenched her hands in her

lap, clearly wishing to be elsewhere, and forced herself to continue. 'I live on a farm and help out a lot. It is my dad's farm,' she added with shy pride, 'and a good living! But I don't get out much and, while my mum wants me to go into nursing, I do not want to go to the city.' Hope supposed she meant Dublin, where the training hospitals would be. Elsa continued breathlessly. 'It is not that I don't want excitement, it's just that I prefer countryside to people. Anyway, I like to sing in the small pubs near home and I know all those people.' Quinn nodded to endorse the beauty of her voice and she glanced at him before continuing with more assurance. 'My dad said I should come to this retreat and he booked it for me and arranged everything, even drove me up to Killalloe and stayed overnight to see I was okay. He said it would do me good to be among strangers from the city and that no country folk would be here because they would have too much sense to come to something like this.' Then, realizing she had quoted far too much of her father's opinion, she subsided.

Hope chuckled and Allie laughed outright. In response to Karen's look, Hope shrugged, still smiling and said, 'I just think I would love to meet Elsa's dad!' She grinned at Elsa, then winked. A bond was forged when the young woman responded with a relieved giggle.

Karen thanked Elsa and turned to Ruari, who seemed as nervous as his predecessor. 'I am Ruari and I have a problem with women.' There, his expression seemed to say, it is out in the open. He glared around the room as if expecting a challenge and, seeing none, stared at his feet, apparently finished. Elsa, exhibiting her warm-heartedness, placed a hand on Ruari's arm and squeezed, earning a small smile of gratitude.

Hope had not really studied Ruari. For all his largeness, he seemed able to melt into anonymity in company. Whatever his problem with women, he seemed comfortable around Elsa, and Hope had heard them laughing together, his warm belly laugh causing her to smile. The only impression that Hope had formed was that he seemed a nice, shy man. Now his admission made her wonder what dark desires lurked in him. Both Ruari and Quinn had confessed to having problems with women and Hope admired them for the risk they had taken. Then it was Allie's turn.

'My name is Allie and I work with computers. My whole life is lived around men and I am like one of the lads.' She looked around defiantly, 'But I am not a lad! It has got so that I don't know how to behave like a woman, and all my lovers are women just as if I were a bloke. I want to be feminine but I just don't know how to behave that way. I either go overboard flirting with men or I beat them in swearing and drinking contests.' Her words were simple and her plea direct, accompanied by an agonized expression, part bewilderment and part irritation. She fell silent and endorsed her words by slapping Rusty on the shoulder, gruffly commanding him, 'Your turn!' Then she slunk back in the armchair, seeking asylum and refusing to catch Hope's look. Had she done, she would have seen a similar confusion.

Startled, Rusty seem unprepared for his words although he had clearly thought them out in advance. 'I am not sure how to put this,' he started, 'but when I heard about this retreat I sat down to think for a long time and decided it would be a good idea. You see, I am a model and all people ever see is my appearance and it affects their behaviour towards me. It is hard trying to look good all the time and I have seen models age, lose their looks and then get depressed and sometimes break down, because they have no idea of who they are. It also seems that women expect an awful lot more from me than they do from other men because I look good.' He seemed to be struggling. 'I need to know who I am under all this fluff, and I need to feel good about myself, because right now I have a low self-profile and it is causing me to behave nastily.'

There it was again, thought Hope, the bad interaction with women. And what did he mean? That he behaved nastily, as he had insinuated to Allie on the launch, or that what he did was okay and it was he who needed to see that? She was surprised to feel quite teary. Rusty was gorgeous, but the thing for which he was admired was superficial and temporary. It had shaped him and those around him, depersonalizing him in the process. Elsa was staring at Rusty in amazement, taken aback at his admission but still awe-struck by his beauty. Hope suspected that it was just this sort of blatant admiration which caused his distress. It seemed that the only thing that would help would be for Rusty to not be so handsome. But Hope suspected that he would look good in a sack, a fact not lost on the media that promoted him. He was in a no-win situation. He had to look good to earn but his saleability was destroying him. It was a tribute to his strength of character that he had come to this retreat before he lost himself completely.

With a shock, Hope realized she was next in line and that the silence had continued too long. She had been aware of the furious thought that had preceded each introduction and realized, with dismay, that she had been listening rather than preparing her own speech. 'This is typical!' she at last burst out, confusing the onlookers. 'I worked in a business at which I was successful, but it involved everyone but me accounting for themselves.' Something stirred deep within her, threads drawing together. 'You see, it is like Rusty in a way: my work shaped me. And it is like Allie, because it was work in which I had to be powerful, so I was working with men and seldom mixing with women, unless it was to control them. But it is also like Angela, because it was manipulative and full of games.'

This earned a hiss from the blonde woman, 'I said no such thing!'

Hope looked confused, then realized that it was what she had read in Angela's behaviour, not heard. 'Yes, you did, just not with words.'

Karen waved her hand as if severing a thread to break the confrontation and Angela subsided, looking angry.

Hope continued, still trying to gather her feelings together. 'Look, I know this is different from everyone, but it feels similar in lots of ways. I haven't had a social life for a very long time, I don't know who I am and I have been celibate for at least five years so I don't know what is normal or what I like. I have a lot of sorting-out to do and, also, I just lost my job so I have to go back home with a new identity and some idea of how to continue.' She shrugged her shoulders at the enormity of her task. Now that she had vocalized her problem, it seemed bigger than before and she suddenly realized that she had come to this retreat for herself. While her original aim had been to meet Willincough, it had become her least important priority. She also realized that she had lied and in the spirit of truth she started speaking again.

'I lied, in a way,' she admitted. 'I *do* know what I like, sexually. It is just that in the past two days I have done new things and liked them all. I think that there are many more things that I would like, given the chance to try them. It feels like I want to do too much, too fast and then sort through it all when I have all the experience.' She became aware that all eyes centred on her and that the looks she had despised earlier, when provoked by Mallot, were welcome now that she had invited them. It felt right to have admitted that she wanted a lot of varied sexual experience, and fast. Where Angela's invitation had been wily, Hope's was forthright and no man in the group, perhaps no woman, was immune to imaginings. Elsa's expression held a deep curiosity as her gaze swept over Hope, her shyness pushed aside as questions rose in her mind. Mallot looked perversely proud, as if it was he who had shaped Hope's admissions, an attitude not lost on Hope who disliked him all the more for his presumed control to which, she resolved, she would not submit. If she clashed with Mallot, it would be she who emerged victorious, with her heel on his neck.

Hope looked at Rat, who was staring at her with something akin to wonder. It seemed that, even after she had exposed her turmoil and insecurity, he had read into it strength and power. Her glance dropped to his crotch and confirmed that he sported his now usual erection. Unable to help herself, Hope scanned the male groins in the circle and learned that her tirade had produced similar results in all but Rusty. None of the men bothered to hide their excitement: it seemed that her honesty had been a confession of the group's sexuality, making it acceptable. The promise implicit in this recognition shattered Hope's barriers and she smiled, her own roused reaction evident in the pink flush rising up her neck and the hard response of her nipples that pushed tantalizingly at the sheer material. She felt exhilarated and longed to rip her blouse and bare her breasts for suckling to all, slip off her leggings and spread her legs so her most secret folds could be publicly examined and shared. It was only Mallot's arrogant grin that prevented her. He seemed to be reading her mind and the last person she wanted nursing at her corolla was him.

It seemed that her outburst had silenced Rat. He was unable to contribute, other than to blurt his name. This seemed acceptable to Brandon, who himself seemed affected by Hope, so it was Karen who next spoke.

'I want to thank you all for your introductions and for the risks you took in telling us your fears and hopes. I think we should stop for a little while, have some coffee and stretch our legs. Perhaps you could all take a quiet moment and think about what has been said.' She rose, signalling permission for the group to disband. 'Please come back in a half-hour and take the same seats.'

When the group filed from the lounge, Mairead beckoned them into the dining room where she had laid out a selection of sweet cakes. Although she had eaten a mere hour earlier, Hope felt ravenously hungry. She was amazed at how much energy had been expended in the first session and helped herself to a generous amount of the sweet offering, plus a cup of strong coffee, which she drained and then refilled. The group milled about silently, no one inclined to talk. Rat followed Hope, wishing that she wore the same small dress as Angela. The desire to invade beneath the hem and fist into her was almost overwhelming and prevented him from holding his cup, his hands were shaking so badly. He had to slump against the wall, breathing heavily until his self-control reasserted itself, before he could approach the table and garner his small feast.

In obedience to Karen, the group split up, taking their cups and plates of cakes to private locations, on small trays. By the time Rat had filled his tray, he had lost sight of Hope and felt both relieved and cheated. With her provocation removed he could try and concentrate on others in the group, but he still longed for her presence and the almost reachable smooth mound of her breasts. He perched on a windowsill, balancing his tray on his knees and gazed at the oil paintings adorning the dining room walls. They were sombre but alluring and every one held a sensual promise.

Hope went outside and sat on the bench near the water's edge. She was joined by Allie, who slid beside her and planted a small kiss on her shoulder, then quietly worked her way through a small mountain of cakes.

'So, who's next for sex?' Allie was irrepressible and there was a hint of laughter in her voice which was reciprocated in Hope's reply. 'Why don't we let the group decide? After all,' she added reasonably, 'we *are* supposed to work it out together.' They laughed, a slightly hysterical beginning building up to a loud crescendo, which drew Rusty from the confines of the hallway and down to their hideout. Without asking the reason for their mirth he joined in with bass burbles. All were surprised by an echo from the quay and discovered Ruari, Elsa and Quinn almost doubled over and unable to breathe with laughter. At last Hope coughed to a halt, wiping tears from her cheek, 'Oh Lord,' she gasped, 'that was heavy!' She referred to the session and no one disagreed.

When they at last fell silent, Allie observed, 'That was the best laugh I have had in years. It is the relief, you know?' They all nodded, feeling joined by confession and bonded with the laughter. Elsa slipped beside Hope and shyly hugged her, a spontaneous gesture that touched her deeply and which she returned, laying her cheek alongside that of Elsa and enjoying the smooth innocence of the flesh on hers and the slight tickle of dark curls on her nose. It seemed that Elsa had chosen her mentor.

After depositing their trays in the dining room, they trailed back into the lounge and resumed their seats. Mallot and Angela were last to enter. He looked irritated and she petulant.

Karen asked, ‘Can someone tell me something they have noticed about the group, from their own observation?’ She glanced around the room and the silence stretched, until Hope spoke.

‘I noticed something at suppertime’. She hesitated until she received a nod of encouragement. ‘Well, we mostly seem to have split into couples.’

‘Yes, that is what Brandon and I noticed. Please do not think us harsh but we would like to rectify that for the purposes of the sessions so I would like to try an exercise. Would the women please swap places with the ones opposite them.’

Hope stared across the circle at Angela, rose and went to stand by her until the blonde relinquished her seat with bad grace and went to sit next to Rat. While far from eager to be close to Mallot, Hope was pleased. She had the makings of a bargaining position with Angela and, to consolidate her position, she smiled at Mallot warmly, delighted when puzzlement flickered in his eyes. She trusted that her behaviour had not gone unnoticed and checked with Angela, satisfied when she received a venomous glare.

Elsa swapped seats with Allie, which placed her between

Rusty and Ruari and did not seem to cause her discomfort. Allie smiled happily at Quinn, now on her left, and relaxed with the same ease she had exhibited in her former seat. Of all of them, the one who appeared most uncomfortable with the new arrangement was Rat. While he had probed between Angela's tantalizing thighs with his eyes when she sat opposite, it was with naturally driven lust and curiosity, but he had no powerful urge to seek closer contact. His expression altered to amazement, then alarm, when she clamped her thigh firmly along his and nuzzled his shoulder. He stared at Hope, his eyes wide and beseeching, but she merely grinned at Angela's sorry attempt to rouse her jealousy. Karen surveyed the group and announced herself satisfied.

'What we would like you to do is become acquainted with your new working partners. I know that these are not your first choice, and perhaps you may feel a little uncomfortable in the beginning, but the object is to have a point of reference, a sort of co-counsellor who will keep you on track and separate you from your emotional bonding as couples.

'Now, had anyone noticed anything else?'

Hope had but, having spoken before with such dire consequence, she remained silent. She felt uncomfortable next to Mallot, intensely aware of his presence. From a distance he exuded power, closer he seemed feral and watchful, even while his attention seemed focused elsewhere. The settee was small and their thighs were pressed together, Hope feeling the burn of his flesh through her thin leggings as if he were naked beside her. The sensation was both repulsive and rousing and she was distressed to find herself responding, her breathing growing shallow and her heart quickening. She was relieved when Mallot spoke and broke the spell.

'It seems,' he said slowly, 'that many in this group have problems dealing with the opposite gender, especially in a sexual way.'

Hope could not criticize his summary, but felt compelled to add, 'But I do not agree with the word "problem" and I think it makes things sound as if something is dysfunctional when it probably isn't!'

'Let's get clear on dysfunction, shall we, so we all understand what that means?' Mallot rejoined. 'My understanding is that is merely means something is not functioning properly and it need not be a negative term.'

'I would prefer that the members of this group don't attempt to be analysts, or use terms which have a specific meaning in psychology,' Karen interrupted. 'Mallot is right when he pointed out that people had expressed problems with interaction and that those problems indicated a difficulty with sexual matters. I wondered if this was a good place to start exploring a road to travel over this fortnight?'

'I want to know what all that means,' Rusty muttered.

'You have to tell us,' Brandon indicated. 'This is about how you decide to go on from here and achieve something to take away with you. I know it is hard, but perhaps someone could state exactly how they feel right now?'

Mallot complied. 'I feel excited. It is like we are opening a door to an adventurous time, with all the barriers dropped. I do not mind admitting that I am a very sexual man and have a lot of experience. I love women and feel very close to all the women I have made love with. I would be very happy to join with any women in this group, in any way they wanted, and I can promise they would be very satisfied.'

'How far would you go?' Ruari questioned.

Mallot spread his hands and shrugged lightly, 'As far as anyone wished to take it.'

'Yes,' persisted Ruari, 'but what does that mean?'

'Okay,' Mallot looked thoughtful. 'Some folk here are shy, right?' He looked purposefully at Elsa, who was staring like a rabbit caught in headlights. 'Well, some aren't, also.' He transferred his gaze to Angela, who returned it stoically. 'As far as I am concerned, it is about "horses for courses". I would make love right here, in the centre of the circle, with any woman who was happy to do so. Those who want more privacy could perhaps invite me to their rooms.'

'What you seem to be assuming,' interrupted Allie, 'is that all the women here want to bonk you.'

'No, what I am hoping is that any woman here can feel she is at liberty to use me if she so wishes.'

The group sat silently for a moment, all staring at the empty expanse of carpet in the centre of the circle as if it indeed contained a sweaty coupling pair. Hope, suddenly remembering the generous proportions at Mallot's groin, shivered and bit her lip. She agreed with Mallot, in a sense.

'I agree with Mallot, in a sense,' she found herself saying, wishing that her mouth would stay shut.

'In a sense?' Rat echoed.

'Well, yes. I mean, we can decide what we want to do in the next two weeks and also how we want to do it. I do not know, if we start exploring this avenue, how it will seem after a week of total sexual freedom. I mean, perhaps it would be exciting to watch people make love in the middle of the group. If they feel good about it, we feel good about watching and it solves some of the problems, why not?'

'Right,' said Rusty with heavy sarcasm, 'and I suppose we can do whatever we like? I said that I behaved nastily – are you up for that in public?'

Hope looked at him, intrigued, 'I don't know what your "nasty" is,' she pointed out, 'and maybe if I did then I would not think it is nasty. Like I said, I am trying all sorts of things at the moment, so even if you told me what it is and I had never done it, I might really like it. As for doing it in the middle of the group, it depends on what the group thinks and would like to see happen.'

'It seems to me,' Allie interjected, 'that we have all sorts of flavours here, and all sorts of levels of experience. Should that not count? What would offend one person may be totally acceptable to another and then, next week, the offended person may not be worried anymore and another level is reached.'

Karen suddenly clapped her hands with delight. 'This is great!' she exclaimed, 'But some people are not saying anything.' She looked at Angela and Quinn. 'And others are saying very little.' She glanced at Ruari, Elsa and Rat. 'I would like their feedback. Perhaps Quinn would start?'

He sat silent for a moment, then said, 'I feel happy with what is happening. I am not sure how my particular problem fits in with this and I would feel better working it out with someone alone before introducing it into the group. On the whole, though, yes. I would agree with what has been said so far.'

'Elsa?'

'Uh . . .' Elsa grimaced, 'I do not know too much about sex. I have not even watched a naughty video.

But I will go along with whatever Hope feels comfortable with.'

Brandon leaned forward and asked gently, 'Elsa, you know that Hope is different from you and may be more experienced in the ways of the world and sex?' Upon receiving a mute nod, he continued, 'You trust her so much that you will agree to do anything she wants?'

'Oh no, it is not like that. I mean, I trust her to lead and then I can follow if I feel okay with what she does!'

'Okay,' Brandon nodded. 'So you are happy for Hope to lead this group along the road it is deciding to travel?'

'Yes.' Elsa smiled at Hope, 'I think that she won't let me get hurt.'

'How do you feel about that, Hope?' Karen asked.

Hope felt uncomfortable and hedged. 'I think that, if what Elsa means is that she trusts I won't do anything that would be destructive, then it is okay. I don't want to feel that I am holding back to protect her, though, and I would feel better if she questions everything before she tries it.' She gazed at Elsa.

'So you want Elsa to be her own person and not depend on you?' Karen translated.

'Yes, I think so, but it is not that harsh.'

'Do you think that is harsh, Elsa?'

'No. I think it sounds better the way you said it and I agree.'

Karen peered at Ruari, who chewed his fingernail nervously.

'I don't know,' he muttered, then frowned. 'I think I am the least experienced bloke here so I would like to talk about it more but I feel odd doing this in front of the ladies.'

'Ladies!' snorted Allie.

'How about you, Rat?' Brandon asked.

'I am with Ruari on this one. I either beat him, or run a close second on lack of experience so I would like to talk about it a bit more.'

'Rusty?'

He shrugged, 'Like I said, I have particular stuff. If someone can reassure me it is not nasty then I don't mind being open about it.'

'Angela, do you want to add to what has been said?'

'Yes! I don't mind what happens or with who and I want to be active in it. I think it will be great.'

'Anybody else want to add anything?' Karen studied the group then, satisfied, continued, 'I think we have achieved a lot in one evening and that this is a good start to the fortnight. This is also a good place to end this session although I am sure that once you leave this room, you will have many questions.

'I know that you will chat among yourselves, and this is a good thing, but I would ask that you do not confine your conversation to your original pairing and try and use your working partners, or at least make sure that they are present in a group discussion.

'I want to thank you all for being so open,' she concluded. 'I feel quite excited by all this and I think we have something really interesting to work with.'

Brandon took over. 'We will not join you for breakfast. That is your time at the start of the day, so the next time we see you will be in this room at ten o'clock. Please be on time and all be here.

'The focus is on sex and the question of how to proceed and how far you wish to take it publicly is still open. Perhaps we can start from that point tomorrow?'

Everyone nodded. Hope suddenly felt very tired. Her head was spinning with thoughts and she wanted to be alone to run through what everyone had said so she could make sense of her own contribution and involvement. There was one task she had to undertake before bed, so when the group rose and started to leave the lounge, she managed to draw Angela away from the mass.

Chapter Eight

Angela cast an undecided look at Mallot's retreating back, but her curiosity was roused so she followed Hope from the house and down to the water's edge. It was dark, the only light coming from the lounge and dining room windows and the silvery moonshine. Hope stayed silent, enjoying the slap of water on the quay, the call of an owl and the crisp rustle of leaves as the breeze played through them. The chill of night was welcome after the oppressive heat of the day, but she shivered, feeling the goosebumps beneath her voile blouse as she rubbed her arms briskly.

'What do you want?' Angela broke the silence. 'It seems to me that whatever I had of value has been already given to you.'

'Mallot is of value to you?'

'You know he is.' Angela sounded resigned, which surprised Hope who had expected a confrontation.

'If it was not me it would be one of the other women,' Hope pointed out. 'He did say he was available to all and sundry.'

'Who? Elsa would run a mile and Allie clearly despises him. You were the only real competition and he wants you.' Now Angela sounded bitter.

'Well, it does not have to be that way. I have a deal.'

'What?' Angela barked a laugh of disbelief. 'I lay off Rat

and you lay off Mallot? Not much of a deal, your young man only has eyes for you.'

'That's not it.'

'So talk!' Angela failed to keep the eagerness from her voice.

'You brought a lot of clothes with you. Have you a suit amongst them?'

Angela fell silent, bewildered at the turn of conversation. Eventually she chanced, 'You want a suit?'

'Yes.'

'With a blouse?'

'Yes, and stockings and suspenders if you have them.'

The pause was longer.

'And, if I give you this suit, with the stockings and suspenders, you will lay off Mallot?'

'Oh, I don't want you to give it to me. I just want a loan of it.'

'Let me get this straight,' Angela sounded confused. 'All Mallot is worth to you is the loan of clothes?'

'Not even that, really,' confessed Hope. 'But I did not bring any working clothes with me and I need some. I'm afraid that, because I know he means something to you, I thought I could do a deal.'

'I am thinner than you, and shorter,' Angela pointed out, practical now.

'Well, could I at least try something on?'

'I will bring what I have to your room a little later.'

'Thank you.'

'It's okay. You're weird.'

Angela turned and strode back into the house, leaving Hope staring after her. The moonlight glittered on the older woman's hair, turning it into a silver shimmy. When she stepped through the doorway, the hall light bathed her in gold, a warm welcome. Hope shivered, suddenly realizing she was not alone. A larger shadow had detached from the sparse shrubbery, moving towards her with measured tread over the pebbled path.

'So,' Mallot said, his eyes glinting, 'I do not seem to be worth a whole lot to you, do I? A skirt and blouse, and not even that if Angela had not brought them with her.'

Hope had recovered from her fright and retorted, 'You said to use you, so I did.'

Mallot hissed and grabbed Hope by the shoulders angrily, his fingers digging into her painfully. Hope cried out and struggled in his grip, without success. She then went limp and he released her.

'That is what it will be like,' Mallot warned. 'I shall have you and when I do you will be limp.' He sounded very calm.

'You can go to hell,' Hope whispered coldly.

'No, my dear, I have already been there.' He laughed, 'But I can take you to heaven. Just let me know when you tire of your skirt and blouse, but bring the stockings with you!' He strolled away, heading down the quay.

Hope rubbed her shoulders. She had refused to do this with him present, but his fingers had left pockets of pain. She stared out over the lake, her eyes wet with anger, and struggled to control her breathing and the rage that roiled in her. Eventually, she turned and entered the house, calmer and more resolved than ever to avoid Mallot.

She was still holding her shoulders, her arms crossed protectively over her breasts, when Rat found her, seated on the choir bench in the hallway. She had stopped to regain her equilibrium before facing the group, who were gathered in the dining room, enjoying late drinks before retiring. To Rat, she looked forlorn and lonely, her hair tousled and her face pale. When Mallot entered the house, casting a brief glance at Hope before joining the group, Rat's suspicions rose.

'What did he do?' Rat sounded calm but he was seething.

'Nothing,' Hope said.

'Ah, shall I ask him?'

'Rat, keep away from Mallot and I shall do the same.' Her tone brooked no refusal, and Hope stared into his face to ensure he agreed. He nodded grimly, a set to his mouth that Hope had not seen before. It aged him and, for the first time, she saw Rat as a man and not an overgrown youth. She wondered if their game was as innocent as it seemed and, recalling his words as they had stood in the shallows earlier, she realized the seriousness of his claim that he could only fuck her, not make love. The silk shirt had tightened over his arm, which lay along the back of the bench, and clung to the sculpture of his muscles. He was six inches taller and significantly stronger than her and Hope suddenly realized that she had entered a pact with him that, with his obsessions driving him, she could not control. She could not understand how the pale, geeky youth had blossomed into this strong, watchful man.

'How come you're so fit?' she asked.

Rat blinked, the boy emerging in confusion, 'I work out, why?'

'I don't know, just that you seem to be in front of computers all the time.'

'There is life outside of Pursuit, you know!'

'There wasn't for me,' Hope sighed. 'At least not until now, and this is hardly realistic.'

'You know,' Rat rearranged his long legs and slouched on the bench, his hands clasped loosely behind his head, 'I think I am luckier than you. You may have travelled the world and earned big bucks, but I knew who I was before I came here, and what I wanted.' He looked sideways at Hope, self-assured, which she chose to regard as smug.

'Sometimes what you dream of is disappointing in reality. Be careful you don't get what you deserve!' she retorted, rising.

The rest of the group was filtering from the dining room, en route to bed, and she received a meaningful glance from Angela who reasserted her ownership by clinging to Mallot's arm as they mounted the stairs. Hope followed, without glancing back at Rat. He stared at her until she turned at the mullioned window and disappeared from view. His eyes had been drawn to the crotch of her leggings, staring while he imagined the soft delight beneath the snug black fabric. How was it, he wondered, that women could walk so easily, their thighs grazing the swell of their lobes, and not be permanently aware and aroused? He imagined that Hope had been aware of his watching her, and that she liked it and grew moist with desire. He thought of her stripping in the privacy of her bedroom, before a mirror, her thoughts centred on him, longing for the harshness of his hands on her breasts as she undid her blouse. It was not the black leggings he envisaged, but pure white suspenders and flesh-coloured stockings, under which her pubis was naked and yearning.

He was not far wrong. Hope undressed before the long wardrobe mirror, sliding the cerise voile from her shoulders to reveal fresh bruising on her shoulders. She felt perversely excited by the marks, recalling the words 'I shall have you . . . you will be limp', except that in Mallot's stead she imagined Rat. She clutched her breasts, as Rat had done in The Piper's Inn, kneading harshly, imagining that Rat would suddenly burst through the door, driven by lust and his last reserves, to ravish her. When she heard the door open, she did not turn around, sure that her fantasy was to be fulfilled. She closed her eyes softly, fear and excitement flooding her, and waited for strong hands to grab her and throw her on her bed.

'I think,' said Angela softly, 'that it was not me you were expecting?'

Hope flushed and turned to see Angela carefully laying some clothes on the satin counterpane. In her embarrassment, still clutching her breasts, Hope was unable to speak. Angela smoothed the garments, then turned to face Hope.

'It's okay,' she said. 'I felt like you do now, for the best part of two years, since my husband left me. I never found a man, until Mallot, who had the sense and experience to subdue me. That includes my husband, by the way, and he left me for someone very much like Elsa.'

'I'm sorry,' Hope stammered at last.

'Don't be,' protested Angela, 'it was the nicest thing that man ever did for me.' She narrowed her eyes and gazed at Hope. 'You're beautiful, you know, especially in your confusion. I think I would like to watch Mallot take you. With me in control, of course!'

'Never!'

'Never say "never".' Angela laughed thinly, 'You may have to renege. Anyway . . .' she gestured at the clothes, 'try these on and see if anything suits you. Whatever you chose, I don't expect it back.' She left as silently as she had arrived.

Hope examined the clothes. All were top brands and she tried them all, finding most, as Angela had predicted, far too small. The zips of the skirts protested as she forced them up and she could not sit down. The least obtrusive suit, a black linen pencil skirt and military-cut jacket, fitted snugly but allowed movement. None of the blouses would button but Angela had thoughtfully included a white fine lace camisole, no doubt as an undergarment. Once Hope had donned the outfit, she was gratified with the effect. The skirt was too short for her, hugging her legs at mid-thigh, and the oversized jacket, when buttoned, hung nearly to the hem of the skirt. Open, the camisole emphasized her breasts. Her white bra would push her breasts into generous mounds that would top the neckline.

A soft bag lay beside the clothes, and contained a lacy suspender belt and two pairs of seamed nylon stockings, one pair flesh-coloured and the other black. Hope had her delicate sandals with her and the low heels would not do justice to the stockings, but the only other footwear she had brought was deck-shoes and trainers.

'Tomorrow,' Hope breathed at her reflection. She unbuttoned the jacket and smiled at her breasts, then swivelled to check the rear view and noted that the vent in the skirt lay just below her quim. Then she stripped slowly, staring all the while at the reflection of her eyes, holding her gaze as if it were Rat's. Naked, except for the lace camisole, she masturbated, balancing with one hand pressed to the mirror, the other rubbing and dipping until she throbbed, leaking her copious fluids over her fingers. As she came she leaned against the cool glass, her breasts flattened, her lips and nipples thrilling to the cold press. Afterwards she licked her fingers clean, imagining that she was dipping into Rat's mouth and his eyes were closed in bliss as he consumed her liquid musk.

She hung Angela's clothes carefully, promising herself she would return them the next morning, then slipped into bed naked, her taste strong in her throat and her scents on her fingers as she curled up, her cheek pressed into her palm.

She woke to insistent knocking on her bedroom door, which then opened to reveal Allie carrying a tray bearing a mug of coffee and butter croissants. The redhead wore a shirt, under which Hope could see a swimsuit.

'Am I going to have to bring you breakfast every day?' she demanded, then sat cross-legged on the bed watching Hope eat and spill croissant-flakes over her breasts.

'I'll get those!' Allie leapt forward to lick them off.

'Tickles!' Hope protested, amending, 'But nicely.'

Allie nipped lightly at a nipple, laughing when Hope squeaked with surprise. 'Haven't got time for this! You have an hour to get downstairs and I am going to swim.' She sat back on her haunches and pursed her lips. 'You smell like old sex, by the way.' She jumped off the bed as Hope threw back the covers and leapt out.

'I'll swim instead of showering.' She gulped her coffee and pulled on a one-piece racing swimsuit. T-backed, with a high scooped neckline, it merely served to emphasize her curves rather than hide them. She slipped on her deck shoes, grabbed a towel and raced downstairs with Allie, their laughter echoing. They did not stop until they reached the water's edge, and then only long enough to kick off their shoes. Allie splashed into the water with her shirt on, shrieking as her warm flesh met the cold, then thrusting from the shallows to flop, gasping as she immersed herself. Hope joined her, sinking to test the depth.

The channel in which they swam was the route taken by the motorboat as they were all ferried from the launch. It was narrow but long, and Hope struck out with an energetic crawl stroke, enjoying the pull on her muscles as she rounded the island. She paused, paddling, to look at the lake beyond the mouth of the bay. There was little wind and the lake was serene. Birds skimmed the surface, creating small ripples, and a large fish jumped, breaking the surface and creating a perfect silver arc. Hope dog-paddled to the near shore and pulled herself onto a rock, to sit staring without any thought of time at the perfect scene.

Allie's shouts drew her back, breaking through her trance and reminding her she was to attend another exploratory session. The island seemed new to her as she slowly returned to the quay and mounted the steps. History and permanence bled into the stone walls of the house, the rocks jutting from the water and the unspoilt bay. Whatever she learned in the coming days, whatever she did, would make little impression and would be shed by this place within minutes of her departure. This was her first lesson, she assumed, that she should make the most of her time at the retreat, launch herself into the experience and at least allow it to make an impact on her own life. She reminded herself that she needed to seek Willincough, but only because Pursuit was paying for this fortnight and therefore she owed them her effort. She wondered why she had wasted the past ten years believing that her work mattered.

'You okay?' Allie met Hope at the quay with her towel

and rubbed her down briskly. She was disconcerted by the intense thoughtfulness of her friend. 'You look like you have seen the light.'

'I have,' Hope replied, laughing, 'and I have never been better. Allie . . .' she swung and hugged her, 'whatever happens from here on, don't be shocked.'

'Who, me? Shocked? No way!' Allie grinned. 'At least I think I won't be: what are you up to?'

'Hedonism,' Hope tapped the side of her nose. 'Just simple hedonism.'

'Can't wait,' Allie muttered as she followed Hope back into the house.

They changed into T-shirts and sweatpants, entering the lounge when the group were all settling. Obediently, everyone had taken the seat in which they had sat before the group broke up the previous evening. Hope did not mind sitting next to Mallot; he now seemed of little consequence. She nodded acknowledgement of his presence and smiled across the room at Rat. She felt confident, with a small edge of nervousness, as she set out on her journey of liberation.

'Has anyone anything to discuss that came up for them in the night?' Brandon opened, and when no one jumped in, continued, 'Fine, then I shall recap on where we were at the end of the last session.

'The group seems to be agreed that a way to proceed during the next two weeks involves examining our sexuality and relationships, but Ruari and Rat would like to discuss it further. Does that sound right to all of you?'

'Yes,' agreed Ruari. 'But I also don't feel comfortable talking about it in front of the women.'

Brandon nodded, 'Okay, we'll take that up in a minute.' He scanned the group. 'Rusty, you want to say something?' He had noted that the model was restless.

'Yes. I think I indicated that I have a particular problem and I would discuss it if I could be reassured that it is okay.'

Karen intervened, leaning forward to face Rusty, 'Can you accept that perhaps it would be okay with some and maybe not with everyone? The only person to whom it must really be okay is yourself and a consenting partner or group.'

Rusty nodded, 'Yeah, but I'm with Ruari, I want to speak about how we are going to handle this first, before I take a risk. I would actually like to talk to people on their own before I bring it to the group.'

'Have you spoken about it with your working partner?'

'Well, that is either Elsa or Angela, and no, I haven't.' He left hanging the implication that Elsa was too inexperienced. All eyes turned to Angela.

'I need to think about it,' she said, 'and will get back to you.'

Rusty seemed disappointed, taking it as a rebuff. 'If you need to think about whether you will speak to me or not then you would not make a good working partner!'

Angela shrugged.

'Will anyone offer to be Rusty's working partner?' Karen asked.

'I will,' Hope offered. 'If he wants a woman rather than a man.'

'And if he wants a man,' added Mallot, 'I will be happy to be his working partner.'

'I think Mallot would just accept it: he has made clear

that he is experienced. I think I would like to take Hope up on her offer,' Rusty looked nervous.

Karen nodded at Hope approvingly and turned to Rusty, 'In your own time, okay? Good.'

'I would like to talk with Hope, too.' Elsa said.

'And me,' added Quinn.

'Hope, you seem to have an awful lot on your plate. You can say "no" to any or all of these requests.'

'No, I said I wanted lots of new experience and I think this is great.'

'One other thing was mentioned last night. There was the suggestion that Hope lead the group on this voyage and her popularity today seems to suggest that she is trusted. Shall we discuss that?'

'If that means that I can just go ahead with what I feel is right then that is fine, but I don't want to influence anyone,' Hope said. 'I do want to say, though, that I decided this morning to launch right in and gain the best experience I can from this fortnight and I won't hold anything back.'

'What does that mean?' asked Ruari.

'It means that it we are going to examine sex and how we feel and behave, and total freedom exists, then I am going to be totally free within this group.'

'Oh, what?' Angela snorted. 'You are going to work your way through all the men?'

Hope stared at her until the pause grew intense, then said calmly, 'Why not? And the women as well, if it goes that way.' She earned a hug from Mallot.

'Right,' Karen smiled at Hope, 'I am glad you decided to throw yourself open to this experience. Given that Ruari, Rusty and Rat want to do a bit more talking about it, how does everyone else feel?'

It turned out everyone felt fine about it and Hope found herself elevated to trail seeker. As the group pledged their commitment, Hope leaned back, enjoying the feeling that they seemed to be bonding. There seemed only the question of how to proceed.

'Perhaps we can, this once, break the group?' Brandon suggested. 'In the coming days, I want *everything* to be disclosed. It is only in that way that we can explore our growth in any depth and learn together. This would mean that any interaction that is pertinent to sexual growth should be discussed openly within this group.

'I would suggest that the women go with Karen into the dining room for the next hour and talk, and the men remain with me. When we regroup, I believe we will be better able to decide on a plan.'

'That is my suggestion, too,' Karen added. 'Perhaps an hour apart?'

Ruari was quick to agree, followed by the rest of the men and, as the women filed from the room, they were already shuffling closer to Brandon.

'All they need is a pint in one hand and a bar under the elbow and they would be well away,' muttered Allie as the women settled in the dining room. They had pulled the dining chairs into a circle and sat quietly, their attention claimed by the possibilities in the lounge.

'And all we need is a sherry and our knitting.' laughed Hope.

Allie grinned. 'Yes, okay. You're right. Let's make the most of it because from here on it is all upfront and not separatist! What are we going to do?'

'Well, far as I can make out, Hope is going to go through the group and then bare all in public.' Angela commented.

'No,' said Hope. 'I think we are all going to tell our experiences because we will all benefit.'

'I feel shy with that. I don't know if I can do it.' Elsa blushed.

'I can,' Allie admitted.

'Me too,' Angela agreed.

'Hope, you seem to have sparked all this off, and I thank you for taking the risks you have and enabling us to find a route so fast. You do not seem to mind being the provocateur so perhaps you can tell us how you feel you would like to continue.'

Hope took a deep breath. 'First of all I am going to have sex with Rat. Then I would like to do that with anyone in the group who wants me – in any way they want.'

'Are you sure?' Karen gazed at her.

'Yes.'

'So,' Allie queried, 'Rat first, then who?'

'I do not know. The only one I do not want is Mallot.' Hope earned a beatific look from Angela.

'Why don't you line them up?' Angela suggested. 'From the least experienced to the most? Rat and Ruari claim they are, and Quinn seems a pussycat. You are Rusty's volunteer partner and he thinks he is kinked so perhaps comes next. Who knows?' She looked directly into Hope's eyes. 'Perhaps something can be worked out with Mallot. He is the most experienced so would come last anyway.'

'What about the rest of you?' Hope asked and turned to Elsa.

'I know that I can talk to you and that will help, but I am happy to be involved.'

'Hey,' Allie grinned, 'I will go to bed with you anytime!'

'I don't know if I would go that far,' Angela said, 'but

I will be happy to run quality control checks on your recommendations.' She earned a laugh.

'This is good!' Karen exclaimed. 'You will all feel your way through this, with open minds, as far as you can. Open and honest, okay, we speak about it all?'

'What about Mallot's comment about doing it in the middle of the group?' Elsa asked.

They all paused to think and Hope was the first to speak. 'I think if we are being open and honest and everyone is aware of what everyone else does then I can imagine it happening.'

'I don't have any problem with doing it in public,' Angela confessed.

'I don't have any problem with watching it,' Allie agreed.

'I would like to,' Elsa added in a small voice and, in response to surprised looks, hastily appended, 'Watch, that is!' She giggled.

'Okay, so we have a deal to put to the men. I imagine they have one for us.' Karen smiled, 'I shall just go and check how they are doing.' She left the room.

Elsa turned to Hope, 'Can I talk to you this afternoon?' she asked eagerly.

'Not this afternoon,' Hope said gently. 'Perhaps later, after the session tonight?'

'Okay,' Elsa said, 'I'll bring the cokes and crisps!'

They all laughed but there was a tremor of excitement and, when Karen returned to invite them back into the lounge, Hope felt as it she was about to face her personal Armageddon. The men had resumed their former seats and once everyone was comfortable, Brandon spoke.

'I understand that we are all more or less in agreement

but perhaps Hope would like to tell us what she believes is agreed amongst the women?'

'We did not say what anyone else would be doing but, for me, I would like to have sex with everyone in the group. I thought that I would start with those who feel least experienced and work my way from there. But I think it is up to the others to decide how experienced they are.'

Angela broke in, 'Rat is first on the agenda.'

'Oh yes,' Mallot queried, 'and who is next?'

'Ruari, then Quinn, Rusty and then, possibly, you.' Angela stared at Mallot.

'Oh, I think I may be less experienced than Ruari!' Quinn protested.

Ruari looked nervous, 'I don't think so, you are married.'

'Doesn't mean anything.' Quinn muttered.

'Have them together,' quipped Allie, earning a horrified stare from Ruari.

The group discussed the ladder of experience easily, allowing each man to place himself on the scale without needing to divulge too much. Mallot, removed from the conversation by dint of his presumed expertise, leaned back with a smug expression. Rat, precluded because he was accepted as first on the list, remained silent, torn by conflict. He was thrilled to think that Hope had chosen him as her initial partner but sick to think that, after him, she would share her sex with the other men. He imagined Ruari, his large mass covering Hope, his buttocks pumping while her slippery cave welcomed his thrusts and her legs curled around his waist. In spite of his jealous misgivings, Rat found himself roused. He wanted to plunder Hope, but with the image of Quinn following hard on that of

Ruari, he suddenly realised he liked the thought of a chain. Perhaps he could share the experience, watch or even slide his penis through Hope's hungry lips while he enjoyed the slick rhythm of a foreign prick taking his woman. And what of the women?

'What of the women?' he found himself asking.

'You mean,' said Allie, 'are we involved with Hope?'

'Not you,' he muttered. 'She's already had you!'

'Hell, and I hope she does again!'

Angela took advantage of the pause. 'What about the rest of us?'

'I suggest,' Mallot chipped in, 'that we appoint a man to go through the women as well.'

'Oh right, and that is you?' Allie snorted.

'No, actually, I was thinking of Rat – after all, he is starting the ball rolling with Hope. So perhaps we can line up the women for him, like you are doing with the men for Hope.'

Rat looked at Hope, who smiled her approval.

'Okay,' he said, a new glint in his eye, 'but the least experienced is Elsa.'

'I cannot do this that fast!' Elsa cried, staring at Hope.

'You don't have to,' Hope answered gently. 'You don't have to do anything at all that you don't wish to.' She addressed the group. 'Elsa and I are going to chat later, so perhaps you will leave her out for the moment?'

'Well then, that leaves Allie and Angela in that order.'

'Suits me,' agreed Allie, 'but what are we going to do, remain celibate until Hope reports back on her progress?'

Mallot laughed, 'Why not?'

'It seems a day-by-day thing,' argued Rat. 'I don't think

we ought to put time limits on it at all, and we can still discuss things with our working partners.'

'Okay,' said Karen, 'what we have at present is a working draft. To begin with, Hope and Rat are going to get together and perhaps we can all hold back until they let us know what happens?'

Everyone nodded. Hope realized that Angela did not mean the restriction to be placed on herself and Mallot, and feeling mischievous, she turned at looked at him expectantly.

'That goes for me, too,' he affirmed, gazing at Angela.

'Tell me,' the blonde improvised, 'when we are talking about no sex, does this also mean no wanking?' She smiled sweetly around the group, satisfied with the guilty blushes. 'After all, it is going to be hard work listening to Rat and Hope bonk all night!'

My fault, groaned Hope to herself. Now everyone would be alert to their involvement. Everyone was looking at her and, later, would be listening.

'There is still a meeting after supper,' Brandon pointed out.

'Yes, and no one said it had to be tonight,' reasoned Karen. 'Right now I think lunch is ready for us. I would recommend that we have this afternoon to ourselves unless anyone has unfinished business?'

No one had, so the group disbanded. Rat hung back and, by silent consent, so did Hope. She crossed to the window and stared through. The heat shimmered on the rocks, the light bright enough to force her to narrow her eyes. She was unsurprised when Rat slid his arms around her from behind.

'I was thinking,' he said and dropped a small kiss on the

top of her head, 'that I do not like the idea of you screwing your way through the group.' He felt her tense to protest and squeezed to keep her silent. 'But it excites me to think of the next guy fucking you.'

They remained silent until Hope said coldly, 'Have you forgotten we have a job to do? We owe this fortnight to Pursuit and my idea was just to get close to everyone so I could find out who Willi is. Seems it is working, doesn't it?'

When Rat dropped his arms in surprise, she swung to face him. 'Please bring your laptop to the library after lunch. I think we should start a report to Reggie and we can do so by writing down everything we know about everyone.'

Hope did not wait for a response. She ducked away and strode from the room, to enter the dining room and take a seat between Elsa and Allie, smiling at them and totally ignoring Rat, who followed slowly with an expression of angry bewilderment on his face.

Lunch comprised melon with Parma ham, followed by cold cuts and salads, self-served from huge bowls lined up on the sideboard. The morning's session had left the group feeling risqué and relaxed, bantering intimately. Karen and Brandon seemed to want to encourage the bonding, themselves provoking interplay and supplying double entendres. Hope picked her way through small amounts of food, her excitement mounting as she attempted to maintain a cool façade. Rat kept glancing at her, frowning, and she hoped he would not disappoint her by not keeping his appointment in the library. After the dessert, chocolate mousse with cream, she helped herself to a cup of coffee and excused herself, carrying it from the dining room and up to her bedroom.

She sat on her bed and sipped her coffee, her excitement

mounting. Rat had no idea of her plan and she wondered how he would respond. Typically, he had chosen to believe that their intercourse would be traditional and that he would lead the game. She had chosen to knock back his expectations and keep him confused. Soon, she would reel him in, even though he would assume it was he who held the power. Her coffee finished, and feeling calmer, Hope showered and patted herself dry. With one foot perched on the seat of the toilet, she carefully clipped her pubic hair with a pair of nail scissors, then shaved. She squatted, put a hand mirror between her thighs and stared at her quim. It seemed alien, smooth and vulnerable. When she stood before the full-length mirror in her bedroom, her labia closed protectively to cover the delicate inner folds. With the removal of her covering of fine blonde curls she felt exposed, the treasures of her secret parts not shielded by a barrier. She felt as if she were announcing her sexuality in a way that words did not convey and inviting a far more intimate response than formerly. With the bridge of curls between the slight slope of her stomach and the tender nether folds removed, all barriers were destroyed and she became one with her secret places. When she glanced into her reflected eyes, she felt renewed, wiser, and her excitement became more than simply physical. The intimacy she felt was with herself, a narcissistic longing and a feeling of love.

Hope put on a light application of foundation, adding mascara, blush and lip gloss. She clipped the suspender belt around her waist and drew the sheer stockings over her legs, rolling them gently over her calves and thighs and smoothing them with flat palms so the seams remained straight. She snapped the suspenders in place and stood to admire herself, twisting to check her seams then gazing at the smooth clam framed by the ribbons of the belt. She put on her bra, scooping her breasts in place until the soft mounds threatened to spill over from their lacy platform, then tugged on the camisole. It hugged her, accentuating her waist and clinging to her breasts. She adjusted the neckline so her overflowing breasts trembled, her areolae barely covered. She slid the skirt up, wriggling until it settled, and closed the zip. From the rear she noted that the tops of the stockings were visible through the vent. She tugged on the jacket and closed the buttons, slipped on her sandals and quickly left the room, realizing that Rat would be waiting in the library.

The place seemed deserted as she descended to the hallway, so she tapped on the kitchen door, which was opened by Mairead. She smiled when Hope asked for directions to the library.

'I am glad to see that someone wants to read! Just go past the dining room and you will find a little passage. The library is at the end. The main light is dim, mind you, so use a desk lamp.' She smiled and shut the kitchen door.

Rat was in the library, hunched over the keyboard of his laptop computer and typing busily. He did not notice Hope's arrival so she took advantage and watched him frown with concentration and sweep his hair back from his face. The light was dim and he had not switched on the lamp, which peered over him like a benevolent, if dark, plant, its scalloped green glass shade petalling softly.

The library was large, the walls clad with shelving crammed with books and further shelving strutted into the room, creating shadowed recesses that Hope ached to explore. A ladder lay against the far wall and smaller steps, on castors, were placed in the corners. Someone had loved books: this was a well-loved place. The floor was smooth, polished wood and two large windows intruded between the shelves, displaying scenes of the bay shore. Dust motes floated in a golden daze along shafts of light. The room was dusty and disused and Hope understood Mairead's pleasure that someone had sought it.

She returned her attention to Rat, watching his fingers fly over the keys. Fingers she remembered digging into the softness of her breasts and which, she anticipated, would invade her most intimate places. They were long, creative and tapering, certain in their mastery of the keyboard, delicate in their touch, pausing and questing. Her desire grew as she continued to watch. Rat had left his hair loose and it hung untidily over his shoulders. He bit his lip in concentration, paused and stared into space, then resumed his tapping.

Hope crossed the room and Rat looked up. His eyes widened and his gaze swept over her, noting her suit. He licked his lips and blinked, then stared to confirm that she was dressed in the way he desired. He felt cast back into his lair at Pursuit, an eager, trembling employee lusting after the unattainable. When Hope reached him, she perched against the desk, as she had done in his office in London. This time, however, she unbuttoned the jacket of her suit, then leaned over to switch on the desk lamp. Her journey brought her breasts level with his eyes and he gazed hungrily at the mounds, sighing softly when a nipple escaped its confines and peeked naughtily at him. When she righted herself, Hope did not bother to tuck the nipple away; it felt nice, caught by the neckline, and hardened in response.

The skirt had crept up, revealing the dark border of

the stocking tops and the clear outline of suspender clips showed against the tight garment.

'So,' Hope enquired, 'shall we get to work?'

She pushed herself away from the desk and sauntered towards the door. She did not tug the skirt down and ensured that Rat received a clear view of the stocking tops through the rear vent. She turned and paced back towards him, fascinated by his stare. He seemed hypnotized, leaning towards her, his hands now idle and clenched in his lap.

'I thought,' mused Hope, 'that we could perhaps write down all we know about our peers. Do you think that would be a good starting point?'

Rat seemed unable to answer. Her words reached him but he made no sense of them, his attention firmly fixed on the hem of her skirt, willing it to ride higher so he could catch a glimpse between her thighs. His head swam. He remembered their conversation in the shallows of the bay the previous day, his later demand that she wear her working uniform. Now she was before him, fulfilling his dreams, her flesh paraded, spilling and available, and he could not speak, let alone move. He could imagine stopping her in mid-stride, sinking his hands beneath her skirt and bringing them together in the moistness of her crotch – he just could not do it. Groaning inwardly, he sought refuge in what he could do. He returned his hands to the keyboard.

Hope studied the back of his head for a moment. She had been sure he would yield to her enticement and felt puzzled. He was clearly roused, his erection prodding at the fabric of his shorts and his breathing slightly laboured. When he pushed his hair from his face she caught a glimpse of the flush covering his neck. What, she wondered, would it take to topple him? She picked up a pencil and tapped it against the palm of her hand. She shed her jacket.

'Let's start with who we know best,' she murmured. 'Allie is from Scotland and works with computers, all her peers are male.' She paused, while Rat typed. He seemed unnaturally still, tensed.

She paced past the back of his chair and heard him shuffle round to look at her. It seemed he was far more comfortable with her rear view so Hope decided to give him a treat. She stopped in front of a window, pretending to enjoy the scenery and the pencil slipped from her hand and landed sharply on the wooden floor. She tutted with annoyance, parted her feet slightly and bent over, straight-legged, to retrieve it.

Rat gasped, unable to help it, as he viewed the display Hope offered. Obligingly, she remained bent over, enjoying the cut of the suspender straps and tug of the sheer stockings. The skirt had ridden to her hips so the cleft of her bottom was exposed, the starry anus and the pink flush of her pudendum. Before him, Rat could see all his dreams come true. He leaned forward, weaving, as if to breathe in her aroma. Hope was almost within reach and, were he to rise and take one step forward, he could touch her. He slid from his chair, a fluid movement that left him on his knees, and shuffled towards her. He drew to a halt level with her quim and stared intently, as if memorizing each soft fold and crevice. He inhaled deeply to savour her scents, then touched her with his tonguetip, drawing it lightly along her moist furrow.

Hope trembled. The muscles in the backs of her thighs hurt from holding her position and detracted from the delicate thrill of Rat's tongue. She bent her knees to relieve the tension and was grateful when she felt his hands span her hips and urge her to her knees. She sank gracefully and felt the press of Rat behind her, his hard rod thrusting into her lower back. He slid his hands over her breasts, pulling her harder into him, then slid them to her hips and suddenly pushed her, so she sprawled forward, crying out with surprise. She flung her arms out and landed heavily but with her face protected, her breasts pressed hard against the bare boards. The floor smelled of dust and old polish, an earthy and reassuring aroma, and she lay still anticipating Rat's next move.

Rat stood up and stepped back. Without removing his gaze, he shed his shorts, setting his erection free. He stroked the hard arc softly, shivering with pleasure while his look grazed along Hope's prone form. Her skirt had pulled up and the stocking tops and suspenders were clear to view, along with an expanse of naked thigh, but the hem shielded her sex. The vent of the skirt lay skewed, one flap tucked between her thighs, further inhibiting his view.

He leaned over and parted her ankles, pushing her legs as far open as the tightness of the skirt allowed and drawing the fabric taut so that her crotch was shadowed but allowed a glimpse of Hope's corolla. He sank to his knees between her calves and gripped the edges of the vent, then gave them a sharp tug so the stitching gave and the seam tore to the base of the zip. Another sharp tug and the zip tore free, the back of the skirt now halved and Hope's bottom bared. It was just as he had dreamed, pale and rounded, trembling and muscled tightly, closed protectively. He cupped his palms over her bumcheeks, enjoying the give of her flesh and the warmth. He pressed his hand into her lower back and drew it down, dipping his index finger into the crease and round until it found her pucker. Hope moaned and wriggled as Rat's questing finger pressed and he was not sure if it was protest or desire, but he was resolute, gently determined, until his fingertip slid past the resistance and sank into the satin-smooth channel. He explored gently, now recognizing that her whimpers were of pleasure, then withdrew and continued his journey, tucking his first and index fingers deep into her willing cave, scissoring as she sought more. At last, satisfied that she was yearning, Rat eased over Hope and rubbed his tip against her damp entry, requesting permission, and she eased up to take him in.

They both groaned with delight as his length slid slowly inside her. He was aching with lust as her hot depths swallowed him. It felt as good as he had ever imagined, tight and welcoming, wide open to his occupation. Hope trembled, curving to him, her bottom weaving and, while Rat loved the sight of her slim body, wanton and squirming beneath him, he suddenly wanted to see her face and watch the pleasure he could give her. He slipped from her, hushing her protests and rolled her over. Drawing her to her feet, he tugged Hope to the desk and then sat in his chair, pulling her towards him. She straddled his lap, facing him, and lowered herself onto his slick prick, sighing as it entered and embedded deep within her.

Hope rocked slightly, then lifted, and both of them peered down, staring at their union. She leaned back, grasping the edge of the desk, and rode up and down, careful with the angle and staring at Rat. His concentration was intense, fascination etched on his young features, and she suspected he had never watched himself penetrating before. It made her want to please him and options floated in her mind before she cast them aside and was caught up in pleasure, the sensations shifting within her claiming her full attention. *Next time*, she promised herself as she floated towards her zenith.

Rat was transfixed. He sought Hope's gaze but found that she had her eyes shut softly and was mewling to the rhythm of her thrusts. A pink blush suffused her neck and she pouted, her lips swollen and red, slightly parted. One of her nipples had popped completely free and her beasts trembled. A thin trap of the camisole had slipped from her shoulders and looped over her upper arms, causing the light top to fall and reveal the cups of her bra. Her stockings were laddered, one suspender clasp loosened and the stocking top gaping. She looked ravished and wild, panting and lusty.

Rat slid his hands over Hope's shoulders and tugged so the straps of her bra slid from her shoulders. He tugged the cups down and her breasts were freed. They perched on the platform of white lace, round and perfect, her nipples puckered and reddened. He grasped her hips and stopped her motion, easing her so that she sat hard in his lap and then he kissed her, his lips hard and muscling against hers and his tongue twining around hers and thrusting. He squeezed her breasts, feeling the sharp dig of her nipples on his palm.

Hope picked up his rhythm, squeezing her vaginal muscles in time to his beat. He settled back into his chair, not releasing his hold, and they maintained the movement, their gaze locked, until Hope sighed, threw her head back and froze. Soon he felt the ringtug of her coming ripple along his length. She swung to look at him, her eyes narrowed, and panted as if she had just run a hard race. He could feel the swift beat of her heart beneath his hand. When she resumed her vaginal muscling it seemed stronger and she massaged his shaft strongly until he burst, crying out as his cream jetted. He slumped, and when his erection waned he felt his juices leak around it and soak over his naked thighs. They sat until his cock slipped from her and their breathing eased. A cool trail of semen dried along Rat's thigh and he rubbed it with his finger thoughtfully.

'That's not what I intended,' he said suddenly.

'What had you intended?'

'I didn't mean it to be so . . .' he cast about for the correct word, '. . . personal.'

Hope eased from his lap and perched on the desk, her feet resting on his thighs. She looked at him thoughtfully. 'You just wanted to fuck me and walk away without feeling anything?'

'I don't know, except that that was not as I meant it to be and I want to do it again and again until I get what I want.'

'I warned you that reality sometimes disappoints.'

He looked horrified. 'God, no! That was not disappointing, it was wonderful. I just think I want to rehearse a bit more.' He smiled, 'A lot more!' He pushed Hope's knees apart and looked between her thighs. 'Are we going to talk about this in group tonight?' he asked nervously, addressing her quim.

'Yes. At least I want you to say how you feel, even if you think it was not as you wanted.'

'And after that, what happens?'

'I go with Ruari and you with Allie, I guess'

'What will you do with Ruari?' A note of jealousy crept into Rat's voice.

'You will learn that in group.'

Rat traced a finger along Hope's cleft, then jabbed into her cave. She flinched but did not move away. As he probed her, he seemed to forget his anger, caught up with the fascination of her juices and inner silkiness.

'Lie back,' he ordered, rising to his feet between her legs, his cock hardening.

Hope lay across the width of the hard desk and stared at the ceiling. Her breasts, exposed, but constrained by the bra, pointed upwards. She stretched her arms upwards and gripped the edge of the table behind her head, bracing herself for the inevitable. Soon she felt Rat push at her opening, and the hard entry of his shaft. He paused to lift her ankles so her heels rested on his shoulders, then started to rut deeply, and she closed her eyes. When he suddenly stopped, Hope was startled, sure that he was not ready to come.

'Keep your eyes closed,' he ordered harshly, breathing heavily.

Hope heard the soft pad of feet cross the library, then the sound of a zip being drawn down. A pair of strong hands tugged her further across the table, lifted her head and tied a hanky over her eyes.

'Who is it?' she whispered.

'You don't need to know,' Rat said. He remained inside her but lifted her hips higher so she was resting only on her upper back and shoulders, then he clambered on the desk and willing hands pulled her further across so her head fell back over the edge. Rat sat back on his haunches, leaned forward and braced his palms either side of Hope's waist. Her legs were now bent hard against her breasts and she found it hard to breathe.

'Grab my elbows, and slip your legs around my waist' he instructed, 'and hold tight or you will fall.' He shrugged her feet from his shoulders, and she drew them under his armpits with difficulty and surrounded his waist, locking her ankles behind his back. Then she let go of the table edge and groped until she felt Rat's arms, and gripped tightly. Her hips were still free of the wooden surface and he started to rock slowly, testing, then picked up speed.

Hands cupped her head to still it and she felt a cocktip brush her lips, swing past and then pendulum back, bumping her jaw. On the second pass she opened her mouth and stuck out her tongue to capture the weaving rod, succeeded and felt the bulb rest between her lips. She stretched her head as far back as she could and opened her throat. Above her she could hear a sudden harsh intake of breath and then the stranger eased forward and his prick filled her mouth. She could feel his hand circling his girth to avoid choking her and then the tentative first strokes as he tried to match Rat's rhythm. Soon the shafting gelled and Hope thrilled, recognizing that the men had achieved synchrony. She sunk into their possession, her holes opening easily, and soon the slick shaft penetrated deep into her throat, the shielding hand removed and keeping her head steady. She felt gloriously plundered, consumed deep within. The air was filled with harsh grunts and the liquid slap of penises tupping deeply.

'Now!' rasped Rat. He shuddered, still thrusting, and Hope felt the liquid burst into her throat while Rat spermed in her cave.

'Yes!' A voice growled above her head.

She felt awash, gulping and muscling, and her own coming seeped in a dull tide, rolling deep inside her and clenching as she ground into Rat, her thigh muscles burning with effort. The stranger slipped from her and held her head up so she could swallow. Cream slipped from the corners of her mouth and trickled over her cheeks and she let go of Rat's arms and stopped the flow with her fingers, massaging the fluid over her skin in small circles.

Rat slipped from her and she released her legs, letting her hips rest on the table top as he slid away. He grabbed her hips and swung her around so she lay lengthways and her head was supported. A hand squeezed her breast gently, then cupped her swollen, hot pudendum and finally stroked her thigh. She knew it was not Rat. Though sated, she realized that, were another to enter and take her, she would welcome his entry. It was as she had suspected, she was built for pleasure and wanted to please. Her legs lay wide open, her sex still rampant, and she felt submissive and yearning.

'This,' said Rat wonderingly, 'is what I intended.'

Hope heard the rustle of garments and zippers and footsteps and she realized she was alone. She felt very tired, warning herself she should dress and not go to sleep, even as she sank into welcoming darkness.

Chapter Nine

'Oh my God, Hope!'

The cry shocked Hope into confused wakefulness. She felt a moment's terror when she could not see, but swift fingers ripped off the blindfold, to leave her blinking in confusion. She sat up, groaning at the ache in her muscles, and rolled her shoulders to ease the stiffness. Awareness flooded in and she cast around to re-establish her surroundings, noting with relief that bright sunlight still filtered through the windows.

Allie rushed to help Hope from the desk and ease her into a chair. Her face was pale with worry. 'What happened? Who did this?'

'What?' Hope stammered, taken aback at Allie's intensity.

'Who attacked you?' Allie hugged Hope, stroking her hair and crooning soothingly.

Hope broke away and stared at her friend. She felt an hysterical swell of laughter threatening to escape but managed to contain it and shook her head mutely. She looked down at her torn skirt and stockings, her breasts still painfully bared and bound by the constricting bra. Her throat felt thick and raw and her lips tender. Fresh bruises threatened on the sensitive flesh of her inner thigh and her hands were grazed from hitting the floor earlier. She became aware of the sorry picture she presented and could not blame Allie, who had also found her blindfolded, for her assumption. She swallowed, then coughed to clear her throat and grabbed Allie's hands, gazing into her eyes.

'No one,' she whispered, cleared her throat once more and then stated firmly, 'No one assaulted me, Allie.'

'You look . . .' Allie gestured, lost for words.

Hope smiled and Allie shook her head, amazed. 'You wanted this?'

'Look, neither of them forced me, or beat me up. It just got a little – interesting. It looks a lot worse than it is.'

'*Them*?' Allie busied herself with tucking Hope's breasts into the bra cups and tugging the camisole into place.

'Yes, them. Except I don't know who the other one was because I was blindfolded. Anyway, how did you find me?' Hope pulled the jacket over her arms, grimacing at the resistance of her muscles.

'I met Rat and Rusty on the quay. They were going swimming, and Rusty told me where you were.'

They stared at each other.

'Ah,' Allie muttered. '*That* sort of nasty.'

'It was not so nasty. In fact, I enjoyed it!'

'I can see that now,' Allie sighed. 'Come on, let's get you tidied up before anyone sees you.' She pulled Hope to her feet and drew her to the door, checking before guiding her down the corridor.

The hallway was deserted and they broke from the passageway and raced up the stairwell, Hope's torn skirt flapping. They were unlucky on the landing. Angela stood in their way. She gave Hope an up and down look and smiled thinly, shook her head and continued mutely down the stairs.

Hope groaned and, responding to Allie's puzzled expression, explained, 'This is Angela's suit.'

She was surprised when Allie burst out laughing. 'You borrowed clothes from Angela?'

'Yup,' Hope confessed. 'In exchange for Mallot.'

Allie was silent when they entered Hope's room. She watched Hope discard the torn clothes and eventually said softly, 'Mallot was on the quay as well.'

Hope swung to face her, looking stricken, 'Not Mallot!'

'I don't know, Hope. Would it really matter that much? After all, you *were* blindfolded.'

'I just don't want Mallot to have that sort of advantage over me.'

'Hey, girl,' Allie hugged her, 'my money is on Rusty, okay? I think Mallot would do things up front and only if you begged for it.'

Hope snorted. 'That is true enough.' She wandered through the bathroom and ran the taps, sitting on the bath edge while the tub filled. 'Join me?' She slipped into the water, then stretched out, sighing happily.

'Love to,' Allie bowed, 'but I think I am too gentle for the likes of you! However, I will wash you.' She kneeled in front of the taps and soaped a sponge, then wiped softly over Hope's shoulders and breasts. 'So, who's next?'

'Ruari,' Hope mumbled, soothed by Allie's ministrations.

'Well, don't try and do them all in one day, okay? Lift your arm.'

'Got to give them something to talk about in group.'

Allie soaped the other arm. 'By the way, Ruari was in the hallway,' she advised, laughing when Hope sat up and slopped water on the floor. 'Look, we are supposed to tell all in the sessions so maybe someone will confess tonight.'

'I don't think he will,' Hope said, 'I think he wants to remain a mystery, but I really think it was Rusty because Ruari would have felt too uncomfortable to do stuff in front of Rat and Quinn is too shy.'

'I am with you on that one. Still, it seems a bit sneaky. Kneel and turn around.'

'Sneaky is the whole point.' Hope grinned wickedly and earned a smack on her bottom. 'More,' she demanded and laughed when Allie groaned in horror, but obliged.

'Is there anything you don't want?'

Hope swivelled to face Allie and said softly, 'I said not to be shocked.'

'I'm not shocked. I'm just a little worried about you,' Allie confessed and kissed Hope on the tip of her nose. 'Anyway, I get the Rat-man next, don't I?'

'Yeah,' Hope smiled at her friend, 'you sure do. Give him hell!'

'Is he any good?' Allie soaped between Hope's thighs gently, noticed her wince, and resisted taking it further.

'Not saying. You tell me in the session, after you have had him.'

'Out.' Allie climbed from the bath tub and held up a towel. She patted the blonde down, tutting at the bruising on her thighs. 'You have three hours before supper so I shall get you a cup of tea from Mairead and then you sleep.'

'I would like that.' Hope hugged her impulsively. 'You are good to me!'

'Why not?' Allie asked. 'You are pretty hard on yourself so someone needs to treat you gently.' She smiled as she spoke but Hope knew she was being serious. She followed

Allie into the bedroom and allowed herself to be tucked under the sheet. Allie left and returned shortly with a big mug of black tea and slices of fruit cake.

'Mairead likes the fact that you used the library,' she explained. 'So you are to be spoilt rotten. I reckon she thinks you read books in there.' She smirked.

They shared the tea and cake, taking alternate sips from the cup. Then Allie set Hope's alarm clock to allow her time before supper to wash and dress.

'I am going to swim and check out the talent. See you in the dining room.' She kissed Hope's cheek and watched her snuggle down. As she made her way to her own room she wondered about Rusty, feeling disappointed. One part of her was roused by him, but she did not think she would enjoy the sort of treatment to which Hope seemed to respond. Of course, she reasoned, it might not have been Rusty, but deep down she believed it was. By the time she had slipped on a swimming costume and joined the group on the quay, she was determined to learn more about Hope's faceless lover and, as the only witness, it would be Rat who would tell her.

She noted that Rat had crossed the bay and was stretched out on the far shore. It was a narrow crossing but thick with rock outcrops. Undaunted, Allie floated on her stomach, peering into the water, and found it shallow enough to wade across. She made slow progress but sank no deeper than her chest. Rat seemed unaware of her approach and, when she tiptoed up the sandy bank, she realized he was sound asleep in spite of the discomfort of his gritty mattress. She stretched out beside him and studied him.

Rat's eyes were hidden. He had flung his arm over his face to block out the sun. His hair spread over the pebbles, still slightly damp, and his chest rose and fell smoothly. His shorts had dried and settled softly over the bulge at his crotch and his legs were stretched straight out, slightly parted. Allie stared at his groin, imagining him hard and pumping into Hope, his neck ridged with effort and the sweat streaming down his chest. She wondered what he had been thinking when the stranger plundered Hope's mouth, presuming that his pleasure was made more intense in being shared. She admitted that the idea of sharing Hope excited her, perhaps more so because she suspected the other man to be Rusty. Not for the first time, Allie wished she was a man.

The site Rat had chosen could be clearly seen from the quay, a gap between fallen trees and a tumble of rocks. Behind her, Allie could see that the bush seemed impenetrable, a thicket of low, glossy-leafed shrubs and sharp, tall grasses. Low tree branches swept the ground to forbid access. Apart from the slight lap of water on the pebbles, it was silent. A length of rope snaked the waterline, snaking gently, one end tangled in the bare branches of a tree that had fallen to lie head first in the shallows, the other end weaving as if seeking escape in the open water. The day had lost its burning heat and the late-afternoon light slanted gently, shadows threatening, as the sun made its way over the hills of the bay. Allie figured they had an hour of warmth left before the shadows claimed them. She returned her attention to Rat, who had not moved.

She had assumed that, when Rat and Hope fucked, she would watch. It was an idea she had formed on the launch trip to the island, after she and Hope had agreed that they wanted to watch each other. She was curious to see how Hope behaved with men but, after her fright when she found her in the library, she was now less certain. However, she felt cheated by the man who lay sleeping easily by her side. Allie did not want to be screwed by Rat, she wanted to watch him fuck Hope. He was attractive, she acknowledged, not up to Rusty's standard but cute and untended. It seemed odd that Rusty, not Rat, seemed the one least couth, when their appearances suggested the reverse.

Now she was lined up to bed Rat. She realized that she could reject him but she did not want to, she just wanted to share him with Hope. He could not have any objection, he had already shared Hope with someone else, and in a way that Allie found disturbing. She gazed at the water, an idea forming. Among the debris washed up on the shore was a miscellany of rags, unidentifiable apart from a faded blue pennant. She slipped from Rat's side and tugged at the rope. It was nearly fifteen feet long, double-twisted blue cord and, apart from a little mud, seemed unaffected by its submersion. She waded into the water and untangled it from the tree branches. It could not, she decided, have been there long, nor the pennant which, rinsed in the bay, proved to be of thick, supple cotton, the sort used for racing signals at mastheads.

Although she was nervous, Allie decided to carry out her impromptu plan, and started by carefully separating the cords, ending up with two lengths. The first she doubled, looping it over a thick limb of the submerged tree and creating two nooses with slip knots, which she laid either side of Rat's feet. She excavated the pebbles under his heels carefully, her breath held, until she could slip the rope around his ankles and gently tighten the loops. Rat stirred but did not wake. She stared at him, considering what to do with the second length and realized that that part of the plan would be far more tricky to engineer. She clenched the wet pennant between her teeth and crept to the edge of the bushes.

Allie looped the rope around an overhanging branch of a tree and tugged. The branch bowed but resisted her attempts to break it. Satisfied, she let go and fastened the loop firmly so it would not slip, then returned to crouch behind Rat's head. She pulled until she felt the firm resistance of the branch, then fashioned two nooses part-way up the length of rope. This would be the worst moment. She had to slip the nooses over Rat's hands, let go and tie the pennant around his eyes before he saw her. If she had judged correctly, he would try to pull and kick only to find himself bound and helpless. She was not certain of the accuracy of her measurements, but judged they would suffice to hold him captive.

She was sweating from the effort of holding the tree branch and her feet threatened to give way on the grit when she suddenly slipped the loops over Rat's hands, scrambled back, and let go of the rope. Rat's arms were dragged from his face sharply, pulled straight up and then back. The branch righted itself and held firm, the nooses tightened and Rat came awake, swearing loudly in shock. He kicked and bucked, as Allie had predicted, and discovered himself captured. Before he could swing around to trace his attacker, Allie scrambled to slip the pennant over his eyes, struggling to tie it in place as his head whipped. Then she scuttled a safe distance away to watch and wait.

'What the fuck!' Rat roared and struggled against his bonds. Then, realizing that he was only increasing his discomfort, he stilled. He tested his legs, then his arms, and neither allowed him more than six inches of play. Allie was concerned that the loops would choke his circulation if he fought too hard, but they did not seem to be cutting too cruelly and there was enough spring in the branch for his shoulders to touch the ground lightly. He wriggled and found the grit beneath him uncomfortable, so he settled, his mouth an angry, hard line.

'This is not funny!' he ground out. 'Who is there?'

Allie remained silent, then crept forward and crouched beside Rat, placing her palm over his heart, ready to spring away if he bucked. He flinched and she could feel the tremor run through him and his heart race. He was breathing swiftly, shallow, angry breaths. She stroked, trying to soothe them, and was rewarded when he seemed to relax. He twisted his head in her direction but could not see through his blindfold.

'Hope, is that you?' He sounded hopeful. 'Look, I can tell it is a woman's hand!'

Allie, sure that he was now under her control, however tenuous, concentrated on calming herself. She had been unprepared for the harsh realities of her action, and for the fear that had charged through her as Rat had woken, furious in his bonds. Now, however, she felt powerful. Rat outweighed her by at least four stone and had twice her strength, yet lay helpless, spread for her enjoyment. She had wanted to show him how it felt to be blindfolded and defenceless, hoping that he would recognize the humiliation and be kinder to Hope if he tried it again.

'What are you going to do?' Rat sounded nervous.

Allie drew her palm over his chest and stomach, then cupped and squeezed his penis through the cloth of his shorts. He was soft and she stroked gently until she felt him respond. When he was fully erect she let go, pleased at his small whimper of disappointment. She tucked her fingers under his waistband and tugged, until he raised his hips and let her slide his shorts to mid-thigh. She stripped her suit off, sliding it beneath him to protect his naked bumcheeks from the stones, then crouched over his chest and shuffled back until her quim grazed his mouth. Allie placed her hands either side of his hips and leaned forward, to take his cockhead between her lips.

Rat's sharp expulsion of breath felt delightful against her now swelling nether folds and, to encourage his participation, she went to work with enthusiasm. She sucked him, nursing at his velvety bulb like a hungry child, wetting him with her saliva and pursing around him with eager lips. She ran her tongue beneath his glans, nuzzling at the flange, and filled her mouth, then sucked in her cheeks. Allie was beginning to enjoy her task and when Rat tentatively licked her pussy, she shivered with pleasure, which resulted in him tonguing firmly among her soft, moist tissues, hunting until he pressed softly on her pearl. She lowered her hips and his lips captured her, sucking gently. They fed until Allie felt herself swell and her demand become rampant. She lifted one hand from the pebbles and wiped it on the swimsuit beneath Rat's hips, then held his cock and pumped gently.

He moaned, losing his hold on her clit but burying his mouth deeper into her cleft, his breath hot and quick. He lifted his hips eagerly, his excitement heightened by his bonds. He was afraid she would stop, leaving him helpless to complete his sexual release, and his fear added intensity. He bucked, heedless of the small stones raking his back and moaned happily when she swallowed more of him and he met the resistance of her throat. He thrust his cockhead into her and hunted with his mouth until he found her entry, then pumped furiously with his tongue. Allie pushed into his face and he was drenched with her wetness, his attention split between the thrilling of his groin and the flow of her sweet juices.

Allie bobbed her head steadily, pumping on his shaft until she felt the swell and tremble that preceded Rat's coming. She inhaled deeply on her next rise, opened her throat and then swallowed his length, her hand falling away to massage his balls firmly. She held firm as he surged and ground her quim into his mouth and chin. Her throat constricted, her muscles fighting for air, and her head grew faint. She was racked with orgasm when Rat spouted, filling her throat and sliding out, into her mouth, to complete his outpouring. She swallowed feverishly, then took a long breath when he slid from her lips. She licked his penis delicately until it lay blushing and sated in a peaceful comma at his groin. Between her legs she could feel Rat reciprocate and when he eased his head back, she rose and tugged his shorts up over his hips, drawing her swimsuit from under him. She pulled it on and, without looking back, made her way to the water's edge.

'I will know who you are eventually, you know,' Rat said. 'I will remember the taste and texture of you.' He listened intently and heard her paddle into the water. 'Wait. You can't leave me like this!' But he received no response except the sound of someone wading away. He rested his head back on the pebbles, resigned, and remembered how he had left Hope alone in the library. He felt a chill creep over him, assuming this was her pay-back. Without sight he became more aware of the sough of wind in the bushes behind him and the trickle of water through the pebbles at the water's edge. He felt vulnerable but strangely peaceful, the tingle at his groin pleasant, although his back felt scored and the muscles of his arms painful.

Rat rubbed the toes of one foot against the rope binding the neighbouring ankle, discovered the slip knot and managed to work it loose to free his foot. He then liberated the other in the same way. He shuffled on his back towards the tree and felt the rope slacken until he could free his hands then ripped the pennant from his eyes, blinking at the brightness then staring towards the quay. He was too late. Whoever had taken advantage of him was nowhere to be seen. He smiled grimly and set out for the quay, believing that he would uncover his assailant later and return the favour.

The quay was deserted and the house silent as he made his way to his room and gathered his toiletries. Rat entered the bathroom to find Allie in the bath, oblivious to his presence. He studied her, then shook his head dismissively. Allie, he felt, would have the courage to do something like that, and she was Hope's friend, but she lacked the nous. He felt sure, too, that she would not act alone.

Allie dipped her head underwater, then rose, shook the water from her hair and turned, startled when she saw Rat in the doorway. Afraid to give herself away if she said anything, she merely cocked her head and shooed him with her hand, but to no avail. Rat simply smiled and drew closer.

'Why? It is you and I next.'

'It doesn't have to be,' Allie protested, holding her arm over her breasts and cupping her mound.

'You weren't this coy with Hope,' he observed, surprising himself with his determination. He recognized that something in him had changed. He felt predatory and driven: his fantasies, once they had materialized, seemed to make all things possible. Hope's confessions of sexual ambition in the group had introduced him to real possibilities and his helpless experience on the shore had left him hungry to reaffirm his control.

'And I think it *does* have to be you and me. I want you. Come on, this is your chance to be the woman you want to be. You wanted to be feminine, why not start now?' His voice had grown persuasive, his eyes warm and his cock hard. He discarded his toiletries and shorts and stepped into the bath with Allie.

She stared at him, sure that he had not connected her with his recent treatment. With the memory of her taste and the texture and composition of her corolla fresh in Rat's mouth and memory, she was afraid to submit but felt herself responding.

'Not without Hope,' she managed at last.

'I am here, don't worry.'

They swung to find Hope framed in the doorway, herself intent on bathing. She was naked, flushed, and her eyes glittered.

Rat leapt from the bath, drenching the floor, and grabbed her shoulders. 'That was not funny.' he growled. He glared at her and realized immediately that she was ignorant of his bondage, her expression bewildered. Embarrassed, he relinquished his hold and stepped back with a mumbled apology.

'What was not funny?' Hope demanded, blazing. 'I only came to bath.'

'Not that. Something that happened to me earlier.' He had lost his erection. In Hope's presence he had shrivelled, his swaggering at Allie countered.

Hope watched him carefully but he did not explain. She

glanced at Allie who was staring at Rat's back with horrid fascination. Intrigued, Hope circled behind him and gasped when she saw the scoring.

'How did you do that?' She touched his back gently, and he flinched and moved away.

'It is a long story,' Rat grumbled.

'I guess,' said Hope, 'that you had better be on top, then.'

Rat turned to face her. 'Are you serious?' he asked and she nodded, smiling slightly, then joined Allie. They made him wait while they soaped each other and rinsed, then invited him to join them, just as the dinner gong sounded.

Allie felt relieved. She had responded enthusiastically to Hope's soapy attentions but not to the point where her appetite for food had abated. She was also curious to see what the group's evening session with the Ormandies would reveal, although she was resolved that she would not confess her part in Rat's bondage.

'Food!' she exclaimed brightly as Rat groaned with disappointment.

Hope agreed and dashed into her room to emerge in sweats and a loose T-shirt, her feet bare and hair still wet. Allie joined her, clad in lycra running shorts and tank top.

'I think our couture is taking a serious dive,' Hope commented, nodding meaningfully when Rat emerged in loose Bermuda shorts and vest.

'Speak for yourselves.' Angela came down the attic stairs, resplendent in a skin-tight black catsuit, her hair plaited and falling over one shoulder. 'I hear,' she addressed Hope, 'that there was some excitement in the library this afternoon? You certainly do not waste time, but I did notice that waste does apply to clothes. Like suits, for instance.'

'Oh la,' Allie interjected. 'Hark at Catwoman.'

She earned a withering look from Angela, who proceeded down the stairs gracefully, in spite of the spiky sandals she was wearing. Aware of her audience, her body language became provocative, the sway of her hips increased and, once she reached the lobby, she bent over, brushing an imaginary fleck of dust from her tightly sheathed thigh. Her tight, round bottom weaved sweetly, free of pantyline. Hope and Allie exchanged grimaces but Rat seemed entranced, which caused them to shake their heads ruefully.

'Maybe,' Allie said, clearly enough for Angela to hear, 'you should take on Angela next, Rat.'

'Why not?' Mallot's voice came from behind them. He stood three steps above, a study in casualness, as his eyes roved over Angela critically, 'I am sure she would like some fresh young meat.' He passed them, expressionless, and drew alongside Angela, lifted her chin with his fingers and stared deeply into her eyes. 'Would you like that?' Without waiting for her response he let go and slid his hand over her small breast, squeezing once, then continuing until he cupped her between her legs.

'I think,' he continued, 'you would like that very much.' He squeezed and Angela lifted to her toes, a pink blush flooding her cheeks. Her lips opened slightly and she wet them with her tongue. 'I think that this little cunt of yours needs a whole variety of cocks and young Rat is a good place to start. I am sure he would be eager, almost as eager as you, in fact.' He turned to face Rat, still kneading Angela's clothed pudendum. 'She's insatiable, this one. In fact, I don't think she even knows who is at her once she gets going.'

'Quit it,' Rat said, although his penis had risen to tent his shorts and he sounded breathless.

'You could take her now, here,' Mallot taunted, 'in front of everyone. In fact, I think the women might enjoy watching.' He raised his eyebrows, glancing at Hope.

Angela had closed her eyes and was rocking gently against Mallot's hand, lending truth to his words. Hope was mesmerized, staring at the swaying woman and feeling an empathy. She almost willed Rat forward, imagining Angela stripped naked and impaled on his shaft, keening as her desire overrode her awareness. The pale blonde was lost in sensation, to the extent she excluded her surroundings. Strangely, Hope felt no anger towards Mallot because it was clear Angela liked his pimping. Not unlike, Hope reminded herself, what Reggie had done with her and the masked man.

Allie seemed less affected: she brushed past Rat and attempted to press past Mallot. 'You're a real snake charmer,' she hissed, then yelped in surprise as his other arm shot around her and gathered her hard into him.

His lips almost upon hers, he enunciated very clearly, 'And you, little tomboy, need to be taught to be a lady!' He ground his mouth on hers while Allie struggled. Then she stilled, suddenly responsive, her lips parting and her tongue seeking his.

If Mallot was surprised, he rallied well. Angela, her mound still clasped, squeaked with excitement, her eyes now open and widely fixed on Allie. It was clear that she encouraged Mallot's mastery and rallied to support his conquest. He lessened his hold on Allie and his lips swept softly against hers, his tongue winding sensualy. He watched her face, his eyes lidded and assessing. Allie suddenly bit hard, then darted from him, her expression blazing with dislike. Mallot flinched and let go of Angela. He touched his tongue and examined the drop of blood on his finger, then licked it, smiling at Allie, who now stood out of reach, glaring at him like an enraged cat.

'Who was it who accused someone else of being "Catwoman"?' he asked, his eyes cold. He moved towards Allie, who again darted out of reach. 'Oh, don't worry,' he said, 'I like a bit of spark in a woman.' His voice dropped and he whispered, 'It gives me an interest.' He laughed and reached for Angela, who moved obediently into his embrace. Catching Rat's eye, he winked, 'I shall keep her on the bubble during dinner, shall I? Perhaps we can make tonight's session a little interesting.' He drew past Allie, seemingly without further interest, and into the dining room.

They all filed in after him, mumbling their apologies to Mairead, who nodded forgivingly and directed them to the *crudités* in the centre of the table.

'Want to tell us about it?' Brandon asked.

Surprisingly it was Angela who answered, her chin held high with pride. 'Yes. Mallot offered me to Rat.' She ignored Allie's snort of derision, 'He said he would keep me on the bubble through dinner.'

'How do you propose to do that, Mallot?' Brandon leaned forward and a silent message seemed to pass, grey eyes soft and interrogatory on the narrowed black.

Mallot nodded imperceptibly and reached behind Angela. The sound of the zipper seemed loud in the hushed tension at the dinner table, and then the top of her catsuit fell away to reveal her naked, outthrust beasts. Angela did not demur. She sat staring into Brandon's face as his gaze swept her.

Mallot casually leaned over and selected a length of celery from the centre plate, dipped its frondy head into a bowl of *guacamole* and painted Angela's small globes with gentle sweeps. He leaned back, like an artist considering his work, and took a bite from the celery stalk.

Angela shivered, the avocado dip cold on her skin, and bit her bottom lip. Her eyes roved across the company, settling on those of Rat, who stared back in fascination. Elsa, to the left of Rat, sat open-mouthed and Ruari, seated next to her, blushed deeply. Quinn wore a puzzled expression, as if unable to comprehend the scene. He blinked and cast about, trying to determine if his peers were more aware than he, but could determine nothing in their expressions.

Hope felt remote, but interested. She had not managed to stand back from the scene in the lobby, and Mallot's continuing titillation of Angela seemed natural. She recognized that these were strange times and that this scene had nothing to do with her. Delighted, she could sit back and watch. It was clear that Rat was targeted and he sat, barely breathing and tense, to her left. Allie, on her right, slid her hand into Hope's, who realized that the young woman was feeling nervous after her clash with Mallot. It seemed that he now controlled the table, with the blessing of Brandon.

It was Rusty who broke the spell. 'Well, I for one have always seen the advantages of watching paint dry!' He leaned back in his chair, his hands behind his head and stared at Angela's dip-dampened breasts.

Mallot laughed, leaned over Angela, and licked her breasts clean. When she attempted to lift her top back in place he snapped, 'Leave it!'

It seemed that collective breaths were expelled when

Angela simpered, then, after seeking permission from Mallot, leaned forward to collect an array of dips on her side plate. She moved without inhibition, as if still clothed, but her small, pale breasts bobbed and commanded attention from her fellow diners.

'This is nice,' remarked Karen, 'perhaps we ought to try being naked together, like we were in a naturist camp.' She beamed around the table, soliciting amazed looks in return.

'I would feel comfortable with that,' Rusty agreed.

'What about, you know . . .' Ruari attempted, then failed.

'Hard-ons?' supplied Brandon. 'What could be more natural?'

'I don't think I want to take off all my clothes in front of everyone. I am too fat,' Elsa protested, then stared at her plate, embarrassed.

'You're not!' protested Quinn. 'You are lovely!'

'I think so too.' Karen clapped her hands girlishly. 'What do you say, folks, shall we try it?'

Allie cast despairing eyes at the ceiling. 'Have you all gone crazy?'

'Well,' Brandon explained reasonably, 'now it has been said, it is in all our minds, so why don't we just make our own choices?' He looked at Mallot, who nodded and stood up, stepped behind his chair and pushed it under the table. Angela immediately followed suit and, one by one, the diners rose. There was a momentary pause on the part of Elsa and a longer one by Ruari, but eventually they joined in.

Angela, already unzipped, merely wriggled, and her catsuit slithered from her. She kicked her sandals from her feet and stepped out of the garment, leaning over to pick it up, smooth it and lay it carefully over the back of her chair. She straightened, tossed her head and her plait swept over her shoulder to nestle, snakelike, between her breasts, its tip arrowing at the sparse ice-blond curls of her mound and drawing all eyes to her cleft. She stared defiantly, a slight curl to her lips, her eyes wide and her expression proud under the massed examination.

Mallot slowly undid his silk shirt, tugging the ends from the waistband of his slacks and allowing it to fall softly from his arms. All had seen him naked aboard the launch but still stared as he dropped his trousers, then his boxer shorts, to reveal his shaven groin and generous genitals. Hope's fingers tingled, eager to trace through the heavy mat of hair mantling his shoulders and chest and as if clairvoyant he smiled and rubbed his palm over his dark nipples, staring into her eyes in invitation.

Rusty was next. He stripped as if he were on stage in a nightclub, his eyes downcast and sultry, his bottom lip pouting. He tugged the clasp from his hair and leaned his head back, closing his eyes to shake his ponytail loose, then tossed his head forward and allowed his copper-gold locks to shroud his face. Another small toss and the glowing curtain opened to reveal his smoky blue gaze, now fixed absently on the centre of the table. He drew his vest from his chest, his muscles rippling, and balled it, tossing it at the corner of the room and then he swept his hair from his face, using both hands and weaving so the audience could enjoy the full splendour of his torso. He unzipped and slithered from his denim cut-offs, then turned and hooked his thumbs in the back of his briefs, sliding them down while bunching his buttocks to produce an hypnotic play of muscles. He kicked his briefs from his feet, over his tennis shoes, then turned back to face the table, his smooth shaft lying peacefully in a nest of thick curls, golden fleece which he fluffed with his fingers into soft clouds, before looking innocently around the assembly.

'So,' muttered Allie, 'tell us all about this modelling you do?'

'That's about it, for beginners,' muttered Rusty and sparked everyone's imagination.

Allie nodded and shed her tank top and Bermuda shorts efficiently. She retained her small panties, patting them determinedly as if daring anyone to try and get them off her. In build there seemed little between Angela and Allie but in stance they were worlds apart. Allie stood naturally, balanced a little aggressively on her heels while Angela was pouting and posing, ensuring she displayed herself at her optimum. The contrast was not lost on the men and they gazed from one to the other in indecision. It seemed that Angela's mixed messages were more alluring, her ice-maiden colouring at odds with her submissive openness. Allie, however, enticed, with her wild red curls and flashing blue eyes, full of heat and slightly frightening. Aware of being watched, Allie stuck her tongue out and crossed her arms, her gaze challenging until most looked away.

Hope felt vulnerable. Her contours were more generous and she was not yet as comfortable as Angela in her sexuality, nor as easy with nudity as Allie. It was her turn and she fumbled as she drew her T-shirt over her head, then draped it gently over her chair. Her round breasts bobbed to stillness, trembling as she bent to slide her sweats over her legs, and swaying as she released one foot and then the other. Her lace panties had drawn down with the sweats and rucked at her groin, leaving her in a torment of indecision whether to take them off or pull them up. Surrendering, she slipped them down, soliciting a sharp hiss from Rat. When she stood straight, she felt she could not catch anyone's eye, so kept her gaze downwards, holding onto the back of her chair for support. Her blush was real but she felt a shy pride in her nakedness. Eventually she chanced a sideways glance at Rat, who was staring at her with unashamed appreciation.

Rat, although he had been drawn by Angela's explicit sexuality and Allie's mild defiance, suddenly recalled why the full brunt of his lusts centred on Hope. She was a Madonna in his eyes, her milky, rounded breasts generous and enticing, the slight round of her stomach pleasing to the palm and her newly shaven pubis soft and hungry. He recalled her long, smooth thighs open to him and her wet folds sucking around him, and his rod hardened in betrayal. With harsh pride he stripped jerkily and revealed his excited manhood to her, his tribute to her womanliness. He revelled in her slightly glazed acknowledgement when her gaze rested on him to examine his weaving bulb. To emphasize his need, he thrust his hips forward and his tip brushed her thigh. She did not move away, in fact she stroked him once, softly, as if approving his cocksure display, then she seemed to become aware of the watchers and allowed herself to look around and make eye contact. No one but Mallot was looking up. He gazed steadily into her eyes and she once again received an uncomfortable feeling of *déjà vu*. Before she could examine this, Elsa slid beside her, muscling in between her and Rat.

'Help me,' the young woman whispered, her eyes imploring. While others strained to hear, these words were for

Hope alone and she warmed to Elsa. She bent near to her ear and whispered, 'Are you happy to do this?' and felt Elsa nod, her dark curls tickling Hope's nose. Hope stood back and unbuttoned the top of Elsa's shirt, while she started from the bottom. They giggled when their hands met and mock-fought over the last button. At once Elsa's strip became fun, like children playing, and they tussled over which arm should first be freed, their laughter now ringing through the room.

Entranced, the group watched as Elsa made a break and scuttled around the table, Hope chasing and capturing her to swiftly unclip her white cotton bra and tug the ends while the young woman defiantly cupped her breasts, resisting its removal. But it was all in fun and Elsa raced to the sideboard, dodging from Hope's approach then tossing her bra, with a jubilant shout, to find it fielded by Mairead, who chuckled and folded it carefully before laying it tidily beside the trifle dish.

'Oops!' shouted Elsa, racing to the bay window, where she was rounded up by Hope and made to sit in the alcove seat and have her leggings tugged from her, her panties following. Shy and subdued, but smiling and her eyes twinkling, Elsa was led back to the table but stationed at Rat's seat, next to Hope. There were approving chuckles and good-natured smiles, a chorus of positive feedback directed at the wildly blushing young woman. Her hair was mussed, the thick black curls tumbling madly around her shoulders and her generous breasts thrusting up in glowing mounds. Her skin was almost translucent, lightly veined with blue, shining with youth and health. She was voluptuous, rounded and soft, the hair of her mound thick and springing and her thighs shivering, enticing cushions.

'Oh, you are so beautiful!' Hope exclaimed spontaneously and hugged Elsa, feeling the delightful soft give of her and the gentle squashing of their breasts. When they parted, laughing and slightly breathless, Elsa looked down at her breasts, startled as her nipples peaked with enjoyment. She clapped her hands self-consciously to cover them and giggled her embarrassment, then, assured by Hope's warm smile, dropped her arms and peered a challenge at Ruari, leaning across Rat to do so. She grimaced at Rat's erection, as if it were a mere irritation, and earned more chuckles.

Ruari, looking painfully shy, stripped to his Y-fronts, his stare fixed blindly ahead and his mouth set in a straight, hard line. The good humour generated by the cavorting women held, however, and he suffered graciously under the assembled stares. He was caught in the gentle wane of an erection, the product, Rat guessed of the massed, naked female flesh. Even Rat had to concede the nobility of Ruari, tall and carved from granite. Not beautiful and alluring, like Rusty, but with a hewn impressiveness, a hard and unyielding strength. It seemed that if he bent he would break, simply because his square-jawed determination would not allow compromise. A mass of curls coated his chest, not thick like Mallot's but inviting gentle fingers to weave through them. He had discarded his clothes with the same unconcern with which he wore them and they lay in a crumpled heap at his feet.

Quinn good-naturedly shucked his clothes, strutting in parody of a stripper and soliciting a slow clap to which he could prance. He ground his hips and sucked in his soft stomach as he tugged his polo shirt over his head, leaving his hair standing in raggedy ends of surprise. He swayed in time as he slid his elastic-waisted shorts over his hips, his bottom weaving and buttocks jostling as he tussled with his sandals and freed his feet. He also chose to retain his boxers, blinking happily and smoothing his hair as he rose, flushed and smiling, to take a bow.

The only ones left dressed were Mairead, Karen and Brandon and it did not seem odd when the housekeeper retained her clothes and scurried about collecting and folding the strewn garments carefully. She seemed unfazed by the nudity, which made Hope wonder how many times she had witnessed this scene. Karen and Brandon undressed without fuss. The American woman sported a tattoo on her left breast, an exquisite rendering of a butterfly in brilliant colours, which she invited all to touch whenever they felt unhappy or confused.

'It is for soothing,' she explained, 'like a woman's breast, for succour and nurturing.' Despite the poetry of her announcement, the result was that the group stared interestedly at her and the other women in more than peaceful interest.

Brandon was slight, smooth-chested, and balanced easily on his feet. He stroked his beard happily and explained that he practised *t'ai chi chuan* for relaxation and meditation. He drew his fingers under his solar plexus and breathed in, his beard rising with his ribcage, and let the air flow to his stomach, pushing it out alarmingly and causing his penis to jiggle. When Elsa giggled, he smiled ruefully and confirmed it was a learned taste, which caused Allie to chuckle and then he gave up, shaking his head in mock severity.

'Well,' Karen said brightly, 'shall we eat?' She drew back her chair and sat down, drawing a linen napkin over her lap.

At first Hope found it bizarre to be naked at a dinner party and it seemed that her feeling was shared: no one seemed to know where to look, each glance chancing upon a breast or nude chest. By dessert it seemed more familiar and, when they rose to take coffee in the lounge, they adjusted easily to the sight of jostling buttocks as they filed from the dining room. Before they were able to take their familiar seats, Brandon held up his hands.

'A suggestion. Perhaps you could choose your own seats, align with the person with whom you feel most empathy, or perhaps wish to know better.'

The group shuffled and Hope sandwiched herself between Elsa and Ruari, Angela found herself between Rat and Quinn and Allie was flanked by Mallot and Rusty.

'Great,' Karen nodded. 'Now tell me why you chose these seats.' She turned to Mallot expectantly.

'I didn't,' he shrugged, 'I have been here all along and I want to know everyone better so there was no right place to be.'

'Nor me,' Allie chipped in. 'It was just the last seat and I don't mind sitting near Rusty.' She deliberately glared at Mallot, making sure that all were aware that the last place she would choose to be, unless forced, was near him.

Karen did not miss it. 'You want to tell us why you don't like Mallot?'

'I think he is arrogant and unlikeable, and I see no reason why he feels entitled to his grossly overrated opinion of himself.'

Mallot stared at Allie. 'Well, perhaps I can give you a reason,' he said. 'See me later.'

'You see?' Allie exploded from her seat. 'That is exactly what I mean!'

'Oh, calm down,' Angela said, 'he has good reason to rate himself.'

'Oh, right! And you, of course, would know, Miss Icy with the wide-open legs.' Allie loomed over Angela, her hands on her hips and her chin thrust out belligerently.

'Yes, I would know, actually. He melted my ice and I have no doubt he would dampen your fire too,' Angela sneered.

'Oh for a chance,' Mallot quipped, his palms pressed together in prayer and his eyes rolling at the ceiling.

'I give up!' Allie sat cross-legged on the floor between Rusty's legs in preference to retaking her place at Mallot's side. As an afterthought she cupped her hands over her naked sex, but not before Rat and Quinn had ogled her. She cocked her head and squinted at them, causing Quinn to blush and Rat to chuckle.

Rusty looked a little taken aback. With Allie between his thighs he was unable to close his legs and was painfully aware, when the attention turned to him, that his genitals were exposed and vulnerable. He was unused to operating without choices. Even when under direction, he chose his own space and now Allie had reduced his options. He liked her, however, her fire and ready wit, her ability to stand up and shout without thought. She seemed determined and active, where he believed himself weak and passive. However tempted he felt, he could not push her away and avoid the stares directed at his groin.

'You guys want to look at my face?' he demanded and felt enormous satisfaction when guilty eyes lifted to his. Once assured that he held their attention, in the right place, he continued, 'I sat here because I wanted to be between Hope and Allie, but I could not get closer to Hope.'

'You wanted to be closer to Hope?' Karen prompted.

'I want to talk with her, as I said before, and she agreed.'

'Good.' Karen looked at Ruari.

'I just sat down and found myself next to Hope. I think she sat next to me.' Ruari sat awkwardly in the corner of the sofa, seeming to be as far from Hope as he could manage. He still felt uncomfortable without his clothes, although he was grateful that his Y-fronts hid his privates.

'I did sit next to him,' Hope confessed. 'He is next on the list.'

'Ah, do you want to share with us?' Brandon leaned forward, interested.

Hope nodded and took a deep breath, then glanced at Rat who shut his eyes softly, his hands clenched nervously in his lap. 'Rat and I did it in the library.'

'So who doesn't know that?' Angela demanded. 'It was broadcast all over the house five minutes later.'

'By whom?' Hope asked softly.

'Yes, by whom?' Allie parroted.

'I heard it from Rusty,' Angela said.

Allie swivelled to face him, disconcerted to discover her eyes level with his golden groin. Recovering, she stared hard into his eyes.

'I heard it from Rat!'

'So who was the other guy?' Allie persisted.

'There was another guy?' Rusty looked with genuine bewilderment at Rat.

'There was another guy,' confirmed Hope. 'We thought it was you, Rusty.'

'How come you don't know who it was?' Rusty asked.

'I was blindfolded.'

'Wait up,' Karen intervened. 'Perhaps Hope can tell us what happened and then we can talk about it.'

'I went to the study to meet Rat. We . . .' She paused. 'We fucked. Then, when we did it again, someone else came in and slipped a blindfold on me and joined in.'

Elsa had turned to face Hope, her expression alive with curiosity. 'How?'

Hope risked an answer, her eyes kind, 'Rat took me and I lay across a table so the other man could use my mouth.'

'Oh,' Elsa blinked and caught her lower lip between her teeth. 'Was that okay?' She seemed to be looking for reassurance.

'For me it was,' Hope answered gently and Elsa gave a tiny nod, satisfied.

'I don't think,' she said in a small voice, 'that I would find that okay, for me.'

Hope hugged her impulsively, laughing. 'We are all different. I did say that I wanted all sorts of things.' She returned her attention to the group. 'However, I do want us all to agree one thing, and that is a safe word. I am used to that being "cave".'

'I agree, and I think that we should all say it out loud.' Mallot said.

'Okay, but what is a safe word?' Elsa asked.

'It is a word we can use and it will mean that, no matter what someone is doing to you, they must immediately stop doing it.'

'Cave,' Elsa said promptly.

'Everyone?' Brandon said, 'with me, ten times then one at a time. Cave, cave.'

The group chanted the word, then one by one, their faces serious, they repeated it.

'Will everyone treat that word as sacrosanct?' Karen asked and received a chorus of consent. 'What does it mean, Quinn?' She chose him randomly.

'It means the strongest of noes and must always be obeyed.'

Hope nodded, relieved.

'Do you want to know who the other man was, Hope?' Brandon quizzed.

'No, I don't think I do want to know. Not right now. I think it would spoil things.'

'I want to know!' Allie burst out. 'I found Hope all torn and blindfolded and I thought she had been abused.' Her voice caught and a suspicion of tears shone in her eyes as she recalled her fright.

Rusty leaned forward and stroked her hair soothingly and she leaned her head back, swallowing to control her tears. Her head rested against his penis, which remained limp.

Rat was amazed. He knew that were he to be nestled against, he would harden immediately. Even now he felt stirred by the sight. His excitement died and he guiltily realized that, apart from the man involved, he was the only one who could identify Hope's faceless fuck, and he had no intention of so doing. Hope was right when she said it would spoil things. He shuffled uncomfortably, drawing attention.

'I was attacked late this afternoon,' he blurted. This was news to the group and they stilled intently. 'I was sleeping on the shore of the bay and a woman tied me up, blindfolded me and gave me a blowjob.'

'Oh my God,' exclaimed Angela sarcastically, 'how terrible for you!'

Unable to avoid it Allie snorted with laughter.

'She left me there!' Rat protested, 'Still tied up.'

'Well, what were you afraid of – velociraptors?' Ruari's sudden humour astonished and delighted the group, who burst into laughter, his own rolling bass joining in.

'No, wait,' Rat protested. 'Why is it okay to sympathize with Hope when she was left, arms and legs free, in the library and think it was funny for me to be left tied up and helpless?' He sounded angry. 'Look,' he stood up and presented his scored back to the circle, 'I was not left unharmed.'

'He is right, actually.' Rat found unexpected support from Mallot. 'It is not okay. But, Rat, had you had the safe word would you have used it?'

Rat sank back into the sofa, thinking, then at last said, 'No. I was angry at first but then I enjoyed it. I also think Hope enjoyed her faceless fuck, and had she just said "no" we would have stopped.'

'I did enjoy it,' Hope offered her support, then, musing, went on. 'Very much. I enjoyed it very much,' she repeated, smiling at the memory.

The group fell silent, staring at her as her face betrayed her thoughts, her tips pouting and a pink flush of desire staining her cheeks. Rat, caught up as he watched, felt his penis harden and felt he would burst if he could not take her again, soon.

Karen broke the tension. 'We haven't finished going around the group,' she reminded them. 'Elsa, you're next.'

'I am going to talk to Hope tonight as we agreed,' she informed Karen proudly.

'Quinn?'

'I also wanted to get near Hope,' he confessed, 'and

this is as close as I got. It is okay though, there is plenty of time.'

'Angela?'

'I fancied having a go at Rat,' she said bluntly, all pretence of seduction dropped. 'After all, I have been offered to him,' she added cryptically.

'Offered?' Brandon looked puzzled.

'Yes, by Mallot.'

'You are no slave!' Allie yelled indignantly. 'Stand up for yourself.'

'Oh, but I am a slave,' Angela informed her calmly. 'It is my choice, and I am proud of it.'

'But he's a dog. He just cats about!' Allie protested, contradicting herself.

'If he chooses to share himself, or me, then I will celebrate for him.'

'Oh yes? So he can just offer you on a plate to whomever he likes?'

'Yes.'

'You're nuts!'

'And you are ignorant.' Angela settled back in a huff, leaving Allie lost for words.

'I think this is a discussion for another time,' Karen said. 'I know it has been an exciting day. My suggestion, if everyone is comfortable with it, is that we remain without clothes unless the weather cools. It seems nice this way.'

'I'll try,' promised Elsa, 'it does feel nice.'

Everyone smiled, even Allie.

'Okay, let's get some drinks in the dining room.' Karen unfurled and stretched, her beasts bouncing happily, and beckoned to Rat. 'You might see Mairead about your back. She has a balm to put on it.'

They gathered in the dining room, each collecting their stack of neatly folded clothing. It seemed too intimate to dress together, so they collected cups of coffee or tea, glasses and jugs of water, and dispersed.

Hope and Elsa climbed the stairs together.

Chapter Ten

'I am fat,' Elsa complained at her reflection in the mirror in Hope's bedroom. She had drawn on her bra and panties and stood, hands on hips, criticizing herself. She turned and faced Hope. 'You're beautiful and I want to be like you.'

'Why?' Hope was tugging a T-shirt over her head, and emerged with a puzzled expression.

'You're slim, successful and sophisticated.'

'No. Angela is slim. So are Allie and Karen. I am curvy.'

'I don't want to be like Angela!'

'But she is also successful and sophisticated.'

'She's mean and trashy.'

Hope studied Elsa seriously for a moment. 'Let me ask you something. You know that, this afternoon, Rat and I fucked in the library. Then another man joined us, a stranger, and he came in my mouth. You know I loved it. How come I am not also trashy?'

'I don't think . . . no . . . I mean,' Elsa floundered, sighed with exasperation and shrugged her shoulders.

'You see? It is really hard to make judgements like that.' Hope drifted over to the bed, sat down and patted the space next to her. 'Come, sit down and let's talk.'

Elsa bounced over and plumped down.

'Okay, what's so bad about you?

'Nothing! I am clever and funny and kind and I sing well,' Elsa said.

'Except you're fat, right?'

Elsa groaned, 'Yes, I am.'

'Where?' Hope pretended to investigate, poking her fingers gently into Elsa's side and eliciting a gale of giggles. 'There?'

'Yes!' Elsa hiccuped. 'I have tyres.'

'Why don't you grab me here?' Hope pointed at her waist.

Elsa cupped the side of Hope's waist and squeezed. A wodge of flesh nestled in her palm.

'Is that fat?' Hope asked.

'No. That is because you are a woman.' Elsa replied, 'You are soft there, like a woman is.'

'Now your waist.'

Elsa cupped her own waist, again collecting a wodge of flesh.

'So, that's fat, is it? Or perhaps it is because you are a woman too?' Hope grinned.

'Oh, okay, but I have big boobs.'

'Lucky you! That's like a woman too.' Hope laughed.

Elsa looked frustrated, thinking hard. 'I don't like them,' she complained.

'Have you found someone who does, though?'

'I had a boyfriend. He was always at them, telling me how great they are.'

'Maybe you should listen to him?'

'He's a man!'

'Oh, and it matters what women think, but not men?'

'I like women more.'

'But not Angela?'

Elsa turned to face Hope, looking crestfallen. 'Look, I am sorry I said she is trashy. I didn't mean that. It is just that she scares me.'

'Well, if you had to grab a bit of her waist, she would feel just like you and me.'

'Can I touch your breasts?' Elsa blurted. 'Allie has, I know.'

'How do you know?' Hope teased.

'I saw you yesterday. When Allie brought you croissants, she left your door open. You dropped crumbs and she licked them from your breast.' Seemingly driven to confess, she added, 'I also saw you on the boat with her.'

'What did you see?' Hope tried desperately to remember if she had noticed where Elsa was on the launch, and failed.

'I saw Allie's back when I was at the wheel with Sean and I came down to join you. You were . . . kneeling down.' She stopped, her face red, and stared at her hands. 'I'm sorry.'

'Were you upset by what you saw?' Hope felt anxious.

'Oh, no,' Elsa stared at her, wide-eyed and sincere, 'I wanted you to do it to me!'

'Would you like me to, now?'

Elsa nodded shyly.

Hope felt amazed. When Elsa had complained about her breasts being too large, Hope had wanted to protest vehemently. She had watched Elsa's breasts surreptitiously all evening, longing to sink her fingers into the generous mounds, heft them and cushion her face in the valley. Elsa's rounded contours and fine, translucent skin drew her in a way that Amy's tight leanness and Allie's slim whippiness did not. There was something more basic in her yearning, a desire to lose herself in the hot, yielding flesh. She recognized that her dawning lust showed in her face. Elsa's wondering look endorsed that much.

'You never looked at Allie like this,' she said shyly.

'No,' Hope breathed, 'I never felt like this before.' Her hands trembled as she laid them over Elsa's breasts. She felt tender and shaken, amazed at the raw craving flooding her.

Elsa fell silent. She had been shy when she made her request to touch Hope, afraid that her own chubby curves would repel, but now she could see that her mentor was full of passion and need, like her boyfriend when he had wanted her. It confused her because she thought a woman would be different, and want different things. The fingers drawing over her nipples were more gentle and exploratory, but the panting and glazed, fixed expression was the same as his had been. Suddenly she knew her breasts were beautiful, and womanly, and her dislike of them fell away to be replaced with pride.

Hope was easing Elsa's bra straps from her shoulders and tugging down the cups, and Elsa quickly slipped her hands behind her back to help by undoing the clasp. Her breasts relaxed heavily, swaying. She lay back and felt the tilt of them to her sides, a feeling she had hated until now, when Hope sighed, gathering their weight in her hands to mash them together and bury her face between their cushions. Her golden hair fell in a broad sweep to cover Elsa's breasts, tickling slightly and creating rippling butterfly kisses over her nipples. Hope wriggled and straddled over her, licking with long strokes along the underside of one breast while she pushed it upwards, then turning her attention to the other. She sucked gently on a nipple, rolling the other between her fingertips, tugging and pulling until Elsa believed she would burst with the sensations. Her nipple had grown so hard it hurt, then Hope's tongue swept over it and her lips nursed and healed, while her fingers transferred to the briefly deserted other teat.

Hope had lowered her hips, her naked quim sliding on Elsa's clad groin, and the young woman could feel the wetness soak through her panties. She was amazed at how good it felt. She had allowed no man to get this far and have her almost naked, bare breasted, and tower over her. She almost longed for the graze of a penis, the bump and slide of it over her mound. Her own nether lips were swelling and moistening, in the way they sometimes did when she bathed and rubbed the sponge over her private places. She had been too shy at first, even alone, to touch herself in any way other than to get clean. Then one day she had lingered, rubbing the sponge harder and harder, until a strange, sweet trembling possessed her and afterwards she had felt guilty and afraid. That was a long time ago, however, and since then she had learned to rub herself to completion whenever she wanted.

Now she revelled in Hope's attention, loving the warm, wet kisses and tonguing on her areolae, the suckling on her nipples and the eager fingers clutching and pressing into her generous flesh. She moaned her appreciation, surprised to hear the soft noise issue from her own throat. She felt faint, as if she was swooning, and ground her hips up to seek firmer pressure, her swollen clitoris hungry for contact. Soon she felt Hope slide down and her pants being drawn from her.

Elsa lost her shyness, her need too rampant. She opened her legs hastily and cried out with pleasure when Hope inserted her finger, swirling her juices gently, then slid in another and scissored slowly. Hope tugged downwards, and Elsa shivered as strobes of dull pleasure shot along her anal wall. Then Hope inserted two fingers of her other hand, palm facing up, and gently tugged towards Elsa's mound while retaining the pressure on the rear wall of her cavity. Elsa gasped and Hope relaxed her hold, only to pull upwards and downwards again. She continued this action, her tempo slow, until she heard Elsa mutter incoherently and then looked up to find the young woman, eyes closed, lost in rapture. Elsa's hands had risen to knead her own breasts and Hope found the sight unbearably arousing. She leaned forward, her fingers sliding and weaving inside Elsa, nudging with her nose until she slid the small clitoral hood from its jewel. She took the small nub between her lips and flicked her tongue. Elsa cried out and arched into Hope's face, shocked as the lust forked through her. Hope flicked faster, digging deeper into the wet cave, not allowing her prey to retreat until she felt the hard clench and roll of Elsa's orgasm.

The young woman mewled and whimpered, then dragged Hope forward, clasping her in surprisingly strong arms and holding her tightly as their breasts rubbed sensually together. She forced her thigh between Hope's and rolled from side to side, trying to maximise her coming and still crying out and jolting as the tide of lust continued to swell, Hope, held fast against Elsa's mound, relaxed and let the pleasure wash through her, her shaven pubis rubbing hard along the thick mat of dark hair. Eventually her own tide burst and she added her keening to the moans and gasps.

As she lay panting, the boiling of her blood reducing to a simmer, Hope remained firmly embraced, prone on top of Elsa. She sank into the soft generous curves and cushioning thighs, feeling absorbed and sensual. Her mouth nestled against Elsa's neck and she kissed her, suckling and enjoying the damp, salty residue of lovemaking. Elsa at last released her, and Hope lifted her head to nurse softly at the young woman's redly swollen mouth, sharing the flavours she had collected.

'I am squashing you,' Hope murmured.

Elsa shook her head, 'It's nice.' She opened her eyes and looked into Hope's face wonderingly. 'It was never like that when I did it to myself,' she whispered. 'That was deep inside me and went on for ever. Is it like that with a man?'

'Sometimes.' Hope rolled gently from Elsa and onto her back. She tucked her fingers between the young woman's thighs and squeezed the surfeit of flesh. The wet residue seeped along her hand and she massaged softly, enjoying the spent lust. She felt wonderfully languorous, happy with her intimate contact, and time seemed limitless. Elsa's breathing had eased and her breasts swayed gently to the rise and fall of her chest, their dark areolaes smoothing.

Hope adjusted her hand, palming Elsa's mound, and dipped her fingers into the well between the damp folds, then started cupping them softly. 'Sleep now,' she murmured, but felt the tissues thicken and seep. Elsa let it happen, the lethargic, lulling ride to a different, less urgent, release. She felt the dull, almost remote, rolling and, as she came, slipped deeply into sleep.

Hope woke slowly, her breath caught with passion, to find Elsa nursing between her legs, her mouth gently moving and dark hair tumbling over spread, wide thighs. Moaning, Hope pressed her head back into the pillows and twisted the sheets in her fists. She arched as Elsa found her clit and sucked softly, then harder as she felt Hope press against her. She was not harsh enough, however, and Hope gripped her head and rode panting to orgasm, fearing she would drown the girl but unable to resist her driving need. As the ringtug still trembled through her, she pushed Elsa away, curved up to her and licked her juices from the soft cheeks, chin and lips.

'I am sorry,' she gasped. 'I nearly drowned you!'

Elsa giggled. 'Was that a nice way to wake up?'

'It was wonderful,' Hope assured her and hugged her warmly.

Elsa sat cross-legged, now totally at ease with her nakedness. 'You taste nice,' she observed gravely, 'and there's lots of it.'

'You, too. And there's lots of yours as well.'

'I think I do like my breasts, after all.'

Hope nodded, pleased, and stroked the large mounds softly, 'They are beautiful breasts.'

'Other people will want to touch them also.'

'Lots of other people will.'

'Everyone in this group?'

'I think so.' Hope wondered what Elsa was aiming at.

'Do you think Rat would like to touch them?'

'Would you like him to?'

'Would you mind?' Elsa looked concerned.

'No!' Hope laughed. 'I would like him to. I would like everyone to touch your breasts.'

'How can I let a man touch my breasts without him sticking his penis into me?' Elsa was serious.

'Don't you want a man inside you?'

'I don't know. I want someone who is experienced when I

give my virginity, though. I thought,' she paused, 'I thought that, as you are going to go with all the men you could tell me who would be best.'

'I can tell you how each of them are and you can choose, if you like.'

'Okay.' Elsa beamed at Hope. 'In the meantime, anyone can play with my breasts and also use their fingers and tongues.'

'Good deal.' Hope smiled and kissed Elsa. 'Shall we shower?'

Allie was already in the bath, soaking, with her eyes closed. Her hand played over her mound and her lips were parted with pleasure. Her tiny movements created swirls that obscured the lines of her body and steam rose to form a mist in the room. It seemed like a scene from a romantic movie, pale gold light shafting through the high, mottled panes of the window and her wet pinkness and damp red hair suggesting torrid anticipation.

When Allie gave a little moan and trembled, Elsa gasped and revealed her presence. Allie open her eyes to gaze at Hope and Elsa with slightly unfocused desire, then invited them to join her. She seemed unsurprised at the young woman's presence, and perched on the end of the bath, her feet immersed, as Hope slipped into the water and slid back between her thighs. Elsa stepped in gingerly and eased down. She drew her knees up and hugged them, her breasts bulging.

'I came to say goodnight to you, but I could see you were both too occupied to notice. I would have joined you but figured three might have been a crowd.'

'It is not a crowd now,' Elsa pointed out reasonably.

'Now it is!' Rat walked in, a towel around his hips.

Elsa squeaked and tried to curl herself tighter, blushing furiously as Rat approached.

'You are taking a risk,' Allie pointed out to him. 'Walking in like that on three lusty ladies.' She winked at Elsa.

'Maybe I should leave?' Rat hovered, his eyes roving and calculating.

'No,' Hope said slowly, looking meaningfully into Elsa's eyes. 'I think you should do exactly what Elsa thinks you should do.'

Elsa stared at her mutely, then cleared her throat. 'You must stay, Rat, and you can touch me.' She slowly uncurled and stood up, her eyes downcast and the water trickling from her, forming tears on her nipples.

There was a silence as Rat examined the young woman, then he murmured, 'Venus, rising from the water.' He moved to Elsa's side and ran his hands over her breasts. 'These are made for spurting over.'

'You cannot put your penis in me,' Elsa cautioned in a small voice.

'That's okay.' Rat's voice was low. 'I want to fuck your tits.'

Elsa looked puzzled, then intrigued. She nodded and allowed Rat to help her from the bath. He grabbed towels from the racks and threw them on the floor to fashion a makeshift mattress, then directed Elsa to lie on them. Before she could comply, Hope slipped from the bath and sat back on her haunches to create a rest on which the young woman could lean her shoulders, her head nestling in Hope's groin. When Elsa lay back, she had the comfort of her mentor's involvement and was able to see. She felt nervous until Allie slid between her thighs and prevented Rat's access, her small hands stroking over Elsa's stomach.

Rat dropped his towel. His erection was already full and weaving and he looked past it at the splay of Elsa's breasts. They lay heavily, the wide rift between offering him a path to fulfilment of a fantasy he had held for a long time. His lust was encouraged by Hope, who leaned over to gather the fleshy mounds and draw them upward and together, so the pathway vanished but the rubbing orbs created a thick, massaging valley for his penetration. Her own rounded globes bobbed over Elsa's face, flanking her cheeks and hiding her eyes. With Allie tugging gently on Elsa's thick nether lips, her fingers circling and pulling, Rat's senses seemed in overload. He stared at the sirens, trying to appreciate his good luck, but his passion drove him to straddle Elsa's waist, his rod tapping for entry between her breasts.

Allie, aware that the valley was dry, in spite of the bathwater, gathered fingerfuls of her own spent fluids and the fresh, creamy fluid from Elsa and slid her hands beneath Rat to smear the paste. Hope, realizing what was happening, loosened her hold so the cushions fell apart and played with the now budding nipples. Allie repeated the process until the sides of Elsa's breasts gleamed with the thick coating.

Rat breathed deeply and evenly, controlling himself as he watched his consort being prepared. Then, when Hope once more pressed the orbs together, he slid forward and, moaning, buried his rod deeply into the trembling flesh. The tip of his penis burst through and he covered Hope's hands with his own and swept the pillows up to cover it, dragging his hips back so his shining shaft withdrew.

Hope pulled her hands from under his, fearing she would

disturb his tempo and wanting to enjoy the sight. She eased from under Elsa's head slightly, and slipped a hand between her own thighs, feeling a jealous vaginal clench as Rat's penis rode, dripping precum over the young woman's chin. With her free fingers, Hope scooped the small drop and traced over Elsa's lips, leaving a snailtrack for her to lick.

Elsa was at first astounded. She had wanted attention but had been afraid that her rounded curves would repel. Now she roused to the clever fingering of Allie among her folds, the quick pulling and small pressings, the sex-scents seeping from between Hope's thighs and the thrilling sweep of the penis shafting her breasts. Rat kneaded roughly at her giving flesh, massaging the pillows harshly to accommodate his thrusts. Every now and then Elsa saw the tip of his penis emerge, slick and satiny, and her cave yearned, in spite of her resolution. He was bigger than she imagined, swollen more than at the start and an angry purple. Creamy tears gathered in his penile eye and then dripped, coating her chin and neck. He smelled rich and musky. His eyes were fixed firmly on her breasts and a ruddy glow suffused his face. Sweat beaded his forehead and tricked down his chest, adding its own pungency, and the cords of his neck were as stiff as the cock gliding between her breasts.

Behind her, Elsa could hear Hope's quick panting and feel the brush of her hand as she dipped into herself. The thighs beneath her head trembled and shook and then she heard the quick rasp and moan as Hope came. She closed her eyes, feeling tugged and pulled until she believed her limbs would fall apart and she would lie, scattered around the room. Her breasts started to hurt, but the pain was intensely pleasurable and the continuing ministry in her folds was a sweet yearning. When Rat spouted, his cry ringing out, she felt the hot splash of come douse her face and neck. He seemed to freeze, then buck, and more heat poured from him. His hands pressed viciously down on her and he rode his cock to softness. Then Elsa surrendered to her own coming, crying out as Allie rubbed hard on her mound, pinching and pulling at her clitoris. It was a sharp, sudden orgasm, almost bitter compared to the deep internal rolling she had enjoyed with Hope, and left her wanting more. She realized that the 'more' she wanted had been spent over her face and neck and now Rat was rubbing his softening prick in it, his tip glancing over her mouth. Obediently, she parted her lips and the warm cylinder nestled, then penetrated. She sucked softly, like a child at an empty teat, comforted.

Elsa felt herself lifted by strong arms and lowered into the tepid water in the bath. She relaxed as three pairs of hands soaped and rinsed her, then helped her from the tub and patted her dry. She wished she could simply drop back into bed and sleep but the breakfast gong sounded and her hunger overrode her tiredness. That, and her eagerness to share her experience with the group. More than ever she longed to be penetrated, to feel the hot leak of a man between her thighs and her vagina was still hungry, longing to possess the strange hard length and suck its life force.

Elsa entered the dining room with her new group of lovers. In deference to Karen's suggestion the previous evening, and the warmth of the day, all had donned light, revealing coverings, but eschewed nudity. Allie had tied a sarong at her waist, Hope had donned her translucent cerise blouse and Elsa wore a baggy T-shirt. The large swell of her unfettered breasts lifted the hem to allow a glimpse of her dark, curling pubic hair. Rat wore silk running shorts. Quinn and Ruari had compromised, donning swimming trunks, but the rest of the group were determinedly naked.

Mallot looked keenly at Elsa, unable to miss her new, pink radiance. He liked the heavy promise of her bust and the peeping moistness between her thick thighs. He knew that she had not lost her virginity but, watching her tender interplay with Hope, realized that their conversation had transcended words. When Elsa's gentle touch settled on Rat, Mallot paused. The young man had blossomed since his arrival and was holding his own in a bizarre and sexual environment in a manner that surprised Mallot. He suspected that much of this liberation was down to Hope. For a moment he was afraid she might escape him and then shrugged dismissively. Hope was his, she merely needed to recognize it, and while she floundered she could play as she wished. Nonetheless his penis stirred and lay in a peaceful half-erection in his lap. Angela noticed and traced her fingertips along him until he clicked his tongue in annoyance. Pouting, she resumed eating her breakfast.

What had she expected, Mallot wondered, that he would take her at the table? Yes, he could do that, push her down so her bum stuck up alluringly and thrust into her with Hope watching, her own desire playing across her face and her longing for his rooting replacing her dislike. He sighed loudly, irritated that the woman had gotten under his skin. Angela, concerned that she had transgressed, was eyeing him nervously and he thought that the sooner he passed her on to one of the other men, the better. Her slavishness was charming but she had not yet learned not to be possessive, and he still felt cross that her cunning had led to the clothes trade-off with

Hope. It never occurred to him that Hope should share the blame.

Ruari ate stolidly, seemingly unimpressed with the interplay of the group. He was next, Mallot recalled, wishing that Hope would get on with it. True to his word, Mallot had resisted sex for the past forty-eight hours, while Hope and Rat seemed to dunk at every turn, Allie riding along. Now it seemed that Elsa had got in on the act.

'Hope,' Mallot leaned his elbows on the table and stared until he was sure he had her full attention. 'This whole exercise seems to be in your hands, you know. So please get the hell on with it.'

Hope flushed angrily. 'What are you talking about?' she demanded.

'You agreed to be the pathfinder. Don't you realize that a responsibility to the group comes with it? While you shilly-shally about, doing much as you please and in your own time, there are folk waiting for you to get sorted. Get with the group, will you?

'Now, the last I knew,' Mallot continued softly, 'you were to bonk Ruari, talk to Rusty and head for Quinn. Have you done that yet?'

'I don't have to answer to you, Mallot.' Hope's voice was icy.

'Oh yes, you do. As you have to answer to each and every one in this group who put their faith in you. You agreed to take an active role and you dispensed with Rat easily enough. You don't think the queue is lying awake at night thinking about what is to happen?' Mallot gestured at Ruari. 'Instead of messing with young Elsa, perhaps you ought to stick to the script.'

'She can't have sex to order!' Allie cried.

'Then,' Mallot snapped, 'she should not have agreed to do so!'

Hope felt angry, but recognized the truth in Mallot's words. She had agreed, and the rest of the group was waiting on her report. She chewed her lip, agitated and hating to have to concede any point to him. Elsa, seated next to her, seemed close to tears and Allie was seething. She had no idea what Ruari was thinking, except she recognized his embarrassment, and Quinn merely looked perturbed. Angela, Hope noted, looked sympathetic.

'Mallot's right,' Hope said softly, soliciting surprised stares, and a gasp from Allie. She stood up and pushed her chair under the table. 'I think we should go to session now.' She waited until the group filed from the dining room, but managed to restrain Ruari. He shuffled before her, unable to meet her eyes.

'Ruari,' Hope murmured, 'we have to make a date. How about after lunch?'

He nodded, then turned away and entered the lounge, leaving her to take her seat next to him. This time he did not move away and she felt the warm, reassuring pressure of his thigh against hers. When he took her hand, holding it loosely, she was surprised and grateful. Ruari, she decided, was a kind, old-fashioned gentleman. She felt a warmth towards him that had been absent in her encounter with Rat. The session progressed in a daze: voices floated around her but she did not pay attention, absorbed in Mallot's words. Once, when she looked up, she found him studying her, his expression unreadable. She looked blankly at him and turned away. When they broke to have lunch she slipped away, not hungry, and sat on the end of the quay. Ruari joined her, offering her an apple. She munched it, enjoying the sweet sap and crisp freshness.

'I am sorry Mallot made you feel bad,' he said at last. 'I don't know how we are going to go through with this anyway.'

'Oh, Mallot is right. But we don't have to do anything we don't want to do, you know. We can just sit and talk or explore the island or something.'

'There's a trail around the house. On the far side there is a small beach, that gets good sunlight around now,' Ruari informed her. He seemed more relaxed and talkative. 'I went there yesterday and it is really private.'

'Shall we go there now?' Hope liked the idea, grateful that Ruari offered the choice.

'I would like to. Stay here, I will be back soon.' He sped off swiftly, belying his bulk with a panther-like grace. He soon returned clutching a canvas bag, which he held up triumphantly. 'Picnic,' he announced. 'Come on!'

They made their way around the walls of the house easily, along a sandy path, climbing at one point over the boulders that lay beneath Hope's window. True to his word, Rauri led her to a small beach, protected from prying eyes by a crescent of tumbling rocks. The sand was fine and the water clear and shallow. There was enough room to settle comfortably and spread the picnic between them.

Ruari seemed slightly agitated and Hope was worried that he might feel forced into being with her when he would rather have been alone, or with other company. She told him this but he merely shook his head.

'I wanted to show you this place.' He did not tell her that his nervousness was due to the fact that, when helping her over the boulders, he had stared at her quim, roused by the pink flush and explicitness of his first sight of a woman's secret places. He felt guilty for looking.

'You're nice,' Hope observed. She smiled at their repast, thickly cut chicken sandwiches, fruit and an illicit bottle of white wine, chilled. 'Where did you get the wine?' she exclaimed. 'I thought it was forbidden here!'

'Ah, well now.' Ruari uncorked the bottle with the corkscrew of his Swiss army knife. 'I made friends with the right person.' He chuckled and filled two tumblers, offering one to Hope, who sipped, then closed her eyes blissfully.

'That is really good wine.' She suddenly felt hungry and polished off two of the sandwiches and an apple. Then, sighing with pleasure, she allowed her glass to be refilled.

'Shall we swim?' She eyed the water.

'It is not very deep here. Which is just as well, considering we are drinking,' Ruari observed, 'but you don't have a costume with you.'

'I am waterproof,' Hope advised him, slipped off her blouse and waded into the shallows. When the water covered her knees she eased onto her back and floated, her arms stretched out for balance, enjoying the heat on her bare skin.

Ruari watched her from the shore, admiring the lift of her breasts and the curve of her stomach and mound. He felt reluctant to join her, sure that his control would snap and he would be damned to suffer in hell, as his priest had said, were he to enjoy carnal knowledge outside of wedlock. It seemed that the group had a different morality and they all seemed to take it in their stride, even Elsa, who had admitted her sexplay with shy, glowing pride. Mallot he could make no sense of, sure that the man was evil and that Angela was a fallen woman. Hope, he believed, was good at heart, a true woman, who had fallen into bad ways because of her association with the city of London. The lure of her womanly parts was natural and she had a sweet temper and humility. It was just a pity she did not share his faith, or they could court.

In spite of his rationalizations, Ruari was roused. It would do no harm, he reasoned, to be sociable and swim with her. In fact, the cold water would ease the hardness that betrayed his impure thoughts. He scrambled to his feet suddenly and lurched into the water, sending large ripples to rock Hope. Surprised, she sank, and bounced up, coughing water.

'Bring the wine!' she called, and Ruari grinned and fetched the bottle, brandishing it triumphantly as he paddled back towards her.

Hope joined him in the shallower water and they sat waist-deep, passing the wine between them.

'I am not much of a drinker,' Hope announced at last, feeling slightly tipsy.

'I usually drink Guinness,' Ruari confessed. 'But Mairead did not have any.' He looked woeful and Hope laughed and tussled his hair.

'Shame on her!'

Ruari splashed some water at her. 'You taking the mick?' he queried and ducked her playfully, pulling her up to face her with a mock-stern expression. He realized his mistake when he felt her soft breasts press into his chest. Her lips were close and he could not resist kissing her. He realized it had nearly gone too far when her arms slid around his neck and she returned his kiss passionately. He groaned in frustration, pushing her away and shaking his head.

'I can't,' he muttered miserably. 'It wouldn't be right.'

'I think it would, Ruari. I can tell you want me.'

They were both aware of his erection: it bobbed treacherously beneath his loose swimsuit.

'I do. But you don't understand. It would be sinful.'

'That is church-speak,' Hope protested softly. 'What could be more natural and healthy than a man and woman sharing pleasure?'

Ruari allowed himself to be persuaded, thrilling as Hope rubbed against him, her lips reclaiming his. He touched her breasts, delighted when the nipples peaked in response. He floated to allow Hope to pull his swimsuit from him and toss it on the beach. She slid onto his lap, as he sat in the shallows, and lowered onto him, her eyes wide and her mouth a small moue. They rocked slowly, the water supporting them, their passion in check.

'This is nice,' Hope sighed.

'I shall burn in hell,' Ruari responded, suddenly not caring. Hope felt exquisite, the contrast of her hot cave and the cool water heightening his senses.

'Burn in me, rather,' Hope whispered into his ear and her soft breath teased.

'I am going deeper in the water,' Ruari announced and slithered forward until Hope was buoyant. He lifted her and made his way into a pool, where he could lean back against a rock and her legs would be all that was necessary to hold his penis in place.

Hope leaned back, her breasts breaking the surface of the water and her hair shifting in a soft veil around her. Ruari grasped her hips lightly and peered down. The water was clear enough for him to see their union in explicit detail, her lips stretched around his rod which was buried in her moist altar. The sight was unbearably rousing and all his reservations fell away. He let go of her hips and fingered her, seeking her clitoris and pulling back the little cover gently, thrilled to find the tiny nub. He ran his finger around it, alarmed at first when Hope moaned, then happy when he realized he was giving her pleasure. He watched her face, experimenting with his fingers, and felt her legs tighten.

Ruari thrust softly, allowing himself to give in to his own demand. He was unsure, but believed that Hope was setting her own pace and was as lost in their lovemaking as he. Soon it did not matter and his balls packed tightly, tendrils forked into his shaft and he burst in ecstasy, yelling his unholy defiance. Hope rose to him, clutching his neck and moaning, and he realized that he could feel her orgasm stroking along his waning, sensitive prick. After a while, with his shaft still in her, she leaned back slightly and looked into his eyes, smoothing his hair gently.

'Are you okay?' Hope asked, concerned at the sadness in his expression. She had not underestimated his conscience but the wine and his obvious arousal had overridden it. The setting could not have been more romantic, the isolation was perfect, and her bloodlust had clamoured. Ruari had been so gentle and giving and she felt close and tender towards him.

'Oh yes,' he replied, 'I am fine. Finer than I have ever been.'

'Your God?' Hope's query hung in the air.

'I will answer to Him in good time.' Ruari kissed her.

They lay on the bank to dry in the sun and Hope was pleased when Ruari did not pull his swimming trunks back on. He fed her orange segments, teasing at her lips with the fleshy sections until she nipped and caught them, their juice running over her chin. He licked it from her and shared the succulent portions in her mouth, their tongues tussling playfully for the greater share. In time he mounted her, his expression serious as he watched her face while he thrust slowly, enjoying her climaxing as much as his own. When the shadows started to creep across their small, sandy place, he washed her in the shallows and helped her to button her blouse.

They embraced, standing for a long time and enjoying the warmth of blending. Hope laid her ear over his heart and was comforted by the steady rhythm and Ruari buried his face in her hair. When they pulled apart, they smiled at each other.

'Now,' Ruari said, 'I must go and make atonement.' In response to Hope's mute query, he soothed her. 'It is okay. I am proud and happy with what we shared, and I will not regret it. It is for my pride alone that I will apologize, not for the sin of unwed sex.'

They made their way back silently, touching often. When they rounded the front of the house they found Mallot standing in the doorway, an unwelcome presence. Ruari kissed Hope, very softly on the corner of her mouth, tucked her hair gently behind her ears and murmured, 'Thank you.' He pushed past Mallot and was swallowed up in the hallway.

Mallot wisely kept his peace. His eyes were strangely gentle, which disconcerted Hope. He stood aside to allow her passage past him. As she made her way to the stairwell, she was sure she heard him whisper, 'I'm sorry.'

Chapter Eleven

A parcel lay on the floor outside Hope's bedroom door. A note was pinned to the brown wrapping.

> Perhaps we can talk after supper? This is an introduction to what I do, and what I mean by 'nasty' . . . Rusty

In her room, Hope tore the wrapping and magazines spilled over the bed. Glossy, colourful covers depicted couples in various stages of sexual congress and the titles were foreign, blazing headlines proclaiming Sodom and Gomorrah. These were not the vanilla publications found on the British shelves and, as Hope riffled through the pages, her eyes widened. Only one magazine seemed out of place, not as garish, and her heart sank as she recognized the cover. It was that in which the article *Hope Springs Eternal* was printed and Salvatore's portrait on the front felt like a stab. A yellow sticky note protruded mid-way and, turning to it, she discovered Rusty.

The article described him as 'New Wave', 'Britain's most desirable bad guy' and 'a man the camera loves'. The photographs were tasteful. He perched moodily on rocks by the seashore, naked but not exposed, with golden evening light pouring over his oiled skin. He leaned against the chimney breasts of a London skyline, sepia-toned, with his hand absently cupping his genitals and a sultry expression that suggested there was no more sensual place to be than among the ashes and guano of the rooftops. One picture was of him and Salvatore partying at Stringfellows. The caption described him as 'Salvatore's latest discovery'.

The other magazines were not so tasteful and Hope was relieved that she could not read the foreign-language captions. In each, yellow notes marked the pages on which she could find pictures of Rusty. The least alarming showed him hovering, fully erect and menacing, over a naked young woman. He carried a large whip and a smile that would chill the blood of Satan. The rear of the magazine carried advertisements for videos, in which Rusty starred prominently.

Hope turned back to the picture of Rusty and Salvatore at the nightclub. They were part of a group and she gasped when she recognized other members of the party. Mallot's sardonic features were captured by the camera as he leaned to whisper something in Reggie's ear. She threw the magazine across the room, as she had done with the earlier copy in her office. Her feature had been towards the front of the magazine and she had failed to look further through the issue, so caught up had she been with her own demise. It seemed too coincidental for both Mallot and Rusty to be at the retreat with her, especially as they clearly had a close association with Reggie. She recalled Mallot's introducing himself at The Piper's Inn and his assumption that she would know him. Presumably, she reasoned, Reggie would have assumed that she had paged through the whole magazine. What was it he expected of her, now that she was locked with these two on a remote island?

Whatever it was, she had failed his expectations and Mallot had neglected to enlighten her. It was therefore up to her to find out, and she would make sure Rusty told her later. She felt angry and manipulated and began to question the existence of Willincough and Rat's part in the intrigue. Giving in to paranoia, she began to suspect there was no demand for a hacker. She had never doubted the existence of Blain, Lechange and Partners, and taken their requirement as the gospel truth – all on Reggie's say-so. But Reggie was a part of the conspiracy and she could not now assume any honesty on his part.

Hope tried desperately to recall all the things Mallot had said to her, or in the group, trying to piece together how he might have engineered her actions through suggestion. He had spoken at the first session but she could not remember his words, merely her own impressions. And what of Angela, was she also involved? Surely not Allie? How did Karen and Brandon Ormandy fit in?

Hope threw herself back on the bed and forced herself to relax. It was too extravagant to think that an entire fortnight had been staged to bamboozle her, and she could not afford to become paranoid to the extent that she suspected Allie of anything. No, she decided, there was a clique who had their own reasons for attending and if it had anything to do with her, then she would learn of it at some time. The situation did not appear life-threatening and she had no substantial reason to suspect that Willincough did not exist. She would tackle Rat on that issue, and Rusty about the party Stringfellows.

By the time the dinner gong sounded, Hope had already showered and donned shorts and a halter-necked top, and was seated, composed, awaiting the summons. She wondered why she had not seen Allie and was provided with the answer when she crossed the landing. Allie and Rat tumbled from his bedroom, obviously post-coital and playful. They drew to a laughing halt beside her and she could not help but share their good humour.

'I know,' Rat said, 'who tied me up on the beach now! All it took was a blow job.'

Allie punched him on the arm lightly and they hugged, giggling, including Hope in their embrace. Lurching down the stairs without separating, they encountered Mallot and Angela in the lobby.

'What is it with you two?' Allie demanded. 'Do you take up station waiting for the peasants to arrive?' She had not noticed Angela's sour expression and the thunder hovering over Mallot before she spoke, as had Hope.

Angela glared at Hope. 'Bit overdressed, aren't you?'

'My choice,' Hope responded without rancour and continued into the dining room. As before, in accordance with Karen's suggestion, most were naked and she was the only one clad above the waist. Elsa's proud breasts monopolized attention and her previous shyness had dissipated. Karen was absent.

'Karen is unwell,' Brandon told them. 'I think we should cancel tonight's session and hope she will rally for tomorrow morning.' He seemed ill at ease.

Hope thought of Rusty's note. He had suggested they talk after dinner, which she had taken as after the session but she now wondered if Karen's malaise had been contrived in order to free the group. She shook her head to try to dismiss her suspicions, deciding that she was not about to succumb to obsession. 'Perhaps Quinn and I can spend this evening together.'

'Oh, so you've had Ruari then?' Angela's voice was sharp and Hope looked at her curiously.

'Hope and I made love, yes.' Ruari's deep voice silenced the table and drew an interrogative look from Elsa.

'Ah,' Angela returned waspishly, 'you "made love". You did not fuck or screw like everyone else, then?'

'We made love,' Ruari confirmed.

Angela seemed about to continue baiting when Mallot intervened. 'That is enough, Angela.' He sounded calm but his eyes were cold. 'You are way out of line.'

'Rat and I fucked,' Allie interjected in an attempt to lighten the atmosphere. 'Does that count?' She drew a snigger from Rat and a relieved snort of laughter from Rusty but it seemed that Angela was not to be appeased.

'God, you are all so self-righteous!' she exclaimed. 'You have no clue what is really happening here.'

'Then,' Hope cut in coldly, 'why don't you enlighten us?' She held her breath, now convinced that Angela was integral to the clique's plans, and hoped that the woman was angry enough to lay them bare.

'I said that was enough!' Mallot cut in harshly as Angela seemed about to respond to Hope.

'You can get stuffed!' Angela rounded on Mallot, then leapt to her feet, sending her chair to the floor with a clatter. She found her arm cruelly grabbed.

'I think you forget yourself, my dear.' Mallot spoke very calmly. 'As I recall, you are my handmaiden and my slave. Perhaps a little lesson is in order.'

Angela subsided, looking anxious. Before, she had invited small punishments and revelled in Mallot's mastery. She knew he was no game-player and had thus far indulged her but this was different and she feared his wrath. She had been schooled well enough to know not to ask for release or mercy and to accept whatever Mallot chose to teach her. However, she felt a small frisson of fear wash through her and she kept her eyes firmly fixed on the table.

'As you all know,' Mallot let go of Angela's arm and learned back to scan the group, 'by this woman's own admission she is my slave. Some of you may not know what that means and that is not really important. What is important is that a slave does not defy her master without punishment.

'Just lately, Angela has consistently forgotten her place and her vows. She has become petulant and possessive and she has mistaken my tolerance for an endorsement. I had hoped that she would see the error of her ways, but this appears now to be unlikely, so I think I have to devise something that will cause her to rethink.'

Hope realized that Mallot was deadly serious, and saw her apprehension reflected in the expressions of most of the group. The exception was Rusty, who simply appeared alert and interested. Not surprisingly, Hope thought, but then she had had the benefit of seeing the magazines. Rat, in spite of his expression of concern, also stared intently.

'I must ask you all not to interfere, there are things going on here that you cannot understand,' Mallot continued.

Again, that reference to plots and ignorance. Hope eased back into her seat, trying to concentrate on the nuances.

'Angela, perhaps you will tell the group . . .' Mallot at last looked at the ice-blode, whose eyes remained firmly downcast.

'Mallot is right,' she said in a small voice. 'Whatever he chooses to do to correct me is something I want, and need to learn.' Despite her misgivings, Angela felt a thrill. She looked up and proudly surveyed the table. 'I will emerge better and more knowing, able to serve and understand – once I am taught.'

'You want this?' Quinn wondered aloud. 'You do not even know what he intends to do.'

'I want whatever Mallot wants of me and I am proud to feel the care and love of his wrath.'

Mallot nodded, satisfied with her answer. 'Then I will tell you what it is.'

As he outlined his idea, Hope felt conflict. What he proposed struck her core of submission and yet horrified her. She felt a dawning envy for Angela and a dull spawning of lust deep inside.

'I propose that even if Karen feels better,' Mallot concluded, 'we do not have a morning session. Angela can have tonight to contemplate her failings and come to the event renewed.'

Brandon nodded mutely. He looked interested.

Hope gazed around the group, trying to judge their reaction. Ruari looked offended but resigned and Hope suspected that he would not attend. Rusty was smiling and Rat looked intrigued, Allie disgusted and Elsa puzzled. Quinn's expression was hard to read. During Mallot's dialogue, Mairead had stayed quietly by the sideboard, but now came forward to serve their meal. Her expression was neutral and Hope once again wondered if she had witnessed this scene before. Without instruction, the housekeeper avoided serving Angela, who remained standing. When everyone else had plates before them, Mairead prepared a tray and offered it to the ice-blonde. She took it and, without a word, left the dining room. Mairead righted the fallen chair and invited the group to eat. It seemed that everyone was consumed with thoughts regarding Angela's fate and there was silence throughout the meal.

Hope was hungry and content to concentrate on her food, the proposed visit by Quinn and conversation with Rusty. She was aware that the male model was casting looks at her, seeking to establish eye contact, and she at last glanced up from her plate into his enquiring gaze.

'Later,' she said softly, drawing a puzzled look from Allie, but Rusty seemed satisfied.

When they rose from the table, Quinn drew alongside Hope. On the landing, Hope paused.

'Do you know which is Rusty's room?' she asked Quinn. He pointed it out. 'I am going to have to go there later,' Hope apologized.

'That's okay. Anyway, perhaps you won't want me around very long.'

'Oh, I cannot see that happening.' Hope smiled at him. 'Why don't you give me five minutes, then come to my room.' She remembered that she had the magazines spread over her bed and felt it would be inconsiderate to display the photos of the model in all his glory. Quinn nodded and backed into his own bedroom.

Hope entered her room, intrigued. Quinn had given no indication of his preferences and she had no idea how to prepare. Once the magazines were safely stowed in the bottom of the wardrobe, she gazed at the clothes and eventually selected a short robe. This felt different from her previous liaisons and, of the men in the group, Quinn was the one who was least known to her. He seemed quiet and polite, perhaps a little self-deprecating, although not ill at ease. Apart from the information that his wife and he had sexual difficulties and that he liked something to which she objected, he had given no clues. Hope, a good judge of character, felt that his interest would not be too radical and, after the scene with Mallot and Angela at the dinner table and Rusty's revelations through the magazine, she looked forward to a relaxing and non-shocking couple of hours. She briefly thought of Mallot's proposed punishment of Angela and again felt a treacherous stirring in her loins.

A small knock on her door alerted her to Quinn's arrival and, when she invited him inside, he thrust a book in her hands.

'Would you mind reading this and pretending I am not here?' He muttered and crossed to the window, peering out to allow Hope time to study his offering.

The title of the book perplexed her: it was *Fuzzy Thinking*. She checked the contents page and was further confused. Surely, she reasoned, however fascinating the theory of fuzzy logic, it was not the stuff of lusty dreams. She riffled through the pages, trying to gain further insight and was astonished when several fifty-pound notes fluttered to the floor. Embarrassed, Hope bent swiftly to retrieve them, her mind working furiously. When she straightened, counting five notes and observing that more protruded from between the pages of the book, Quinn had turned from the window and was regarding her neutrally.

He had watched Hope gather the notes from the carpet, her buttocks trembling and her pink quim displayed. He was nervous but he had never been rejected for paid service, only by his wife, and while he knew that Hope was not a prostitute he hoped that she would play his game.

'Whatever it is,' Hope said softly, 'you do not have to pay me for it.'

'Perhaps you should decide afterwards.'

'What shall I do?'

'Please lie on the bed and read the book. Pretend I am not here.'

Hope gazed at him, wondering if that was all that would happen and that Quinn would merely watch her for as long as he wanted while she pretended to be alone. She could not see how his wife would object to such a thing, nor why he paid such a large sum of money to indulge in a little innocent voying. Perhaps she should masturbate, a thought she found oddly pleasing. He wore only his swimming trunks and had brought nothing but the book, so it seemed unlikely that he intended to approach her with any instrument. Still wondering, she plumped the pillows and nestled back into them, propped the book on her bent knees and started to read. She found it hard to ignore Quinn but started to concentrate on the words and gradually became involved in the analysis of the fuzzy principle.

After a while she felt the end of the bed sink. She steadfastly kept her eyes on the print but peripherally saw Quinn kneeling at her feet. He grasped her knees and parted them, which caused her to grab the book as its rest was removed. This enabled her to hold it high enough to cover her face but still allowed her to look down at her splayed thighs. A corner of her robe modestly covered her mound and he lifted it gently and folded it back so that she was fully exposed.

Quinn felt elated. Hope's inner thighs were soft, pale and smooth and between lay the jewel that was always denied him. He studied the petalling corolla before him, licking his lips in anticipation. Her outer lips were pale, like rose-coloured Turkish Delight, giving way to deeper, blushing folds, hints of mauve. As he parted the thick lips with trembling fingers, her moist inner core beckoned him and before he bent his head, his tongue was already protruding and his mouth filled with saliva. He drew his tonguetip over the large, fleshy lobes first, delaying his first taste of the delight of the damp interior, and breathed in the mushroom scents with deep appreciation.

'Oh, Matty,' he murmured, and surrendered, sinking his tongue into her rift and seeking to drown in her juices. He commenced a delicate feeding frenzy, aware and proud as Hope's thighs hugged his head and trembled with need.

Hope had, at first, been amazed when she realized that all Quinn desired was to worship at his wife's altar. His tongue was gentle and questing, his hunger obvious and his ministry devout. She felt she could not judge Matty, but hoped the woman would learn to open to Quinn and let him serve her as sweetly as he was tending to Hope. As his supping continued, Hope tried to concentrate:

> '. . . events are black and white, they occur all or none.'

If Matty would not succumb to Quinn's oral ministry, Hope wondered, did that mean his wife had never really surrendered sexually? If Hope let the pleasure of his tongue wash through her, did that mean that her whole sexuality was fluid and occurring? She obeyed Quinn and, therefore, because she obeyed, was her sexuality a whole event? All Hope could grasp, as shivers of delight spread from her groin, was that she felt free even as she bowed to Quinn's demand. Matty must feel fettered.

'Free Matty,' she whispered involuntarily, and the head between her thighs stilled.

'Matty,' Quinn groaned, his nose buried in Hope's drenched folds.

'Free *me*,' Hope demanded and the book slipped to rest on her stomach, her hands loosely grasping the covers. She laid her head back against the headboard and closed her eyes.

Quinn peered over the edge of the book, gazing at Hope's arousal. Her eyes fluttered, her lips red and swollen and slightly parted. The mounds of her breasts framed her face, their nipples pouting, and a pale blush of lust crept over her neck. Not the real Matty, but as he wished she could be, pliant and delighted while he feasted for her pleasure. He bent to his task with renewed energy, his mouth absorbing the female secret flesh and nectar, his nose sifting the freshly wafting lust. He was barely aware when the connecting door opened and Allie paused, wide-eyed, in the portal. Even had he been more aware, he could not have stopped feeding.

Hope saw Allie through a haze of desire, her eyes hooded and glazed. She lifted her hand and languidly waved to her to join them. The redhead stood poised for shy flight before treading lightly to the bedside and easing down beside Hope, charmed by the quiet passion of her expression. She nestled softly into Hope, gazing up to witness her release, and soon the blonde trembled, sighing, and shuddered softly, her eyes closing in appreciation.

Quinn felt Hope come, his tongue savouring the tremble of her inner muscles. He lapped the small spill of her juices, the cream thick in his mouth and coating his throat as he swallowed. His hunger was not assuaged and his eyes shifted, seeking between the slim thighs of the newcomer. Another fleshly platter was possible and he gently pressed to see if it would be offered, groaning with delight when Allie's limbs opened to him and her folds were made available. New scents and flavours were positioned before him, a different arrangement of folds and the hard round bobble of a new clitoris, swollen greatly beneath its delicate hood. Heaven loomed and he was permitted entry, his faith restored. He quaffed the food of angels, alternating between the sweet and musky valleys of worship until his face was coated and his hunger sated. Splayed, stomach down on the bed, he felt his seed boil and his juices leak and coat his groin, a dull rush of sticky, hot cream as evidence of his joy.

Hope and Allie lay side by side, openly viewing Quinn's rapture, the book lying neglected between them. He continued to suck and lick long after his own release and kept their flesh alive and shuddering with small repeated releases. To ease his eating, Hope encouraged Allie to lie on top of her, her muscled bottom pressing into Hope's taut stomach. She embraced Allie, her hands crossed and grasping the small breasts tightly, her own soft mounds trapped and pressed under the other woman's slightly shifting back.

Quinn was presented with an easily accessible double feast and his head bobbed and his tongue probed until their joint coming leaked and blended. At last, his jaws and tongue aching, he slid from the bed and stood gazing at the wanton spread. He looked beatific, renewed, and his face was free of concern and lines, moistened with the benediction of the women's cream. He smiled broadly at Hope and Allie, then made to leave.

'Wait,' Hope murmured. 'Your book.'

Quinn shook his head.

'I think that Elsa might like to read it.' Hope slid from beneath Allie and rose. She padded across the room and pressed the book into Quinn's hands. 'I really think that you should offer it to her.' She kissed Quinn on his cheek, then looked meaningfully into his eyes. She smiled: 'I know she would like the fuzzy principle very, very much.' She held the door open and watched Quinn cross the landing, pause before Elsa's door and look back at her. She nodded her encouragement and softly closed her own door as he knocked on Elsa's.

'I have to go to Rusty.' Hope had led Allie into the bathroom and they now lay companionably facing each other in the warm suds.

'Take care with that one,' Allie warned.

'Do you think there is any way it was him, in the library with Rat and me?'

'No, I feel sure it wasn't him. But I do not know who else it could have been.'

Hope sighed. 'Well, apart from Mallot I have been with everyone else.'

'Is it important now?' Allie looked slightly concerned. 'I thought you said you did not want to know. That it may spoil things.'

'I am worried about what is going on here, especially as there seems to be a mystery man among us.'

'What's going on?' Allie looked genuinely puzzled. 'I mean,' she grinned, 'apart from the obvious.'

'Have you ever heard of a guy named Willincough?' Hope felt treacherous but needed to assure herself that Allie was not part of the clique. She was satisfied when her friend simply stared at her blankly.

'Hope, are you okay?'

'Yes, I am fine. Things just don't seem to add up, somehow.'

'More like you are overdoing things. Why don't you take the rest of the night off?'

'No. I want to get to Rusty before Angela's event tomorrow morning.'

Allie swirled the water with her foot, pretending great interest in the rippling patterns. 'Are you planning to be there?'

'Yes.'

'Why?'

The pause stretched until Allie was forced to look up and she was taken aback at the vulnerability of Hope's expression. 'You want to be in Angela's position, don't you?' Her voice was soft.

'Yes,' Hope admitted, afraid of Allie's censure, but hoped that their fledging friendship would withstand any critical judgement.

'I don't really understand,' Allie confessed. She leaned across and cupped Hope's face. 'But if that is what you want and it makes you happy, then I'll be there for you.' She was rewarded with a miniature tidal wave when Hope lunged across the bath to envelop her in a soapy hug.

'Also,' Allie said, 'I figure that is why you want to go after Rusty tonight. I saw his face at the dinner table. It is his sort of thing, isn't it?'

'You like Rusty,' Hope pointed out.

'Yes, I do. I just don't feel so keen on what I suspect is his preferred sexual behaviour.'

Hope debated with herself for a moment. 'There are some magazines in the bottom of my wardrobe. Why don't you take a look at them while I dress?' She slipped from the bath and wrapped herself in a towel, exiting the bathroom to retrieve the English-language magazine from the pile before Allie followed. She wrapped the towel around it, not wanting Allie to learn of Rusty's association with Mallot, and placed the remaining magazines on the bed. She was staring at her meagre collection of clothes when she heard the rustle of pages.

'I have no clue what to wear,' she complained.

Allie snorted. 'If you're dressing for a sadist, I would suggest only a few well-placed welts! Will you *look* at this guy?' she exclaimed, and held up a picture of Rusty laying about him with a crop. A group of leather-clad, well-endowed girls cavorted to either avoid or encourage the treatment. 'Hope,' she slammed the magazine down, 'are you *really* sure you want this maniac?'

'I don't think that is what he does off camera,' Hope said thoughtfully. 'I suspect that once the lens is off him, he behaves in quite a different way.'

'I hope you're right. Just in case, I am going to find Mairead and get some of that salve that she put on Rat's back.' She sauntered over to peer into the wardrobe, plucked a black vest and wide leather belt from the shelves and offered them to Hope. 'I think these would do.' She winked and, grabbing the top magazine, left the room.

Hope pulled the vest over her head. It hugged her tightly, cupping firmly around her breasts and clinging to her flaring hips. When she buckled the belt around her waist the hem lifted to display her clam, so she slipped on some sheer bikini panties. She looked raunchy. The belt accentuated her wine-glass femininity but was menacing, the large buckle cruel. She dragged her hair back from her face and secured it in a tight bun. She stared at her reflection for a minute, then, before she lost her nerve, she swiftly gathered up the magazines, including the one she had hidden from Allie, and left her room.

To her dismay, Mallot was framed in Rusty's doorway. The two men spoke quietly, then, following Rusty's gaze, Mallot turned to face Hope. His eyes swept her briefly as she hovered uncertainly on the landing, then he strode towards the stairwell, his face grim. Rusty invited her in.

'What has this got to do with Mallot?' Hope demanded as Rusty closed the door softly behind them.

'Nothing.'

'Then perhaps you can explain this picture?' Hope fumbled, dropped the stack of magazines, retrieved the issue and thrust the picture of the group at Stringfellows towards him. 'You are all playing some sort of damned game with me and I am fed up!'

Rusty sat on the bed, looking miserable. He was naked, except for a small towel wrapped at his waist, and beneath it Hope could see the soft swell of his limp penis, an odd contrast to the blazing display of his erection on the cover of a lewd magazine that was splayed at his feet.

'I don't know what is going on,' Rusty muttered unhappily. 'I was just told to be at this retreat and pretend I did not know Mallot. I know who you are and that you worked for Reggie and know Mallot, but I thought you had received the same instructions as me.'

'But I *don't* know Mallot! I came here to look for someone for Reggie.' Hope noticed that Rusty was staring at her strangely. 'What?' She threw up her hands in frustration.

'You *do* know Mallot,' Rusty stated.

'No, I don't. I presume he has something to do with Salvatore, or Reggie. I have never met him, however, even though he seems familiar at times.'

Rusty continued to look puzzled, then his expression gave way to dismay and he crossed to the window and stared, even though the blackness beyond the window hid the scene. Hope watched his reflection in the pane, softening as she realized he seemed like a child about to cry.

'It is like I said in the group' He spoke so softly that Hope had to draw nearer to hear. 'I fell in with this bad bunch because all I had was this pretty body and everything has been dictated from that.'

'Oh, right,' Hope clapped her hand to her forehead in mock surprise, 'I forgot. You're a victim? Silly me, of course you have no choices!'

'You despise me,' Rusty stated. 'You think I am bad and weak and deserve whatever punishment I get.'

Hope was about to protest when Rusty turned from the window and she glimpsed a sly undertone in his expression and the unmistakable first tenting of the towel betraying his burgeoning erection. She swiftly turned and strode up and down the room, desperately thinking. She was right, she congratulated herself, off-camera Rusty wanted the tables turned. The big, bad sadist wanted chastisement. She felt strangely elated, ill at ease with the mean hunger that rode her, but overwhelmed with the drive to explore this new development. She felt powerful and sensual, and slightly cruel. She stopped and glared at Rusty, her hands on her hips.

'Yes, you're bad.' She agreed. 'I think bad people ought to receive exactly what they hand out, don't you? Perhaps if they know how it feels they won't be so eager to do it again.'

Rusty nodded, his head hung down. His shaft was now fully hard and poking through the folds of the towel.

'Drop your towel and bend over.' When Rusty hesitated, Hope slipped off her belt. She grasped the buckle in her palm and wrapped the strap once around her hand, flicking experimentally. The thick band licked the air lazily, its passage followed by Rusty's hungry gaze. He quickly turned his back and bent over, presenting his muscled buttocks to the strap. Between his parted thighs, Hope could see the smooth round sac of his tight scrotum and a suggestion of the falling arc of his penis. He gripped his knees, his elbows bent.

Hope had never imagined she would be meting out punishment to Salvatore's latest discovery, never mind any other man, and the connection increased her interest. Somehow she associated the long nights of futile yearning, her abstinence, burning and repressed sex-drive with Rusty. He was the vessel for her release and, despite his avowal that he was as ignorant as she of his role at the retreat, she sensed duplicity and that cunning overlay a host of associations with the men she had trusted. She drew the belt slowly over Rusty's waist, curving it so it snaked over one bumcheek, then she turned and repeated the process from the other side. Rusty trembled, his buttocks clenching.

Taking a pace back, Hope tested the belt, flicking it lazily into the air. It was heavy and she determined not to strike too hard. However, when she flicked, again it arced with a life of its own and landed harshly across Rusty's bared buttock, drawing a gasp.

'That one was for Mallot,' Hope said calmly. She drew the belt back and delivered a stinging blow across the other buttock. 'That one was for Reggie.'

Bands of vivid white crossed Rusty's buttocks, then bloomed pinkly. She laid her palm on the markings and felt a mild heat. *Not too hard*, she decided. The belt licked again, sweeping across the markings and this time provoking a moan.

'That one was for Allie,' she improvised. 'For disappointing her.'

The next band was laid across his mid-thigh, causing Rusty to sway, and it was delivered harder.

'For me,' Hope attested. The next would be the last. Broad red welts crossed Rusty's perfect flesh and Hope thought carefully about where to lay the final strap. She let the belt fall straight down, practised, then jerked her wrist. The leather whipped into an 'S'. The tongue licked between Rusty's thighs, curved under and, when she pulled sharply, it glanced along the erect length of his rod, skimmed over his sac and then halted, its momentum lost. It seemed to cling, for a split second, between his thighs then, as his cry rang out, it dropped limply.

'That one,' Hope said, 'was for Salvatore.' She unwound the belt from her hand and tossed it to the ground, marvelling that Rusty's erection still weaved lustily. 'Stand up and face me.'

Rusty groaned and turned to look at Hope. His eyes were wet from the pain and narrowed with desire. He panted, whimpering when Hope retrieved the belt from the floor. She backed slowly until she could feel the hard wedge of a chest of drawers bite into her waist, braced her hands on the surface and swung to sit on it, leaning back until her shoulders met the wall.

'Now you are going to please me,' she instructed. 'Come here.'

When he was close enough, she looped the belt behind his neck and tugged so he leaned over her, his breath panting on her stomach. She wrapped her legs around him and started to slide from the surface. He immediately embraced her, taking her weight as she slid down his torso. When her waist braced the edge once more, Hope curved towards him, her arms surrounding his neck. The belt lay in a loop between her hands. She felt the nudge of his penis through the sheer material of her panties and rode his length, enjoying the slippery give along the fabric and, looking over his shoulder, she caught their reflection in the mirror on the wardrobe door.

Rusty's broad, muscled shoulders gave way to his sculpted back. His buttocks, crossed with blazing crimson welts, stood out. Her calves hugged around the vivid stripes and she clenched suddenly, the rub of her flesh abrasive. He braced his legs and leaned back, taking her weight, then slid one hand down to finger the crotch of her panties to one side. Breathing heavily, he entered her.

'Christ,' he exclaimed, 'you're wet!' He carried her to the bed and threw her down, his penis sliding free, then rolled her over and whipped the belt from her grip, only to drag her wrists together with one hand while he slid the tongue through the buckle. He slipped the noose over her arms and tightened it at her elbows, then flipped her onto her back.

'You're just like all the other bitches,' he muttered, straddling her, then cried out as she kicked and her knee slammed into his groin.

They wrestled and Hope knew that, with his greater strength, he was merely tussling with her and allowing her to get some licks in. She, meanwhile, made no concessions, kicking and connecting mercilessly with any sensitive area she could reach. Eventually he had her pinned, the weight of his chest pressing against her cheek. She went limp, as if in surrender, and when he eased from her she whipped her head around and bit his nipple hard, refusing to let go. He jerked, his breath a hard expulsion, and groaned.

'Oh God, that's good,' he moaned, freezing above her.

Hope let go in shock, while Rusty writhed above her, lost in rapturous pain. After a moment he leapt up and raced to the wardrobe, ripping it open and scrabbling through the shelves. When he returned, he rolled her onto her stomach and released her arms. He dragged her from the bed and onto her back, then stood over her and dropped a small whip on her stomach. She clutched the blunt stock and wriggled from between his legs, glancing at her weapon. A short, thick handle gave way to thin leather thongs, each tipped with knots.

'Now we're even,' Rusty growled, although his hands were empty.

Quick to take advantage, Hope sprung to her feet, only to find herself knocked back. She knelt and flicked the whip blindly, shocked when she looked up in time to see the tassels connect with Rusty's pouch. He moaned delightedly and threw himself at her and again she struck. This time the strips flashed across his stomach. She slashed again, across his chest, and the knots bit into his nipples. Now Rusty was groaning, but his weight pinned her. He rested his elbows either side of her head and his penis was a hard demand along her rift.

Hope fought him, her teeth bared, and slashed the whip across his back and waist. The pain drove him into a rampant frenzy, his demands incoherent. His knees forced themselves between her legs and he penetrated her, his angle of thrust forcing the crotch of her panties aside. He pounded into her, bucking as her swipes landed across his already marked buttocks.

'Oh, you glorious bitch!' he shouted suddenly and shuddered, swiftly withdrawing and kneeling so his cream geysered over her breasts. He milked at his shaft until the last silky drops coated her stomach.

Hope slumped, breathing heavily. He was done but the pressure of his shafting remained in her and she writhed in frustration, her need thwarted. Rusty grabbed the whip and slid beside her, his legs capturing hers in a scissors-like grip. He drew the stock of the whip down her stomach and over her mound, coating it with his sex-liquor, then slipped it between her lobes and jiggled until it entered her. Crazed as she was, Hope lifted to take it in, sobbing her relief as he worked it inside her, slowly thrusting. He leaned over and parted her vulva, sunk his head into her groin and nipped lightly at the inner flesh of her succulent nether lips. She came with force as he held her bucking hips down, tupping with the surrogate cock, his teeth fixed around her hooded clit.

Afterwards they slumped apart, the sweat soaking into the carpet. When he could speak Rusty said, 'You are amazing.' He traced the myriad of thin welts on his chest with his fingers and wet his finger to rub it gently over his smarting nipples. Hope eased into a sitting position, her head ringing and aware of the start of the aches of exertion. She tugged her vest back down, pulled the crotch of her panties into place and tried to smooth her hair. Surprisingly the bun had held. She looked dully at the whip, its handle slick with her juices, but when she reached to pick it up, Rusty's hand shot out.

'No.' He grabbed it and drew his tongue along it, then sucked the end, closing his eyes in bliss.

'You're very . . .' Hope cast around for a word, 'fundamental.'

Rusty stared at her. 'Are you disgusted?'

She shook her head, afraid to confess how she felt.

'What then?' Rusty persisted. He sat to face her, his eyes roving over her face intently.

'Excited,' Hope confessed. 'Like something new has been added, something in me.'

'It was always there,' he said, strangely gentle. 'As it is in me. Don't let them make it something bad,' he added cryptically.

'Like Mallot did with you?'

'No, not Mallot.'

'Who?'

'It doesn't matter now.'

Hope knelt before him and grabbed Rusty's face, forcing him to at her. 'It *does* matter! Who?'

After a pause he relented: 'Reggie.'

Hope stared.

'Reggie,' Rusty stated more firmly, 'is the introducer. He introduced me two years ago, and you a week ago. Just don't end up where I am.'

'How did you know about Reggie and me?'

'You had an audience.'

Hope sat back, her mind whirling. 'I couldn't see,' she murmured. 'I was blindfolded.'

'Through the window. The building opposite.'

There was silence, then, 'I see. Were you there?'

'Yes.'

'And Mallot?'

'Yes.'

'Angela?'

Rusty looked surprised. 'No! She really is a member of the retreat.'

'But there are others involved, aren't there?'

'Yes,' Rusty said miserably, 'but I am not sure who.'

'I see,' Hope repeated, although she did not.

'Look,' Rusty said sincerely, 'if it is any consolation, you were magnificent, both in Reggie's office and here. There is something special in you.'

Hope recognized his compliment in spite of her chagrin, and a part of her gloried in it. 'Thank you.'

He nodded.

There seemed no more to say so Hope rose and, gathering her belt, left Rusty sitting on the floor. She found Allie curled up in her bed, fast asleep, fifty-pound notes scrunched loosely in her hand. Hope washed and slipped under the sheet, wrapping her arms around the soft form and delighting when the small body shifted sleepily to mould to her contours.

Chapter Twelve

'You're bruised,' Allie greeted Hope as she opened her eyes. She was seated naked and cross-legged next to Hope, and had drawn the sheet down to examine the marks.

'You should see the other guy.' Hope rose to lean on her elbows and survey herself. She was disconcerted to note large purpling splodges on her thighs and waist. A sprinkling of smaller discolorations freckled her arms, and her muscles ached.

'We heard.'

Hope blushed.

'In fact,' Allie continued, 'some of us were so concerned that we were going to break the door open and save you but Mallot appeared and stopped us.'

'Ye gods!' Hope pulled a pillow over her face and groaned.

'Serves you right!' Allie laughed and pulled the pillow away. 'I can't wait to see Rusty. It was his yells we heard, mainly.'

'Does that mean you are going to attend Angela's event this morning? I have no doubt Rusty will be bared and ready.'

'You obviously learned something about him last night.'

'And something about me,' Hope confessed.

'Later? Let's get breakfast.' The gong had sounded.

The atmosphere was strained at the breakfast table. Hope received curious looks but said nothing, and had covered her bruising with sweats and a loose T-shirt. Rusty was less reticent and his striping was still vivid. Hope could only see his upper front torso but was aware that some had viewed his rear and their reluctance to meet her eyes came as no surprise. Quinn, however, beamed at her, still entranced with his night's success. Mallot nodded and continued to eat his breakfast calmly. Angela was not present. Rat grinned at Allie and patted the seat next to him.

'What of Karen?' Elsa ventured at last.

'She is still indisposed. We shall see Brandon at the punishment.' Mallot's reference stilled Elsa. 'In fact,' Mallot looked at his watch and rose, dabbing his mouth with a serviette, 'it is nearly time.' He left the room and the air seemed lighter.

'Is anyone going to be there?' Elsa asked, her voice timid.

'I am,' Rusty said.

'I would have thought, from the look of you, that you had had enough punishment!' Rat retorted.

'I'm not on the receiving end this time,' Rusty responded cheerfully.

'Well,' Rat conceded, 'I am going to be there, too.'

'As am I,' Hope said softly.

Elsa looked at Hope shyly. 'Can I come with you?'

'If you are sure that you want to see this, then okay.' Hope felt concerned but realised that Elsa was bursting with curiosity. The young woman had seemed to accept a great deal very quickly and Hope put it down to the blessing of innocence. Still, it seemed a crazy way to be introduced to the arts of love.

'How can I not be there?' Allie muttered.

'Very easily,' Ruari countered. 'I intend to stay well away.' He glanced at Hope and in his expression she saw reproach.

'What happened last night had nothing to do with this,' she said.

'It is all part of the same thing,' Ruari argued.

'What?' Rat intervened, 'Sex?'

'Yes. That is all this retreat seems to be about.' Ruari seemed upset.

'It is me you're really getting at, isn't it?' Elsa squared up to the big Irishman, her eyes flashing. 'Well, I don't think you and Hope were just about sex and nor were Quinn and I. If you wanted sackcloth and ashes you should have gone to Holy Island. You just remember that I am as Catholic as you and I don't think I have committed any sin!'

'You will have if you watch Mallot's carry-on.'

'Oh, right,' Elsa responded angrily, 'and watching is sinning, right? Just like thinking is sinning? Will you grow up, you big *eejit*!'

Ruari subsided, humbled by Elsa's onslaught. It was clear that his views were fixed but he found it difficult to face the wrath of the young Irishwoman. 'Well,' he conceded, 'please yourself but I won't be there.'

'Sure, we don't want you there!' Elsa promptly replied, her voice haughty.

'You go, girl!' Allie chuckled, earning a dark look from Ruari and a snigger from Quinn.

'Hey, folks! Let's not squabble amongst ourselves. We have serious business going down in a half-hour!' Rat protested.

'Great! Time for another piece of toast,' Allie was unrepentant.

For all their humour, Hope sensed a nervous excitement. She felt anxious, even after her session with Rusty. What Mallot proposed was very remote from the experience of the members of this group, with the possible exception of Rusty. Hope also suspected that Mallot was banking on Rusty's performance ability. She ate in silence, allowing her anticipation to build. When Rat rose and tapped his watch, she followed him from the house, barely aware that Elsa and Allie were following.

The air was still. Not even a breeze ruffled the glass surface of the water and the leaves hung limp and thirsty in the morning heat. It felt like Nature was holding her breath and the glare was painfully bright, causing Hope to narrow her eyes and shield them with her hand. The venue chosen by Mallot was the small patch of lawn that featured the bench, but it was deserted.

'Maybe Angela chickened out,' Rat suggested.

Hope tried to recognize the shy geek who had accompanied her to the retreat and failed. It seemed that a surfeit of sex had revealed an uncaring young man. *But then*, she reasoned, *how different I am from the woman he knew at Pursuit*. She, like he, was eager to witness the punishment of a slave and the only difference was that Rat had expressed his thoughts aloud. Hope had to admit that the same wish had crossed her mind.

'It's too hot,' Elsa volunteered. 'Maybe they found somewhere cooler.'

As she spoke, Rusty came up behind them. 'No, it's here all right. You had better find somewhere out of the way.' He gestured to some rocks flanking the lawn beyond the bench.

They formed a small natural amphitheatre and puddles of shade, for which Allie was grateful. She was wearing her sarong and, while she had wrapped it under her armpits, she could already feel her skin burning. Hope perched on one of the rocks, her back to the sun, and she was better able to view Rusty who remained standing near the bench, his back towards her. His buttocks looked raw, but she noticed that he had oiled his body and was unable to decide if that was for show or for protection from the sun. Elsa crouched beside Allie, at Hope's feet, and Rat sat a little apart, as if between camps.

Brandon appeared, carrying a video camera. He waved at the small assembly and settled in a lotus position, hands resting palm upwards on his knees, and started to hum.

'You're not planning to tape this!' Allie exploded, after staring at him for some seconds in disbelief. She interrupted his flow, and Brandon looked up wide-eyed.

'Yes, of course. I have permission and this is very valuable material,' he responded mildly.

'Material!' Allie was appalled. 'We are talking about real people here, not guinea pigs.'

Brandon unclasped his legs and rose. He picked up the camcorder and moved closer, his eyes sincere and fastened on Allie's. 'I know and I respect people. Please believe that I would never, ever betray the faith of this group. This film is purely for my own files and education. I am here to be supportive, but otherwise I am a spectator, just like you.'

Allie seemed appeased. There seemed nothing but good in Brandon and his sincerity was disarming. She shrugged and settled back. Brandon smiled his thanks and checked the camera, hoisting it to his shoulder when Mallot strode from the house and faced them. The camera whirred.

'You know what I told you last night, so if anyone has any problem they should leave now because interference will not be tolerated at any stage.' He was met with silence and, for him, the onlookers then ceased to exist.

Hope's silence was caused by shock. Mallot wore a black leather balaclava and tight leggings. The zip that ran from beneath his chin to fasten the collar was undone but the voice piece glinted in the loose flap. As she stared, slack-mouthed, Mallot fastened the neck, tapped on the inset and muttered, 'How's that?' His voice came out distorted and mechanical. It was only then that Hope allowed herself to face the realization she had suppressed.

'You!' Her word was strangled. The camera turned on her.

Mallot swung to face her. 'I was most disappointed that you failed to recognize me without my clothes on.'

Hope's eyes swung to his groin. Beneath the fine leather leggings, the bulge of his manhood rounded proudly.

'Oh, don't worry. I was not shaven when you visited down there.'

'You know him?' Rat asked her.

'Indeed she does, young Raith,' Mallot answered for Hope, his eyes not leaving her face.

She stared at him, dumbfounded, trying to work out how she had failed to recognize the dark coldness of his eyes. It was only with the mask and mechanical distortion of his voice that his identity was made clear to her and the memories of London flooded back. She felt faint, grappling with the effort of trying to accept his presence on the island.

Mallot had not expected such a radical reaction and he softened, unzipped the throat collar and spoke to Hope in his normal voice. 'Don't try to work it out right now,' he murmured, reaching to stroke Hope's cheek. 'We'll talk later.' He rezipped and turned from her.

The small contact grounded her and Hope gazed at his back, recalling the feel of him in her mouth and his large, hard cock filling her cave. Her desire resurfaced, warring with her dislike of him, to further confuse her. The whole scene felt dreamlike and this effect was compounded when Angela stepped from the front door and made her way down the path towards Mallot. She stepped delicately onto the lawn, approached and drew to a halt before him, her eyes downcast.

Her long ash-blonde fall of hair was gone and only fine, silvery wisps curled around her head, no more than an inch in length. She looked wraithlike and fragile, an effect heightened by a stiff leather collar that surrounded her neck. A short chain hung from it and Angela held the end, which she now proffered to Mallot. In her other hand she held a birch switch. He took both the chain and the lash and led her to the bench, making her stand before the seat, while he stripped his leggings and then sat on the back, facing her.

'You shall please me now and from this moment until midnight you shall be handmaiden to all in this group. At no time shall you rise higher than anyone's waist and you shall be available to them on demand,' Mallot instructed. He braced his feet, slightly parted, on the seat of the bench, and the heavy curl of his limp penis moved softly between his thighs. He waved the switch at Rusty who was quick to step forward and accept it.

Rusty stationed himself behind Angela and tapped between her shoulder blades. She bent forward and leaned into Mallot's groin, her hands grasping the back of the bench on either side of his hips. The dark man drew the chain around so it lay in a snake along her back and let his hands fall beside hers, then nodded at Rusty, who drew forward and caressed the small globes of Angela's pert, bared bottom.

Taking this as her cue, she dipped her head and started working on Mallot's limp rod. She nibbled along its soft length, then sucked the silky tip into her mouth, holding it lightly with her teeth as her cheeks distended visibly. It grew and, as its girth and length increased, Angela grazed along it, her lips pulled back. When she reached the swollen tip she released it and nibbled down the underside, then buried her face into the heavy pouch, her tongue muscling into the fleshy joining. Mallot's shaft trembled and weaved heavily over Angela's cropped head. He let go of the bench and stroked himself softly, with clear enjoyment, as she gently sucked in one ball, nursed it, and then did the same to the other. When she drew her head up, Mallot grasped the root of his cock and laid a hand on her head, urging her to take his length in her throat. She stretched her neck, bobbed her head and the shaft slid deeply in, stopping only when Mallot's hand prevented further insertion. He sighed and stroked her bent head gently, then flicked a finger at Rusty who drew the birch softly across Angela's bumcheeks, causing them to clench in anticipation

Rusty idly traced an imaginary pattern of her bottom, then flicked his wrist to lay a line. The thin, sharp slap of the birch was heard by all and Elsa gasped, her hand rising to seek Hope's, who clasped it reassuringly. In the glare of the sun it was difficult to see the stripe left by the switch, but Hope recalled her own pleasure at the hands of the young whip-master in Mallot's London home and she squeezed her buttocks together jealously.

Angela moaned around Mallot's shaft and wriggled her bottom eagerly. Her head had risen on receipt of the first blow and, as Rusty continued to rain criss-crossing stripes, she dipped to his beat, her head rising and falling to take Mallot in more deeply each time. His head was now thrown back, his groans of pleasure distorted by the metal voice-piece. His hands returned to brace against the bench and he surrendered to his lusts, allowing Rusty to set the pace.

The model continued to switch until his penis hardened and then he cast the birch aside and slapped Angela's smarting cheeks with open palms to ensure she maintained the rhythm of the plunging. Satisfied, he then cupped her quim roughly, thrust his fingers into her cave and wet them, then spread her liquor between her bumcheeks to anoint her starry anal pucker. He explored with his index finger, slapping her sharply when her bobbing head faltered, and then penetrated past her firm sphincter, his bulb now cupped in the palm of his exploring hand. When he withdrew his finger, he pressed firmly and the shining tip of his cock slid inside her.

They both stilled and Mallot opened his eyes and looked down. Rusty's hands spanned Angela's hips, and her bumcheeks were parted by the girth of his rod. He stared into Mallot's eyes and gently eased deeper, withdrew, then started to tup slowly until Angela relaxed and opened to him. His thrusts increased in speed and she tensed her thigh muscles and braced herself more firmly to take the impact of his jabs. Satisfied that she now held firm, he released her hips and returned to slapping her, his palms once more establishing the rhythm. Her head resumed its plunging.

It was not long before Mallot came: he groaned, his voice distorted mechanically, and grabbed Angela's head, holding it hard into his groin as he shed his cream. When he released her, she spluttered, swallowing, then gasped for breath, shuddering as her own orgasm rushed through her.

'Bitch!' Rusty suddenly shouted and ground harder into her arse, his fingers cutting into the flesh of her bottom. He surged from her and his silk spun, lacing her back. He stood, breathing heavily for a moment, then stumbled back and slumped to the lawn.

Angela whimpered softly but remained in place, her head buried in Mallot's spent groin, lapping him clean. Mallot glanced around the group and his gaze settled on Rat. The young man's rod was a hard demand and his eyes were slits as they roved over Angela's slim form. Unable to resist his urge, Rat leapt forward and positioned himself behind Angela and bucked forward: his prick was swallowed in her. He rode her mindlessly, his hands grabbing and abrasive. His body stretched in a tight bow, hips thrusting, and his narrowed stare concentrated on his erotic pummelling, his mouth stretched in a feral sneer. His breath was expelled noisily with each sharp jab and when he came his cry seemed foreign and anguished, his fluid wrung from him. As the echoes died, he spun and raced to the water's edge, waded in and sank beneath the water. When he surfaced he seemed angry. He wiped his face, paddled back to shore, then made his way to the quay and sat moodily staring at the bay.

Angela sank to her knees, her arms sliding down the bench. She rested her head on the slats and Hope could see the sweat trickling down her back. Mallot eased from the back of the bench, picked up his discarded leggings, unzipped the balaclava and pulled it from his head. He then turned and walked away and soon Rusty followed. The waif was left discarded by the bench, slumped and used, in the searing heat of the midday sun.

Brandon had been forgotten during the event, his filming ignored, but as he turned the camera to tape the slumped slave Hope slid from the rock, pushed rudely past him and slipped alongside Angela. Brandon backed off up the path to the door, then disappeared inside the house.

'Come,' Hope said, resting her hand lightly on the small shoulder.

'Lead me,' Angela's voice was soft.

Hope lifted the chain and almost dropped it again. The heat had soaked into the links and the pattern was burning into Angela's back. She felt horrified. While Angela had been ministering to Mallot and Rusty had been buggering her, a deep well of lust had roiled in Hope and her blood had been as hot as Rat's when he raced to relieve his aching need. Hope had nearly slid from her perch to wrest his hardness from Angela's soft folds and herself claim its burning length. However, she had remained frozen in desperate arousal, watching the scene unfold, trying to make sense of the whirling thoughts and feelings that almost drowned her passion. She recognized her empathy with Angela, her envy of the submissive woman's position, but she also recognized herself in the punishing Rusty, the mastering Mallot and the desperate Rat. Now she allowed her angst to surface. She would accept and welcome the birch and surrender to harsh sexual ministration but she would never countenance the thoughtless cruelty that led to abuse through a burning chain left thoughtlessly draped on bare skin or desertion when care should be tendered. When a woman offered her valuable service in slavery, she did so with trust and the obligation on a master was absolute. He had to return care and nurturing as readily as he meted out punishment. Mallot, she determined, did not deserve Angela.

She gently guided Angela to the water, understanding when the woman crawled beside her and slid, her body low, into its healing coolness. She had been told not to rise above anyone's waist that day and intended to heed the command.

'You've also been told,' Hope murmured, as if she had spoken her understanding out loud, 'that you are everyone's handmaiden for the day. Please therefore sit in the shallows and feel comfortable with being level with me.'

Angela paused and then sat up, shifting slightly until she found a comfortable way to rest on the pebbled lakebed. Hope scooped handfuls of water over the link pattern on Angela's burnt back and the marks faded slowly. Angela had flinched with the first pouring but sighed as the ache receded. Hope then slopped water over the collar and shifted it around until the chain fell forward for Angela to hold.

'Lie on your tummy.'

Angela stretched out and then rolled over. She was buoyed by the water and her striped bottom broke the surface like a small rounded island. The thin mesh of the birching criss-crossed in a crimson network and Hope soothed it with her cool palms. By this time Allie and Elsa had crept to join them. Allie looked outraged, but bit back her words, and Elsa merely looked puzzled although the evidence of her own arousal was still present in the redness of her swollen lips and the pucker of her nipples.

'Allie,' Hope turned to the redhead. 'Did you get that salve from Mairead?' Hope received a curt nod. 'Will you fetch it?'

Allie scuttled away.

'Here,' Hope addressed Elsa, then guided her hand to Angela's back. 'Just scoop little amounts of water over Angela. Wash off Rusty's leavings and make sure the chain marks are all gone.'

Elsa gently obeyed.

'Angela,' Hope said softly, 'You can speak freely with me.' She had suddenly remembered that the permission was needed and looked intently at Elsa.

'And around me!' Elsa mimicked and received a smile from Hope.

'Me, too.' Allie had returned with the salve, her panting betraying the fact that she had run to fetch it.

Hope stripped off her T-shirt and gave it to Allie. 'Pat her dry and put the salve on her back and bottom, okay? I have to go and talk to people.' She stood up but found herself anchored by Angela's surprisingly strong grip on her ankle.

'Not Mallot!' Angela cried. She surged from the water and gripped Hope's shoulders, her expression imploring. 'There are things you don't understand.' Angela was almost weeping.

'I know,' Hope soothed. 'But there are also things *you* don't know. I am not going to tackle him about you, but about me.' Hope hesitated, then led Angela into the shade of the rocks and urged her to lie on her stomach. While Allie dabbed her dry and smoothed the lotion over her buttocks, Hope explained.

'Mallot and I met recently, in London.'

'Why didn't you tell me?' Angela demanded.

'Because I did not remember him until I saw him in his mask.'

'He is your master?' Angela sounded aggrieved.

'No. Mallot will never be my master,' Hope said firmly. 'And I realized today that I will have no master, only an equal.'

'So why do you want to talk to him?' Angela blurted, then suddenly remembered her place. 'Oh,' she muttered in a small voice.

'Tell me, Angela,' Hope asked, 'have you heard of Reggie? Or Salvatore or Willincough?' When Angela shook her head, Hope said kindly, 'Then it is none of your business and I think you should keep it that way, or you may find yourself in a lot more trouble than you are already.' She rose to her feet.

'Wait! Please. One last thing . . .' Angela peered up at her. 'What has Rusty got to do with Mallot?'

Hope tried to find the right word, especially since Allie also seemed to be holding her breath for an answer. Eventually she said, 'I think the best description is that Rusty is Mallot's lackey.' She knew she sounded bitter, so she added, 'But at least Rusty knew it, which is more than I was allowed to know. You see, somewhere along the line I have been played for a fool and no one had the grace to spell it out for me.'

As Hope strode away, Allie shoved the salve into Elsa's hands and raced to join her. She rounded in front of Hope at the front door and prevented her access.

'You don't want to do this,' she said urgently. 'These guys are not pussycats!'

'This from you, Allie? If it was you being played with, I would think you would be the first one racing to tear them limb from limb!'

'No,' Allie shook her head. 'Not this way. These guys are real trouble and I don't know who the others are but it doesn't sound safe. Why don't you just try and get the hell out of here and confront this in London where you at least have some protection?'

'What do you know, Allie?' Hope peered into her friend's eyes, alarmed at her reaction. 'I don't think there is danger here, but you seem to think I am putting myself at real risk.'

'Wake up, Hope! We both watched what happened with Angela. After last night Rusty is a mass of welts. This retreat has gone to hell in a bucket, and fast! What's next – a ritual sacrifice? You are dreaming if you think it stops here. Mallot is a cold bastard and capable of anything and Rusty would help him do it, too!' Allie propelled Hope into the lobby and pulled her over to sit on the choir bench. 'Who are these Ormandies, anyway? Don't you see, we're *all* being set up. We still have a week to go and it's Mallot who seems to be saying when we meet and when we don't.'

'Okay,' Hope said, with a small laugh, 'now who is being paranoid?'

Allie threw up her hands in a gesture of frustration and despair. 'All I'm saying is that we both know something fishy is going on. So why don't we just ease back a little bit and take a good look at what is happening? Don't you think it's a bit coincidental that Mallot just happens to be on the same retreat with you when you told us that you met him recently as that masked man? And don't think I haven't realized that there is a history between you and Rat! At least let me help you find out what is cooking. Don't just go barging in like the Winged Avenger.' She slumped back in the pew and studied Hope.

Hope returned the appraisal. 'You're quite a gal,' she said at last, and giggled. 'This is becoming a real one-act drama.' As Allie continued to stare at her, she relented, 'Okay, think first, act later.' She held out her hand and Allie shook it, appeased.

'What shall we do first?' Allie's words were almost drowned by the luncheon gong.

'Eat?'

They both laughed, sobering when Elsa came through the door, leading the crawling Angela by the chain. There was a mixture of helpless confusion and repugnance on the young woman's face and she cried out, 'She made me! She said she was not allowed to walk and would get into trouble if no one led her.' Elsa was almost in tears.

'Hush,' Hope leapt to take the chain, hugging Elsa with her free arm. 'It's okay. See, I've got her.' She grimaced at Allie and led Angela into the dining room.

They were the first to arrive, though Mairead was bustling around, setting plates of cold meats and bowls of salads in the centre of the table. She glanced at Angela and beckoned Hope to lead her beside Mallot's usual chair. A cushion was already laid on the floor and Angela sank to sit cross-legged on it.

'You can leave her now,' Mairead whispered, 'I know what to do.'

Elsa gave Hope back her T-shirt. It was damp and crumpled but she pulled it over her head gratefully as the rest of the group entered. Only Rat glanced at Angela. He seemed about to say something but Hope shook her head.

'I only wanted to apologize,' he whispered as he passed Hope.

'No need. It's okay.'

'How come you know so much about this?' He kept his voice low.

Hoped tugged him to the window and rounded on him. 'Now you tell me honestly,' she hissed, 'is there really a Willincough?' From the expression that crossed Rat's face she received her answer before he spoke.

'Yes, of course!' In his surprise, Rat failed to keep his voice low. 'What's going on?'

'Later.' Hope strode back to the table and took a seat between Allie and Elsa.

Karen had again not appeared, but Brandon sat quietly, gazing around the table.

'I have good news for you,' he said, 'Karen is feeling much better and we shall have a session after supper tonight. Unless we have a reason not to do so, perhaps we can talk about how we felt this morning?'

'Oh, right,' Allie retorted, 'and you can pass the photo albums!'

Ruari looked up. 'What?'

'I made a video of this morning's event,' Brandon explained.

And he had my full permission,' Mallot cut in.

'He did not have *my* permission,' Rat protested, 'and I don't think I want to be on that tape.'

Brandon sighed. 'It will be a great pity, because your actions were spontaneous, but I pledge to cut that footage from the tape. I do assure you that this is for my own research collection and no one but Karen and I will view it.' He looked mournful.

Rat subsided.

'What about Angela's permission?' Allie persisted.

'She does not need to offer her permission. Mine is sufficient,' Mallot said coldly.

Angela remained seated on her cushion, only the top of her downcast head visible. The conversation regarding her rights seemed to be irrelevant to her. Mairead offered her a plate of food but, before accepting it, Angela waited for Mallot to mutter his consent. She took the plate but, without cutlery, was forced to eat with her fingers.

'I want to speak with people in the library after lunch,' Ruari said suddenly.

'Fine,' said Mallot.

'Not you, Rusty or Brandon.'

'What is this,' Mallot laughed, 'a mutiny?'

Ruari stared at him, his jaw set. 'I think you are a bad person, Mallot, and that you are breaking this group apart. We came here for a reason and you have constantly pushed it too far.'

'Seems to me that the shaker and mover in this group is Hope,' Mallot pointed out. 'It was she who started the ball rolling and one only has to observe Rusty to see her handiwork. So tell me,' he leaned across the table and faced Ruari, 'how come she is invited and not me?'

'Hope had held us all together and we trust her. We do not trust you,' Ruari said.

'And you do not trust your hosts?' Brandon asked softly.

'Where were they when we needed them today? Brandon was making dirty movies and Karen was swimming on the far side of the island.'

All eyes turned on Brandon. 'She has been infectious,' he advised, 'and was careful to keep away but she was feeling much better and risked a little exercise.' His sincerity was beginning to wear thin.

Ruari shook his head in disbelief. 'Well, that's it. Nobody has to be there but I think it is time the ordinary folk spoke together about what is happening.'

'I am against it,' Mallot said angrily.

'Tough,' Allie retorted. She smiled at Ruari, 'I'll be there.'

Nods followed and Hope, caught in the blaze of Mallot's harsh stare, added her own assent. He pursed his lips, sighed, and continued eating.

'I feel disappointed,' Brandon added mildly, 'but I hope that, whatever you decide during your meeting, that you will feel comfortable discussing it later with Karen and me.'

The library was cool and dim and Hope explored, thankful to have the opportunity before the group assembled. It was only a week since she and Rat had consummated their lust but the room seemed untouched, the dust covering their trespass. She climbed a ladder and gazed at the leather-bound books on the high shelves, their titles almost obscured with wear. Her original feeling returned. Someone had loved these books. Absorbed in her task, she nearly fell when Ruari's deep bass surprised her.

'It's dangerous up there, without someone holding the ladder for you.'

Hope felt the trembling when he gripped the sides firmly, but decided to descend now that the peace was broken. She climbed down, surprised when Ruari failed to let go, and when she reached the ground he pressed along her back and she could feel his firm rod between her bumcheeks, through her sweats. His knuckles were white, his hands still tightly circling the struts.

'I cannot get you out of my mind.' His voice was low in her ear and he bent to kiss her neck, his lips hot and firm. He let go and slid his arms around the ladder and his hands beneath her T-shirt, to cup her breasts and softly pinch her nipples.

Hope moaned. Her desire had barely been in check throughout lunch, the legacy of her morning's voying. Heat expanded though her and she realized that, in spite of his religious conviction, Ruari was filled with a lust that he could not control. Beneath the gentle touch, he was trembling with need. Neither of them was in a position to stop. She had drawn to a halt, within his embracing arms, her hands secure on a higher rung and her feet on the ground and now she pressed into the ladder, her breasts protruding between the rungs. She weaved her bottom against his shaft, encouraging his passion.

Ruari groaned, released a breast and wrestled Hope's sweats down to mid-thigh, dragged his swimming trunks down, sufficient to release himself, and tried to guide his burning cock between her closed thighs. It was awkward and Hope heaved herself up so her feet rested on the first rung. He aligned his cock and slipped into her wet welcome, with a sigh of deep pleasure that matched hers, then returned his hand to her breast. The ladder sprung when he started to fuck, his weight leaning full into her, and Hope relaxed, surrendering to his shafting. She dreamily noted the arrival of others, not caring, her concentration centred on the swelling delight inside her.

Ruari rode without haste, shedding his reserves and

emerging into a new world of sensation without stress. He marvelled as he banished the dicta of the priests from his head and soul and was free to breathe in the scents and flesh of the woman between whose willing thighs he felt the thrill of a mutual taking. His rod was hot, engorged with a human lust and stroked with silk. He sunk into Hope without conscience, knowing that she was as rampant as he, and when his groin clutched and the heat rose through his cock, he felt her drive down on him, to meet his release with hers. Their small animal cries shattered the stillness of the library, reducing to sobs as they slumped, and the old wood of the ladder creaked discordantly with the broken tempo of their last thrusts.

Ruari eased back, allowing his waning length to slide heavily from Hope. He realized how tightly he had been gripping her breasts and felt a moment's alarm, but she stepped down and wriggled to face him, her face glowing and her eyes softly enquiring. He nodded and kissed her lightly to reassure her that he was not going to fly into religious remorse. He felt very tender towards her, enjoying the last pleasured press against her mound before his penis slept.

Over his shoulder, Hope could see Allie and Elsa, their faces intent as they scanned the sated pair. Elsa's face was flushed with arousal and Hope guessed it would not be long before she demanded congress and the liberation of her virginity. To Hope, Ruari seemed the perfect lover for Elsa, but her mind niggled at the memory of the young woman's excitement as she had watched Angela with Rusty. In Elsa she saw herself, her own adventurous sexuality, before the wasted years. Perhaps Ruari was too gentle and sweet in his lovemaking, and Elsa with her burgeoning lusts would demand a harsher ministry. Whatever she chose, the young woman did not lack for possible suitors. Rat was also present, his hand idly pressed to his groin and his eyes misty. The only one not viewing them was Quinn, whose gaze was roaming the spread of Allie beneath the sheer fall of her sarong.

Ruari smiled, stepped back and tugged up his swimming trunks. Hope knew that he was aware of their audience and he was embarrassed but unrepentant. He drew her sweats up and kissed her once more, before turning to face the group.

'Shall we get started?' he asked.

'Looks like you already did,' Allie quipped and winked at Hope.

'I never did.' Elsa's voice was sad.

Hope recognized that the girl was ready to make her bid. She glanced a warning at Ruari and slipped beside Elsa.

'You okay?'

'No,' Elsa shook her determinedly, 'I'm not.' She looked around the group. 'You're all involved and, whenever I look anywhere, I see people bonking without any problem. I want to do it too and I don't want to go back to the farm and settle for some galoot with cowpat on his wellies who only knows to stick it in.' She subsided, blushing.

'Who do you want?' Hope asked softly, sure that Elsa would chose Ruari. She was stunned when Elsa replied.

'Mallot.'

'Jesus!' The exclamation came from Rat.

Hope stared at the young woman, unable to speak.

'I know what you all think,' Elsa said. 'Mallot is a bad guy and I am a virgin so it would be horrible. But he would do it the best way because he is so experienced and, if Hope will help me, then I'll enjoy it. Anyway, it's what I want,' she concluded defiantly.

Allie surprised them all. 'I think Elsa's right. If I was the virgin then I would choose Mallot.'

'But we don't know what is going on here!' Ruari persisted. 'All of us think there is something dodgy about this retreat, and the connection between the Ormandies and Mallot, so why are we going on with this?'

'Because there are two separate issues,' Hope said. 'This is about what Elsa wants and I think we should help her. I don't think Mallot will be surprised: he *did* offer himself to everyone. If there is something dodgy going on then there's plenty of time left to uncover it. One night is not going to make a whole lot of difference.'

'Well,' Ruari said desperately, staring at Elsa. 'Won't I do, or Rat or Quinn?'

'Oh yes,' Elsa gazed at him, 'I want you. I just want to come to you in Cork without this silly virginity getting in the way!' With this she sealed their future promise and Ruari smiled broadly.

'What about this discussion we're supposed to be having?' Rat demanded.

'I think we've been sidetracked,' Ruari muttered.

'You may have been, I haven't!' Rat protested. 'Look, I just need to get to a telephone line for a couple of hours.'

'For what?' Quinn looked genuinely interested.

'I've a modem with my laptop, so I can look around for information on all of them. Maybe something will give us a clue.'

'You're that good that you can access personal information in secure databases? As far as the Ormandies are concerned, they are probably American citizens. How are you going to get details on them?' Quinn was now studying Rat carefully, his eyes narrowed. He no longer looked the shy, bumbling husband but shrewd and powerful.

'Yes.' Rat returned Quinn's stare. His eyes held a warning and the American, who seemed about to continue his questions, reconsidered.

'The only telephone line is in the Ormandies' room. That is what Mairead told us, anyway,' Elsa offered.

'Well,' Hope suggested, 'it may help if we started off knowing who owns this place.'

'It used to belong to some Earl,' Rat said, 'but I understand it changed hands recently. They told me that at the hotel in Killalloe.'

'In England,' Hope said pensively, gazing around her, 'this would belong to the National Heritage Trust or some such.'

'They're starting to tighten up in Ireland but some places slip through the net. Still, it shouldn't be too hard to find out who bought it.' Quinn said. 'Far as I know this place used to be used for *religious* retreats. That is what I learned before I came here.' In response to the curious looks, he continued, 'I'd never go anywhere without looking into it.'

'Hang on a moment. Who knows we're here?' Rat asked suspiciously.

'My wife and possibly two colleagues from work.' Quinn shrugged.

'My dad and friends,' Elsa said.

'Folk at work,' Allie said.

'And for Hope and I the same. People at the office.' Rat turned to Ruari.

'Well, no one really,' Ruari confessed, 'I just went on a walkabout during my work leave.'

'There's also the people from the windsurfing centre,' Hope protested, 'and Bear at The Piper's Inn. I also put it down on the form they gave me on the flight to Shannon. Let's not get carried away with some conspiracy theory!'

'So, what's the deal, then, if there is no conspiracy?' Ruari asked.

'Maybe there is no *deal*. Maybe this retreat is exactly what it said it would be in the advertisement. Mallot will have seen the same magazine as me, as would Rusty. I know Rat saw it so perhaps it *is* just coincidental that some people seem to have a link.' As she spoke, Hope did not really believe it. 'Well, if anything is afoot, it is hardly world-shattering, life-threatening stuff. We only have five days left, so why don't we just relax, enjoy them and vow never to meet Mallot or the Ormandies again?'

'I'm for that.' Allie grinned, 'Let's concentrate on the deflowering of young Elsa!'

'Oh you!' Elsa hugged the redhead affectionately.

'I still want to get to a telephone,' Rat muttered.

'I'm with you,' Ruari agreed.

Quinn joined them as they wandered off, sotto-voiced and hatching schoolboy plots.

'Will you talk with Mallot?' Elsa beseeched Hope.

'Oh, Elsa. That is really something you ought to do,' she protested, then softened. 'Tell you what, we shall speak to him together.'

'Need an arbitrator?' Allie stuck her head between them.

'An arbitrator,' laughed Hope, 'also has to be a bit diplomatic. I don't think you qualify as far as Mallot is concerned.'

'Right, I know when I am not wanted! You will find me on the quay.' Allie marched off in mock anger.

Hope squeezed Elsa'a arm. 'You sure about this?'
'As I'll ever be,' Elsa murmured. 'It's time.'
'I understand. Well, let's go do it!'

They found Mallot, Rusty and Brandon in the lounge. They were stretched out on the sofas, chatting idly. Angela was leaning against Mallot's knees, playing with the end of her chain.

'It's such a special thing, giving one's virginity,' Brandon observed seriously after Hope had made the proposal.

Mallot was staring at Elsa with a mixture of calculation and disbelief. 'This is what you talked about in the library?' he questioned at last.

'Yes,' Elsa replied.

'I see.' Then, remembering his manners, he patted the seat next to him and Elsa joined him on the sofa. He looked deep into her eyes. 'I will be happy and privileged to be your first lover.'

'You see,' Elsa smiled at Hope, 'I told you he would do it right.' To Mallot, she said, 'Hope must be there.'

'Well, as the group seems to be split apart, why don't we take this opportunity to celebrate together? That will involve everyone and maybe we can make this a joyous event?' Brandon seemed excited. 'If you want I can also make a videotape especially for you.'

Hope was about to protest when Elsa clapped her hands.

'Yes! Like a proper ritual,'

Hope added the word 'sacrifice' silently but, loath to burst Elsa's happy bubble, kept her peace.

'Angela can be your handmaiden and Hope can give you away,' Mallot suggested. 'Allie can be the one who protests when Brandon asks for any reason not to proceed and Ruari can officiate.'

Hope sought signs of sarcasm in Mallot's words but found none. He seemed as charmed by the prospect as any frustrated thespian offered a part in *A Midsummer Night's Dream*. Even Angela was smiling softly at Elsa, obviously pleased.

'Well, what can I do?' Elsa demanded, then blushed when everyone chuckled.

'Just be there,' Mallot said gently. 'We'll do the rest. You'll be like the sleeping princess and we'll all celebrate your waking.'

'That makes you my prince, doesn't it?' Elsa asked shyly.

'It does. And I thank you for the title. Usually I am the wicked king!'

'And, if Angela is to be my handmaiden, then we should do this before midnight. Then we can also celebrate her release from that yoke!'

'You are a very sweet person,' Brandon observed. 'Perhaps we can all learn that from you. Come,' he looked around, 'we have to get Mairead to prepare something special for dinner and apprise the rest of the men! We have four hours until supper, and afterwards, a passage of innocence – for us all!'

'Angela,' instructed Mallot, 'go with Hope and Elsa and help the women. When we all meet again at the dinner table, each group must know its role. I intend to sleep and re-energize and I suggest my princess does the same.' He dropped lightly to one knee and kissed Elsa's fingers.

As he left the lounge, flanked by Rusty and Brandon, Hope heard him mutter, 'This could not have worked out better!' She could not decide if he meant well or ill, but her main concern was that Elsa should be the princess and she believed Brandon was correct: Elsa's initiation would bond the group.

Chapter Thirteen

The circular table had been pushed to one end of the dining room and cushions and low stools had been scattered over a large Persian carpet. Light from a high, dimmed chandelier cast a molten gold illumination over the assembly, supplemented by the warm flicker of dozens of candles set in silver candelabra on the sideboard. The group were directed by Mairead to recline in a semicircle on the cushions and she placed finger bowls of warm, scented water on the low stools, with small white towels. The housekeeper seemed energized by the occasion, slipping silently among the loungers to lay platters of *hors d'oeuvres* and sweetmeats within convenient reach. Tiny porcelain pots of caviar with minute spoons, and rich pumpernickel bread followed. Then gleaming buckets holding champagne on ice, trays of sheer crystal flutes and fine bone china side plates. Finally, Mairead bore covered dishes which, with the lids removed, were revealed to hold steaming quail and woodcock, a whole poached salmon and piles of artichoke hearts and asparagus spears, with hollandaise sauce nestling in the silver gutters. Delicate forks bristled from the dishes and Mairead tore the small carcasses into jointed portions. At last satisfied, the housekeeper slipped away.

'This is the feast that was to mark the end of our retreat,' Brandon explained, 'but I think this night warrants the celebration. Please eat, and let's drink to Elsa and the special night to come.' He lifted a bottle of champagne from a nearby icebucket and poured the starburst liquid into a flute. 'To Elsa,' he intoned softly, his warm eyes resting in sincere admiration on hers.

Hope murmured her toast with the others, smiling at the young woman who blushed prettily, accepting the accolade with grace. She looked like the innocent princess Mallot had predicted. Angela had helped Elsa dress, offering garments from her own wardrobe, and the girl reclined proudly in a pure white voile robe tied at the waist with a twisted gold belt. The sheer material clung to her large breasts, her areolae brazen. Beneath the robe she wore white silk thong panties. She looked flushed, beautiful and very young, flanked by Mallot and Hope, with Angela settled at her head.

Hope was naked beneath a simple cream silk sarong. She had resisted Angela's offer of more exotic clothing but succumbed to the gilt clasp that held her hair in a topknot. Angela wore only her leather collar and chain, but had been permitted to don a gold anklet. Allie had tied a large purple scarf around her waist and drawn it, like a nappy, between her legs and secured the ends with a glittering marcasite brooch. Karen sat at one end of the semicircle in a black leather basque, her breasts uplifted and the butterfly tattoo displayed. She sat cross-legged and her shaven, dusky pink quim was bared and open.

The men were all dressed in black, fully clothed, apart from Mallot who wore his leather leggings. His oiled chest, covered in its riot of curling dark hair, gleamed in the candlelight. He was first to reach for the succulent breast of quail, the juices leaking between his fingers and running over his chin. He licked his fingers, then heaped artichoke and asparagus spears on a side plate, spooning hollandaise sauce over the mound. His example inspired the others and soon there was rippling movement, the pleasure of bobbing bare breasts and bottoms and the stealthy shift of black-clad forms. A lot of caressing occurred: asparagus was traced over breasts before the spears were sucked into male mouths and tongues lapped the residue of sauce from soft nippled flesh.

Angela served Elsa, feeding her morsels of food and sips of champagne, wiping her face with a cloth dipped in the perfumed water and ensuring the young woman was happy, before herself indulging in the finger-feast. The atmosphere was heady and sensual, the group making their way through the fare with murmurs and quiet laughter, at ease with the congress of warm flesh.

Hope felt relaxed. She realized that the men, schooled by Mallot, were orchestrating the pleasure of the women. Ruari had slipped alongside Hope and was tantalizing her with shreds of woodcock and spoonfuls of caviar. He caressed her breast, his hand slipping beneath the edge of the sarong, and breathed softly in her ear, his tongue lightly jabbing. When she had sighed, aroused and seeking more, he had withdrawn, his desire warring with the need for constraint. Rat attended to Allie, his hand slipping under the scarf, and Hope could see his fingers worming beneath the sheer material. He withdrew when the redhead lifted her hips to encourage penetration, instead offering champagne, then sweetmeats. Quinn replaced Ruari, his tongue circling Hope's nipples after he had carefully spread caviar over her areolae. But he withdrew as she leaned towards him, and merely refilled her glass. He turned to Angela and, bidding her kneel, parted her bumcheeks and drew a candied, sticky sweetmeat along the crease, then lapped the sugar from her. Karen was teasing her own nipples, her fingers circling softly, pinching and urging the small peaks to hardness while Brandon smiled and stroked himself gently through the cloth of his trousers.

The ebb and flow of rampant desires flooded the group, the men struggling to control their bursting erections and the women musky with arousal and pushed to fever pitch. Elsa's eyes were wide as she watched the sexplay. She remained untouched, except for the hot gaze of Mallot appraising her. A faint bloom covered her neck while her nipples grew pointed with frustration as she shifted, trying to pleasure her swollen nether folds against the cushions.

When Mallot nodded at Rusty, the model quickly slid the empty platters from sight to clear the carpet. The party fell silent, breath caught in anticipation, when Mallot knelt at Elsa's feet, massaging the soles. He bent to take each toe into his mouth, sucking softly, then looked up, his gaze hot, and murmured, 'It's time, my princess.'

Elsa sighed, wriggling forward to lie flat on the carpet. She stretched one arm out in search of Hope, who grasped the hand and squeezed softly. Hope kissed Elsa, her lips soft against the young, swollen mouth, and was rewarded when a tonguetip quested against hers. Angela reached for the other arm and caressed it.

Brandon murmured, 'Is there any objection within this group to the sacrifice of Elsa's maidenhood tonight?' Receiving none, he reached behind him and then lifted his video camera to his eye, sweeping the group, then settling on the gentle massage of Elsa's foot between Mallot's dark hands.

'Lift her,' Mallot whispered, 'so she can see and share with me.'

Angela and Hope moved together to form a bridge of knees against which Elsa could rest. Their hands roamed over Elsa to assure her of their support. Mallot stripped off his leggings and his large cock sprung free, causing Elsa to whimper and wriggle.

She felt nervous, even though she burned with need. He looked so huge after the small insertions of Hope's fingers. Her head was light with champagne and, despite the comfort of Hope's hand on her breast, Elsa felt dreadfully alone. Then Mallot was lifting her robe to bare her legs, his lips grazing her flesh and his tongue seeking along her inner thigh. The fascination of his mouth approaching her dark, curling muff kept her silent. When he slipped his hands between her thighs, they parted seemingly of their own volition, and her moist virgin folds were exposed to him through the sodden silk of the delicate thong.

Mallot tugged the wispy cloth aside and sank his mouth between the thick curls, his tongue testing. His blood was hot with the knowledge that he was the first man to cast around this patch and he held his cruel streak in check. He wanted to rear over the girl, plunge past her tight virgin ring and feel it tear along his cocktip, then pummel her with the huge girth of his hot rod until her moans of distress and pain turned into sobs of pleasure. Under his lips, he could feel the slick readiness of her and the shiver of her cunt muscles when his tongue penetrated. A glance upwards revealed that Hope was rhythmically squeezing one of Elsa's breasts, Angela teasing the other. Their ministration was not gentle and Hope's eyes were narrowed, staring in covetous desire at Mallot's prick when he rose to his knees to widen the spread of Elsa's legs. Elsa's eyes also were fixed on his groin and fear flitted across her face. Her lips were parted and she panted, squirming but restrained by the women's hold on her breasts. Despite her alarm her lips were red and swollen and a lustful, moist glaze covered her eyes.

Hope felt disturbed. Her own need, fuelled during the meal, burned hotly and she longed for the thrust of the smooth, heavy penis weaving before Elsa's trembling rift. She also felt a harsher edge sweep through her, the desire to watch Mallot's generous rod pierce the pure folds of the pale girl she held for sacrifice. She wanted to witness Elsa's resistance and hear the whimper as the tip plunged into her tight cave and then tore, unheeding, past her innocence. She found a similar lust mirrored in Angela's expression and the two gazed at each other in common acknowledgement. A slight smile curved Angela's lips and she leaned forward, her mouth widening, to meet with Hope's eager breath and hot, twisting tongue to seal their sisterhood. Hope broke away to stare at Mallot, again recognizing herself in the hard darkness of his eyes. She felt guilty, but nodded slightly and grasped Elsa's arm tightly, noting that Angela followed suit.

This was all the signal that Mallot needed. He forced a cushion under Elsa's hips so that her quim was raised for easy access. He grasped his cock and slid his bulb over her labia, forcing gently through, then rubbing among, her folds until it was slick and positioned at her entry. Dipping his fingers inside her to wet them, he stroked along his shaft until it gleamed with her fluid. Then he reared over her, taking his weight on his straight arms.

'My princess,' he whispered, before plunging smoothly into her tight tunnel, the force of his thrust driving past her maidenhood as she cried out in shock and pain. He froze, waited for the cries to die away and allowed himself his pleasure, heedless of her cries of distress but nonetheless alert in case she tried the safe word.

Elsa struggled in the grip of her captors. She started to sob, the tears running freely over her cheeks when Mallot began to plunge within her, his huge invasion forcing along her virgin tunnel. Soon, however, the pain lessened and his deep, smooth stroking provoked a hungry yearning. She felt consumed, powerless and pinioned, and she surrendered, barely noticing when her head fell back and her mentor slipped away.

Rusty had approached Hope from the rear, tugging her to her knees and pulling her bottom eagerly towards him. He thrust his fingers rudely between her thighs, digging them into her already wet cave, and then forced his tongue between her bumcheeks, muscling firmly against her starry anal pucker. He penetrated and swirled the satiny walls of her most secret channel until she was wet and pushing at him. His tip barely grazed her bottom before she was thrusting back, seeking the punishment of a shameful entry. He soldiered in, another tight entry, then fell to his side, pulling her with him. He grabbed her thigh and drew it back so her leg hooked back over his, her wantonness clearly displayed.

Rat was magnetized. He scuttled forward, eyeing Rusty's burial of his shaft beneath the taut, swollen wetness of Hope's orphan cunt. He lay on his side with Hope's leg beneath his waist, grasped his prick and nudged for entry without preamble. His tip penetrated and Rusty, feeling the press of Rat's cockhead inside Hope's entryway, forced her leg over Rat's waist.

Hope groaned, afraid of Rat's entry but driven crazy by

her need for it. When he slid tightly into her and paused, she slumped, surrendering to the massive simultaneous invasion of the two pricks. She was sure she would tear and felt almost that she would welcome the release from the burning pressure, should that happen. When the two men started to seesaw in her, her head swam. She felt pinioned and helpless, her bottom impaled on Rusty's slowly pistoning prick and her cave possessed by Rat. In the background she was aware of the climax to the union of Mallot and Elsa, regretting that she missed it, and the whimpers of Allie who, she assumed, was enjoying the ministrations of Quinn or Ruari.

In fact, Allie was enjoying the attention of Brandon. Karen had taken charge of the video recorder and was training it on Brandon, who was supping eagerly between Allie's slim thighs. The tumble of his large, unruly beard shifting over her thighs added a new dimension to her enjoyment and she had the bizarre wish to plait it and push it into herself. The image caused her to laugh, until she was silenced when Quinn's stocky prick slid into her open mouth. He had straddled her chest and, cupping the back of her head with his interlaced fingers, had lifted her so that his scrotum slapped softly into her chin when he started to fuck her mouth eagerly.

Ruari watched the double invasion of Hope with mixed feelings. Having possessed her sleek interior he felt jealous and protective, but he was also painfully roused, his prick swollen, sensitive and longing for release. He gazed at Elsa, happy that she had finally surrendered to the pleasure of Mallot's shafting strokes after the obviously painful first thrusts. When the man had burst through her precious maidenhood, Ruari had flinched, his fists clenched. It was only the restraint of Quinn's hand that had prevented his surging forward to knock the evil bastard away from his intended. He had taken Hope's place at Elsa's head, soothing her as he watched her eyes fill with blind pleasure and listened to her little mewling noises announce her sexual awakening. When she came, her expression grew contorted in surprise and joy as the thrills shot through her. Afterwards, when Mallot had slumped from her, it was Ruari who cuddled her in his strong and tender embrace while tears trickled down her cheeks. He kissed her eyelids and breasts, murmuring praise and comfort. Then he let her crawl into the comforting warmth of his generous contours, spent and childlike, while he watched Hope.

She made guttural noises of demand, the jolting inside her increasing as she urged her lovers to harsher attention. Rat exploded, almost breathless with effort, the exultation of shared fucking ringing around his head. He had discovered his joy in his penchant for shared encounters, the memory of Rusty's member moving against his through the thin tissue separating Hope's cavities. He withdrew from Hope so he could watch Rusty's completion, delighting in the slide and suck of the heavy member between Hope's bumcheeks. His breath held, he watched Rusty's last frozen stroke and the trembling of his thighs preceding his coming.

Hope was thrusting back urgently, her hand scrabbling at her clitoris. She moaned, her mouth stretched in a wide rictus of pleasure as Rusty creamed. She added her groan to his, and shuddered violently while he plunged and voided his precious spill. They slumped, his spent organ inside her until he softened, then rolled away. Hope collapsed onto her back, her legs spread wide and her quim blazing.

Unable to resist, Quinn came and gently supped, cleaning

up the traces of her pleasure with a gentle excitement. His own coming had been delightful, spewing thickly into Allie's tight throat, but his first love lay in feasting on female musk. Ruari permitting, he hoped to serve Elsa in this way and share the delight of her virgin coming. It was his supplication and his joy, and the richer leavings of the men added pungent luxury. When Hope shifted, revived, to smile at him, he felt jubilant. He moved away and settled in front of Ruari, eyes downcast, until the large Irishman realized his wish and released Elsa.

Elsa gazed at Quinn. With him she had shared *Fuzzy Thinking* and an evening of pleasures so she understood his need. She eased her legs open and, leaning back into Ruari's strong chest, watched Quinn tend to her. The memory of pain had vanished and she felt no loss. Something had been added to her value and she was thrilled that the confused awkwardness of her virginity was a thing of the past. Mallot meant nothing to her and, while not regretting her choice, she had no desire to repeat the coupling. She felt ready to leave the island, looking forward to her next encounter outside of the stone walls with the man against whose broad chest she rested. She turned her head and kissed Ruari softly on the arm, enjoying the response of his chin rubbing against the top of her head.

'It's nearly midnight,' Brandon advised.

The group rallied, delighted when Mairead appeared with frosted glasses of cold spring water and bowls of fresh fruit salad. Shortly afterwards, she collected the empty trays and replaced them with steaming mugs and slices of rich fruit cake. They toasted Elsa and cheered when the leather collar fell from Angela's neck.

* * *

To Hope, the aftermath seemed an anticlimax. With five days of the retreat left to go, she wondered how they could top the evening and felt reluctant to spend hours in session hashing out the meaning of her encounters. She wanted to return to the world, taking her new-found liberties with her, to test them out in a larger environment. Above all, she wanted men and women who were less familiar, more space – and she longed to start her new life. She felt an overwhelming urge to tie all the loose ends, the last remaining matter being Willincough. Surely, she reasoned, he or she had now had ample opportunity to come forward, even if nervous. Hope had been available and intimate with all the group, bar the Ormandies and Mallot, but even with him she had been alone. Her mind turned again to Reggie and Blain, LeChange and Partners, and his involvement with Mallot, Rusty and Salvatore. From what Rusty had told her, he was as ignorant of the situation as she, having merely been instructed to attend the retreat. It seemed obvious that he was being used, but the purpose was unclear.

There were separate issues involved in this retreat. The sex she dismissed as being too coincidental. It had arisen out of the first evening's session and was too spontaneous in growth to be part of a plan. No, she decided, the link had to be Willincough and she surmised that he had not come forward because he was afraid. The only reason she could think of, to support such a fear, was that she was not the only one seeking him and his other pursuers must not have as innocent a purpose for their hunt. Willi was a hacker. Had he caused electronic damage to someone at the retreat?

She recalled Quinn's interest in Rat in the library when

the young programmer insisted that all he needed was a telephone. Rat hacked and his connection with Willincough was the reason she was here at all – he was in Ireland, so she was in Ireland. That was the deal. Quinn lived in Dublin but was American. His occupation was vague and he seemed benign except when his eyes had rested on Rat in the library. Then she had noted his shrewd and sharply assessing gaze, his understated but persistent interest and his eager accompaniment of Rat.

Hope stared at Quinn. He lay on his back, staring at the ceiling, seemingly sated and supremely content. Was it an act, she wondered, or was something more sinister being cleverly disguised? If he was interested in Rat as a hacker, then was he really after Willincough? And, if so, why? She sat up suddenly, wincing at the burn between her thighs. She needed to talk to Rat, and fast, the suspicion dawning in her head far from conclusive but sufficiently formed to alarm her.

Her movement had drawn unwelcome attention from Mallot. He slid beside her and murmured, 'Are you hurting?' It was obvious from his question that his attention had not been fully fixed on his deflowering of a princess and his view of Hope's double taking had been clear.

'Yes.' Hope wanted to get away from the penetrating dark gaze, but seemed drawn, her thoughts faltering and the urgency of her need to speak with Rat fading under Mallot's hypnotic allure. She longed to ask him about his relationship with Reggie but realized he would obfuscate. Whatever his motives for attending the retreat, she could not find a connection with Quinn.

'There's only you and I left, you know?' Mallot studied Hope carefully. 'Of course, we were really first.' His allusion to their coupling in London was calculated and he was satisfied when Hope's eyes filled with remembrance and a pale flush rose in her cheeks. Pressing home his advantage, Mallot continued, his voice low and soothing, 'I said you were wonderful, I set you free.' His oblique reference to the chastity belt was symbolic. 'Free to return to me.' Mallot stroked a finger across her lips, traced it down her neck and stroked the shivering globe of her breast, settling at her nipple. His eyes remained on hers, noting the widening of her pupils. When he began to circle her areola, she licked her lips.

Mallot had misjudged. While Hope felt her trembling need build and recognized her submissive attraction to him, her desire to know the truth of his presence on the island overrode her need for congress. When he continued his hand's journey over her stomach and gently fingered past her mound, seeking her pearl, she moaned and shrank from his tantalizing touch. Undeterred, though surprised, Mallot eased his hand between her loosely clasped thighs and slid along her crease, noting the wet spill of juices and eager opening as his fingers penetrated. Hope gasped, a strangled sound he took as the presage of surrender, the moment before her rationality deserted her and the animal desire in her would surface to consume her last reserves. Already he envisaged her splayed and bucking mindlessly, his rod pistoning. For his own sheer pleasure, he would enter the painful channel Rusty had ridden and hear her cries while his larger cock aggravated the burning tissues. In anticipation, his rod was hard, his expectation rampant and his blood tingling with cruel intent. He owned Hope – she had been given to him by Reggie and the tiresome wait for her surrender was past its due date.

'Cave.' Hope's loud cry hung in the air like a whiplash. It seemed wrung from her, anguished and vulnerable.

Mallot stared at her, uncomprehending. He was obedient to the command but his fingers remained in her, stilled, and his expression was shocked and disbelieving. 'Cave?' He whispered the word, shook his head angrily and snatched his hand away. 'Why? This is no game, Hope. Deny me now and you lose me.'

Hope gulped, afraid of the wrath in the dark man's face. She breathed carefully, stamping down the lust. 'I don't want you, Mallot. I am going after Salvatore.'

In the split moment it took Mallot to leap to his feet and curse her, Hope was shocked at the expression of pure fear that crossed his face. Her own fear was replaced by jubilant realization. Mallot was Salvatore's pawn, just as Rusty was Mallot's pawn. Mallot was afraid of Salvatore and now, without any notion of why, Hope had power over the dark man. She dismissed him, he was vanquished, and her mind now sought Reggie's place in the scheme. Rusty had called him 'the introducer' and she suspected that Reggie's manipulations were subservient to Salvatore as well. It remained to connect Reggie with Quinn. She stood up slowly and confronted Mallot, who was glowering and breathing hard to restrain his anger.

She stared into the narrowed menace of his eyes. 'Cave,' she repeated, softly yet more firmly.

She sought Rat, realizing as her gaze swept the group that her rejection had caused ripples of shock. All were staring at her with wide looks of amazement. She had used the sacred word, and on Mallot. Angela looked horrified, her gaze swerving between Mallot and Hope, as if waiting for violence to erupt. She had risen to a crouch, like a terrified animal waiting to see if flight was necessary. It was Mallot who broke the suspense: he turned and strode abruptly from the room, signalling to Angela who scuttled behind him, terrified but eager to bear the brunt of his malicious temper.

'Rat,' Hope found him tensed beside the speechless Allie. 'I need to speak to you.'

'I think,' murmured Quinn, 'that you need to speak to me, too.' He rose to his feet and padded over to face her. Leaning into her neck, he whispered, 'You've made the connection, haven't you?'

Hope shook her head, whispering back in astonishment, '*You're* Willincough?'

'Good God, no!' Quinn burst out laughing, forgetting to whisper.

'Well, then,' Hope retorted testily, 'you're FBI.' She watched as Quinn almost doubled over with mirth.

'No,' he gasped when he was able. 'We really do need to talk.' He grabbed Hope's arm and led her from the dining room, seemingly oblivious of the bewilderment they left behind.

Rat followed nervously.

Quinn guided the pair into his room, directed them to a seat on the bed and lifted a heavy valise from his wardrobe. Opening it, he produced a cellular telephone that rested in the cradle of a complicated box. He untangled some cabling from the skein nesting in the bottom of the case and attached a laptop. Once the apparatus was assembled, he gave Rat an enquiring look.

'I knew you would be here so I borrowed this, but it is

up to you to work it. Am I right in assuming you know how to?' He handed Rat a small notebook.

Rat whistled, flipping through the contents with wide eyes. 'Where did you get this?' he demanded.

'You should know,' Quinn shrugged.

'Okay, how did you get hold of it?'

'Does it matter?'

'Can I keep it?' Rat was eagerly firing up the system, his eyes alight. 'After all, it *is* mine to start with.'

'Like hell,' Quinn retorted. 'As I recall, you stole all the software and broke every law in the free West getting the hardware.'

Hope glanced in amazement at the two men. 'I thought you were tracking Willincough,' she accused Quinn.

'I didn't have to,' he explained, 'I already knew who he was.'

Hope stared at Rat who glanced up from the small screen long enough to offer a small grimace of apology.

'You're Willincough?' Hope stammered. 'Why . . .?'

'Because I wanted to bonk you so badly,' Rat muttered, his concentration fixed on the screen's swiftly scrolling text. He paused, lifted his hands from the keyboard and swivelled to face her. 'What can I say? I'm human.'

'Oh, I see. So you lied, deceived and manipulated me just so you could get into my knickers?' Hope's voice rose dramatically in disbelieving outrage.

'Yup.' Rat stared at her with a puzzled expression. 'You have no idea how much I wanted you,' he said. 'I would have drugged, gagged and kidnapped you just to have you. Then, when we were here on this island, I didn't have to.'

Hope fell back on the bed. 'You're sick,' she muttered, but laughed.

Rat looked relieved and returned to the keyboard.

'How do you fit in?' Hope looked at Quinn.

He was distracted, peering over Rat's shoulder. He took a small handheld computer from the valise and tapped impatiently. 'How's that?' He offered the machine to Rat, who nodded briefly and entered some digits. Shortly the shrill tones of a modem invaded the room.

'Bingo!' Rat slapped the box in delight.

'Let's just say that I am an old pal of Willincough,' Quinn murmured. 'Settled down.'

'Crossed over, more like!' Rat muttered cryptically.

'You're another hacker?' Hope questioned.

This caused Rat to peer at her in amazement. 'He's not just another hacker. He's a *wizard*!'

'Okay, our electronic paths have crossed, but I don't think Hope needs to know more,' Quinn cautioned.

'I don't want to know more,' Hope decided. 'Except what you are doing now.'

'Exactly what you suggested. Seeing who owns this house.'

'Corporate,' Rat said.

Hope leaned forward to peer at the screen, before Rat shifted to block her view. She caught a glimpse, however, and said, 'Hang on, I recognized them.'

'Which?' Quinn looked at her eagerly.

'Delwinnish, they acted as proxy when I was in South America recruiting Salvatore.'

Quinn forced Rat out the way so Hope could see the next screen.

'No, I don't recognize those.' A list of company names floated before her. 'Hang on, can you find something on that?' She pointed near the end of the list.

'It's secured.' Rat advised, indicating that the next screen was flashing a warning. The file was encrypted. 'This could take a few minutes but judging by the administrator's pattern, the code is probably something like his wife's birthday.' He snorted his contempt, tapped a few keys and sat back, relaxing while text and numbers flitted frantically.

'How do you know his wife's birthday?' Hope asked.

Rat laughed, 'I looked. His password is pretty stupid. It's just his initials and his car registration number.'

'You looked?'

'Yeah, he has this hidden directory full of his personal details. Bank account numbers, cars, birthdays, tax number and such. I am running combinations of that file now.'

Hope gazed at Rat, horrified.

'Don't look like that.' Rat grinned at her. 'He's a fool for putting all that stuff within reach. Besides, I am not going to do anything with it.'

'You already are!'

'Yeah. But I'm not going to steal his money. He hasn't got a lot anyway.'

'Okay,' Hope said softly, 'what do you know about me?'

'Nothing.' Rat responded too quickly, blushing. He was saved when the screen beeped. 'Told you. It's his dog's name and the street number of his house.' He entered the password and the file de-encrypted.

It contained addresses, cross-referenced to linked files held in remote registers. None seemed familiar to Hope, but she stared at the words hoping they would offer more information if given enough concentrated effort. They did.

'Wait!' she exclaimed as Rat prepared to hit another key. 'Can you find out more about that one?' She pointed to a company called Resolvata Ltd.

'Sure.' Rat tapped and another screen filled. 'It's an environmental preservation subsidiary with an overseas parent. Hang on.' He typed in the name of the parent, studied the screen, then suddenly cut the connection. 'Ouch!'

'What?'

'A trace,' Quinn supplied the answer. 'Seems that someone didn't want us to peek in there.' He looked at Hope curiously, 'Why that one?'

'It's an anagram of Salvatore.'

'There's another way,' Rat was thoughtful and reconnected the modem, tapping his foot impatiently while it stuttered shrilly.

'What are you after?' Hope repeated her earlier question to Quinn.

'The Ormandies.'

'I don't understand. How do they fit in with Reggie?'

Quinn shook his head. 'I don't know yet, all I have to do is find out what the Ormandies are up to.'

'But you know that Rat and I both work for Reggie?'

'Yes.'

'You're a cop?'

'No.'

'What, then? Are you really married and upset with your wife? Or is that just another false trail?'

'No, that's true.' Quinn looked downcast and Hope felt guilty. 'I am a trader.'

'Where did you get this equipment?' Hope was suspicious.

'It's part of a trade.'

'This is like drawing teeth,' Hope complained. 'I feel like I am caught up in some plot and you won't tell me anything. I think it is only fair to trust me with something that will put my mind at rest.'

Quinn sat beside her on the bed. He stared at Rat for a moment, satisfied that the young man was busy, and softly explained his position to Hope. She learned he was an exile from his native Cleveland, a victim of the FBI hacker crackdown in 1990, though not a main player. They allowed him to leave his homeland, providing he traded information. His wife was Irish so he chose to live in her homeland. Right now they needed something on the Ormandies.

'It is Salvatore,' Rat intruded.

Hope stared at the screen. 'And Reggie.' She stared at the list of directors of Resolvata Ltd. 'I do not recognize the others, however.'

'I do.' Quinn looked grim.

'Who?'

'The Ormandies.'

'I don't see them.' Hope checked.

'Anne Gothly and Desmond Wellington Jnr.' Quinn tapped Rat on the shoulder. 'Stop now, for an hour.'

'But they'll pick up the permissions,' Rat protested.

'There are no permissions,' Quinn said bluntly.

'You said you got this equipment on loan,' Rat persisted. 'Surely it's kosher?' He groaned when Quinn shook his head and disconnected his modem line. 'Damnit,' he complained, 'it is my stuff, after all.' He threw himself across the end of the bed in a sulk.

Hope ignored him, deep in thought. 'It looks like this house is owned by a company that includes Salvatore,

Reggie and the Ormandies as directors. The Ormandies are our hosts and we know that Reggie is linked with Mallot and Rusty, who are both here.' She mused, then looked at Quinn. 'What are they after the Ormandies for?' When Quinn looked reluctant to answer, she insisted, 'Come on, Quinn. It hasn't escaped my notice that, because Rat and I work for Reggie, we are in trouble by association.'

'You what?' Rat shot into a sitting position and glared at Quinn. 'She's joking, isn't she?'

'No, she's right. You are both going to have to prove you are not involved.'

'Involved with what?' Hope now grabbed Quinn's arm and implored him.

'Vice. The making of pornographic movies. Even snuff movies.'

Rat and Hope stared blankly at each other.

'They're tracking the Ormandies about a vice thing?' Hope looked bewildered. 'I thought it would be income tax evasion or something.'

'Well, that too.' Quinn squirmed. 'It's the link with the others, though.'

'Let me get this straight.' Rat's brow was furrowed in concentration. 'They have this house for vice reasons. That doesn't explain why we're here.'

'It explains why Hope and Rusty are.'

'Rusty's Mallot's kiddo,' Hope protested, then blanched. 'Oh, I see,' she said miserably.

'What?' Rat look worried.

Quinn supplied the answer. 'Hope is supposed to be Mallot's kiddo too. She was recruited in London after an introduction by Reggie.'

'But she said "Cave",' Rat returned triumphantly. 'Anyway, I'm a witness to why she is here.'

'No, you're the lure, Willincough.'

'They know about me?'

'Of course.'

'Is there a Blain, LeChange and Partners?' Hope demanded.

'Yes, they're legitimate.'

'And they do want a hacker?' Hope pressed.

'No, they want a technical security manager.'

Rat sniggered.

'I still don't see it,' Hope muttered. 'Why plan this elaborate set-up?'

'I don't think there was much planning,' Quinn said slowly. 'The Ormandies moved quickly, and they were not alerted much in advance. Mairead has worked with them before.' He looked up when Hope groaned at the admission of the housekeeper's complicity. 'My guess,' he continued, 'is that this was cobbled together. At least this retreat was, although I suspect the house was set up for things like this when Resolvata took it over.

'I saw that article about you and Salvatore and I think that you've underestimated your role in this fortnight. If I were to hazard a guess, judging from Mallot's reaction when you said you were going to go after Salvatore, you have opened a whole can of worms.'

'I still don't understand.' Hope shrugged.

'Let me spell it out for you,' Rat said. 'You know how I lied and dragged you here under false pretences?' He waited until Hope nodded, 'Well, imagine what a rich guy would do if he wanted you as badly as I did.'

Hope stared at Rat, 'No way! He did this because he wants to get into my knickers?'

'Yes.'

Hope looked to Quinn for help, but he agreed with Rat. 'I think there is more, though. Rusty is valuable property. He earns a lot for the cartel he works with. Forgive me, but you're a raunchy and beautiful woman and you are independent and quite an exhibitionist. They may be seeing money in the bank as well.'

'I'm being groomed for pornographic stardom?' Hope was appalled. 'I mean, I don't mind the idea, in principle. The method stinks, though.' She groaned. 'Is this how they have hooked me? I mean my association with Salvatore and Reggie looks so bad that I get dragged in because they would threaten to expose me otherwise?'

'It's possible,' Quinn agreed.

'No, it's not,' Rat said. 'We have it on record at Pursuit why we're here.'

'Sure, but that could be taken as a cover story,' Quinn pointed out.

'Well, then we're stuffed,' Rat stated.

'Only if those videos get out.' Hope muttered.

Quinn stared at her, 'You're right. That is the only real proof of what happened on this island.'

'It's simple, then: let's go get Brandon.' Rat jumped to his feet.

'They needed those movies as evidence to convict the Ormandies,' Quinn said miserably.

'Tough,' Rat informed him. 'Until I found out who owned this place you did not even know about the connections. You just tell your bosses that this retreat was a stroll in the park with a lot of sobbing hysteria and no one wanted to play sexy. I'll come back to Dublin with you and trace all the links again, as if I had just found them for the first time.' When Quinn still looked reluctant, Rat glared at him. 'I don't think you were pretending when you stuck your nose happily in Hope's crotch,' he stated crudely. 'Way I see it is that you owe her.'

'And,' Hope chimed in, 'you can do it again.' She deliberately slid her legs apart and fingered her exposed corolla suggestively.

Quinn moaned, staring at her display. 'This is not fair,' he protested.

'All's fair. You get to eat me whenever you want and Rat and I, who are both victims by the way, get out from under these stupid entrapment games.'

Quinn wavered. He leaned between Hope's knees, breathing deeply, but before he could get closer, she slid back and snapped her legs closed.

'Videos first, chow later,' she asserted.

Rat shook his head. Muff-diving was good but to be as hooked as Quinn was bewildering. Still, he thought happily, if they would share with him then that would satisfy his passion also. He helped Quinn stow the equipment back in the valise, then followed Hope from the bedroom.

Allie and Elsa were sitting despondently on the stairwell.

'What's up?' Rat asked them.

'Ruari's gone after Mallot,' Elsa said unhappily.

'Good show. We need him.' Rat turned to head up the stairwell to the attic room that Mallot and Angela had selected.

'Not that way,' Allie called. 'Mallot went off with the Ormandies.'

Rat looked at Hope and they dashed down the stairs.

'Have you any idea where their room is?'

They collided with Angela in the lobby. She was crying and angry. 'They're buggering off,' she wept, 'and I was left behind.'

'Where?' Rat shook her, his hands digging into her shoulders.

'Outside,' Angela gasped.

Ruari ran from the corridor leading to the library. 'Where the fuck are they?' he roared at Angela.

'Come,' Rat ran through the front door and raced towards the quay.

'No. This way!' Ruari rushed towards the path he'd taken with Hope the day before. There was barely enough moonlight for him to pick his way along the sandy ribbon but he moved fast, ignoring Rat's curses as he hit his elbow on the old stone walls. Hope used Rat's misfortune as her guide and stumbled after him without mishap. When they reached the fallen boulders, Ruari scrabbled over, breathlessly explaining.

'They have a boat on the other side of the island. They would have to pass our cove, Hope.'

Hope heard the urgency in his voice and pushed past Rat. She was aware that Quinn was panting behind Rat and trusted they could catch up, but realized that they had to get to the bay fast or the chance of preventing the Ormandies from leaving was slight. She heard Ruari's footsteps drawing away ahead of her and sprinted to catch up, then scrabbled down the small slope to the cove, hard on his heels. They could not see any sign of the boat and Ruari bent over to catch his breath.

'Hush,' Hope commanded. She heard a stealthy dip of

oars and slid into the water. The channel through which the boat would have to travel was near the rock against which Ruari had leaned to fuck her and she swam silently behind it and stopped to listen. Ruari joined her.

'I'll overturn them,' he whispered. 'There's a motor but I guess they wanted to keep it quiet until they reached the lake.'

'We have to get the videos,' Hope whispered urgently as the sound of oars got closer.

The boat came into view. A zodiac, its air cushion gleamed gunmetal-grey in the moonlight. They made out the shape of four figures crouched in the well.

'We can't overturn that!' Hope breathed in alarm.

'Watch me.' Ruari muttered, then slipped around the rock. The water was still only chest – deep and he ducked until only his head was visible. Hope copied him, but he pushed her away and she obediently gave him room.

A shout from the shore alerted those on the boat. It was Rat, trying to get his bearings and hoping for a response from Hope.

'Shit!'

The curse came from Mallot and the boat was much closer than Hope had realized. It rocked violently as one of the figures rose and tried to fire the engine. It spluttered, but then caught on the second attempt. Hope recalled that, beyond the next rock, the channel widened and they could easily build speed and escape if they got past Ruari. She flung herself from the rock and grabbed onto the cushion of the zodiac.

'Here,' she shrieked as Ruari surged from the water, braced his back against the rock and kicked mightily at the jolting boat.

Hope was thrown clear and, for a moment, she glimpsed the bottom of the boat. Then it rolled sluggishly, the engine blaring until the propellers bit back into the water. Karen was screaming and Mallot bellowing curses but the zodiac surged forward until it hit the last rock before freedom, tilted crazily, bounced and regained the surface. It dug in solidly and then slid into the channel and roared away.

Hope slumped against the rock, downhearted. She heard the thrashing in the water as Rat sought them.

'Have you got the videos?' he gasped.

'No.' Hope was almost crying. They had had only one shot and that was now lost.

Quinn waded past them. 'You could not see this from where you were,' he called, 'but their gear went overboard. Some of it, anyway.' He ducked beneath the water and emerged holding a small bag, which he chucked to Hope. 'Karen's gonna miss her make-up.' he quipped.

'Please, God,' Rat breathed and pushed Hope forward. 'Can't swim, remember?'

She glared at him and joined Quinn, ducking and feeling along the stony bottom until her hand struck a soft surface. It was a knapsack, and alongside she discovered a suitcase. She towed them to shore and tore them open. The knapsack turned out to be the hold-all for the video camera, but there were no tapes with it. The suitcase revealed little but sodden female clothing.

'Well, it would have been too easy,' she muttered to herself miserably, then sat shivering and wet, waiting for Quinn.

Ruari and Rat emerged from the water, each tugging luggage, with Quinn not far behind. They forced the cases open and scrabbled through the contents.

'I think,' Quinn said, 'that this is what you're looking for.'

The case contained plastic boxes sealed against the wet and, through the opaque covers, Hope could see the unmistakable shape of video tapes. She laughed with relief and hugged Quinn.

'Let's get this stuff back.'

The journey back was slower, burdened as they were, but happier. Hope allowed herself to believe that they had the incriminating tapes even before they prised the covers off and read the neatly-written labels. It seemed that Brandon had been busy and further investigation revealed cameras hidden in the bathroom and all the bedrooms.

Angela seemed too outraged for them to suspect her of complicity. She was furious with Mallot and now, outside of his power, she seemed to mourn the loss of her hair more than the intrusion of the camera on what could be deemed her private space. Allie was philosophical.

'At least we have the videos,' she pointed out.

'What is to stop them coming back for them?' Ruari asked. 'These people are criminals and may have rather more than fists.'

'I think you're right but I have an idea.' Quinn outlined his suggestion.

'Well, we cannot play the videos to check what's on them but going by the labels . . .' Hope stared at the tape in her hand, then read softly, '"Hope/Rat/Brandon in Library".' She spun to face Rat. 'Brandon?' she yelled. 'You shared me with him?'

'"Hope/Ruari in Cove",' Rat read, ignoring her. 'Bet if I watch this tape I will realize how come you never noticed you were being filmed!' he said pointedly.

'Look, Quinn. "Elsa/Quinn Cunny",' Elsa giggled.

Hope shook her head. Only three of them realized how badly their lives could have been damaged if these videos had reached the black market. She felt violated. Apart from the 'Deflowering Elsa' movie, no permissions had been sought for these productions and, while she did not regret any of the experiences, she wished she could bring retribution on their hosts.

'Enough,' Ruari muttered. 'Let's do as Quinn said.'

They carried the baggage down to the quay, carefully packing the empty tape covers back into the suitcase. The sounds of water, an owl hooting and their own movements were all that broke the night silence, but Hope sensed they were not alone. She jumped when Ruari shouted.

'You can come and get your things from the end of the pier. I'll even light a bonfire to guide you.' He stepped back and strode to the pile of tapes heaped ten feet from the stack of suitcases, struck a match and flicked it into the celluloid they had unravelled to ensure the flames would catch. Once he was sure the pile would burn properly, he joined the rest of the group huddled by the bench.

Hope was shivering almost uncontrollably. She felt frozen until Rat stripped his shirt off and wrapped her in it, discarding her sarong. They did not have to wait long. Mallot bounded up the steps of the quay and tried to stamp out the fire but only succeeded in setting alight his trouser-leg. Cursing, he leapt into the water. No one laughed. They made out the shape of hands lifting the baggage and dragging it into the zodiac. The engine roared into life and they were left, listening as the boat escaped along the channel and into the open lake.

'If you ask me,' Quinn said, 'we got away lightly.'

'Not really. We're still stuck on this island,' Elsa pointed out. 'Sean is only coming back on Friday.'

'I can fix that,' Rat advised her, 'with a phone call.' He paused, then added, 'In the morning.'

'Why not leave it until the afternoon?' Quinn suggested, linking arms with Hope, 'I think I deserve a hearty breakfast.'

'Good thinking.' Rat linked with Allie. 'Perhaps we'll join you.'

'I think we should get away from here as soon as possible,' Hope warned. 'I am sure Bear would accommodate us. I have a horrible feeling about the ownership of this place.'

'You guys know a lot more than you're telling,' Allie observed shrewdly.

The hallway seemed alien when the group entered, stripped of its mystery, the retreat destroyed. Hope, noticing Elsa's downcast expression, clasped the girl to her gently.

'Nothing can destroy what happened between us, you know,' she assured her. 'No matter what they did, that was real.'

'I know,' Elsa smiled at her. 'I don't regret anything, not even Mallot.' She squeezed Hope gently, and moved into Ruari's arms.

'What are you going to do?' Allie asked Hope. 'I mean, you haven't a job to go back to. I just want you to know that there is a welcome for you in Edinburgh.'

'It's like I told Mallot,' Hope said. 'I am going after. Salvatore.'

'Who's Salvatore?'

'Doesn't matter,' Hope grinned. 'What does matter, though, is that Rat is heading up your way.'

'I am?' Rat looked puzzled.

'Sure, Edinburgh is where Blain, LeChange and Partners have their offices.'

'I see,' Rat nodded. 'Of course. The cannibal devours again. As it happens, I think a change of work place may be a very good idea.'

Hope climbed the stairs to her bedroom alone. She stood for some moments, staring through her window at the silver pathway created by the moon on the waters of Loch Derg. She had no way of knowing how Salvatore would react to her but, if Quinn and Rat were right, he would welcome her and, stripped of his hold via the video tapes, would be forced to meet her on equal ground.

No, she amended, on *her* ground. She realized, with surprise, that her intention was only to consummate the promise of that night on the bougainvillea-clad terrace. She still yearned for Salvatore and was unimpressed with his hold on Mallot or Reggie. If the power of her womanhood held him in thrall then she would take advantage, indulge her lusts and simply walk away. The additional thrill would be keeping one step ahead of him and for that she needed information, therefore she needed Willincough and his box of tricks. Therefore, she reasoned further, she also needed Quinn because he could supply the equipment that Rat coveted. She turned from the window when she heard her bedroom door open.

'I think you owe me a snack,' Quinn observed, delighted when Hope perched on the windowsill and spread her legs. She watched him kneel and snuffle eagerly between her thighs. 'Feast well,' she murmured as the pleasure surged through her. 'Have seconds and I shall tell you what I want from you in the future.'

Quinn paused, then surrendered, his hunger overriding his good sense.